MONTANA WRANGLER

BEAR GRASS SPRINGS, BOOK SIX

RAMONA FLIGHTNER

GRIZZLY DAMSEL PUBLISHING

Cover design by Jennifer Quinlan.

To the Glynns,
Thank you for your ongoing support, your never-ending enthusiasm for the
stories I write, and for sharing your stories about Montana with me.

CHAPTER 1

Bear Grass Springs, Montana, November 1886

It was an inauspicious way to die. Sorcha MacKinnon stared at the sky as storm clouds overhead obscured the sun, heralding a change in the weather. A gust of wind caused the pine trees to sway. She took a deep breath and tried to move, biting back a scream of pain as she barely progressed an inch. "Sugar?" she called out to her horse.

She closed her eyes and listened for any sound, tears coursing down her face and wetting her hair. "Why should I want a horse that threw me?" she asked in a quavering voice. She continued to mutter to herself so she didn't feel so alone in the large, empty forest.

Her eyes snapped open at a creaking sound, her heart racing. A strange snip of a memory came to her, a man's voice. *She died too soon.* Her heart raced, and her breath emerged as pants as she strained to remember anything further. After a moment she took a deep breath, realizing the pine tree had made the noise after a strong gust of wind sprinkled needles off its branches. In her pain-induced state, her mind jumped from memories of holding her niece, Skye, to arguing with her youngest brother, Ewan, to laughing with her sisters-in-law at the bakery. "I dinna want to die alone." She tried to move again and fainted from the pain.

〜

Frederick Tompkins paused on his way from the ranch house to the horse barn to watch the large fluffy white clouds followed by a band of darker storm clouds move across the brilliant blue Montana sky. Along with his two brothers, Peter and Cole, and his grandparents, Harold and Irene Tompkins, Frederick owned the Mountain Bluebird Ranch, or the MBR as the men preferred to call it.

Near the main ranch house stood two large barns. One housed Frederick's prized horses, while the other held milk cows, goats and pigs. In front of the horse barn was the blacksmith shop with a hand pump for water. Large interconnecting paddocks and corrals were behind the barns and to the side of the larger horse barn.

Frederick pulled on his hat and strode to the barn. The MBR was the largest and most successful cattle ranch in the valley near Bear Grass Springs, Montana. His grandparents and father had founded it in the 1860s and then given it to the three brothers. Whereas Frederick chose to remain in Montana, Cole and Peter preferred the adventure of driving herds up from Texas each spring. They were currently in Chicago to sell the cattle they had cut from the home herd. Frederick knew from previous years' experience that his brothers would return to Texas rather than winter in Montana.

He smiled to himself as he considered winter in Montana. Rather than look to a calendar to determine the season, Montanans glanced out the window to ascertain the season and often joked there were only two here—summer and winter, with winter lasting up to six months. He glanced at the foreboding dark clouds on the horizon again, and he knew that winter was about to arrive. He said a silent prayer that it would be a mild one, like last year's.

Frederick gave a small grunt of satisfaction that his elder brothers had missed the recent harvest dance held in town. He glowered as he thought about the dance he had shared with Sorcha MacKinnon. He tugged at the red bandanna tied around his neck, flushing as he remembered storming away from her after she had called him a "simpleminded wrangler." Her mocking stare—as she had intimated that any woman living on his ranch would be miserable—had filled him with such ire that he had been unable to speak.

A cool breeze blew, scattering fallen leaves and rustling the prairie grass thawing in the fleeting warmth before the storm hit, helping to cool his momentary anger at the memory. After the long harsh summer with temperatures in the nineties and little rain, the grass was thin and sparse on the range. There would be little for the cattle to eat over the coming winter months. Fresh snow shone like a beacon on the nearby mountain peaks, while the hint of more snow to come remained in the air itself as well as in the nearing clouds. He focused on the land around him, forcefully putting the memory of Sorcha from his mind.

Frederick called out to Dalton, one of his hands. "I'm taking Boots out for a ride. To clear my head and to let her run before the storm hits. Might be my last chance to roam the range before winter arrives." He rubbed a hand along the neck of one of his prized horses, a beautiful chestnut filly with white forelocks. He clicked and murmured, "Come on, Boots. Let's see how fast you want to run." Although the MBR was a cattle ranch, Frederick raised prized horses and had begun to earn a reputation for them in the area.

He barreled down the drive before veering off and slowing Boots to a trot onto his more undeveloped land as they headed toward the mountains. Boots tossed her head, as though upset with the slowing of their pace, before she settled into a gentle canter. The frost on the grass melted as the day warmed, and Frederick saw hawks circling overhead in search of any small creature foolish enough to be on the prairie. Few of his cattle were visible as they had scattered on the range after the fall roundup. He stared in dismay at the brittle grass and again prayed for a mild winter.

As he followed a well-worn trail, Frederick's sense of unease heightened rather than diminished. The trees thickened as he approached the base of the mountains, and he heard the soft trickle of a nearby stream. The air cooled, and the scent on the breeze was sweeter with the fresh smell of pine trees mixed with mossy undertones from the creek. He reined in Boots, closing his eyes to breathe deeply, as worries about the ranch and his fledgling horse business faded. The soft wind moved through the trees and caressed his hair and face, further easing his tension. After a few more moments, he patted Boots's neck and was about to turn for home when he saw a piece of burgundy fabric caught on a nearby bush.

He jumped from his horse to grab it and then heard a sound. He closed his eyes. The noise came again. *A moan.* After a moment he heard a whimper. Walking with Boots's bridle in his hand, Frederick turned the corner of the trail and came to an abrupt halt. Someone lay crumpled in front of him, and he took a deep breath after seeing the figure move. "Don't be frightened," Frederick whispered.

"Dinna touch me!" a woman's voice said, her voice tremulous, weak and pain-ladened.

"Sorcha?" He tied his horse to a nearby tree and dropped to his haunches. He ran a hand over her head and back, frowning when his palm came away bloodstained. "Let me turn you over."

"Dinna touch me," she said again as a sob burst forth. "It hurts too much. Just let me die."

"You dramatic fool," he muttered. "I won't let you die in the wilderness, a target for the wolves and bears. Is that how you'd like to meet your maker?" He waited until he saw a small shrug of her shoulders. "Is that your greatest desire? To become a tall tale in Jessamine's newspaper?"

Sorcha MacKinnon, the only unmarried MacKinnon in Bear Grass Springs, had arrived from the Isle of Skye in Scotland over two years ago to join her brothers Cailean, Alistair and Ewan. The youngest brother, Ewan, was married to Jessamine, the town's reporter.

Sorcha pushed herself up enough to glare at Frederick, her light-blue eyes lit with animosity. "How dare ye turn what has happened to me into a farce?"

"I'm not the one begging to be left in the wilderness to die." He reached forward and eased her onto her back, earning a yelp of surprise before she passed out. "Sorcha!" he screamed. "Sorcha!"

She was as white as a freshly bleached sheet, and he frantically placed his fingers at her throat, anxious to feel any sign of life. He leaned over her, his breath calming as he felt her soft exhalations on his cheek. "Wake up, you devilish woman." He ran a hand over her arms and then blanched as her burgundy wool skirt had risen up high on one side, and he saw the odd angle of her upper right leg. "Oh, dear God, what have you done?"

"I dinna do anything," she whispered, her eyes still closed.

"What happened?" he asked as he breathed out a sigh of relief that her faint was short lived.

"It was Sugar. She bolted and threw me. Somehow I hit a rock, and … I dinna remember the rest."

"You could have broken your neck."

"Aye." She took a deep breath, her mouth tight with pain. "Then I wouldna be in such pain."

Frederick made a noise of disgust that rivaled any her Scottish brothers made. "Do you think your family wouldn't mourn you? How could you be so selfish?"

Tears seeped out of the corner of her eyes. "I ken I have a broken leg, Frederick. I ken I'll be a cripple the rest of my life." She swallowed a sob. "I dinna want that." Until this moment, they had always snarled and circled around each other when they met at his grandparents' café or at a town dance.

He leaned forward and swiped at her cheeks, meeting her startled gaze at his tender touch. "You will not die. You will not be crippled. You are strong and determined and as irascible as anyone I've ever met." He looked deeply into her eyes. "You will fight."

She nodded and then flushed. "Dinna tell them that I was so weak, aye?"

He smiled. "Never." He looked to his horse and then at Sorcha. "I can't get you to the ranch with a broken leg on my horse." He pulled off his long jacket and covered her and then tugged the bandanna from around his neck, tying it to help staunch the bleeding at the back of her head. "I have to leave you to get help."

Her eyes were frantic for a split second before she closed them and nodded. "Aye, I understand." She opened them with a start when she felt him place a revolver in one of her hands.

"I hope you have a basic understanding of how to use this." At her nod, he gently squeezed her arm. "I'll return as soon as I can, and I'll call out, so you will know it's me."

"Hurry," she whispered.

He leaned forward and kissed her forehead. "Fight, Sorcha." He rose, grabbed his horse's reins and was off before she could react to his impetuous action.

He raced down the trail as fast as he thought safe for his horse. When he was free of the forest, he caught sight of riders in the distance, approaching the ranch. He pulled his rifle from the back of his saddle, stopped and fired once in the air. The riders turned in his direction and raced toward him.

As they approached, Frederick recognized the three MacKinnon brothers, Cailean, Alistair and Ewan, along with their good friend and partner, Bears Renfrew. Bears was a one-third partner in the livery which Cailean and Alistair owned in town, while Ewan was a carpenter who ran a successful construction business.

"Sorcha," Cailean MacKinnon said on a gasp. "She's missin'. I ken somethin's happened to her." His hazel eyes wild with fear, he watched Frederick rein his horse to a halt in front of his brothers and friend.

Frederick nodded. "Yes. She's back there, in the woods, with a broken leg." He grabbed at his friend's reins. "Cailean, wait! We must get a wagon or something to transport her back to the ranch."

"We'll bring her home," Cailean said as the wind blew gusts of frigid air across the prairie, heralding the nearing storm.

Frederick held onto his friend's reins to prevent him from riding off. "No. She's badly injured and such a journey would only harm her more. The ranch is much closer than town. We mustn't jostle her more than is necessary. And she can't ride a horse in her condition."

"Ye get the damn transport. I'm goin' to my sister," Cailean growled as he took off at a gallop toward the location Frederick had indicated.

"Call out to her when you approach! I gave her my revolver," Frederick yelled. He saw Cailean's acknowledgment of his words by a raised arm in the air as he raced away.

Frederick watched Bears and Ewan galloping off after Cailean and turned to share a look with Alistair, who remained beside Frederick. "Do you mind being the one to help me?"

"Nae," Alistair said. "Sorcha doesna need three MacKinnons worryin' over her with no way to move her." He rode alongside Frederick at a breakneck pace as they approached the barn, Frederick yelling for his men to prepare a wagon.

Soon the wagon pulled by two of his strongest draft horses was ready, as were his men. One ranch hand rode into town for the doctor, and another readied a sickroom for Sorcha at the main ranch house. A third ranch hand cooked food to feed all the unexpected visitors. The two most junior men prepared stalls for the visitors' horses that would need tending upon their arrival. Soon, Frederick was driving the wagon with as much speed as possible out of the stable yard toward the mountains.

When Frederick and Alistair reached the base of the trail that led up into the mountain, they had to abandon the wagon. From the wagon bed, they extracted a large piece of wood and hauled it with them up the trail.

As they approached, they heard Ewan and Cailean speaking; Bears and Sorcha were silent. Frederick shared a worried glance with Alistair as they rounded the bend.

"How is she?" Frederick asked. He glanced at Sorcha and frowned to see her sweating and shaking.

Bears had pulled off his shirt and had torn it into strips. He had long straight branches set beside her misshapen leg.

Cailean shook his head in despair. "Come. Let's get her away from here."

"No," Bears said. "We must bind her leg first." He motioned for

Ewan to hold her shoulders as he pulled up her long skirts, showing a finely stitched hem on her knickers.

"Hush, Sorch," Ewan said as he bent over her and murmured in her ear. He held her tight as she shrieked and swatted at them, struggling when they moved her leg. Frederick grabbed her hands, holding them immobile until she fainted again.

Once she was insensate, Ewan let out a stuttering breath, and Bears worked with efficient movements as he braced her leg. He supported it with sticks and then had Cailean tie them in place. When Bears was satisfied that her leg was as stable as possible, he motioned for Frederick and Alistair to bring over the large flat piece of wood. The MacKinnon brothers picked up their sister, placing her gently on the board before all five men picked it up and carried her back down the trail to where the wagon awaited them.

After a few sections in the forest where it was a challenge to fit the pallet through the narrow trail, they arrived at the wagon. Once Sorcha was settled in the wagon bed, Frederick hopped up to drive the wagon. Ewan sat beside him, while Alistair and Cailean sat at the rear of the wagon with their sister.

Bears nodded to the brothers. "I'll get the horses and follow you to the ranch." Bears ran off into the forest. When Bears rejoined them, the reins of the brothers' horses tied to his saddle, they were halfway back to the ranch.

During the trip, Frederick asked Ewan, "How did you know Sorcha was missing?"

"Sugar came back alone to the livery." He shook his head. "How that horse kent where to go, I dinna ken. As soon as it showed up with no rider, Alistair kent Sorcha was in trouble. Cailean ran for me as Alistair and Bears prepared our horses."

"Do your womenfolk know something happened?"

Ewan nodded. "Aye. Cailean stopped at the bakery to tell them."

Frederick shook his head. "How did you know to come out here?"

"Bears kent she'd headed out of town past the church. Karl saw her race past the sawmill afore noon today. I dinna ken what made her so upset." Ewan glowered at the passing scenery, his expression gloomier with each bump they hit and with each stifled moan heard from his sister. "She has a fiery temper, aye, but she isna foolish."

"Perhaps that horse isn't as docile as you think." Frederick tried to remember what the horse was like but couldn't remember Sugar from his brief visits to the livery in town.

Bears spoke up. "There isn't a more docile horse on earth. Something or someone upset it." He shared a glower with Ewan.

"Aye, an' Sorcha is sufferin' because of it," Ewan said. He glanced over his shoulder to find Cailean and Alistair talking to each other on the back of the wagon. They weren't able to sit beside Sorcha out of fear of jostling her as the wagon swayed. "An' someone will pay for hurtin' our baby sister."

～

Helen Clark, the town midwife, ran from Frederick's ranch house as soon as the wagon pulled up the drive. "Sorcha!" she yelled as the men moved to pull her pallet from the back of the wagon.

Frederick hopped down and grabbed Helen's arm. "Helen, give us a minute." He met her worried gaze. "Take a moment to calm yourself so you can help her." He watched as she took a few deep breaths, and any panic was now hidden away as she transformed into the competent healer she was renowned for. "Is the doc here?"

"Yes, he's inside. He's ordering your men about." She flushed. "I didn't care for him to think of me as his hired staff, so ..."

Frederick smiled for an instant before frowning as he looked at Sorcha, who clenched her jaw as each step jostled her and provoked pain. "Help her."

Helen stroked a hand down his arm as she followed the men carefully moving Sorcha into the house. She directed them into the first-floor room where she had slept when she had lived here earlier in the year. Helen waited outside for them to transfer Sorcha to the bed as the room was too small for all of them. Bears emerged, but the MacKinnon brothers remained inside.

"You should leave. The doc and I will tend her," Helen said as she poked her head in. She met the MacKinnons' mutinous frowns and motioned for them to wait in the parlor. "After the doc leaves, I'll bathe her and get her in some clean clothes." Each brother kissed Sorcha on the forehead and whispered something in her ear before leaving.

Cailean was the last to depart, and he paused, staring at Helen intently for a few moments. "I ken ye and the doc will do all ye can. Come for us, with any concern," he said, his voice hoarse and thickened with a Scottish accent that was generally muted after many years of living in the United States. His eyes glistened with tears, and he swallowed before he dropped his head and marched out of the sickroom.

Helen moved toward Sorcha, instinctively grabbing a clean, dry cloth. She swiped at Sorcha's brows and frowned at her fever. She heard the doctor enter behind her and said, "I'll brew some willow bark tea."

The doctor waved away that offer. "I've already sent one of the ranch men to do that. I need your steady hands to help me set the bone. And we need a man in here who will hold her down and not become too emotional."

Helen paled. She poked her head out and looked into the parlor. Bears paced around the room, as though feeling trapped or cataloging the fine contents of the living space. "Bears." As Helen called his name, he was instantly alert. "We may need your help." She met the brothers' stares, and their shared despair shone in their eyes.

Bears nodded and followed Helen into the room. He saw the doctor removing the makeshift splint and met the doctor's gaze.

"Whoever thought of this might have saved her from being permanently crippled," the doctor said. He motioned for Bears to hold Sorcha's upper body.

Bears shook his head. "We need more help." He moved out the door, and soon the brothers were in the room again. Ewan and Alistair held her shoulders while Cailean held her middle and Bears her other leg. "Do it, Doc," Bears said.

With grunts and groans, the doctor manipulated her leg, causing an unconscious Sorcha to jerk and fight him. Thankfully her brothers and Bears kept her steady enough so her involuntary movements did not interfere with the doctor's attempt to set her bone. Finally the doctor straightened, nodding his head with grim satisfaction.

"I think it's in place. There is already quite a bit of swelling, so I cannot be completely sure. But she has a chance that she will only walk with a minor limp." He looked at her brothers. "Whatever you do, do not move her until she is completely healed. It will take months for a larger bone, like a fractured femur, to mend itself." He looked at the brothers with grave intensity. "To break that bone again would render her crippled for life." He paused as he met each brother's thunderstruck stare. "Or kill her."

The wind rattled the windows, reminding them of the impending storm and winter's early arrival.

"I must leave at once to beat the storm." With that, the doctor washed up quickly and departed.

"I ken our wives and Fidelia would be willin' to take turns carin' for Sorcha out here," Ewan said. He paused as another gust of wind battered the house. "But I dinna ken if I could live without Jessamine if she were to be stranded here for a long winter."

Cailean shook his head. "A week without Belle would be long. I can't imagine an entire winter."

"But Sorcha canna stay here alone with only ranch hands. A single woman on a ranch?" Ewan sputtered.

"'Twould ruin her reputation," Alistair breathed.

Helen put a hand on her hip and glared at the brothers. "Did it ruin mine? Was I found to be damaged goods because I lived here before I married Warren?" She nodded as they flushed. "No, I wasn't. And Sorcha won't be either because the men here are honorable."

"Aye, I know," Cailean said as he shared a wild look with his brothers. "But we want her close so we can care for her, aye? And what happens when she needs more personal care?"

A throat cleared in the doorway. "I will care for her. I will ensure no harm comes to her," Frederick said.

Cailean turned and shared a long look with Frederick. "Aye. I think you believe that, but …" He shook his head. "We will visit often."

Frederick nodded. "I would expect nothing less." Frederick shared a fatigued smile with Helen. "Thank you, Helen, for being here today. I know that you didn't have to come."

"But I did," Helen whispered as she pulled the blankets around Sorcha. "She watched over me as I struggled this spring. It's the least I could do for her." Helen looked at the MacKinnon brothers. "Warren already knows I will spend the night here tonight. I will keep vigil to ensure she does not worsen, but I must depart tomorrow before the storm fully arrives."

"Aye," Ewan said. "An' I will stay with ye. Ben can run the sites for me tomorrow, an' Jessie kens where I am." He looked at his brothers. "I'll send word immediately if anything changes."

Cailean and Alistair nodded before they exited the room. Bears had already departed to ensure their horses were ready for the return trip into town.

Ewan sat in a chair near Sorcha and held her hand. "She struggles with the pain, aye?" he whispered to Helen.

"I fear she will for some time." She smiled at the man she considered a close friend, if not family. Her husband, Warren Clark, was the town lawyer, and he was an honorary member of the MacKinnon clan. When she married Warren, they had welcomed her into their family too. "The tea will help her, and I'll see if Frederick has any ice left in the ice house."

"For the swelling," Ewan said, nodding, as his sister whimpered. "Ye ken we'll never forget yer help today."

Helen squeezed his arm. "I know. I'm just sorry it was required." She left him to keep his vigil to rest for a few hours.

❧

A deep burning pain lit her right leg. Waves of agony filled her, and nothing caused it to abate. Sorcha reached toward her place of torment, only to have her hands caught in a tight grip. She groaned as she did not have the strength to overpower whoever restricted her. "Let me," she rasped as she moved her head side to side.

"No, Sorcha. No," a deep, melodious voice whispered in her ear.

"Who?" she rasped as she struggled. "Why?"

"You injured your leg, and you will not undo all we have done to help you heal properly."

"Please," she begged as tears leaked out. "Make it stop." She sighed as a cool cloth swiped over her forehead and face.

"Make what stop?"

"I feel like I'm on fire. Like my leg is burnin' up from inside out. I canna take this." She frowned as she felt him moving away from her. "Dinna leave me. I'll try to be stronger."

"Oh, you are plenty strong."

Sorcha felt another soft swipe over her face and then a gentle hand to the back of her neck and shoulders.

"Drink."

She swallowed, and her lips puckered at the bitter taste. "Are ye tryin' to kill me?" She frowned at his chuckle.

"No, you little demon," the man with the melodious voice said. "I'm trying to help your pain and fever. It's willow bark tea. Helen said to add honey. I'll add more next time."

"Please," she whispered as she collapsed against the cushions. "Why am I too tired to open my eyes? What happened to me?" She relaxed as a hand swiped over her head again and then cool fingers clasped hers.

"You were bucked off your horse, and I found you in the woods. The doctor had to set your leg."

"My leg," she whispered as she seemed to realize her reason for panic.

"*Shh*, Sorcha. The new doctor is competent. And Helen was here to ensure he did everything right and to get you properly cleaned up."

"Helen?" Sorcha whispered. "Why can I no' remember?"

"You had a head injury too. But relax for now," he murmured. When she settled again, he sang to her softly, never leaving her side until she was completely asleep.

⁓

The following day Sorcha woke and stared with bleary eyes around the room. Curtains were closed against the cold and to prevent the bright sunlight from disturbing her rest. She touched the heavy blankets, tucked up under her chin, and frowned. As she attempted to move, a searing pain lit up the right side of her body, intensifying in her right thigh. Unable to help herself, she gave a small scream of dismay.

"Sorcha!" Helen gasped as she thrust open the door. "What have you done?"

Sorcha frowned as she stared at Helen. "What are ye doing here, Helen? And where is *here*?"

"Frederick's ranch. You were injured, and this was the closest place."

"What day is it?"

"November fourth. A Thursday. You fell yesterday." Helen bustled into the room, filling a small bowl with fresh water from the ewer and grabbing a clean cloth. She set the bowl of water on the small bedside table and dipped the cloth into it. She raised an eyebrow when Sorcha thrust her hand out to take the cloth. "You shouldn't move or you'll only cause tremendous pain, like you just had."

Sorcha frowned and nodded. After a moment she asked, "What happened?"

The door creaked open farther, and Ewan stood in the doorway. "I was hopin' ye'd tell me, Sorch." He shared a long look with his sister as she stared at him in confusion. "What caused Sugar to bolt and to toss ye against a rock an' break yer leg?"

"Sugar?" Sorcha whispered. "I dinna ken. She is docile, aye? I never had trouble with her before."

"Bears swears that someone must have spooked her for her to act like she did."

Sorcha shook her head. "I dinna ken. Not now." She rubbed at her head. "Mayhap later?"

Helen glared at Ewan. "We already discussed this, Ewan. You know that it may be some time before Sorcha remembers everything. She has suffered a trauma to her head."

Ewan sighed and glowered at them. "I ken, aye. But I dinna like knowin' someone is out there who hurt my sister. No' when I dinna ken who he is and. Not when I ken he isna bein' punished."

"Ewan," Sorcha whispered. She held her hand out to her brother. "Am I … Will I …" She bit her lip.

Her brother, youngest in age to her, frowned. "Will ye what, Sorch?" As he saw her struggle to find the words, he nodded in understanding. "Will ye walk again?" As her eyes filled with tears, and he saw her battle an inner terror, he clasped her hand. He knelt beside her, not wishing to sit on the bed and jostle her. "Aye, ye will walk again and no' be a cripple, *if* ye do what the doc and Helen say."

He traced away a tear as she waited for him to explain further. "Ye must remain here, Sorch. We canna move ye into town. Yer leg could break again, and then ye may never walk again."

"No, Ewan, ye canna leave me here." Her eyes overflowed, and tears coursed down her cheeks. "Ye canna leave me with strangers."

"Ye have to understand, Sorcha. If we move ye, an' yer leg breaks, ye could die. None of us will risk that." He nodded as she stared at him in astonishment.

"Besides, Frederick is no' a stranger. He found ye. He saved ye. We could still be lookin' for ye." His eyes were wild with fear. "Ye dinna ken what it did to us to have Sugar return without ye."

"I'm sorry, Ewan. I'm so sorry. Dinna punish me by leaving me here," she sobbed.

"Oh, ye daft wee thing, 'tis no' a punishment. 'Tis what we must do to ensure ye heal. The doc said so. Can ye no' see the difference? Can ye no' imagine how it's tearin' us apart to no' have ye near us?"

She accepted his handkerchief, swiping at her eyes and nose. "Promise me ye'll visit. As often as ye can."

"I promise," Ewan whispered. "I ken we'll have a hard time limitin' the visitors. Frederick will grow daft with all who want to visit his ranch. I want ye to ken the only thing that will keep us away is a fierce storm. Pray for a mild winter, aye?" He smiled as Sorcha fought tears, and he traced away a tear on her cheek. "Every week one of yer sisters will help ye with yer personal care an' catch ye up on gossip from the bakery." He referred to her sisters-in-law who Sorcha considered her sisters.

"I ken that's the best ye can do, Ewan, but I fear I'll go mad between your visits," she whispered.

"Ye are my beloved sister, Sorcha. There is little I would no' do to see ye safe. I promise ye that ye will be protected here. I trust Frederick to keep ye safe. Ye ken?"

Sorcha battled a sob. "I ken, Ewan. I ken."

"*Shh*, Sorcha," Ewan said, patting her softly.

When Sorcha began to fall asleep, Ewan eased from the room. He found Frederick pacing in the parlor and heard Helen teasing Frederick's workers in the kitchen. "I forgot that Helen would be friends with yer men."

Frederick nodded. "Yes. She was adored by them." He took a deep breath. "Sorcha doesn't remember what happened to her, does she?"

Ewan shook his head. "Nae. She doesna remember anything except wakin' up this mornin'." He paused a moment. "What did Bears say to ye yesterday afore he left?"

Frederick shared a concerned look with Ewan. "He advised me to be vigilant. That not everything was at it appeared and that Sorcha was still at risk."

Ewan flushed with anger and then stared hard at Frederick. "I ken ye promised Cailean that ye'd protect her." He saw Frederick tense under Ewan's severe gaze. "Ye ken all that that means?"

Frederick nodded. "Yes."

Ewan strode up to Frederick until he was nearly chest to chest with him. "I ken ye are Irene's and Harold's grandson. I ken ye treated Helen with respect when she lived here on the ranch." He took a deep breath. "But ye did no' desire Helen. No' like ye desire my sister."

Frederick's eyes flashed. "Do you truly believe I would attempt to seduce Sorcha when she is hurt?" Frederick met Ewan's glower. "I will ignore your insult because I know you are worried and truly care for your sister. I keep my promises."

They stepped away from each other as Helen entered the room, confusion in her gaze at the apparent animosity between the two men. "Ewan? Should we return to town soon?"

"Aye," he whispered with a tortured glance toward his sister's door. "I would like to wait until Sorcha wakens to say goodbye. An' then we should leave, before the next storm hits and traps us here—or worse, finds us on the road."

CHAPTER 2

A week later, daily snowstorms had impeded her sisters-in-law from spending more than a few hours at a time with Sorcha, as they feared being stranded at the ranch too. Frederick looked into Sorcha's room and growled. "What do you think you're doing?" he snapped.

She glared at him. "Are ye daft? I'm tryin' to find a comfortable position. If I can move around an' no' just lie on my back, I ken I'll feel better." She gasped as he pressed on her shoulders, pushing her down against the mattress.

"I know this means you are improving and that you feel restless. However, it's no reason for you to risk reinjuring your leg. The doc wanted you to have complete bed rest for at least two months to allow the bone to heal properly, and that is what you'll have." He stared at her and watched her flush. "Do you want to limp? Or worse, do you want to cripple yourself? Do you wish to disappoint your brothers?"

"Ye dinna have the right to keep me here against my will," she snapped. "An' dinna imply I'm disappointin' my brothers."

"*Against your will?*" Frederick leaned forward and placed his hands on either side of her pillow as he loomed over her.

"Aye, I dinna want to remain here with a bunch of farmhands! I want to be in town, with my family. With people who ken me." Her cheeks flushed with aggravation. "I'm tired of havin' to depend on ye for care when my family is no' here."

"None of us mind the work, Sorcha," he murmured.

"I mind!" she shouted and then glared at him. "I want to go home, where I ken I'll be well taken care of."

"Fine," Frederick said, his blue eyes flashing with anger. "Slims!" At his bellow, the large man entered the room. "Our guest no longer wishes to remain here. Please carry her to a sleigh and bring her into town before the winter weather prevents any such travel."

"But, Boss," Slims said, with a shake of his head.

"Do it!" Frederick ordered and stormed from the room.

Slims stood, staring at Sorcha lying on the bed, the covers tossed aside, exposing her in a flannel nightgown. "Is this what you wish?" At her defiant nod, he moved to her side and scooped his arms under her, one under her shoulders, the other her knees. "Put your arms around my neck."

"See, Mr. Slims? I kent there was no reason I shouldna ..."

As he lifted her, she gave a small scream and then fainted.

Slims settled her in the bed again, pulling the blankets over her and turning to meet Frederick's agitated stare. "You proved your point, Boss. Don't expect me to help you again." He pushed past Frederick and returned to the kitchen.

"Damn stubborn woman," Frederick muttered as he sat beside Sorcha's bed. He gave a nod of thanks to Slims as he brought in a cup of willow bark tea. Then Frederick held her hand as he waited for her to awaken.

"I'm sorry," he whispered to her. "I'm sorry I lost my temper and allowed you to feel a moment of pain. Wake up, Sorcha." He waited a minute, and he saw her eyes flickering. "Come back, love." He flushed as the endearment slipped out.

"Cailean?" she rasped.

"No, it's Frederick," he said as he swiped at her sweaty brow. "You're at my ranch, and we just argued." He waited until she opened her eyes. "I'm sorry."

"I thought I heard ye say that," she said with an impish smile. "Oh, how my leg hurts." She held a hand to her broken leg. "I was the fool who wanted to leave."

They stared into each other's eyes for a moment. Finally he said, "But I am uninjured, and this is my home. I should have had better sense than to rile you."

"I have a temper, aye?" She flushed. "I'll be the one to pay for my folly." She moaned as he eased her to a sitting position to take a sip of the willow bark tea. "Thank ye."

He sat there in the chair beside her sickbed for many minutes as he watched her take deep breaths as she fought through the pain. "I know my men and I are not who you would consider for nursemaids, but I like to think we are doing a decent job."

She gave a half smile and nodded. "Ye are."

He paused and scratched at his day's growth of beard. "I'm sorry you feel like a prisoner here, Sorcha, but you can't leave. It's in your best interests. You understand that, don't you?"

She nodded and opened her eyes, a deep resignation within. "I ken I can no'. I'm frustrated an' uncomfortable an' no' used to being restricted to one room. I'm crotchety when I'm no' sick. Ye can imagine how much worse it is when I am." She smiled ruefully at him.

"I fear there's little I can do to make your situation any better than it is."

"I ken," she whispered as her eyes filled. "I ken. An' that's what makes it so difficult."

Two weeks later as November waned, Sorcha sat in bed in her ranch bedroom, staring at the wallpaper. She had memorized the design, counted the number of flowers that bloomed in one branch from floor to ceiling, and she had learned the patterns of the ranch by the sounds the men made. Early morning was punctuated by groans, grunts and the sound of the coffeepot slamming over and over onto the stove. Then the house quieted until noontime, when the kitchen door slammed shut repeatedly as the men entered for their midday meal. They conversed in low voices, a rare laugh heard in her room. In the evening, their voices were louder and more relaxed as they sounded satisfied after a day's hard work.

Throughout each day, someone poked a head into her room to check on her, brought her food and water, but rarely spent any time with her. Her brothers, one by one, had come for short visits as the recurring snowstorms broke. During one visit, Annabelle had ridden in the sleigh with Cailean to check on her sister-in-law and to bring Sorcha her knitting needles and wool. During another visit, Fidelia had brought fresh clothes including two winter dresses and three nightgowns. Jessamine, during her visit, brought tall tales and gossip. All of the women helped Sorcha bathe and ensured she had fresh sheets and had changed into a clean nightgown before they left.

While Ewan and Jessamine were at the ranch, they had to cut short their visit and leave with precipitous haste due to the sudden arrival of a particularly severe storm. With each departure of her family members, Sorcha fought against begging them to bring her home.

Thanksgiving had been a quiet affair, with none of her family able to visit. The following day someone had entered her room and had cracked the window curtain open for her while she dozed in the midmorning. She turned as the floor creaked near her doorway. "Hello?" She waited, heard nothing and then sighed. "There's no one there, ye daft woman," she said to herself. "An' why would there be? They've a ranch to run. They've no time to spend worryin' over ye."

She frowned as she heard a muffled chuckle. "Who are ye to listen to my ramblin's?" She leaned forward as far as she could, grimacing as the movement provoked increased pain in her leg.

Frederick poked his head in. "Hello, Sorcha." His smile broadened as she gave a grunt of disgust at his appearance. "You seem to be improving."

"I'm bored," she snapped and then flushed. "Why do ye no' ken I need somethin' to do other than count flowers on the wall?"

Frederick frowned and then laughed. "I wondered what you were muttering about in your sleep. Arguing with yourself between thirty-seven and thirty-eight."

She flushed. "'Tis of great importance."

"Why not knit with the yarns that Annabelle brought you?"

Sorcha shook her head. "I canna focus enough to keep up with the count of my stitches."

"Thus you count the flowers on the wallpaper instead. I imagine it's much like counting sheep. No wonder you sleep so often." Frederick's gaze lit with humor as he teased her.

Her blue eyes glinted with defiance and challenge. "Ye'd do the same were ye stuck in this bed."

Frederick sobered. "I fear I'd do far worse." He sighed and pulled out the nearby chair, sitting beside her. "Every time I come in here, you're asleep. I'm sorry if you've been bored." He ran a hand through his hair. "No womenfolk are on the ranch just now. The men who had wives left for the winter to see their families." After a moment's silence between them, he said, "What would you like to read? There is a library of sorts in the parlor."

She frowned and shrugged. "Do ye have any Dickens?"

Frederick frowned as he stared at her. "Dickens?" At her challenging stare he nodded. "Yes, we have a few of his novels. I thought you'd want to read Jane Austen or something like that."

Sorcha shook her head. "Nae. Dickens's books are long, an' I need the longest books possible right now."

Frederick nodded as though understanding her reasoning. "Consider it done."

"Why do ye no' have a cook? I thought all ranches had cooks."

He sighed, rubbing at the back of his neck. "Well, Helen filled that position for a little while before she returned to town to help your sister-in-law and to marry Warren. Then the next man I hired as a cook turned out to be a drunk and a rascal." He sighed again. "I sent him away before the weather turned."

"Why? I'd have sent him off in the middle of a blizzard."

He stared at her so long that she blushed. "You say that, but, when it comes to it, I doubt you could be so cold-hearted as to send a man to his certain death. I believe you would have done as I did."

"Ye just sent him on to bamboozle another unsuspectin' person."

Frederick nodded. "Yeah, that may be so. But I think he's paid a high price for his devotion to alcohol." He waited for her retort and studying her when she bit her lip, as though deep in thought.

Sorcha frowned. "Is that why ye rotate between three meals? Slims seems upset when he brings me the meals he's cooked." She flushed at her impertinent question.

Frederick chuckled. "Yes. Slims is a decent cook, but he's upset I want him in the kitchen rather than working in the barn with my horses. He's trying to make me so sick of his cooking by only cooking three meals that I'll have another one of the men cook." He shuddered. "But they're horrible cooks."

"Why do ye no' cook?"

He shrugged. "I could. I might have to."

"So ye can cook?" She raised an eyebrow.

"Yes."

She watched him a long minute. "Yer mother must have taught ye well." Her smile froze as he glared at her.

"Nothing worth learning was ever taught by that woman." He rose and slammed his chair into the corner. "I'll ensure you have more company during the day."

She watched as he strode from the room, her brows furrowed as his bootheels clomped down the hall. As she relaxed against her pillow, she muttered to herself, "No need to act as though ye're the only one who ever had trouble with yer mother."

～

During the next two weeks Frederick and his men visited Sorcha frequently. Howling winds and over two feet of snow heralded the arrival of December. When the latest blizzard calmed, everything in sight was covered in a thick layer of snow. Drifts of snow made for treacherous travel by foot and on horseback, impeding all travel to and from town.

Although Sorcha listened for her brothers' voices, she did not see them after the December blizzard. Instead, she heard the low rumble of the ranch hands and Frederick's deep baritone. Sorcha spent hours knitting socks, sweaters and scarves with the wool Annabelle had brought to the ranch. One afternoon Sorcha looked over her shoulder to find one of the men, Dixon, staring at her from her doorway. He studied the burgundy scarf Sorcha worked on, which was almost complete.

"Do you only make new clothes?" He stared at her and frowned as he rubbed his head.

"Nae, but 'tis what I have to do now." She set aside her needles and motioned for him to enter the room. "Ye're Mr. Dixon, aye?"

He flushed and nodded. He stood tall, as tall as his middling height allowed. Although slender, he had a sense of restrained strength in him as he stood watching her.

"How long have ye been at the ranch?" she asked.

"Going on five years now, miss. Boss didn't have to take on a greenhorn like me, but he said he saw potential." His chest puffed out at that. "Now I train the other greenhorns who show up each spring lookin' for work."

She smiled. "Yer family must be proud."

He shook his head. "I don't have no family, Miss Sorcha. They all died when I was a boy."

"I dinna understand how ye can be as optimistic as ye are," she said as she watched him with wonder.

"If I've learned one thing in this life, miss, it's *live for today*. I have no faith in there bein' a tomorrow."

"How can ye be so optimistic and so jaded all at such a young age?" she asked.

"I'm twenty-eight, miss." He shrugged. "An' I doubt I will have my own family as I doubt I'll marry."

They remained in companionable silence for a few minutes, and then she frowned. "Do ye like workin' as a cowboy?"

He shrugged and sat after she motioned for him to settle on one of the chairs near her bed. "Yes, although I like the horses more. I understand some have no interest in horses. Except in carin' for their own so it never lets them down." He stared at her hard. "To abuse your horse is the worst sin."

She frowned at his censure and then flushed with indignation. "I may no' remember what happened, but I ken I did nothin' to harm Sugar."

"Riding like a bat out of hell is no way to treat a fine animal." He nodded as she clamped her jaw shut rather than lie to contradict him. "I heard your brothers talkin'. Wonderin' what got you so riled that day."

She crossed her arms over her chest and glared at him. "Is that all ye men do out here? Gossip about me?"

He laughed and scratched at his blond hair. "What else is there to do in this cold winter that has just begun and seems like it will never end?" He smiled with satisfaction. "It's as though you were sent here to ensure we wouldn't die of boredom."

She gave a small shriek of frustration and threw a ball of yarn at him, hitting him on his head. It unfurled and fell down over his ear and shoulder, before landing with a *thud* on the floor.

"Sorcha, are you all right?" Frederick asked as he poked his head in. He frowned as he saw Dixon with yarn tangled over one side of his body. "Dix?" When Dixon just shrugged and untangled the yarn from around his head and arm, Frederick turned to Sorcha. "Would you care to enlighten me as to why one of my men is sitting here covered in your yarn?"

"I threw it at him." She glared at Frederick. "I willna be little more than entertainment for ye and yer men." She flushed as she saw Frederick's startled expression.

"Entertainment?" He shared a quick look with Dixon, who only rolled his eyes. "We've only treated you with respect. Never like ... never like ..." He sputtered a moment before flushing and meeting her irate gaze. "Never like a woman from the Boudoir." Betty's Boudoir was the whorehouse in Bear Grass Springs.

"*Argh!*" Sorcha growled as she slapped her hands onto the side of the bed. "Ye'd better be thankful I'm stuck in this bed an' canna chase ye down for insinuatin' that ye'd treat me no better than a Boudoir Beauty!"

Frederick bit back a laugh and took a step backward, aware that her knitting needles were long and sharp. "I never did. *You* did."

"I did no'!" Sorcha bellowed loudly enough for the men in the kitchen to hear. "Ye jumped to that conclusion." She took a deep breath, glaring at Dixon's back as he made a hasty retreat. "I dinna want to be your latest source of gossip."

Frederick chuckled, leaning against the wall near the chair Dixon had just vacated. "You are, and you will be until you leave. The men are fascinated by you. By your stories of Scotland. The fairies and legends. The descriptions of lochs and moors and mountains. How it is different but similar to our life here." He met her startled gaze and noticed when she calmed.

"They compare stories. Life on a ranch is isolating." He paused. "Life on a ranch in the middle of a brutal winter is like purgatory. You're making it bearable. For them." He met her gaze, his eyes expressing a deeper truth that he did not say out loud. He paused as she bit her lip and tilted her head, studying him. "Be patient with them." After a moment he murmured, "For you are becoming precious to them."

Her breath caught at his words spoken in his gentle tone as she watched him slip from her room. "Precious only to them?" she whispered to herself. "Or to ye too?"

The following day Slims entered her room with a tray of food. Slims was the tallest man she'd ever seen, standing at six-and-a-half-feet tall. He had broad shoulders and a barrel chest with hands twice as big as hers. However, he was one of the gentlest men she had ever met.

Today she frowned at the food on the tray, as it was not one of the usual meals that had been delivered so far during her stay at the ranch. Rather than meat loaf, beef stew or something she'd heard the men call *slop*, a serving of fried chicken, biscuits and mashed potatoes was on her tray with a slice of cake beside it. "Did ye decide to stop borin' us?" Sorcha asked with an appreciative sniff at the tray of food.

Slims laughed. "No, Dalton slipped into town between snow-storms, and Mrs. Tompkins sent back food. And the bakery sent us cakes."

She fought an instinctive envy that she had not returned to town with Dalton, although she knew she would be bedridden for at least another month. She watched Slims curiously. "Do they do that often? Send cakes?"

"'Bout as often as never, miss." He set the tray on her lap. "Seems those in town are worried about you and want to ensure you're eatin' well. It's my dumb luck that means they sent food along for all of us."

She studied him a moment, holding her hands together so she wouldn't devour the food that instant. "Ye seem more content today, Mr. Slims."

He chuckled. "It's just *Slims*, miss." He sat on the chair near her bed and motioned for her to eat. "And I am. Rather than be chained to that tempestuous monstrosity Frederick calls a stove, I spent the afternoon in the barn." He sighed with pleasure.

She tilted her head to one side. "They're yer first love, are they no'?"

He nodded. "I've yet to meet anything or anyone I love more."

After she swallowed her first bite of chicken, she asked, "Has this always been a ranch that raises horses?"

Slims kicked out his legs, shaking his head. "No, that's Frederick's doing. His father was a cattleman, as are Frederick's brothers. Cole and Peter enjoy the challenge of driving a herd from Texas. They don't have much interest in Frederick's notion of raising fine horses."

Sorcha frowned as she ate a mouthful of potato. "Why does Frederick no' travel?"

Slims shrugged. "Seems there was some sort of bet between the brothers, and Frederick lost. That was a while ago, and I think he now prefers to live and work here, rather than deal with the increasing difficulty of bringing a herd north."

"'Tis a long journey, aye, but 'twould be a grand adventure." Her eyes gleamed at the thought.

Slims shook his head. "There ain't no use tryin' to make sittin' in a saddle, eatin' dust for over two thousand miles and waiting for cattle to stampede sound romantic or like an adventure." He failed to hide a smile and then grinned at her. "Although sleeping under the stars around a campfire with the cows lowing nearby is unlike anything else."

"An' ye say 'tis no' romantic," she teased. "I dinna remember meetin' his brothers."

"Oh, when they're home, they rarely go into town." He fought a grimace. "I fear there would be bloodshed if they did."

Sorcha frowned and shook her head in confusion. "I dinna understand. Why would they no' want to see their grandparents?"

Slims slapped his hands and stood. "They have other family in town, Miss Sorcha. I've said enough. If you're this curious, you should speak with Frederick."

She grabbed for Slims's hand as he was about to leave the room. "Can ye no' understand that I'm as bored as any of ye? Mayhap more?"

"Boredom doesn't give me the right to gossip about my boss and friend." Slims nodded and strode from the room.

She savored the rest of her meal, attempting to discern who or what would keep Frederick's brothers from town. When she only succeeded in giving herself a headache, she gave up and enjoyed the slice of white cake with almond-flavored frosting. When she had finished her meal, she set the tray to one side of her bed and began knitting again as she sang a sad love song in Gaelic.

"Are we treating you that poorly?" Frederick asked from the doorway.

She looked at him with curiosity. "I dinna ken what ye mean. I've just eaten a delicious supper, and now I'm knittin'. What more could I want?"

He sighed and sat on the chair near her bed. "Company. If you're resorting to laments in your native tongue, then I know we're doing something wrong."

She laughed. "'Tisn't a lament, Frederick. 'Tis a song about lost love." Her gaze softened as she fingered the plush wool. "My da loved it when I sang, and he taught me many songs. We were no' supposed to sing in Gaelic, but he kent few would notice a lass on Skye, singing in the house. I was to only sing in English when I was outside, working the croft."

"Why wouldn't you sing in Gaelic outside?" he asked with a confused frown.

She shrugged. "After the Battle of Culloden, everything that made us Scottish was banned, includin' our language. We were no' supposed to speak it or sing it, and my father risked quite a bit teachin' me old songs. But he kent how much I loved to sing, so he taught me everythin' he kent, includin' the songs that had been passed down to him. He dinna want them lost, as too much of our heritage had already been lost."

"Your father sounds like a remarkable man." Frederick relaxed into the chair. "He'd be proud of how close you and your brothers are."

"Aye," she said with a smile. She glared at the window. "I dinna like the weather changin' so rapidly that my brothers will no' visit me each week."

Frederick sighed. "I fear they won't visit for some time, Sorcha. Winters are often harsh here, but I've never seen anything like the last blizzard. It looks to be an especially vicious winter this year. I doubt we'll make it into town more than once or twice until the thaw."

She blanched as she stared at him. "But that is no' 'til April."

He nodded.

"Ye canna mean I'm to remain here all this time!" She dropped her knitting needles. She grabbed his hand in supplication. "Ye canna be so cruel."

His eyes flashed. "It isn't cruel of me to want to see you well, Sorcha. And you have a long recovery ahead of you before you can contemplate returning to town."

She swiped at a tear on her cheek, her light-blue eyes mournful. "I had hope, ye ken?"

He nodded. "And you still do, Sorcha. Even if your return is delayed because of this harsh winter by a month or two, you *will* return to your family."

She gave him a weak smile. "Aye, of course ye're right." She closed her eyes a moment. "If ye dinna mind, I'm tired."

He rose, taking her dinner tray with him. "Rest, Sorcha. Nothing will seem as bad in the morning."

When he had closed the door behind him, she let her tears silently pour down her cheeks. "Months of this," she whispered to herself. "How will I bear it that long without my family?"

The next morning Sorcha looked up at Frederick entering her room with a warm basin of water, towels and a fresh change of clothes for her. She looked behind him for one of her sisters-in-law and frowned when none of them followed him in. "What do ye think ye are doin'?"

He set down all he carried and pinched the bridge of his nose. "Sorcha, you need a bath. We'd agreed to wait for your family to visit in early December, but they haven't been here for over two weeks. I doubt they're coming again anytime soon because the winter weather has firmly set in, and they shouldn't risk becoming trapped by a blizzard on the road with no shelter." He shared a knowing look with her.

"Nae, I dinna want them takin' such risks," she murmured, shivering at the thought of any of her family members freezing to death in a storm out of a desire to visit her.

"They might not get out here again until the spring thaw."

She ignored the last of his comments and threw a handkerchief at him. "Ye are no' helpin' me bathe! Do ye want to ruin my reputation?"

"Be reasonable, Sorcha. You need a bath. I can help you." He waited for her agreement and frowned as she continued to glare at him. "You aren't able to stand long enough to wash, only balanced on your good leg. You'd fall over from exhaustion and reinjure your broken leg."

"Ye're daft if ye believe I'll let ye help me." She shook her head as she met his disgruntled stare.

Fine," he snapped. "I'll ask Slims or Dalton to aid you. Or would you prefer Dixon?" His eyes glowed with indignation as he challenged her.

"Dinna be so daft," she sputtered as she tugged the blankets around her. "I ... Ye canna help me, Frederick. Nor can any of yer ranch hands."

He sat on a chair, getting his anger under control, and watched her with forced patience. "If I don't, you'll get bed sores and be worse off. Be sensible."

She stared at him and shook her head. "Ye canna ask such a thing. I'm respectable, aye?"

He scratched at his head. "I refuse to believe, if our situations were reversed, that you wouldn't help me if I were the one in the sickbed."

She flushed and shook her head again. "That is conjecture. I dinna ken how I'd act."

"Don't you want a bath? To be in fresh clothes and fresh bedding and to feel clean?"

She nodded instinctively before she remembered she should say no. After a long pause, she pointed to the chair he sat on. "Place the basin of water atop the chair, with the towels an' soap, and push it all closer to my bed." She flushed. "An' my nightgown too."

He did as she asked and stood, waiting for her next instruction.

"Now get out. I'll bathe myself."

"You can't wash your back," he murmured.

"I'll survive," she snapped. "And dinna enter again until I give ye permission." Her eyes flashed with anger as he chuckled and then slipped out the door, shutting it firmly behind him. She pushed her weight on her left leg, lifting her nightgown up and then over her head. She dropped it to the floor and then pushed the sheets down. With a huge sigh, she waited for her strength to return, astonished at how little she had. Grabbing the washcloth, she wet it and quickly washed every inch of skin she could reach. She then toweled dry as quickly as she could in the chilled air in her sickroom and tugged the fresh nightgown over her head.

She pulled the sheets up over her and gave a sigh of relief to have finished her ablutions before Frederick tapped on the door. "Come in," she said. Her triumphant smile faded as she saw him enter with Dalton and Slims. "I dinna need their help," she sputtered.

She shrieked as Slims picked her up gently, holding her in such a way as to not reinjure her leg as Dalton and Frederick stripped her bed and quickly remade it. Slims set her down again on the bed, patted her shoulder once and allowed Frederick to pull the fresh sheet and blankets over her.

"It made no sense to me that you'd have a bath and yet remain on dirty sheets." He frowned as he saw her fighting tears. "Did Slims hurt your leg?"

"Nae," she whispered.

"Good," he murmured, his gaze intense as he stared at her. "For there's only one thing left to do." He smiled as Slims returned with a fresh basin of water and more towels. "I'm to wash your hair."

She froze at his words. "There is nae need."

He smiled. "On the contrary, there is every need."

Sorcha sat on her bed, her hands playing over her fresh sheets, her clean flannel nightgown and then threading through her now-clean hair. "Heaven," she whispered. Somehow Frederick had known she needed a bath and had found a way to help her while preserving her modesty.

Her eyes closed as she remembered the soft caress of his fingers massaging her scalp and washing her hair. She wondered how he knew to wash her hair without soaking her pillows or her bed. She shivered as she recalled his gentle words, his soothing touch, his impromptu shoulder rub. Blushing, she remembered groaning as he worked out the knots found along her spine.

"Why him?" she murmured to herself. Any of the other ranch hands could have touched her in a similar fashion, and she would have felt gratitude for their thoughtfulness. Never an unremitting desire for more. She groaned again and then shrieked at Frederick's voice.

"Are you unwell, Sorcha? Did your bath give you a chill?" His concerned gaze took in her reddened cheeks.

"Nae. 'Twas what I needed. Thank ye." She kept her gaze downcast as she tugged the bed linens to her chin. When she met his gaze, she saw his amused smile.

"Slims is making tea," Frederick said. "And I know he hopes you'll share another story about Skye with him."

She frowned, thinking about her niece. Then she nodded as she realized Frederick meant her home on the Isle of Skye in Scotland. "Aye, I enjoy talkin' about the fairy pools an' the legends of Skye."

He gave her shoulder a squeeze. "Rest well," he murmured as he left her alone.

She closed her eyes, breathing in his retreating scent, a mixture of musk, horse and something that was all Frederick. "Good night," she whispered.

CHAPTER 3

"For God's sake, who died?" Frederick demanded as he entered her room. His abrupt entrance put an end to her low, haunting singing that sounded like a funeral dirge.

"Why should ye care?" she demanded as she wiped her face.

"The men nominated me to come and see what was wrong."

She glared at him, her crying abating as she grew more angered. "Because a sad woman is no' good for yer appetite? Am I ruinin' yer dinner?"

"Don't be …" He broke off as he sighed and ran a hand through his hair. "The men care, Sorcha, but they don't like strong emotions." He met her mocking stare. "Nor do I. Now what has happened? I can't imagine you've had any news from town. I know you haven't had any mail in the past week. None of us has." He frowned as she shook her head in dismay.

When she remained quiet, he grabbed the nearby chair and pulled it over, so that he sat beside the bed, facing her. He took her hand, giving it a squeeze. "Tell me. What has happened?"

"I'm bein' daft. I've just realized I willna be home for Christmas. 'Tis less than two weeks away, an' I willna be there." She sniffled and glared at the window, rattling with the gusting winds outside. "An' my family willna be able to visit me."

She closed her eyes as though envisioning what will be missed. "I willna be there to sing carols with my brothers. To see Skye an' Angus on their first Christmas. To spoil them as an aunt should. To receive Cailean's blessin'." She opened her eyes and met Frederick's confused stare. "Every Christmas, the eldest in the family blesses the others. And then he finds time with each of us to commend us in some way. My granddad started the tradition and then my da. It … I loved it."

"What did he tell you last year?" Frederick asked, his voice soft.

Sorcha sniffled, and her eyes lit with pleasure as she remembered a year ago. "Jessamine had just joined the family, aye? An' it was such a celebration to see Ewan happy." She paused and then flushed. "Cailean assured me that I'd find my way."

Frederick frowned at her words. "I'd think he would have been more eloquent."

She glared at him. "He was, aye? But ye have no right to learn what he said."

"I see." He released her hand and sat apart from her, no longer canted toward her. "I will assure the men that you are well. And, although I know we will be poor substitutes for your family on Christmas, we will do what we can." He marched out the door, ignoring her softly calling out, "Frederick," as he continued to the kitchen.

"Well, what's it to be, Boss?" Dalton asked, his gaze shadowed as though fearing another loss. His wife and child had died in childbirth in February.

"Is she pestering?" Dixon asked.

"It's *festering*, you idiot," Slims said with a slap to Dixon's head. "How is she?"

"She's fine. Emotional. But otherwise fine." Frederick sighed. "Worried about missing her family's Christmas celebration. There isn't much we can do for her."

"Sure there is," Dixon said. "We can make sure she has a great time with us."

"And how will that happen?" Dalton asked. "She's stuck in that bed, with a wicked winter raging outside, and I doubt we'll even make it to the forest for a tree."

Dixon shrugged. "My mama always said it was the people you were with, not the food or the pretty decorations."

Dalton rolled his eyes. "And that's the point, Dix. She won't be with her family but with a bunch of ranch hands."

Dixon shrugged again. "Well, ain't we better than nobody? Can't we be a bit entertaining?"

Frederick smiled at his upbeat ranch hand who had the optimism and tenacity of a puppy. "Yes, we are here and can entertain. And I agree. We haven't celebrated much in recent years. We should put more effort into it. We could put out some Christmas decorations. Maybe bring in a felled pine limb to adorn with ornaments." He sobered as he looked at his men. "But I want none of the older decorations."

"No, sir," they said in unison as they shared knowing looks.

The ornate Christmas ornaments from Frederick's youth, his mother's ornaments, had been in storage since she had left the ranch.

"The simpler, the more festive," Dixon said with an impish smile.

Slims worked beside Frederick in the barn a few days before Christmas and paused from mucking out a stall. He swiped at his sweaty forehead and then shivered as the frigid temperatures made any sweat turn to ice almost immediately. "Do you think we'll have everything ready in time, Boss?"

Frederick smiled. "With Dixon and Dalton organizing things, I have no idea. But Dixon has the eagerness of a four-year-old, so I hope Sorcha will be pleased by our efforts." Frederick speared his rake in a pile of hay and then hammered at the water bucket to free some of the ice atop to reach the water underneath. "Damn, that hurts my teeth," he gasped after taking a sip of the frigid water.

Slims nodded. "It's cold, Boss, and only gettin' colder."

Frederick gave a grunt at his friend's statement and waited for him to say what truly worried him.

"Shorty's never contacted us. Never come back." His eyes were wild as he thought about his best friend and fellow ranch hand.

Frederick nodded. "I know. I've made inquiries. The MacKinnons are aware that I'm worried about him, but I've received no news about him. My hope is he went south for the winter."

Slims frowned. "What if he didn't? What if he was caught out there"—he waved to the outside of the barn where the strong winds blew—"trapped on the prairie as the first storm hit?"

Frederick shook his head. "Shorty can read the weather as well as you or I. We must continue to hope he is well."

Slims clamped his jaw shut and picked up his rake. "I wish I could do more than hope."

Frederick nodded, and they continued to work as winter raged outside.

~

On Christmas morning, Sorcha woke, feeling sorry for herself. She envisioned what the day would be like at Cailean's house. The presents the family would exchange. The stories they'd retell. The gossip they would share as the women worked together in the kitchen. Sorcha's heart ached, missing her family, and she wished she could curl up on her side. Instead she was stuck on her back with her broken leg immobile in a splint from her hip past her knee. She took a deep breath and tried to imagine something positive so that she would not descend into a spiral of sadness.

She took another deep breath and sniffed at the air. Why did her room smell like a pine forest? She leaned to her bedside table and turned on the lamp, gasping as she saw the evergreen boughs slung on her curtains and on her bureau. A small pile of presents was atop her bureau, and she shook her head in confusion.

"Frederick?" she called out. After a few moments, she heard his footsteps. When she glanced up to see him grinning at her in the doorway, she smiled in return. "What did ye and the lads do?"

"We brought Christmas to you," he said. "It was Dixon's idea. After your mournful singing, we decided to make Christmas as special as we could for you here." His eyes widened in alarm as he saw the sheen of tears in her eyes.

"Nae," she rasped, reaching a hand out to him. "I'm touched. I had nae idea ye would care enough to do this for me." She looked at the bureau. "I dinna have presents for ye."

He chuckled. "Ye've made each of us a scarf over the past month. We've no need of any more presents." He turned and yelled down the hallway. "Boys! She's awake!"

Soon Dalton, Dixon and Slims entered, each carrying something for her. Dalton, a perfectly brewed cup of tea. Dixon, a plate of pancakes smothered in honey. Slims, a plate of eggs, bacon and potatoes. They looked at their offerings with pride.

"We wanted you to have a good breakfast," Dixon said. "Our feast is later in the day."

"Feast?" Sorcha asked. "I canna eat all this an' another big meal later."

"It's Christmas," Dalton said. "You should eat up and then open your presents."

Sorcha watched them with fond amusement and sampled everything they had brought for her to eat. Although she ate her fair share of the pancakes, eggs and bacon, the only thing she finished was the tea. "I canna eat another mouthful," she said as she set down her fork.

Dixon jumped up. "Time for presents!"

Sorcha giggled at his enthusiasm and accepted the first present, one from Dalton. She opened the carefully wrapped package, extracting a new pair of knitting needles. She held them between her fingers and smiled at him. "Thank ye, Dalton. They are a different size than my other ones, an' I can make other clothes with them."

He blushed and nodded his head as he backed away.

The next present had a dun-colored piece of string holding the brown paper wrapping closed over the package. She smiled as Dixon watched her with glee. She chuckled as she pulled out a heavy pair of blue wool socks.

"Your feet are always cold, Miss Sorcha," he said.

Slims rolled his eyes. "You're hopin' to get out of bringin' her hot bricks each night to warm the foot of her bed." He gave Dixon an affectionate tap on his head. "You'll still have to do it."

Dixon shrugged and grinned at her. "Yeah, but maybe not quite as often?"

Sorcha laughed and smiled her thanks.

Slims handed her his gift, flushing as it was not wrapped. "Sorry, Miss Sorcha. I couldn't find paper."

She stared at the wicker basket and ran a hand over it. "'Tis beautiful."

Slims's chest puffed out with pride.

"Ye made this?" She watched him with a trace of wonder, ignoring Frederick's disgruntled stare.

"Yes, miss. I enjoy an odd project when there aren't as many chores in the winter. Although cookin' has kept me busier than usual." He shrugged and flushed. "I thought you could use it to hold your knitting things."

She beamed at him. "'Twould be perfect. Thank ye."

Frederick stepped forward with his gift, wrapped in a blanket. "I'm afraid I wasn't as thoughtful as my men. I didn't get you something for your knitting or to wear." He handed her the blanket-covered item.

She frowned as she saw him looking unexpectedly nervous. After a moment's hesitation, she lifted the blanket away and gasped. "Oh my."

She stared at the small painting before her in wonder. Rather than the bleak winter raging outside, it showed the beauty and majesty of the valley in summer. Fields golden with the late-afternoon sun shining down. Cattle distant on the range. The mountains looming in the background. Her fingers shook as she traced over a part of the painting. "'Tis beautiful," she whispered. "Did ye paint this?"

He shrugged. "I'm like Slims. I sometimes have too much time on my hands in winter."

She grabbed his hand and squeezed it. "Thank ye, for ye remembered how tired I was of starin' at these four walls." She held the painting out to him and then pointed to the space across from her. "Will ye place it on the wall between the windows? I want to look at it every day."

He smiled and gave a nod to Dalton as he tapped a nail into the wall and then hung the painting. When it was hung perfectly for Sorcha, the men traipsed out, leaving Frederick and Sorcha alone.

"Thank ye," she whispered.

He shook his head. "We wanted you to have a bit of Christmas while at the ranch, Sorcha."

"Nae, ye are makin' it so I dinna miss my family as much today. Ye are takin' away my sorrow." She blinked to hold her tears at bay. "I willna lie to ye. I still feel their absence keenly. But I ken it could be so much worse."

He gripped her hand. "Don't thank me. The men wanted to do this for you."

She smiled as he flushed under her scrutiny. "Nae, I ken ye had a role to play. Ye are the leader of yer men, an' I ken they wouldna have done all this without yer proddin'. Thank ye."

She sat holding his hand, for many minutes, as a quiet contentment filled her.

In early January, Sorcha sat in a daze on the bed. She rubbed at her aching leg and shook with fear. Flashes of memory and visions of the day she was thrown from Sugar flickered in her mind as she slowly remembered what had happened that day in early November. Her confrontation. Her despair. Her flight from town. The wondrous feeling of freedom as she had raced away. The terror as Sugar reared, and then bucked, throwing her into the air.

She jerked as her mind replayed that moment, hearing the *crack* of her leg hitting the rock as loudly now as she did when she had fallen two months ago. Her hands shook as she brushed away tears. She failed to notice Dalton entering and jumped when he touched her arm.

"Miss Sorcha?" he whispered as he stared at her. "You look like you've seen a ghost." She stared at him blankly, and he bellowed, "Boss!"

Groaning and muttering could be heard from the direction of Frederick's office, and then footsteps approached. "What's the matter now?" Frederick poked his head in and stilled as he saw a glassy-eyed, pale Sorcha trembling on the bed. "What in God's name did you do?"

"Nothin.' I swear, Boss. She was like this when I came in here."

Frederick nodded and motioned for Dalton to leave. "Make her some tea." He sat on the chair, pulling her hands to hold between his. He frowned at how clammy and cold they were. "Everything will be all right, Sorcha. You aren't alone."

"Ye," she whispered. She shook her head at the sound of his voice. "It's been ye."

He leaned forward, resting his elbows on his knees, his brows furrowed with concern at her nonsensical words. "I don't know what's happened, but you're safe."

She closed her eyes as tears cascaded down her cheeks. "Ye've been here, ensurin' I was well. When I had fevers. When I was in so much pain that I thought I would die from it." She opened her eyes to meet his guarded gaze. "Ye were here."

"Yes," he murmured. "I promised your brothers I would care for you."

"Every time I needed ye, ye were here." Her tear-thickened voice broke. "I dinna understand. I thought ye dinna even like me."

He ignored her last comment and squeezed her hands. "What happened? What brought this on?" His blue eyes shone with concern.

"I remembered." She nodded as he canted forward with keen interest. "I ken why I acted like a fool."

When she remained quiet, he let out a deep breath in frustration. "Do you know who hurt you when you were on the trail?"

She closed her eyes as though concentrating on that part of her memory. "I remember a loud noise, and then Sugar rearin'. A clang or a clatter." She shivered. "I hit my head too, aye? I think I was knocked senseless for a bit." She shuddered. "But there was a voice. No' yers. A voice upset that I'd been killed ..." She whispered, *"Too soon."*

"Whose voice?" Frederick whispered, his eyes gleaming with rage. "And too soon for what?"

"I dinna ken. ... I dinna ken if I'm dreamin' that part." Her eyes shone with frustration and fear.

After a moment he asked, "What do you remember after that?"

Tears continued to fall down her cheeks. "Pain. Such terrible pain. An' wishin' I had died. An' then panic as I heard someone approachin'. I kent I had no ability to protect myself." She sniffled. "An' then it was ye."

He reached forward, his thumb swiping at the tears on her cheek. "Thank God I found you when I did."

She nodded. The memory of him running to her, of the tender way he had treated her, all was in her gaze, mixed together with wonder and uncertainty.

He stared deeply into her eyes and whispered, "Why did you flee town?"

Her gaze filled with shame. "I met Mrs. Jameson. An' she reminded me again that I was the unwanted spinster sister of the MacKinnon clan, destined to remain unmarried and unloved." She lowered her eyes. "I ken that woman speaks lies and half-truths in her desire to provoke harm. But I was feelin' vulnerable that day. An' her words hit their mark."

His gaze, previously filled with righteous indignation, was instantly filled with ardent passion he was unable to mask. "But you are cherished, Sorcha."

She closed her eyes. "I ken I have a good family. An' I ken they love me." She bit her lip and shrugged.

"But you want more," he whispered, and she opened her eyes. He nodded at the truth shining there.

"Aye." She waited, taking a deep breath. "Was it only because of your promise?"

He tilted his head to one side as he thought through her question and then flushed. "No. With or without a promise to your family, I would have been here to ensure you improved." He waited a long moment and then whispered again, "You are cherished."

Her breath caught at the intensity of feeling in his gaze, and she snatched her hand from his hold as Dalton entered with tea. "Thank ye, Mr. Dalton." She took the mug of tea and blew on the steaming liquid. She kept her gaze lowered until Dalton left again; then she set the mug of tea on the side table.

"I keep my promises, Sorcha," Frederick whispered, waiting until she met his gaze again. "You will be safe here."

A sole tear tracked down her cheek, and he swiped it away, his soft caress with callused fingers provoking a shiver from her. "I … I dinna understand why someone would want to hurt me. I've a temper, aye? An' I ken I am no' easy to care for, but …"

"Hush," Frederick demanded. "Stop that nonsense." He shook his head in frustration. "I fear you interrupted someone doing something illegal. I've heard rumors of cattle rustlers on my land, although there are always those rumors. If you did stumble upon them, I suspect they panicked, and they were afraid of being caught."

She stiffened as she grabbed his hand in panic. "Then they're still out there. They ken I'm no' dead. They dinna ken I have no idea who they are." She pointed to her leg. "I'm as vulnerable now as when I was on that trail."

Frederick took her head between his large palms, his stare intent on her. "We are always vigilant for strangers. For anyone who might bring harm or calamity to the ranch." He stared deeply into her eyes. "The weather prevents my men from being on the range to look for such men, but then I know no rustlers will be out there either."

"But I fear I canna be …" her voice cracked.

"You *are* safe here, Sorcha. No one will harm you. My men are loyal. To me and to you."

He moved to sit on the bed beside her and pulled her into his embrace, holding her as she cried. "*Shh*, darling, it's all right."

"I hate that woman …" she stuttered, until she quieted after the last of her sobs.

He grunted his agreement as he thought of Mrs. Jameson. "You and everyone else."

"Nae," she said as she rubbed her face against the soft cambric of his checkered shirt. "I hate that I allowed that woman to affect me. That I wasna strong enough."

"None of us can be strong every moment," he whispered into her hair, kissing her head softly. He let out a sigh as she eased away from him. "Better?"

"Aye," she whispered as she flushed. "Seems I always ask ye no' to tell the others about my moments of weakness."

He paused in caressing her cheek, dropping his hand to the bed beside her hip. "You don't always have to bear your burdens alone to prove you are strong, Sorcha. Sometimes strength comes from allowing others to see your weaknesses."

She gave a small smile. "Ye sound like yer grandmother when ye speak like that."

"Anything worth learning, I learned from her or my grandfather." He rose. "Rest, Sorcha." He squeezed her shoulder and then left, closing the door softly behind him.

She eased down on the bed, her head comfortable on the pillows as she thought about Frederick. His quiet strength and support. His ability to provoke her temper to spur her out of bouts of melancholy. His whispered word, *darling*, as he held her as she cried. Her eyes closed as she relived the soft kiss to her head.

Her heart raced with the thought of being cherished by a man like Frederick. Then, just as quickly, she remembered her past and tamped down any ill-advised fascination with the man who merely showed her kindness in her time of need. As she lay in a half daze, she wondered how many other women he'd called *darling*.

CHAPTER 4

Awarm breeze blew in mid-January across the frozen land, coming off the mountains and melting everything it touched. Frozen streams now gurgled as though spring runoff were about to start; snowdrifts shrank as they melted, and the land turned into a nearly impassible morass of mud and muck.

Frederick stood with his arms slung over the rails of a fence, staring at the puddles forming in the paddock, shaking his head over and over again. He wore a light coat, open to the warm wind, and he couldn't help but tilt his head toward the brilliant blue sky. The winter sun and the temperate breeze heated his face, and he sighed with momentary pleasure. He turned his head to meet Slims's worried gaze, who had joined him at the fence. "What do you think?"

"It's too damn early for a chinook," Slims said as he glared at the mud. "Don't mean it don't feel good to be warm, but this ain't right, Boss."

Frederick nodded, his hands gripping the wooden railing. "Either it'll freeze up or this means a severe drought this summer."

Slims snorted. "It's January in Montana. Ain't no way we won't have more snow and cold coming our way. This chinook should have come in March."

"Or April," Frederick murmured. He closed his eyes as he heard the hooting and hollering of young Dixon on the other side of the barn. "What's he doing?"

"Playing in the mud. I swear, it's as though he's five." Slims rolled his eyes as Frederick looked at him in astonishment.

"Fool," Frederick muttered.

Slims shrugged. "Maybe he's smarter than all of us. He enjoys *right now* without worryin' too much about tomorrow."

"Still no word from Shorty?" Frederick asked. Shorty was one of his most trusted ranch hands, and they'd had no word from him since late October.

Slims glowered at a mud puddle. "No. I've received no letters. Damn fool, heading out for a routine ride around the range in October."

Frederick shrugged. "It's what he does every year, Slims." Frederick sighed. "I've had no news from town for a few weeks, but I know the MacKinnons or my grandparents will inform me if there is any word regarding Shorty. For now, we have to assume he's fine, Slims." Shorty and Slims were best friends, and Frederick knew Slims would worry about Shorty until Slims had knew how he fared—one way or the other. "We'll know soon enough how he is."

Slims shrugged and nodded. "As long as he didn't get caught out on the range when the first storm hit."

Frederick shivered involuntarily at Slims's persistent worry about his friend. A moment later, as he heard the sound of horses approaching, Frederick turned toward the drive leading to the house. "Who would travel now?" He shared a confused look with Slims and made his way around the barn with Slims at his heels. He stood with an amused look as he watched Warren and Helen Clark trot their horses down the lane.

After Warren and Helen came to a halt in front of him, Frederick said, "Never thought you were so foolish as to risk harming a pair of horses or yourselves by riding out here in the midst of a melt."

Warren pointed his thumb at Helen. "She made a plan to visit Sorcha again after her last visit, and she insisted we not alter our plans. Originally we were to travel here in a sleigh. When we woke to the chinook, we decided to ride out on horseback."

Frederick helped Helen down and gave her a hug. "Next time, be more sensible. There's every likelihood you'll be marooned here for a few days."

Helen flushed and refused to meet Frederick's gaze. "I fear that is my husband's hope. It's the only reason he went along with my hare-brained idea." Her blush deepened as Slims let out a belly deep laugh, and Frederick chuckled.

Warren took off his hat and ran a hand through his thick brown hair. "You'd think in a town as small as Bear Grass Springs that I would be guaranteed a lull in business in the middle of winter."

"Not when you're the only competent lawyer from here to Helena," Slims said as he nodded hello to Helen and shook Warren's hand.

They remained outside, as it was pleasant with the warm wind blowing. "Why were you insistent on visiting now?" Frederick asked Helen, a woman he considered a sister after the time she had spent on his ranch the previous year. Helen had fled Warren's home, after he had saved her from the Boudoir, when Warren was unaware of her talents as a midwife and when he had thought she had spent the night with Frederick. Helen had found friendship and an inner fortitude while living at the ranch before reconciling with Warren.

"Warren gave me medical texts for Christmas," she said, her eyes lighting with joy. "I've read as much as I can on the most recent recommendations for care after a fracture."

"You gave your woman books?" Slims asked, stupefied.

"And she's pleased?" Frederick asked, his brows furrowed.

Warren laughed. "The key is knowing what she desires. And Helen has a thirst for knowledge." He shrugged. "It was easy to write associates in Pennsylvania and to have them ship me the books."

"Caring and thoughtful," Helen said as she looped her arm through her husband's. "And now I know what I can do to further help Sorcha. It's been over two months. Her bone should be knitted together enough by now that she can get out of bed. She needs to move about."

"Oh, God," Frederick muttered. At Warren's and Helen's inquisitive stares, he said, "She's enough of a handful when she's relegated to one place. I can't imagine what it will be like when she can roam the whole house." They chuckled, while Frederick smiled and led them inside.

After taking off their overcoats, Helen motioned for Frederick and Warren to remain in the parlor, and she entered Sorcha's room alone. Frederick led Warren into the kitchen, to the ever-ready pot of coffee, pouring them both a cup.

"Why are you really here, Warren?" Frederick asked.

"Well, it is as Helen says. She has new ideas to aid Sorcha's healing." He held up a hand before Frederick could comment. "She discussed them with the doctor, and he agreed with her. However, he did not feel he could risk being stranded here, when he has patients in town who need his care." Warren nodded with satisfaction. "We found a good one this time."

"You have every right to be pleased after what the previous doc did to Helen." They shared a glower as they thought about the former doctor of Bear Grass Springs who, in reality, was a charlatan. When he was exposed in one of Jessamine's articles, he had attacked Helen, causing a head wound where she had been unconscious for days. After fleeing from town, the former doctor's corpse had been found in the woods, although uncertainty remained over who had killed him.

"Our new doc wanted adventure in the 'wilds of Montana' after years of living in a city, but I fear life in our small town might prove boring for him." Warren shrugged. "As you can imagine, the young women enjoy having another eligible bachelor in town."

Frederick laughed. "I know that will be a relief to Cole and Peter."

Warren shook his head at his friend. "You're too blind to see the unattached women act the same way around you."

After shuddering at the thought of the eligible women in town chasing after him, he focused again on Warren. "Why are you really here?"

Warren grabbed his cup of coffee and motioned for Frederick to leave the kitchen. "I believe your office is the place for this conversation."

~

S orcha beamed as she saw Helen in the doorway. "Helen!" she exclaimed, holding her hand out to greet her friend. "I canna believe ye are here."

Helen leaned forward and hugged Sorcha. "You look well."

"Ye dinna need to sound surprised. The men are takin' good care of me." She grimaced as she moved to sit upright in bed, provoking Helen to frown.

"Are you still in pain?"

"Nae, I'm uncomfortable. I havena moved in too long."

Helen smiled. "Then you should be delighted as to why I am here. Warren gave me medical books for Christmas, and, since your fall, I've also corresponded with a few doctors in Philadelphia. Contacts that he had and that he introduced me to."

"Ye're glowin' with happiness," Sorcha said, unable to hide the envy in her voice. "Ye're fortunate to have wed a man committed to makin' ye happy."

Helen nodded. "Yes, well, in my studies, my correspondence and my discussions with the new doctor in town, it's time for you to start moving again. You must get out of this bed, or you truly will be a cripple from the atrophy of your muscles."

Sorcha paled. "I thought the purpose of me stayin' here, bedridden, was so that I'd recover."

"Too much of anything can be detrimental. And that includes lying in bed. You've had over two months for that bone to heal. You're a young, healthy woman. It's time for you to slowly start putting weight on it again, using those muscles again."

"I'm afraid. What if it's too early? What if the bone snaps? I'm no' a small woman."

"Enough dithering. I know you well enough that you could talk anyone to death. We could be having this same conversation in three days, when I need to leave, and you'll still be bedridden." She pulled away the bedcovers, revealing Sorcha's clean flannel nightgown. Helen looked around the room and saw a robe hanging off a peg and set it on the bed. She moved to the right side of the bed and unfastened the straps holding the binding in place on Sorcha's right thigh. Helen ceased her competent movements when Sorcha grabbed her hand.

"Ye believe I'll be fine?" When Helen nodded, Sorcha whispered, "Ye'll help me so I dinna fall on my face?"

Helen smiled. "Yes. You'll be weak, weaker than you can imagine for a long time. But slowly your strength will return."

Sorcha released Helen's hand and gave a nod. "I trust ye, but I'm scared, aye?"

"If you weren't, I'd think you a fool."

After the men had settled into comfortable chairs in Frederick's office, Warren sighed. "I always forget how sore I get after riding a horse." He glared at Frederick as his friend laughed. "Not all of us were meant to be horsemen." Warren took a deep breath and sobered. "I've heard rumors. About your ranch."

Warren waited as Frederick leaned forward, wholly focused on him.

"There are those who are indiscreet when they drink. I've joined Ewan a few times at the Stumble-Out when Helen is busy on a call." He half smiled in self-recrimination. "I find I don't like being home at night when she isn't there."

"Your lawyer books aren't good company anymore?" Frederick asked.

Warren shook his head with another half smile before sobering. "I've heard a rumor. Someone, and I don't know who, has crafted a brand that looks like yours."

"Are you saying you have proof that someone's rustling my cattle?"

Warren nodded. "No, as I have no proof the rumor is true. But I fear that might have been what was occurring when Sorcha was injured. I'd be vigilant."

Frederick stared at his friend, although in his mind he relived that day. The horse ride, the exhilaration of the early fall weather. The sense that something was wrong once he entered the woods. "I can't remember anything out of the ordinary to do with my cattle that day. All I remember is Sorcha. Injured and alone, waiting for help."

"Well, all they need is to poach one here, one there, and you wouldn't be any the wiser. Especially after a winter like this."

Frederick sighed and leaned away. "I've never had loss rates any higher than normal. In fact, I've always thought my cattle hardier because so many survived our Montana winters. If this rustling rumor is true, it must have just started." He watched Warren closely. "My men are always on the lookout for strangers and rustlers. It's the nature of running a cattle ranch. Although there's little to discover now in the midst of such a harsh winter. Do you have any ideas who could be the rustler?"

"Oh, I have plenty. I may advocate not jumping to conclusions, but Walter Jameson's been a bit … edgy lately."

"Don't you believe that could be because his favorite cousin is about to hang for the murder of five women in Helena?"

Warren shook his head as he thought about his wife's brother, Walter Jameson. Where Helen was friendly and eager to help those around her, Walter reveled in any pain or discord he could provoke in others. Walter resented Warren for protecting Walter's favorite target from his cruelty once Helen had married Warren. "No, the man doesn't understand the concept of loyalty. He would only mourn his cousin because he'll no longer have a partner in crime for his cruelty. Such grief would be short-lived as he's bound to find another associate soon."

"What other reason do you have to suspect Walter?" Frederick's jaw ticked with his agitation. "I don't like the man. Hell, I hate him and wish he were dead." He saw Warren shake his head at that statement. "Forget I said that."

"Don't say incriminating things around a lawyer or a man of the law when there's a good chance you'll come to blows with the man in question," Warren said with a wry smile. "As for Walter, he's flashing money again. And I know for a fact he hasn't been working in the mines. He has no income, so it makes no sense for him to have money to spare."

Frederick sat in silence for a long moment. "He resented me for helping Helen last winter. And he did threaten to hurt whatever or whoever I cherished in retaliation." He closed his eyes. "My grandparents know of his threat, but I never imagined he'd come after Sorcha." His gaze was filled with fury. "This is all speculation, Warren. There's no proof to who's behind any of it."

Warren nodded. "No, but I've learned in all my years as a lawyer that, when my gut is telling me something as strongly as it is now, something nefarious is afoot. And Sorcha is a target."

"I want to retain you as my lawyer. And I need you to speak with the MacKinnons. They work in different parts of town, and Jessamine hears all sorts of things in her work."

"Why do you believe you need a lawyer now?"

Frederick let out a deep breath. "It's like you say. My gut is telling me something isn't right. And if there is a need for a lawyer, I don't want Walter or his mother to think they can come to you. I want to know you are working for me."

Warren nodded and then smiled. "Mrs. Jameson has always been delusional in her belief that I would work for her or her son. I'll always choose the MacKinnons or their associates."

Frederick met Warren's smile. "You never know with family."

"As I've said many times, Helen is my family. Not her mother or her brother." He clenched his jaw as he considered his wife's unfortunate relations.

"I never thought I'd be thankful that Sorcha broke her leg, but now I am," Frederick whispered.

"It's kept her safe and out of town."

Helen continued to chatter as she removed Sorcha's bindings. "Did anyone send you some of Leena's *pepperkake*?" At Sorcha's confused look, Helen gave a sound of regret. "That's a pity.

It's a Norwegian type of gingerbread, and it was delicious. Warren made a point of visiting the bakery before Christmas to buy me some every day she sold it." Leena Ericson, now Leena Johansen, worked with Annabelle as one of the two bakers at Annabelle's Sweet Shop, the bakery in Bear Grass Springs.

Sorcha gasped as her leg was freed from its binding for the first time in months. "Oh, look at my poor leg," she exclaimed. Her right thigh appeared smaller than her left, although there was no swelling. She shook her head as Helen tentatively poked at her leg. "Nae, no pain."

Helen then slowly bent Sorcha's knee and moved her leg.

Sorcha gasped at the movement but again shook her head, denying pain.

"Give me a moment," Helen said. She reached for a satchel that Sorcha had not even seen and pulled out a jar.

When Helen opened the lid, the faint scent of lavender filled the air, and Sorcha sighed with pleasure.

"You need lotion on your skin."

"'Tis like ye brought summer here in the middle of winter," Sorcha murmured as Helen tended her.

"Today is more like spring outside," Helen said as she met Sorcha's startled gaze. "We're in the midst of a chinook, and it's months too early. I've never seen one in January, but I think it does not bode well for the rest of winter."

"What does *chinook* mean?"

"When warm winds blow down off the eastern side of the mountains, warming everything and bringing springlike conditions. But we can't have spring in January because the melted snow will turn into ice when the vicious winter weather returns." She shared a look with Sorcha as she replaced the lid on her lotion jar. "Come. I want you to sit up, with your legs bent over the side of the bed."

When Sorcha sat as Helen had instructed, Helen smiled at her. "Now prepare to stand, but put your weight on your left leg."

Sorcha fisted her hands beside her and then firmed her jaw. "I'm nae coward, aye?" When her friend laughed, Sorcha glared at Helen.

In a fit of pique, Sorcha stood rapidly, the world spinning. She gave a small shriek as she fell, landing on the soft bed, the world going black.

She woke, seconds later, to find Frederick looming over her. "Frederick," she whispered, her hand brushing back a strand of black hair that had fallen over his forehead. "Why are ye worried?"

"You screamed," he said, his blue eyes filled with concern. "Are you hurt?"

She flushed as she saw Helen and Warren behind Frederick. "Nae, I tried to stand up too quickly."

"You don't have to prove you are brave," Frederick whispered. "We already know that." After a moment he backed away and held out his hand. "Here. Let me help you."

She took another deep breath and firmed her shoulders. She rose slowly, now clinging to his arm and stood, teetering as she found her balance on her left foot. "Oh, 'tis wonderful to be out of that bed, even for a moment."

"Dalton!" Frederick yelled. A moment later, Dalton poked his head in. "Get fresh sheets and help make Miss MacKinnon's bed."

Dalton nodded and moved away.

"Now what?" Sorcha asked Helen.

"Now, lean on Frederick and take a small step on your right leg." Helen watched Sorcha with fierce intensity.

Sorcha nodded as she hobbled forward a step. She faltered, recovering when she moved to her left leg. "If ye want me to make it to that chair, I'll arrive tonight." Sweat beaded on her forehead. "An' I canna expect one of the men to be around every time I wish to move."

Dalton came in with sheets tucked under one arm, pushing Warren to the hallway to make room for changing the bedsheets. Dalton nodded to what he held in his other hand. "I found these, Boss, in the storage room the other day. I thought they might be useful."

Helen gave a squeal of delight at the crutches Dalton handed to her. "Oh, these are perfect." She put them under her arms, showing Sorcha how to use them. "Have you seen crutches before?"

Sorcha nodded. "Aye, there was a cripple on Skye." She glared at Helen. "I thought ye said I was no' goin' to be crippled?"

Helen gave her arm a squeeze. "You aren't. These are to help you walk so that you can slowly put more weight on your right leg. And they will give you freedom from depending on one of the men here."

Sorcha nodded, grabbing one crutch and then the other. She looked at Frederick. "Stand behind me, aye?" She slowly moved toward the chair, hopping on her left foot to turn around and then to sit down.

She flushed as she swiped at her forehead. "That should no' be as hard as it was."

"You're weak from all your time in bed. Your strength will return," Frederick said. "But I don't want you overdoing it now that you can move around on your own." He gave her a stern look. "I also don't want you moving around unless you know someone else is in the house, and they are aware you are going to move around."

She nodded and then smiled at Dalton as he was about to slip from the room. "Thank ye, Mr. Dalton, for finding me these. An' for makin' my bed."

"Was nothin', Miss Sorcha," he said as he smiled at her and left.

Helen winked at Sorcha. "Seems you might have an admirer in Dalton." She fought a chuckle at Frederick's glower. "Now I want you and Warren to go to your office, your barn, anywhere but here. We have work to do, and neither Sorcha nor I want an audience."

Frederick gave Sorcha's hand a last squeeze before leaving to join Warren in the hallway.

Helen looked at her friend. "First, I will teach you a few exercises that I have learned. Then I will help you have a bath, and I'll find clean clothes for you. And afterward I'll catch you up on the town gossip."

Sorcha sighed as though she had just been given the promise of her heart's desire. "Thank ye, Helen, for bein' such a good friend."

A week later toward the end of January, Frederick stood, staring out the parlor window as the wind rattled the window frames. Rather than the warm breeze from the previous week, this bone-chilling cold from the north froze everything in sight. Anything that had melted was now refrozen, and the snow on the prairie had turned into a thick, impenetrable mixture of ice and snow. Icicles hung from the eaves, some two to three feet long. The men kept the area over the door cleared lest an icicle snapped and fell on one of them as they slammed the door shut.

"What's the matter, Frederick?" Sorcha asked, frowning as he tensed at her voice. She hobbled into the parlor, still struggling to find a graceful way to use her crutches as she followed Helen's advice to slowly add more weight to her right leg to build up strength. She stood a few feet away from Frederick as he kept his back to her.

"It's too cold."

She gave a snort of incredulity. "'Tis winter. What do ye expect?" She blanched as he spun to face her, his gaze filled with anger and panic.

"Do you have any idea what this winter might do to the cattle?" He stared at her as she shook her head dumbly. "My herd is out there, on the range, struggling to find something to eat."

Sorcha moved to a chair and sighed with relief as she sat. She massaged her leg as she thought through his words. "Do they no' just paw through the snow and eat the grass?"

He gripped his nape and stared out the window again as another window rattled. "In normal years, that is what they do. We always lose some. I've been taught to believe that is expected." He paused. "But it always seems a waste to me."

He spoke in a low voice. "This year, there is little for them to eat. The warm summer and ensuing drought caused the grass to grow more sparsely than it has in the past. And now, after the chinook, there's no way for the cattle to reach what grass there is."

Sorcha paused in digging at a knot in one of her muscles in her thigh. "I dinna ken what ye mean."

"During a lull in the storm today, Dixon and Dalton walked a short distance away from the paddock. Not far enough to get lost. Dalton made sure they could always see the ranch." Frederick took a deep breath. "They carried pickaxes."

At her headshake in confusion, he said, "I wanted them to confirm how hard it is to break through the icy layer coating the snow. To see if the cattle have any chance of penetrating it with their hooves. And they don't." He rubbed at his forehead as he leaned his shoulder against the wall and looked at her. "They are strong men, used to hard work, and they had a near impossible time busting up the ice with a pickax. And then the snow is still inches deep on top of whatever grass remains underneath. How do you think the cattle will fare?"

Sorcha whispered, "They'll perish."

Frederick nodded. "Yes. And there isn't a damn thing I can do about it."

Sorcha watched him, his frustration mixed with impotence, and she reached a hand out to him. When he did not move toward her to clasp her hand, she dropped it to her lap. "'Tis no' yer fault."

"I know that," he hissed. "I know that in every logical way that matters, but that doesn't mean it's easy to accept that I sent that herd out there last fall to die."

She shook her head. "Ye had no way to ken such a winter was comin'. An' ye had no way to feed such a number of cattle."

"Being rational doesn't help when I'm filled with rage."

She shrugged, seemingly unfazed by his uncontrolled emotion. "I ken, in a small way, what ye fear," she whispered. When he frowned, staring at her, she twisted her fingers together. "Do you think I dinna ken the fear ye feel at the thought of losin' yer home? Of losin' the place ye love most?" Her eyes shone with the memory of the loss of her homeland.

Frederick sighed. "Maybe it makes me seem spoiled in your eyes, but I can't imagine living anywhere else."

She smiled. "'Tis why ye dinna mind remaining here when yer brothers travel to Texas each year."

He gave her a startled look at her insight. "Yes. For a while, I thought I should want the adventure, that I should want to toil for months on the trail." His self-mocking smile made her breath catch. "Although I wouldn't mind missing a Montana winter here and there."

"But why should ye miss Montana in the spring? An' who would care for yer horses?"

He nodded. "All true."

"Ye have a home here, Frederick. One ye generously share. If ye speak with yer men, most of them ken what it's like to feel rootless. Most ken what it is to drift, only hopin' to find a home again. 'Tis why they are so loyal to ye."

He flushed at her words. "Thank you."

"Anyone who kens ye, an' yer grandparents ken ye well, will never doubt ye did all ye could. Some things are out of our control. Like the weather."

He sighed and nodded. "It doesn't make the waiting for March or April any easier."

They sat in silence a few moments. "Why are ye no' married?" Sorcha blurted out and then flushed beet red.

He chuckled. "I have my reasons, Sorcha, just as I suspect you have yours." He headed out of the parlor toward his office. "Take it easy on your leg. It's only been a week since you started moving around." He left her, staring after him, as he shut the door to his office on her and any further opportunity for increased intimacy between them.

"What's put you in such a sour mood?" Slims asked. He closed the office door and sat in the chair across from Frederick.

"Besides the rumors of rustlers, the fate of our hungry catte, the precarious survival of this ranch and the safety of our friends Shorty and Sorcha?" Frederick snapped, and then tapped at a letter on his desk. "Warren and Helen brought letters. In the confusion of their visit and the excitement over Sorcha moving around on crutches, I missed one."

Slims stared at the letter in front of his boss. "What'd it say?"

"It was a reminder of the promise I'd made," he whispered, his gaze filled with anger and regret. "I ... I had hoped her brothers would come to trust that I'd never hurt her."

"Who wrote it?" Slims asked. "And what did you promise?"

Frederick's gaze was bleak as he pushed away from the desk and bent over, his forearms on his thighs. "Cailean, the eldest wrote it. I promised them that she'd be safe here. That I'd protect her reputation." He whispered. "And protect her from me."

Slims sat back in his chair. "Seems to me, by reminding you of that promise, they're causing her more pain than if they released you from it."

Frederick shook his head. "I refuse to act dishonorably." When Slims snorted, Frederick glared at his friend.

"Desirin' a woman does not mean you dishonor her." He glared at the younger man. "Ignorin' your feelings, and hers, is more hurtful, and you know it." He shared a long look with Frederick. "You aren't your parents. I'll say it as many times as is needed until you believe it."

"What do you know of love, Slims?" Frederick asked as he remained with his elbows on his knees.

"I know what it is to lose everyone I'd ever loved. You know the story of how my family died in the War."

Frederick nodded and saw the shadow come over his friend's gaze at the memory of finding his family murdered for their livestock during the War. "Yes."

"I thought I'd be alone forever, until your grandma took a shine to me and insisted I travel with you from Fort Benton. I've no need for any other family."

Frederick shook his head in silent disagreement and then sighed. His gaze flicked to the letter again, and he frowned. "I should have sent her home with Warren and Helen."

Slims shrugged. "You didn't. She's here for another few months until we have the real thaw. You'd do better to figure out what you want from her." He raised his eyebrows. "As you dither, there are those who take a greater interest in her."

Frederick gaped at Slims as he rose and closed the door behind him. Frederick rested his head on his desk, battling the urge to go to her.

~

January 12, 1887

Dearest Sorcha,
    I heard Helen was to visit you and wanted to write you a short letter. Angus is asleep, and Hortence is busy with her schoolwork. Alistair has promised us a supper at the café, and I think he hopes to hear any news of you from Irene and Harold. Please send a letter to us when Helen leaves, even if it is only a few short lines, assuring us that you are well.

Oh, I hope you are well! I hate this weather that prevents any of us from visiting you. From hearing your stories and your laughter. Your presence in the bakery is missed every day, and I see Fidelia glancing at the door, as though looking for your arrival. She always seems disheartened when she remembers you will not be with us.

The New Year's Eve Dance was a success! A miner bought Leena's pepperkake house for twenty-five dollars! Can you imagine? J.P. was upset that she and Ewan could not bid high enough for it, but Leena surprised all of us by hiding a small gingerbread house in each of our homes while we were at the dance. Ewan told me that J.P. danced with joy upon seeing their own gingerbread house and ate a large portion of it that very night!

Do not worry about any of us. We are all well. Our only problem is that we are missing you, dearest Sorcha.

I hope you feel better every day and are able to return to us soon.

Your sister,

Leticia

PS: I pray daily that Frederick is wise enough to break any promise he made to your brothers.

Sorcha traced over the final words in the letter and fought tears as she reread Leticia's letter. She frowned as she focused on Leticia's postscript and then shook her head.

At the gentle knock on her door, she called out, "Come in." She maintained a welcoming smile, although it failed to brighten her eyes as Dalton entered. "Hello, Mr. Dalton."

"It's *Dalton*, miss," he said as he flushed. "I hoped you had more stories to tell about Scotland."

She took a deep breath and set aside her letter. "Oh, I think I've told ye all the stories I ken," she said with a chuckle.

"Are the mountains like our mountains?"

Her gaze became unfocused, as though seeing a faraway, distant scene. "Nae, they are covered in grass an' heather, and they shimmer purple in August, like a sunset in midday. An' the loch and sea are no' far away. Ye never had to worry where water is." She smiled at him. "But, aye, they're tall like the mountains here an' flirt with the clouds an' snow."

"Do you miss home?"

"I miss the smell of a peat fire on the breeze as I walk home. The glint of the sun shining on the lochs. The songs of the birds—they're different here, ye ken?" Her smile was tinted with nostalgia. "But I'd miss my family more were I there."

Dalton looked at the small sweater she was knitting in deep green and fought a grimace. "For your nephew?"

"Aye, although I worry he'll be too big for it by the time I see him again. I can always sell it, if that happens."

"You're very talented, Miss Sorcha."

She flushed and lowered her gaze. "Oh, get away with ye," she said with a laugh. "'Tis simple knittin'. I ken ye are teasin'." She flushed and then gaped at Dalton as he gripped her hand and kissed the back of it. "Mr. Dalton," she gasped.

"Good evening, Miss Sorcha," he said with an intense stare and then slipped from her room.

"Oh my," Sorcha whispered, raising a hand to her hot cheeks.

Frederick glared at Dalton a few weeks later in early February as he exited Sorcha's room with a contented smile on his face. Frederick had listened to their chatter and laughter while sitting by the fire in the parlor and had finally decided to join them. Dalton had taken to visiting Sorcha every evening after supper, and Slims's words haunted Frederick. "*Dithering*, my foot," he muttered.

"Sorcha," he said as he entered her room, Dalton now out of earshot. Frederick frowned to see her sparkling blue eyes, flushed cheeks and hair pinned back in a more elaborate coiffure. "What are you doing?"

"I dinna ken what ye mean, Frederick," she said as she barely spared him a glance.

"Why are you flirting with Dalton every night?" When she merely glared at him, he glowered at her. "Why are you allowing him to think he's courting you?"

Her eyes bulged a moment, and then she shook her head. "He couldna possibly believe that. He's my friend. Or am I no' supposed to have friends here?"

"Don't be ridiculous. Of course you can have friends."

"But no' you, is that it? An' no' Dalton?" She shook her head. "Why are ye treatin' me as though I dinna exist? Before Helen and Warren came, ye visited me. Ye talked with me." Her eyes clouded with confusion. "Now every time I enter the parlor, ye go to yer office an' shut the door. Even now, you stand upright in my room, no' taking a seat, no' intendin' to stay or to share a conversation. What have I done?"

Frederick's jaw ticked, and his eyes shone with yearning. "It's not because of you." He ducked as she threw a pillow at him.

"An ye wonder why I like visitin' with Dalton? He doesna lie to me. He actually likes bein' in my presence. He does no' act as though he's bein' tortured." Her eyes gleamed with tears. "Leave, Frederick."

He straightened and stood even taller. "I don't want Dalton visiting you every night in here. Your leg is better. If he wants to talk with you, he can talk with you in the parlor with the others."

She shook her head in disappointment. "How can ye no' ken that I need to get my leg up? That sittin' in a chair too long still hurts? Why do ye no' care enough to ken that?" She watched as he paled at her questions. "I asked ye to leave. Please, Frederick."

He fisted his hands at his side as he paused by her bed. "Sorcha," he whispered, his voice breaking off as she turned her head away from him.

He closed the door behind him, fighting the urge to return to her and to enfold her in his arms.

~

Thesh next morning Slims stood leaning on a hay rake in the barn as he watched Dalton work in one of the stalls. Frederick was in the house in his office while Dixon milked cows in the other barn. Both Slims and Dalton wore heavy coats, scarves, hats and gloves in the barn to combat the cold as the temperatures outside dipped well past twenty below zero. Frederick, worried about his horses, had found old blankets to throw over them to try to keep them warm. When possible, they also stabled them in shared stalls for them to share body heat.

"What are you doing with the boss's woman?" Slims asked Dalton. Slims stood as tall as his imposing six and half feet allowed, crossing his thick arms over his chest as he challenged the man.

"Why should it be any of your concern?" Dalton flushed as he met his friend's censure. "And who says she's the boss's woman? She wasn't acting like that last night."

"Acting out … that's what she was doing. You tell me. Did she start flattering your ego before or after Boss showed up?" He nodded when Dalton clamped his jaw shut with agitation. "Those two have been circlin' around each other longer than you were married. Don't get involved."

Dalton swore and ran a hand through his thick brown hair. Embarrassment shone in his blue eyes. "I should have known a woman like her wouldn't be interested in a cowboy."

Slims chuckled. "You know that ain't true as she likes Boss just fine. She's got her aim elsewhere on another cowboy." He sobered as he studied his friend. "Besides, you ain't over your Mary yet."

Dalton closed his eyes. "There will never be another woman like my Mary. But I have to try, Slims. I'm not content alone, like you."

Slims's gaze shadowed a moment. "I've never found a woman worth the headache. Unless that one in there had a cousin." He nodded his head toward Sorcha's bedroom window. "Then I might be tempted."

"Is Boss angry with me?"

"No, he knows she was the one to blame. *This time.*" Slims gave Dalton a warning glance. "I don't know if he'll be as understanding the next time."

Dalton nodded. "I don't want to do anything to risk working here. This is the first place that's been like home since I was a boy."

Slims nodded "I know. And if Boss has sense and marries that girl, we'll still be treated like family."

"Then that's something we should hope for. A wife can change things, more than anyone can, as her man tries to keep her happy. Miss Sorcha knows what it's like to be surrounded by family, and I think she likes it here."

Slims slapped Dalton on his shoulder. "Not just that but she knows what it is to be surrounded by men, growin' up with her three brothers." They moved to the next stalls to muck them out, their conversation turning to the hoped-for thaw.

When Dalton knocked on Sorcha's door that evening, she sighed. "Come in." She smiled at him, but she saw an answering hesitancy in his gaze. "What is it, Mr. Dalton?"

He sat on the chair near her bed and frowned when he saw her massaging her healing leg. "Did you overdo it today?"

She shrugged and then smiled. "I walked a bit farther, an' it hurts more than I thought it would. I ken it will be better tomorrow." She continued to rub at it as she watched him. "Is something the matter?"

He scrubbed at his brown hair and then acted as though to trace the rim of his absent cowboy hat. Instead he ran his fingers over his pant leg. "I want you to know how much I have enjoyed speaking with you. I enjoy our friendship."

She nodded. "Aye, but I ken ye can no' continue to visit me. For we are just friends, aye?"

He gave a brisk nod. "Yes. I'm still mourning the loss of my wife and child." He shrugged. "It was nice to imagine I wasn't alone."

Her eyes filled as she reached her hand out for his. "Ye ken ye are no'," she whispered. "Although I ken 'tis a different sort of alone." She sighed. "I did no' mean to cause you trouble with the other men. I …" She shook her head. "Frederick is angry at me for leadin' ye on."

Dalton gave an affronted growl. "You did not. You've only shown me kindness and friendship. Two qualities I hope I find in a woman in the future, if I am fortunate enough to marry again."

"I hope ye are, Mr. Dalton," she whispered.

He paused a moment and took a deep breath. "Remember that the man giving you advice last night has a distorted view of you and any man who might be your friend. He's not rational where you are concerned."

She shook her head. "I fear it doesna matter." She smiled at Dalton as he stood and rose, leaving her to her thoughts.

CHAPTER 5

By mid-February, three and a half months after her accident, Sorcha moved around the ranch with the aid of only a cane. She fought weakness in her right leg daily but knew that she was slowly regaining her strength with every attempt to push herself farther. When she had walked up and down the hallway in the ranch house ten times, she leaned against the wall in the parlor a moment as she caught her breath.

"What are you doing?" Frederick asked. He frowned as he took in her sweat-streaked face, flushed cheeks and triumphant gleam in her eyes.

"I just finished a task I set for myself," she said with pride as she took a few steps toward him. "Now I'm tryin' to decide if I should rest or do it again."

"Don't push yourself too much," he muttered. "I wouldn't want you to reinjure yourself and to remain here any longer."

She paled, any joy in her recent accomplishment fading at his words. "Do ye want me to leave?" she asked, her breath emerging in stutters and her breasts rising and falling rapidly as though she had just galloped across a field.

"Yes." His eyes shone with anger and a mixture of deep, unfathomable emotions. "I wish you'd never come here."

She backed away, her gait uneven, and collapsed against the wall as though she were unable to support herself. "I ... I'll leave as soon as the weather breaks."

He shook his head, his gaze never leaving hers. He frowned at the devastation evident in her gaze wrought by his words. "Don't you understand? This winter is never going to end. Not until ..."

She shook her head. "I dinna ken why ye are so angry with me." Her whispered words were more powerful than any shout.

"Do ye no'?" he asked, mimicking her accent. He stalked over to her, pinning her in place with his intense stare and then by leaning forward and placing his hands on either side of her shoulders. "Do you not know what you do to me?" His glare turned to confusion as he continued to stare at her. "How can you not know?"

She shook her head and then shrugged. "Ye want me gone. I irritate ye. I ken ye dinna like me." She frowned as he gave a snort of disbelief.

"That's rich." He let out a deep breath. "Considering you're the one who'll dance with every ranch hand and miner with a bright smile and then glower at me for having the gall to ask you to dance. That you flirt with every man who works for me, and save your temper and ill humor for me."

Her cheeks reddened, and she hit him on his shoulder. "Ye're the one flirtin' with a married woman!"

His head jerked back as though she had struck him. "I've never done such a thing."

"Well, as good as," Sorcha grumbled. "Visitin' the bakery every day to see Leena last spring when ye lived in town to help yer grandparents. She was already engaged to marry her Karl!"

He chuckled, and his eyes lost a bit of their intensity as he saw her irritation. "So, it worked," he muttered to himself.

"I dinna ken why ye bothered. Ye've avoided me as much as possible in the past month." She sputtered into silence as she gazed into his eyes. Passionate, covetous eyes.

"You have no idea, do you?" He fisted his hands beside her. "No idea at all." Before she could speak, he leaned forward, kissing her. He kept his hands on the wall, his lips the only part of him touching her.

However, Sorcha showed no such restraint. She grabbed at his shoulders and tugged him closer. Soon her hands were tangled in his too-long hair, and she kissed him back with equal passion.

After many minutes he pushed away and spun from her. "Dammit," he rasped. "I promised …" He took deep, stuttering breaths. "I promised …"

She grabbed her cane and tottered over to him, his back still to her. "What did ye promise?"

"To keep you safe. Even if the person you need to be protected from is me." He looked at her over his shoulder with a passionate desire and then marched from the room.

Sorcha flailed a hand out, searching for a seat. After a few steps, she found a chair and sank into it, groaning with relief to be off her mending leg. She rubbed at her cheek, scrubbing away a tear and sniffling once. Her hand dropped to her leg, massaging her thigh and the weakened muscles.

She welcomed the pain as it distracted her from the confusing interaction with Frederick. As though against her will, her hand rose and traced her lips, as she remembered gripping him to her. "What was I thinkin'?" she muttered to herself, flushing beet red. He had remained separate from her, except for his lips.

More tears threatened, and she attempted to blink them away, but they began to fall. "'Tis as my mother said," she whispered to herself. "No man will ever want a woman like me."

She rose and leaned heavily on her cane as she made her way to her room to cry in private.

Frederick stormed out of the house with barely the sense to grab his coat and hat, yanking them on as he struggled against the wind and headed toward the barn. Swearing to himself at having forgotten his gloves, he yanked on the rope tied between the house and the barn and used it to orient himself as he made the journey there. After he arrived, he blew on his hands and rubbed at them to warm them up.

"What's got you so riled that you forgot gloves in below-zero weather?" Slims asked. "Or should I say *who*?"

"Not tonight, Slims," Frederick growled. He walked over to the stall with his prize mare, Bonnet, and waited for her to approach. At her whinny of welcome, he stroked a hand down the center of her snout. "Hello there."

Slims gave a snort and shook his head. "If you paid half as good attention to the woman who interests you, you wouldn't have to resort to flirting with your horse in the middle of winter."

Frederick closed his eyes and took a deep breath. "Slims, when I want your advice, I'll ask for it."

Slims, a man who'd earned his nickname from Frederick's father, hung up the tackle he'd worked on and approached Frederick—a man he considered his boss and his friend. They were alone in the barn and were unlikely to be interrupted. "You're not your mother."

Frederick spun and glared at Slims. "I sure as hell hope not."

Ignoring his anger, Slims said, "And you sure as hell aren't your father."

Frederick gripped his hands together as though wanting a fight, but he was smart enough to know better than to challenge the large barrel-chested man. Frederick would end up knocked out until the real spring chinook finally hit months from now. "Do you think I don't know that I will never be my father?"

Slims frowned as he studied his younger friend. "I'd rejoice at that fact." He held up a hand as he understood he was pushing Frederick to the point of attacking him. "Your father was a good man. A just man. And he treated his men well." He paused as Frederick nodded. "You are the same. Where you differ is that you aren't taken in by a pretty face and the promise of an easy wife." Slims scoffed at his own words. "There ain't such a thing, as any man would tell you." Slims smiled.

"And what man would want an easy wife? The tempestuous ones are the ones who keep life interesting."

Frederick frowned. "How would you know? You've never been married."

"I've lived, boy." Slims paused a moment. "That woman in there"—Slims pointed to the house—"she isn't your mother. And, if you have any sense, you'll see you aren't your father for wanting a woman like that."

Frederick's jaw clenched. "I promised her brothers."

Slims made another derisive noise and rolled his eyes. "Yes, we all know about it. It's like a shield you've wrapped around yourself so that you don't have to do anything about your feelings for her. Your promise was not to hurt her. To protect her. Seems to me, you probably hurt her as much tonight as that broken leg did."

"That's not fair." He fisted his hands and glared and took a step toward Slims. "I did not debase her."

"You know better than anyone that the worst pain isn't the physical kind." Slims patted Frederick on the shoulder. "You aren't being fair to yourself or to her."

Frederick sighed and turned toward his horse, listening as Slims walked away. His horse butted his hand, and Frederick patted her, but his mind raced at what Slims had said. Closing his eyes and taking a deep breath, Frederick tried to rid himself of the restless anger that always filled him when he thought of his mother. Lately he'd thought of her too often.

His mother, with her red-blond hair and sparkling brown eyes. Her wide smile and infectious laugh when she was happy. The joy in her children when they were young. Her scowl and dulled eyes as the realities of working and living on a ranch took their toll on her. The anger and disgust in her expression as she stared at her boys as they grew into mirror images of their father. He held a hand over his eyes as he tried to block out the memories of the constant fighting between his parents. The desperation in his father's gaze. The despair when his father had realized that his wife had left him for his cousin, who was like a brother. The sorrow when Frederick realized his mother was never coming home. Frederick's anguish when he heard the news of her unexpected death.

Frederick hit the stall door with his hand, the ache from the blow centering him. He pushed back the memories of the taunts and jeers from the children who should have been his friends during the breakup of his parents' marriage. The interminable church services where the pastor had droned on and on about fidelity and duty. The pitying glances from the townsfolk. "I will not be that man."

He pushed away from the barn door and decided to muck out a few stalls. Anything to prevent him from acting on what he felt should be ignored.

~

Sorcha lay awake, listening to the winds howl as her mind continued to replay the scene in the parlor with Frederick. Uncertain what she could have done differently, she castigated herself for her actions. For her passionate response. "Your true blood shines through," she whispered to herself.

She punched at the bed and then listened to the weather outside as the winds calmed. She rose, grabbing her cane as she hobbled to the window. A full moon shone, and the winds were now gone, revealing a beautiful winter night for as far as the eye could see. Pristine white snow glittered under the moon's rays, and a sense of peace, rare in this tempestuous winter, pervaded. Sorcha bit her lip as she saw Slims returning from the barn. Suddenly irrational anger filled her, and she pulled on a pair of boots. After finding a coat, a scarf and a hat, she limped with her cane toward the front door.

When she pulled open the door, she realized the impression of a calm night was misleading as a low wind blew again, stirring up the snowfall and clouding her view. Tugging her scarf and hat more tightly around her, she grabbed the rope and began the slow walk to the barn. Halfway there, sweating and exhausted, she paused and glanced back to the house, barely visible with the snow blowing around her.

After a moment, now shivering in the cold, she firmed her shoulders and began to walk again, her limp more pronounced. Images of the warm barn, of seeing Frederick's horses, of seeing *him*, motivated her.

Strong winds roared to life and stirred up the snowdrifts just as she resumed walking again, blinding her and disorienting her. She stumbled, falling to her knees and losing her cane. "Dammit," she muttered as she felt around for her cane, unable to find it. "Ye *bluidy* fool," she chattered as her teeth rattled from the cold.

Giving up on finding her cane, she rose, reaching for the rope. As she tugged on it, she heard a *crack*, and suddenly the rope went slack in her hands.

She stood there, halfway between the barn and the house, uncertain which way to go, with neither structure visible. She yanked on the rope and pulled it to her until it was taut. Praying that the rope would not give out on both ends, she pulled herself along in an uneven gait until she eventually tripped up the steps to the house. She reentered with a clatter, falling to the floor as she shook with cold.

"Miss Sorcha!" Dixon shouted as he emerged from the kitchen. "What were you doing outside?"

She trembled, unable to form words as her body shivered uncontrollably. Dixon lifted her, carrying her to her room and setting her on her bed after shucking her sodden outerwear.

"Can you undo your buttons, or do you need help?" He frowned as he looked over his shoulder when Dalton glanced in the room.

She batted away his hands even though her fingers shook too much to work at the buttons on her clothes.

Dixon looked at Dalton and said, "I don't know what to do. She was outside in the blizzard."

"Get her dry and warm," Dalton said, striding farther into the room. "Go get a hot brick." Dalton ignored Sorcha's protests, unbuttoning her dress with precision and stripping her dress down. He tugged off her soaked socks and rubbed at her feet. "Jesus, they're as cold as ice." He moved to her chest of drawers and pulled out a pair of woolen socks, tugging them on her feet. When she was stripped to her damp shift, he set a flannel nightgown beside her. "I'll leave so you can change out of your wet underclothes. If you haven't changed in two minutes, I'm doing this for you."

She watched him with eyes as big as two full moons, and he left, leaving the door slightly ajar. She tugged upward on the hem of her shift, sighing with relief when it was off her body. She then pulled on the clean flannel, shivering at the dry warmth it provided. As she smoothed her hands over her thighs, Dalton entered and nodded.

"Good," he said. He eased her up, pulled down the bedcovers and helped her under them. "Lay down and tell me a story. You aren't sleeping for a while."

"I'm tired. Leave me alone, Mr. Dalton."

"Not on your life, Miss Sorcha," he said as he looked in a trunk at the foot of her bed for another blanket. He nodded as Dixon entered with a brick. After jerking up the bottom covers, Dalton placed the warm brick at the base of the bed to keep her feet warm. "Don't put your feet too close. You don't want to burn your skin. Let your body warm up more gradually."

Sorcha shivered and nodded.

"I'll brew coffee," Dixon said and exited the room again.

Sorcha shrieked as Dalton clapped his hands. "Why are ye makin' so much noise? Can ye no' let a body rest?"

"You are not resting. Not yet." He met her glare with a gaze filled with intense purpose. "What was your family like in Skye?"

"Ye ken my brothers. They are no' much different now than when lads." She shuddered and burrowed farther into the covers. "Protective older brothers. Treated me well, although I dinna ken Alistair and Cailean well, as they left when I was still young."

"And your ma and pa?" He tucked covers around her neck and waited.

"Da was a good man. A hard worker. A gifted storyteller." She frowned. "Mother thrived at finding faults. With everyone and everything." She sighed as she closed her eyes. "Where is your family?"

He shrugged, although she did not see the motion with her eyes closed. "They're all dead. Died of hunger or disease during the War between the States."

Her eyes opened at that, and she stared at him mournfully. "Oh, Mr. Dalton. I canna imagine no' havin' my brothers and now women I consider my sisters." A tear leaked out. "I'm sorry."

His chuckle was mirthless. "Yes, well, I thought I had a chance for happiness again. For a family when I married my missus. It takes little to realize your own insignificance."

They sat in silence a moment, listening to the wind howl a mournful song.

Sorcha shivered, then asked, "What will Frederick do? The rope broke. He canna attempt to walk from the barn to the house without the rope."

Dalton groaned. "Is that what happened? Well, he'll spend the night in the barn. It's warmer than outside, and blankets are there in case someone gets marooned out there. But he'll be a bear when he returns to the house."

"Why a bear?"

"The man hates the cold." Dalton chuckled. "Lives in Montana and hates the cold. Can you imagine?"

"Aye," Sorcha whispered. She looked up as Dixon arrived with a mug of coffee. She pushed herself up on one elbow and took a sip, moaning with pleasure as the warmth filled her. After a few more sips, she laid on her side again. She now rarely shivered, and a gentle warmth pervaded her. "I'm no' cold anymore. Thank ye," she said to both Dixon and Dalton.

"If you don't mind, miss," Dalton said, "I'll sit here for a while longer to ensure you are well." He waited until Sorcha began to doze. He motioned for Dixon to remain. "What aren't you telling me, Dix?"

Dixon dropped his voice, whispering, "I found a straggler hanging about. Asked him to move on. I'll tell the Boss as soon as I see him."

"Boss'll be more worried about Miss Sorcha, but you must tell him." Dalton's worried gaze flickered to the woman resting comfortably on the bed. "You know he wants us to be vigilant."

Dixon nodded and left Dalton to watch over Sorcha as she slipped into a deeper sleep.

~

"Dalton, what are you doing in Miss MacKinnon's room?" Frederick asked. He wore clean clothes, and his hair was wet from a recent washing. His brows furrowed, he glanced from Dalton to Sorcha and then back again. Bright sunlight glinted off the icy snow outside, sparkling into the bedroom.

"Hi, Boss," Dalton said as he groaned and stretched in the hard wooden chair. A wide yawn escaped before he spoke. "She nearly froze to death last night, trying to make it to the barn."

Frederick stilled and shook his head as though confused. "I think I misheard you. Why was she outside last night?"

Dalton rose and slapped Frederick on the shoulder. "As to that, I have no idea. She's slept soundly. Hopefully she will be fine with no illness."

"The rope broke," Frederick rasped.

"Yeah, and, from the sounds of it, she barely made it back inside."

Frederick paled as he watched her sleeping soundly. He barely nodded as Dalton left to find a cup of coffee. "You idiot," he berated himself as he sat and ran his hands through his damp hair. He watched the gentle rise and fall of her chest as she breathed deeply in her sleep, her hair a jumbled mess on her pillow. He gripped his hands, rather than give into temptation and slip a hand through her soft hair.

When Slims came with a cup of coffee for Frederick, he nodded his thanks and continued his vigil. When she began to stir, he leaned forward, meeting her confused stare as she gasped and yanked at the blanket that already covered her from toe to neck. "You aren't indecent," he snapped.

"I dinna ken why ye believe ye have the right to be angry with me. Ye're the one actin' like a boor." She glared at him. "Please leave."

"No," he hissed, his eyes flashing with satisfaction as she gasped at his refusal to do as she bid. "Not until you explain what you were doing outside last night in the middle of a blizzard."

"There was no' a blizzard the whole night."

He let out a deep breath, as though clinging to his temper by a thread. "You've lived in Montana long enough to know that just because the winds die down for a bit, it doesn't mean the blizzard is over."

She shrugged. "Well, now I ken better."

His temper snapped just as the rope to the barn had last night. "Dammit, you could have frozen to death last night, and none of us would have thought to look for you until this morning, since we didn't even know you had wandered outside." He watched as she paled. "By then it would have been too late."

"I ken I was foolish," she whispered. She lowered her gaze to avoid meeting his disapproving frown. "But I was angry."

He ran a hand through his hair. "At me. At what I did." He waited until she met his gaze. "I'm sorry."

Hurt flashed in her eyes. "For actin' as ye did or for kissin' me?"

"Both."

She nodded and pulled the blanket even more securely around her. "Aye, an' I'm sorry I acted a fool, so we're even." She snuggled into bed. "Now that ye ken I'm fine, will ye leave?"

He rose and then stood for a moment. "Sorcha, I ..." He watched as she feigned sleep before he turned on his heel and marched to his office.

He stood behind his desk, staring into space as visions of her frozen and helpless last night filled his imaginings. Then he thought of her coming inside, nearly chilled to the bone and in need of care, and an irrational anger filled him that he had not been the one to tend her. To warm her. To keep vigil to ensure she recovered.

Dalton poked his head into Frederick's office. "Is Miss MacKinnon well, Boss?" He yawned again. "She gave us all a fright last night."

"Who helped her?" Frederick asked. "Who helped her change out of her wet clothes?"

Dalton paled at the anger in Frederick's tone. "I did. But she was alone when she changed from her wet shift into a nightgown. Nothing improper happened."

Frederick pinched the bridge of his nose and then looked at his trusted ranch hand. "I know, Dalton. Thank you. I'm angry I wasn't here to help her too."

Dalton nodded. "You may not want me sayin' this, Boss, but she has no interest in any man on this ranch but you."

Frederick nodded. "Thank you, Dalton, for ensuring she was well last night." After Dalton left, Frederick sat in his chair, and rather than write letters or continue to make up projections about the ranch's future—which may or may not have any basis in reality once the thaw hit—he sat and thought about Sorcha.

He had stood outside the kitchen the previous morning, listening to her chat with Slims and Dixon, charming them with tales of Scotland. Her laughter had filled the room and had lifted his spirits, as Dixon and Slims had exchanged stories with her.

Now that she was mobile and freed from her bedrest, the evidence of her presence in his house was everywhere. From a newly knitted red scarf on the peg by the front door to lace doilies on the tables in the parlor, to her knitting needles poking out of a ball of yarn by the chair she had claimed as hers by the large fireplace, her presence was palpable. He found himself pausing at the threshold of the parlor every time he entered the house, listening for her singing or her laughter or her chatter. A panic that he did not know he even had eased each time he was reassured of her presence.

"What am I going to do?" he muttered to himself.

CHAPTER 6

F rederick sat at his desk in his study, looking blankly at the number of cattle that had been on the range before winter started. He sighed as he calculated again how many they could lose before running into financial difficulties. The telegram from his brothers the previous week had only further soured his mood.

Won't come back with herd this year. Hear rough winter. Keep enough alive for market this fall.

The memory of the skeletal, staggering cattle wandering through the ranch a few days ago haunted him, as did his inability to provide them the hay they needed to survive. He looked to the door at the tap. "Yes?"

"Boss, we have a problem," Slims said as he entered and shut the door behind him.

Frederick frowned, understanding instantly that it was a serious concern as Slims sat down. The shut door heralded the need for privacy, something rarely required among his trusted ranch hands. "What is it?"

"I made it into and out of town today between storms. I stopped by the livery." Slims shook his head at Frederick's silent inquiry. "They have no extra hay. All they have they'll need for their horses and business."

"Damn," Frederick muttered. "I'd hoped we could find someone with a bounty of hay." He closed his eyes in frustration.

Slims nodded, tapping his hand on his leg. "Do you want your horses to suffer as well as your cattle?" He met Frederick's gaze and shrugged. "The hay is for the horses. It always has been. Don't jeopardize everything because you now know how bad it is on the range."

Frederick nodded. "I understand, but it's hard to accept the cattle are dying, and there's nothing that can be done." He glared at the slip of paper in front of him. "Peter and Cole aren't coming back with a herd this year. The cattle sold at auction in October didn't bring enough to purchase another herd."

Slims closed his eyes, and his shoulders stooped. "I'm sorry, Boss."

Frederick nodded. After a moment he frowned at his friend's tense posture. "There's no need to shut the door for this discussion. What else did you learn in town?"

"When I left the livery, where the brothers were still friendly to me, I made my way to the saloon. The Watering Hole." He flushed. "Seems a rumor has started that Miss MacKinnon had a man spend the night in her room a few evenings ago."

Frederick froze. "What?"

"Yes, the man sipping his whiskey was delighted to realize that she was open to dalliance. Took all I had in me not to bust out his teeth." Slims fisted his hands. "Seems someone here talked about the night she nearly froze, although I can't recall anyone besides me making it into town the past month." He shared a long look with Frederick.

"I know you wouldn't tell such a tale at the Watering Hole. But I wonder who did ..."

Slims continued, "I spoke to another man, who congratulated me on the fact Dalton had found another bride."

"Idiots." Frederick's mind raced, and his heart pounded. "Her brothers don't know?"

"By the way the brothers who work in the livery acted, they ain't got a clue. I imagine the youngest one soon will. He frequents the saloons, looking for stories for his wife. Someone will only be too pleased to whisper in his ear."

Frederick dropped his head in his hands. "Dammit. What can we do?"

Slims shrugged. "Dalton likes her. Knows he doesn't have much chance of meeting another agreeable woman. He'd marry her."

Frederick growled and shot to his feet, pacing behind his desk. "How chivalrous of him," he snapped.

"You got another solution to this type of rumor for a woman staying alone on a ranch with nothing but men?" Slims demanded.

"She doesn't know you went into town?" Frederick relaxed at Slims's headshake. "I should be the one to tell her." He pinched the bridge of his nose and thought for a minute before exiting his office.

The house was quiet, as most of the men were either in the barn working or taking it easy. Frederick heard Slims enter the kitchen behind him, where he unpacked the supplies he had picked up in town. Sorcha's bedroom door was nearby and ajar, and he knocked on the frame.

"Aye?" she asked, her voice reedy.

"Are you ill?" Frederick entered and touched her forehead with little thought to propriety.

"I dinna ken," she whispered. "Since a few nights ago, I do no' feel well." She shivered and pulled a blanket around her. She met his worried gaze with a shrug, her cheeks flushed and her eyes bright. "But 'tis always worse at night."

"You've a fever," he whispered as he put the back of his hand to her cheeks. "Why did you say nothing and suffer alone?"

She shivered. "'Tis out of my own stupidity that I got a chill. I'll survive." Sorcha closed her eyes and curled on her side. "What's the matter, Frederick? Since I've arrived, ye've become more an' more dour, an' now circles are under yer eyes."

He sighed. "Give me a moment." He strode to the kitchen. "Slims, make Sorcha willow bark tea. She's a fever." At his friend's grunt of agreement, he spun away to return to her.

He sat beside her on the bed as he waited for the tea. "You've hidden in this room since … since the night I kissed you. And I've avoided you." He waited for some acknowledgment of his words, but she remained quiet. "If you had joined us for dinner or been in the parlor, you would have heard us talking about the cattle wandering near the ranch that were so starved that their ribs showed. Stumbling and lowing for food, as though barely with the strength to move."

"Oh, no," Sorcha murmured, pulling her hand out from underneath the covers to grasp his.

"I might lose the ranch." He took a deep breath. "Of three generations who owned this land, I might be the one to fail."

Sorcha shook her head and squeezed his hand. She tugged at him until he lay beside her, face-to-face, and she wrapped an arm around his middle, pulling him close. He lay on top of the covers, and she underneath them. "Ye are smart and resilient. Ye'll find a way through this. And yer grandparents will never see ye fail."

He sniffed. "For once, just once, I'd like to succeed without them." He flushed as he met her eyes, intelligent and filled with clarity, even in the midst of a fever.

"Then ye're a fool. For few have the fortune of having such support." She shivered and her arm around him tightened. "I ken what it is to desire my independence away from my family. And I've never felt more alone."

"You aren't alone," he whispered, as his fingers traced along her hairline. He watched as her eyes drifted shut, either from his caress or from the fever. "Sorcha?"

"Aye?" She turned into his touch.

His hand lowered, tracing his fingers over her cheek. "There's something else I must tell you." He frowned as he saw her start to fade. "But you need sleep and willow bark tea for now. It will keep, and then we'll talk more."

"Stay," she whispered. "Dinna leave me."

He let out a deep breath as his fingers continued to caress her head and face. "I fear you are capable of causing me to break my vows, Sorcha. But I won't leave you." He looked up at Slims as he stood with a mug of tea. "First, drink your tea. Then sleep."

He helped her sit up to drink her tea and then eased her back to her side. She preferred to sleep on the left side as her right leg still ached. After a few minutes, she was asleep, curled in his arms.

"You are a fool if you let her go," Slims said, startling Frederick from his reverie.

Frederick ran a hand over her head before kissing it. "I know."

The following morning, Sorcha woke feeling more rested than she had in weeks. She gave a soft sound of contentment and curled forward toward the source of heat at her side, gasping in shock as she came awake to realize a man was in her bed. She sat up and glared at the offending person, her glower intensifying as a sleepy chuckle emerged from him.

"No need to act indignant when you've slept on me like a cat in a patch of sunlight all night," Frederick's raspy voice said. He opened one eye, filled with amusement to stare at her before closing it again and breathing deeply.

"Ye can no' be in my bed. Ye must leave now!" She gave him a push, but he didn't budge. It felt like she was attempting to dislodge a boulder. "Why would ye think I'd want ye here?"

"Oh, how you wound me, Sorcha. You begged me to join you here in this bed and then pleaded with me not to leave you. Or can't you remember?" He watched as she flushed with memory. "Or perhaps you can."

He yawned and stretched. "Come. Relax. The men won't bother us." He held his arm up for her to relax against his shoulder, and, after a moment's contemplation, she did.

"This means nothin', ye ken?" she muttered.

He sighed. "I fear it might mean a great deal." He held on to her hand as she tensed. "It seems your fever has broken, and you are lucid. Is that correct?" He waited for her to mutter "Aye," and then he waited another moment. "Slims went to town yesterday. Snuck in and out on a quick trip for supplies."

She hit him on his chest with her fist. "Why did he no' bring me in? I could be at home now with my family."

Frederick raised his other hand and rubbed it over his face. "I should never have attempted this conversation without first having coffee." He met her gaze as she lay in a position so she could glare at him, propped on his chest. His breath hitched at her innocent beauty, her red-brown hair free of its braid and spilling down her back. Her cheeks were flushed, with irritation rather than fever, and her eyes shone with challenge and intelligence. "You are beautiful."

She glared at him. "Dinna think an attempt at false platitudes will placate me. Why are ye keepin' me here, a prisoner?"

He frowned, and then his expression blanked. "You're not a prisoner. And my words aren't false. However, Slims wasn't sure he'd make it into town, much less back to the ranch, and I did not want to risk you suffering any more in the freezing cold than you already have. If he got stuck or had to seek shelter in a hut ..." He shook his head. "I would not risk your safety."

"Did ye no' believe I had a right to decide for myself?" She pointed at her chest. "I'm a grown woman. I can make decisions."

"Yes, and twice those decisions have almost gotten you killed." He flushed with anger. "Heed me well, Sorcha. I will not risk your safety. Ever."

She sobered at the solemnity of his words. Finally, she nodded.

"Now I know what I'm going to tell you will anger you, but I need you to listen." He waited until she gave another subtle nod. "Slims had time to visit the Watering Hole while our order was filled at the store. A patron there told him that he had heard how you'd spent the night with a man while out here on the ranch."

Sorcha's eyes rounded, and she pushed away from him, gasping in pain as she landed on her weak leg. "Get out. Get out of my bed."

"Sorcha, listen. It's not me they're talking about. It's Dalton." He waited for her panic and anger to abate. "The night you went into the snowstorm. The night you nearly froze, and he spent it on a chair to ensure you were healthy." He shrugged. "Someone, somehow, found out about it, and they've made it seem salacious."

She stared at him with a wounded gaze. "Ye kent what they were sayin', an' ye stayed here anyway last night. Did ye think me fair game?"

"Dammit, no!" He leaped from the bed and tugged the chair over, plopping onto it as he faced her. She had curled into herself, as though protecting herself. "Somehow, we must find a way to protect you from this gossip."

"Take me home. Take me away." She flinched at the pleading note in her voice.

"That will only make the rumors worse, Sorcha. If you leave here now, there are those who will always see you as ..."

"A loose woman," Sorcha whispered. "My *puir* brothers. What must they think of me?" She wrapped her arms over her head as she cried.

Frederick touched her, leaping back as she struck at him.

"Dinna touch me! Dinna think to woo me to whatever idea ye have now. Ye had yer chance to be honorable. To ... to ..." She burst into sobs, unable to continue speaking.

"I'll leave you for now, Sorcha, but this is far from resolved between us." He gripped his hands together tightly—rather than to offer her comfort as he yearned to—and slipped from the room.

F rederick walked into the kitchen and met Slims's grim stare. "Slims, can you confirm that the two junior ranch hands have not been to town in the last month?" At Slims's nod, Frederick said, "Gather Dixon and Dalton. I want to talk to the three of you." He watched as Slims nodded and left to find the other men. Frederick paced around the kitchen, finally pausing to pour himself a cup of coffee.

The men entered the kitchen and immediately served themselves cups of coffee. Dalton stiffened when he saw Frederick's foreboding stare, but Dixon remained relaxed and continued to prattle. When Dalton nudged his buddy with his elbow, Dixon looked at Frederick and quieted.

"What is it, Boss?" Slims asked.

Frederick motioned for them to join him at the table. "I want to know how a rumor about Miss MacKinnon reached town in the middle of the worst winter we've ever had. I want to know who among the three of you was indiscreet." He looked at each man, frowning when he saw Dixon flush. "Dix?"

"Don't you remember me tellin' you about that straggler I found the night Miss Sorcha nearly froze?" Dixon asked. He frowned as Frederick shook his head. Dixon looked to Slims and Dalton, who also shook their heads. "I told you about finding a man in the bunkhouse, holed up, an' I told him that he had to skedaddle when the weather broke. We weren't lookin' for no more help, and we weren't a charity, givin' out free meals."

Frederick's gaze cleared, and he nodded. "I remember now. After I knew Sorcha was fine, I went to speak with him, but he was gone."

Dixon nodded. "I think he's the one who could have told tales. You know I chatter, and I think I told him about Miss Sorcha and her misadventure when I brought him a blanket and some coffee." His gaze was filled with trepidation and fear. "I never meant to cause no harm, Boss."

Frederick gave a curt nod. "I know, Dix. This isn't your fault." He sighed, rubbing at his forehead. "However, it seems her reputation is now in question, due to that drifter's story."

Dixon flushed with indignation. "I'd never have given him food if I knew he'd hurt Miss Sorcha."

Slims gave a grunt of approval. "You did nothin' wrong, Dix. We always help those who show up, even if they can't stay long. I'm surprised he didn't freeze on his way into town."

Dalton shook his head in confusion. "I don't remember tending an extra horse. How did he get here? And why venture forth in the middle of such a harsh winter on foot?"

Dixon shrugged. "I don't know. He was here, and then he was gone. He wasn't much of a talker, although he did seem interested in anything I had to say about the ranch."

Frederick gave his men a piercing stare. "From now on, I want to meet any drifter." As his men quickly agreed, Frederick rose to return to his office, deep in thought.

～

Cailean snuggled into bed on a cold Sunday morning in February, enjoying his lazy morning with his wife, Annabelle. His sister-in-law, Fidelia, had offered to watch their daughter, Skye, that morning, and Cailean and Annabelle had time to relax and to enjoy each other. He pulled Annabelle back so that she was snug against his front and let out a contented sigh. "Heaven," he whispered.

"Yes," she whispered, wriggling against him. "It's been ages since we've had time for us." She let out a gasp as he tickled her belly. "I love you, Cailean."

He kissed the side of her head, his hand moving to caress her when he heard heavy footsteps and raised voices downstairs. He lifted his head and frowned. "'Tis Alistair. And Ewan. They never interrupt their Sundays if it can be avoided."

"Something must be wrong," Annabelle whispered, just as a tapping started on their door.

Cailean kissed her neck and slipped from the bed. He opened his bedroom door to meet Alistair's glower. "Aye?"

"We need ye downstairs. Now." Alistair's eyes were filled with rage.

"Aye." Cailean shut the door and grabbed his pants and a shirt. "Sorry, Belle, but something's wrong. I've never seen Alistair this angry. Not since his problems with Leticia." He kissed her. "Rest."

She rolled her eyes and pushed out of the bed. "If you think I'm resting when the family is in the middle of a crisis, you don't know me." She rose, pulling on her dress and a pair of thick wool socks.

Soon they had joined Alistair, Ewan, Jessamine and Fidelia in the kitchen. Jessamine held Skye while Fidelia cooked breakfast for them all. Leticia had remained at home with Hortence and Angus. "Thanks, Dee," Annabelle said as she sat next to Jessamine. She watched as Alistair and Ewan paced and attempted to share a smile with Jessamine. When she shook her head and remained sober, Annabelle frowned.

"What is it? Why have you called for an impromptu clan gathering?" Annabelle asked. Cailean had leaned against the counter, sipping coffee, waiting patiently for his brothers to speak, but she had no desire to wait out an irritated Scotsman.

"I went to the saloon last night," Ewan said. "Jessie had heard a rumor, an' she dinna ken it to be true. But I wanted to make sure it was no' true." Ewan ran a hand through his blondish hair. "The men at the Watering Hole and the Stumble-Out were only too delighted to tell me of our sister's downfall."

"What?" Fidelia asked with a gasp as she dropped the spatula. She flushed and picked it up, setting it in the sink to wash. "They must be mistaken. No one on the ranch would take advantage of her."

The brothers all exchanged looks. "Except for Frederick," Cailean rasped. "I'll kill him."

"Nae," Alistair countered. "I'll kill him."

Annabelle hopped to her feet and stood between the brothers. "No one is killing anyone. There must be more to this story. How can there be any gossip from the ranch in the middle of the worst winter ever?"

"I dinna ken," Ewan said. "But that giant of a man who works there was in town yesterday. He slipped in for supplies but dinna manage to bring our sister back." He glowered at the floor.

"Perhaps they dinna want her to leave," Alistair said.

Jessamine cleared her throat. "Before you start your own vigilante party of three, Ewan heard the story that Sorcha had been in the presence of a man named Dalton all night long." She looked at each brother a moment. "That could mean anything. And it could mean absolutely nothing. You are jumping to conclusions."

"Aye, the conclusion that one of them is a dead man," Cailean growled.

Annabelle rubbed at her temple and closed her eyes. "You are not killing anyone." She met his gaze. "Must I remind you that you were caught acting on your own passion and that's why we had to marry? Everything we have heard so far is pure gossip."

"Aye, an' this town thrives on it." Ewan scrubbed at his head. "I'm headin' to the ranch today. The weather looks a bit clearer, an' I need to see how Sorcha is."

"I'll go with ye," Alistair said.

"And me too," Cailean said.

Annabelle pinched at her brows. "You can't both leave Bears with the livery. One of you must stay."

After wolfing down their meal, Cailean and Ewan departed for the livery to prepare a sleigh for their journey, while Alistair ran off on an errand. Bears met them inside and shook his head. "You'll regret your rash actions." He looked at the sky. "This calm will only last a few hours."

"What would ye have us do, Bears?" Ewan said. "She's been out there without a visit from us for over two months. There's a rare letter that arrives as few travel from the ranch to town in winter."

Bears began to speak and then rolled his eyes instead at the sight of Alistair with the pastor in tow. Bears marched away from them, as though deciding any wisdom would be lost on them today.

"Now, young men, I don't know what you have planned, but I will not travel with you to that ranch. It is a den of iniquity, after what I have heard is occurring there."

Alistair glared at the pastor and then shared a long look with his eldest brother. "If what ye've heard is true, then that is why we need yer presence. To ensure our sister is saved from such iniquity."

The pastor shook his head. "No, not in the middle of this winter. I will not be stranded in such a place. With such heathens for men." He looked at the three brothers. "I commend you, for caring for your sister, even though she is now a fallen woman."

"How dare ye?" Ewan took a threatening step toward the pastor. "She is honorable and good. More than can be said of ye, if ye are spreading such vicious words about her. Ye dinna even ken if what ye've heard is true, but ye've already judged her."

"Aye," Cailean said. "What would your Bible say about that? I thought there was something in it about not casting stones, Pastor. Perhaps you should learn that lesson. Or your wife should. As I fear there may come a time when stones will be sent in your direction."

He glared at the man until the pastor stiffened his shoulders, tipped his head back and marched away, as though he had been sorely abused by the MacKinnon brothers.

"*Bluidy* man," Alistair swore. "How dare he?"

Cailean let out a deep breath. "Well, he may have saved us from a horrible battle with Sorcha. She would have never forgiven us had we arrived with a pastor in the sleigh."

Ewan frowned. "Isna marriage without a pastor legal in Montana Territory?"

Cailean nodded. "Aye. Warren married last year at the ranch." He smiled at Ewan, his gaze devious. "Perhaps we dinna need the pastor."

"Nae," Alistair said as he finished cinching the horses to the sleigh, "but ye need a willin' bride, an' I doubt Sorcha will be pleased with what ye have in mind. An' the pastor blessin' their marriage would have calmed the gossip. 'Tis why Helen and Warren had two celebrations last year, even though the second was no' required." He watched as his brothers got in the sleigh and handed Cailean the reins. "Good luck. I'll watch for ye this evening."

Cailean nodded and gave the horses a flick of the reins. After leaving town, they passed by the sawmill that did little business in the winter and then turned down the lane to the ranch. Large drifts of snow covered the rangeland, and Cailean was thankful for the sleigh tracks still visible in the snow to follow to the ranch. He knew they would cross a creek, but it was invisible due to the ice and thick layer of snow. The mountains in the distance were shrouded in white, as was everything in sight.

"I've never seen anythin' like it," Ewan murmured. "Can ye imagine gettin' lost out here? Ye wouldna ken where ye were."

"Besides the fact you'd be dead in a matter of minutes due to the cold," Cailean said. He urged the horses on and moved with greater speed toward the ranch and their sister.

When they arrived, they brought the horses to the barn, and a man met them. Cailean handed over the reins and followed Ewan as he marched toward the ranch house. He grabbed Ewan's arm before he barged into the house uninvited and knocked on the door. After a few moments, a huge man opened the door.

"We're here for our sister," Cailean said as he met the man's curious expression.

The man stepped aside, allowing them into the warmth of the house. After taking off their jackets, Ewan moved toward Sorcha's room, while Cailean asked the tall man, "Where is he?"

"In his office." Slims pointed to a doorway near the parlor. "I'm Slims."

Cailean barely acknowledged the other man's greeting, walking toward the ajar door. He paused as he saw Frederick, sitting with his head in his hands in absolute despair. "You've a fine way of keeping your word."

Frederick bolted to his feet and flushed. "Cailean. I had no idea you'd come to the ranch today."

"How would I not, when the town is talking about my sister in an unflattering way." He took a deep breath as he saw Frederick flinch. "How could you not keep your promise?"

"She hasn't been harmed. She hasn't been touched, I promise." His gaze flit away, and he swore under his breath. "That's not true. I kissed her. Once."

Cailean took a moment, allowing his anger to subside as he studied the man. He frowned as he saw how miserable Frederick looked. "Was it to get her to stop talking?"

Frederick let out a small laugh and then shook his head. "No. I can't act like it was in any way out of self-preservation." He paused. "Or maybe it was." He shook his head. "I'm sorry. I shouldn't be talkin' like this to you." He paused as he heard Sorcha shouting.

"That would be her yellin' at Ewan." Cailean sighed and pointed to a chair. "May I sit? I fear we've acted like fools, just as Bears said we were."

Frederick motioned him to a chair and collapsed into his behind his desk. "How are things in town?"

Cailean shrugged. "Boring. The townsfolk are tired of this harsh winter and will delight in any gossip. Our rushing to the ranch will only make many believe there is truth to the rumors." Cailean sighed and rubbed at his head. "I'm sorry. I wasn't thinking this morning when Ewan and Alistair arrived at the house. All I could think of was Sorcha. Of ensuring she was well."

Frederick watched him. "No one needs to know that your trip here was unplanned. You could let everyone know that you had always planned on visiting her today."

Cailean cleared his throat and flushed with embarrassment. "Except for the fact Alistair dragged the pastor to the livery, intent on having him travel to the ranch with us." He saw Frederick's shoulders sag. "The gossip will only become more pronounced after he gives his sermon today."

"I've never understood why we've yet to have an understanding, compassionate pastor," Frederick said. "We've always had the ones who relish in making us feel smaller and worse about ourselves and our neighbors."

Cailean nodded. "Aye, well, we've made it all worse for Sorcha, rather than better." He paused and then changed the subject. "How are your cattle?"

Frederick groaned and rubbed at the back of his neck as though attempting to relieve tension. "Dying or dead." He shared a tormented glance with Cailean. "I … There's nothing I can do. I don't have hay set aside for them, and I can't risk the health of my horses by giving their portion of hay to the cattle."

"Nae," Cailean said in rapid agreement. "Your horses are beautiful and will help see this ranch through hard times. Don't jeopardize them."

"Well, that's easy to say but hard to do when starving cattle roam onto the homestead hoping to be fed."

E wan eased open Sorcha's door to see her lying atop her bed, reading a book. Or acting as though she were reading. She stared into space, out the window crusted over in snow and ice. His alert gaze took in her loosely braided hair, her clean clothes, the tidy room. "Sorch," he whispered.

She dropped the book and looked to the door. "Ewan!" she reached for him and pulled him down to the bed to hug him. "Oh, I canna believe ye're here, today of all days. I missed ye so!"

He laughed and hugged her, his smile fading as he felt her shudder in his arms. "Dinna cry. All is well."

She shook her head. "Ye can say that because ye dinna ken what they're sayin' about me in town." She looked at him and then froze, as she saw the banked anger in his gaze. "Ye do ken?"

"Aye. 'Tis why Cailean an' I are here today." His fingers twitched as he raised his hand to push back a tendril of loose hair. "Ye are well? Ye are unharmed?"

She nodded. "Aye, although I dinna ken what to do." She leaned into his embrace. "Where's Cail?"

"Talkin' sense into that bastard," Ewan said, his voice betraying his anger.

She pushed away and studied her brother a moment before her eyes widened. "Oh, no, Ewan. Ye can no' be serious! I will no' do it!"

He grabbed her hand to prevent her from moving away and potentially moving too fast and hurting herself. "Think about it, Sorch. Ye ken ye will always be a source of gossip in town if ye do no' wed. Why no' wed him?"

"Which one would ye have me wed? Dalton or Frederick?" She snatched her hand out of his and hit him on the chest. "For both men have spent a night in this room." She saw her brother's eyes kindle with rage. "What would the townsfolk say if they kent that?"

"Stop talkin' like a daft woman. Ye ken all they'll care about is that ye are wed. We couldna get the pastor to travel here with us—"

She shrieked loudly and belted him on the shoulders at that comment, Ewan raising his arms to defend himself. "Ye fool! Ye thought to bring the pastor!" She hit him again. "Ye could no' have assured gossip any more than if ye'd had Jessie write a story about me."

Ewan hopped off the bed and paced the small room. "Sorch, we're trying to ensure that you are safe. Free from gossip."

She collapsed onto her back and let out a deep, stuttering breath as a few tears leaked out of her eyes. "I ken what I am, Ewan. An' the fact the townsfolk have yet to discover I'm the bastard daughter of the MacKinnon is a surprise."

Ewan growled and moved to the bed. He loomed over her, his face mottled with rage. "Ye are no' a bastard," he said in a low, lethal voice. "Ye are my beloved sister, an' I will ensure ye are treated as ye deserve. As ye still do no' ken ye deserve to be treated."

She closed her eyes and shook her head. "I'm no better than *she* was, Ewan."

He frowned at the despair clinging to her. "What's happened, Sorch? Ye've written letters describin' how ye've driven him mad with yer chatter. Is any of it true?"

"Some of it. Mainly he avoids me. I think he doesna like me. He's only payin' attention to me know because he has to." She looked at her brother and flushed and looked away.

"Ye ken we've always been the closest, Sorch. What is it ye want to know?" He sat beside her on the bed and waited as she calmed.

"Am I shameless for desirin' his kiss? Am I a wanton woman for wishin' he'd see me as more than the invalid stranded at his ranch?"

Ewan sighed and took her hand. "I dinna ken who yer birth mother was. But I ken she must have been good and kind and loving for Da to ever consider breaking his marriage vows for her." He looked at his sister. "If ye have a chance with a good man, take it. For ye canna ken when that chance will come again."

She sniffed and rested her head against his shoulder. "I never want him to look at me and wish he'd waited for another."

"Ye need to have faith, Sorch. In yerself. And in him." He held her as she relaxed for a few moments. "What do ye want to do?"

She shrugged. "I dinna like the idea of anyone feeling obligated to marry me." She was silent for a minute. "But I dinna want to return to town to face that gossip." She peered up at him. "Mind ye, I could. I ken I could." She settled again on his shoulder. "Yet I've found I enjoy the peace on the ranch."

Ewan smiled. "Then I think ye've found yer answer. Now ye must decide which one it will be." He grunted as she hit his arm. He kissed her head and eased her onto a pillow. "I must talk with Cail."

She blinked back tears as she saw her brother rise to leave her room. "He won't leave without seeing me, will he?"

Ewan chuckled. "Of course no', ye daft wee thing. He's anxious to see ye, but I stormed in here, and he had to deal with Frederick afore he could see ye." He paused and raised an eyebrow. "'Tis Frederick ye want, no?"

She flushed and nodded.

"Aye, well, we'll see what happens." He winked at her and left her to her book.

Ewan tapped on the office door twice before opening it. "Glad to see violence was no' necessary in here."

Cailean raised an eyebrow as he watched his youngest brother with amusement. "Unlike the yelling needed to speak with Sorcha?" He sobered. "How is she?"

Ewan gave a half shrug and sat in the chair next to Cailean. "Confused but with no desire to return to town. Seems she's an affinity for the quiet life on the ranch." He speared Frederick with an intense stare. "Do ye plan to do anythin' about that?"

Frederick's mouth dropped open, and then he faltered a few times before speaking coherently. "She threw me out of her room today. Wanted nothing more to do with me and only wanted to return to town. To escape this ranch. What changed?"

Ewan chuckled. "Aye, well, ye have to ken she's a temper. An', when it's in full steam, she says things she doesna always mean or even kens she's sayin'. Especially if she feels backed into a corner or vulnerable." He paused as he saw Frederick thinking through his words.

Cailean waited a moment and then spoke, his voice soft in the quiet room. "You scare her, so this is how she acts."

Frederick shook his head. "I … I never planned to marry." He looked at the brothers to see them share an incredulous look. "I didn't."

"That's not how it appears when we see you and Sorcha butt heads," Cailean stated.

"Do ye need a visit with yer grandparents to help ye see sense?" Ewan asked. "Ye have a good woman in there, who cares for ye. Who's cared for ye for some time. I dinna understand."

Cailean watched Frederick for a long moment and then nodded. "Only you can free yourself of this prison you alone have crafted. You understand?" He waited until Frederick nodded.

"I must ask," Frederick said, "would you still want your sister to marry a man who might be bankrupt in a few months?" He met the brothers' shocked gazes. "This winter ..." Frederick shuddered as though the cold had penetrated his multiple layers of wool clothing. "This winter might be the end of us."

Cailean canted forward, his hands on his knees as he watched Frederick intently. "I know Irene and Harold have been worried. I've seen the strain in their eyes as they try to hide it with their ready smile when I visit them for coffee." He shook his head. "I'm certain you'll survive."

Frederick pinched the bridge of his nose. "If we do, it will be some time before we thrive again. I make daily calculations of how many cattle we can lose without declaring bankruptcy. Of how low the price of beef can remain." He shook his head. "The price dropped last year, and I fear the easy profits of the past decade will remain a cherished memory."

Cailean shared a look with Ewan and then met Frederick's gaze. "I see now that there is more than your past that worries you."

"Aye, yer future," Ewan said. "But ye can no' ken what will come. All ye can hope is that ye'll have the support of those around ye. An', if ye have the care of a good woman, it makes it all bearable."

"Besides, you have your horses, don't you?" Cailean asked.

"Yes, of course, but I will do what I must to save the ranch for the family." Frederick met their gazes.

"I understand well enough loyalty to family," Cailean said. Ewan nodded his agreement. "But there are times when you must act for yourself. When acting in your best interests is not selfish. You deserve to find your own happiness."

"My brothers sent me a telegram saying they aren't coming north with any fresh cattle this year. We earned little profit at the auction in Chicago this fall," Frederick murmured. "Whatever survives here is what we'll have."

Ewan gazed at Frederick in an assessing manner. "Life is a gamble. Every day we take a risk, Frederick. The question is, will you take a risk on our sister?"

Cailean waited as the silence became pronounced and shared a long look with Ewan. Ewan shook his head as Cailean was about to ask Frederick a question.

"Did she tell you that she remembered a little of what happened that day?" Frederick asked Ewan in a soft voice, his gaze unfocused. "About her accident?"

The brothers canted forward with curiosity. "Nae," Ewan said. "What happened?"

"Someone startled her horse in the woods. Made a loud sound." Frederick's eyes blazed with anger and hatred. "Stood over her as she lay unconscious and was upset that she'd died *too soon.*"

Cailean's gaze was molten with his fury. "Do you know who it was?"

Frederick shook his head. "Sorcha didn't recognize the voice. She didn't see the man." He rose and paced to the window, his shoulders tense. "I hate the thought of anyone hurting her."

Cailean nodded. "Aye," he whispered as he sat in quiet contemplation. "Sorcha can't leave the ranch. She's safer here than she'd be in town. We can't protect her every moment in town, but here"—Cailean looked around—"here, she'll be safe."

"*Safer,*" Frederick said as he met her eldest brother's worried gaze.

"Ye made us a promise," Ewan said as he stood and met Frederick's gaze. "Ye promised to always protect her. We expect ye to keep that vow."

Cailean nodded. "Aye, and it's not from you that she needs protecting." He waited a long moment for Frederick to nod his acknowledgment of those words, and then he rose. "How long have you known what Sorcha remembers? Was it before Warren visited you?"

Frederick nodded.

"Why did ye no' tell Warren about Sorcha's memory? About the man standin' over her?" Ewan asked.

"She's not even sure it really happened. Thinks it could have been a dream." He let out a breath. "And I wanted to tell you in person." His intense gaze flit from one brother to the other. "I wanted you to know that, if it was Walter, he's mine."

Ewan shook his head. "Nae. If he dared hurt a MacKinnon, he's ours."

Cailean looked at Frederick, met his determined stare. "Why do you think you have the right to deny us our desire to defend our sister?"

Frederick swallowed and then said, "She'll be my wife. I've been coming to this point for over two years."

Ewan shook his head. "An' she's been my sister for twenty-five years."

Cailean glared at his brother. "Ewan, if this were Jessamine, you'd fight anyone who dared threaten her."

"Fine, but I want to ken I can inflict some damage on the man. Ye dinna get to do it alone."

Frederick grinned at the men he knew would become his brothers. "Yes." He sighed. "And that's another reason I didn't tell Warren what I suspected and what Sorcha isn't sure was just a dream. I didn't want to place my lawyer in a difficult position."

Cailean rubbed at his brow. "Your problem now is finding a way to convince my sister to marry you."

"And to keep her safe," Ewan said.

Frederick nodded to both men. "There's one more thing. The night Dalton sat by her bed, keeping vigil, a drifter was on the ranch. I didn't see him, but the friendly ranch hand, Dixon, did. I think Dix inadvertently told him about Sorcha and Dalton, and that's how the rumor started."

Ewan shrugged. "Ye can never ken how rumors start."

Cailean shook his head. "Nae, something more is worrying you."

"I can't prove anything," Frederick murmured, "but I have this gut instinct the man who was here was Walter Jameson." He shared a bleak stare with the brothers. "I've instructed my men that I must meet any straggler who comes through from now on."

"Do any of yer men ken Sorcha remembers?" Ewan asked.

"I'm certain Slims does, but I'm not sure about Dalton and Dixon." Frederick shared a long look with the brothers. "It makes no sense for Walter to come to the ranch in the middle of winter."

"Nae, it doesna. But that man rarely makes sense. I'll say it again, Frederick. Keep Sorcha safe," Ewan said.

Frederick nodded. "I will do everything I can."

"Aye, well, 'tis all any man can do," Cailean said. "I must see Sorcha, and then Ewan and I need to leave before the winds return. Our wives would be dismayed to be denied our presence for long."

After his eldest brother left the office, Ewan stared at Frederick as the quiet sounds of the ranch filtered into the room. Slims banged pots and pans on the stove while singing songs he usually sang on the range during roundup. Another man hummed as he read, while two more bickered amid playing checkers. "I thought ye'd have them lodgin' in the bunkhouse," Ewan said with a frown.

"This winter has been brutal. I decided to conserve wood and have them stay here. There's only five of them here this year through the winter and this house is plenty big." He shook his head. "Besides, in the beginning, I needed their presence to help me with your sister."

"I ken she can be ... challengin'," Ewan said.

"No, that's not it. She needed frequent care. And the men took a shine to her. Wanted to ensure she was always well and wanted for nothing." He met her youngest brother's curious gaze. "None of them would have hurt her."

Ewan nodded, his eyes filled with a hint of mischief. "Of course no'. No man is daft enough to flirt with the boss's woman." He raised his eyebrows. "Ye might have denied it, but it's been plain to all for some time."

When Frederick groaned and dropped his head into his hands, Ewan frowned. "Ye are a good man. An' I hope ye treat my sister well. For, if ye dinna, ye will no' live long." Any mischief or levity was missing from his gaze as he met Frederick's. "That is a promise."

～

Sorcha lay on her side, staring at the door as she awaited the arrival of her eldest brother. She listened intently, but she heard no shouting from the office. The only sounds were the usual ones from a wintery day at the ranch. She sighed and lowered her head in resignation, closing her eyes.

"Come, Sorch, it can't be as bad as that," Cailean teased as he entered her room. He pulled the chair up closer to her bed and reached forward to squeeze her hands. His gaze roved over her as though to ensure himself that she was, in fact, well. "Please tell me that I wasn't a fool for talking with him rather than beating him, as I wanted."

She choked out a laugh before scooting over and throwing herself in her brother's arms. "Nae, ye are no' daft." She clung to him for a moment as he held her close. "I've missed ye, Cail."

"As we all have. Even Fidelia speaks longingly of your chattering." He laughed when Sorcha swatted him on his shoulder as she sniffled. When she whispered in his ear to tell him about home, he cradled her on his chest and spoke in a low voice. "Belle and Leena have worked out a schedule so Belle now works at the bakery four days a week. 'Tis good to have a schedule. To know when she will work and when she'll be home. Fidelia works there every day and seems to enjoy it. Skye grows and grows."

He leaned back to meet his sister's gaze. "She called me *Da* the other day, and she knew who I was!" His gaze was filled with wonder and a touch of terror. "I don't know what I would do if anything ..." He broke off and shook his head.

Sorcha tugged him close. "Ye love yer daughter. As does her mother. 'Tis wondrous."

Cailean pushed Sorcha away and looked into her tormented gaze. "Your mother loved you. Not the woman who raised you. *Your* mother." His gaze was filled with a desperate truth. "I met her, and she was a good woman, Sorcha. She only let you go because she died."

"It doesna matter." Sorcha shook her head, stilling the motion when Cailean clasped her head between his hands.

"Aye, it does. You've lived with the belief that you are unworthy of love and devotion because of how *my* mother treated you." He shook his head. "Why can you not focus on how much Da loved you? On how the thought of you being harmed caused all three of your brothers to wish to rush to the ranch in the middle of this harsh winter? Let the pain of the past go, Sorch."

"'Tisn't easy," she rasped as a tear coursed down her cheek. "I dinna ken how."

Her eldest brother nodded. "It takes time. And patience. And the pain and doubt will sneak up on you, again and again. But, each time, it will be a little less painful. Weaker in its potency."

She smiled as she looked at her brother. "Ye are fortunate in Annabelle."

He grinned. "Aye, although she's as fortunate in me." He winked at Sorcha before sobering. "What do you want? Do you want to remain here? Do you want to marry?" He paused as she bit her lip and seemed deep in thought. "For, if you are to remain here, you must marry."

She closed her eyes and took a few deep breaths. "Do ye ken why I rode Sugar so hard that day?" At his subtle shake of his head, she met his curious gaze with no trace of censure. "I'd spoken with Mrs. Jameson." She grimaced as he hissed in a breath. "I ken I shouldna listen to anything that woman says, but sometimes her words can pierce into soft parts that ye hadna realized were vulnerable."

After a moment Cailean whispered, "What did that witch say?"

Sorcha looked at her hands, refusing to meet her brother's gaze. "That I was the pathetic MacKinnon spinster who no one could love and that I would always be alone without a family of my own." She shrugged. "I dinna ken why it affected me so much that day, but it did."

Cailean growled once and waited in silence for his sister to raise her gaze.

After many moments, she finally did.

"You know she spoke lies, aye? That you are cherished by us? By many in town?"

She nodded. "Yes. But, in that moment, it seemed as though my dream for what ye have with Annabelle would always be unfulfilled." She flushed. "She laughed at the way Frederick had run from me at the Harvest Dance. Said I'd be the crazy spinster aunt, singin' of lost love and a wasted life as I spun yarn in a back room. As forgotten as the old baby furniture that crowded the room with me."

"That *bluidy* woman!" Cailean growled.

Sorcha sniffled. "I ... I ken I overreacted."

"She brought your fear to life, Sorch." He gripped her hand. "None of us is rational when that happens. Look what I did to Belle and me when I was faced with what I most feared." He looked at his sister with understanding and compassion.

"How can ye no' be angry with me for what I did? For what happened?" Tears streaked down her cheeks.

"You've more than paid for your anger and fear." His eyes glowed with rage. "That gossipy woman has not." He took a deep breath and met his sister's gaze. "What do you want, Sorcha?"

"I dinna want any man to feel forced to wed me." She took a deep breath. "But I would like time for courtship."

"Courtship," Cailean said and then smiled. He shook his head ruefully. "You make me wish I was to be marooned here so I could see Frederick's attempts." He kissed his sister's forehead. "Be kind to him as he tries. He must face his own fears too, Sorch. You aren't the only one with a past that torments you." He rose. "I'll find Ewan, and then we must leave if we are to return to town in daylight before the next storm hits." He ran a hand over her head. "Never forget how much your family loves you, Sorcha."

She nodded, battling tears as her eldest brother left to find Ewan.

Frederick sat in his office for a long while after Sorcha's brothers left. "Courtship," he muttered. "What would I know about courtship?" He stared blankly at his desk as he thought about his grandparents. Of his grandfather coming in with a handful of lilacs for his grandmother every May. Of her baking him his favorite pie. Of his grandfather never leaving the house without giving his grandmother a kiss. He frowned as he never remembered his father or mother doing those little things for each other.

"I should look to my grandparents," he whispered. "Look to those who knew how to show their love." After running his hands through his hair a few times, he rose and moved toward Sorcha's room. Outside her door, he smoothed down his hair and tucked in his shirt. After knocking, he waited until she called for him to enter.

He poked his head inside, his breath catching at her beauty as she looked at him with faint embarrassment. Her cheeks were rose pink; her red-brown hair was tied back in a neat braid, and her hand fidgeted with a button on her dress.

He clenched his hands together, suddenly wishing they weren't empty. He silently reprimanded himself for not bringing her something. "Do you need anything?" he asked and then flushed at this new awkwardness that had risen between them.

"Nae." She shook her head and studied her fingers. "I've plenty to do with my knitting."

After moments of silence, he cleared his throat. "Did you enjoy your brothers' visit?"

She shot a glance at him and flushed. "Aye. 'Tis always wonderful to see them. But I ken ye are bein' forced into doin' something ye do no' want." She looked down again. "I'm sorry."

He reached forward, stopping his movement just as he was about to take her hand. Instead he tapped the quilt by her hip. "May we talk? Without you yelling at me to get out?"

She blushed a brighter red and nodded.

After he sat on the chair, she made herself comfortable, sitting on the edge of the bed. However, he saw her grimace. "Sit back with your leg stretched out. It still bothers you, doesn't it?"

Sorcha nodded and was on the verge of tears. "Aye. I dinna ken what to do to make it stronger. I'm walking again, but I have no strength."

He gripped his hands together, wanting to touch her but forcing himself not to. "You have to be patient. Continue to do what Helen taught you, and soon you will be as strong as you ever were."

She grinned at him wryly. "I ken by now ye realize that patience is no' one of my strong points." They shared a rueful smile. "What did my brothers say to ye, Frederick?"

He looked at her a long moment and then spoke. "They want you happy. They want to ensure that whoever you marry will bring you more joy than heartache."

She moved until she lay on her left side, facing him. "Why do ye believe ye would no' make me happy? Why do ye think ye would no' be that man?" When he only stared at her in silence, she whispered, "Why do ye no' like yer mother?"

He shook his head. "I will not answer all your questions today. But I do not deny that you have a right to them. And that you should expect me to answer them." He paused for a moment. "I believe you deserve a man who will be able to provide for you."

"I dinna understand why ye do no' think ye are that man." She bit her lip a moment. "Ye ken that I was only actin' out when I flirted with Dalton afore I kissed ye, aye?"

He smiled. "I know that now, and that's what is important. However, you should be thankful that Dalton understood too and that you aren't crushing his hopes."

Her gaze turned mournful for a moment. "He's still mournin' his wife and the dream of what he hoped would be. He willna be alone forever, but he isna ready yet."

"This is why you are adored by my men. Because you pay attention. Because you care." Frederick took a deep breath and clasped his hands together and leaned on his knees as though he were praying. "Sorcha, you need to understand something." He looked around the fine guest room she occupied. "All of this ..." He cleared his throat. "All of this might be lost."

She frowned and stared at him in confusion. "I dinna understand."

"Do you know what I do in my office every day?" At the shake of her head, he explained. "I make charts of how many cattle we had on the ranch, how much we would have gotten in the market had I been sage enough to sell them last year and how many we must have come spring to have the hopes of survival."

Her eyes filled with compassion and concern. "Frederick," she whispered as she reached her hand out to him. "Ye will still have yer horses. An' ye always have yer grandparents behind ye. Yer men. Yer brothers. An' ye have me." Her jaw firmed with resoluteness.

"In a few months, I fear it will be confirmed that I have failed. My men. My family." His voice broke, and he closed his eyes.

"Ye are no' a failure," she said in a strong voice as she tugged at his hand, urging him closer. "Ye are a man, livin' through an extraordinary time, doin' the best he can. No one can ask more of ye than that."

"You should want someone who has better prospects."

Sorcha smiled and shook her head. "Nae, I shouldna." She waited until he met her gaze. "Ye are honorable and hardworking and diligent. I ken ye will do all ye can. No one could ask more of ye—or of any man."

Frederick flushed under her praise.

"Have my brothers released ye from yer promise?" She bit her lip at her bold question as his head jerked up at her question. She met his intense stare, the passion and interest in her gaze easing the worry and regret in his.

"Yes." He scooted his chair closer to the bed and leaned forward until they were nearly nose to nose. "Yes, they did."

She pulled on her hand, now linked with his. "I thought they might have, as they seemed in favor of ye courtin' me."

He grinned, raising his free hand to trace his fingers over her hairline and then down the side of her face. "Court?" He shook his head, his smile widening as she tilted into his touch. "I fear I will be a grave disappointment to you if you want any grand courtship. I'm a simple man, Sorcha. I run a ranch."

She glared at him. "Are ye tellin' me that ye are so daft ye dinna ken how to court a woman ye like?"

His smile broadened, and he saw her breath catch at his full smile. "No, I'm not daft, unless it is from the desire to kiss you." He felt her quick exhalation as his frank words surprised her. "Do you want that too, Sorcha?"

At his words, she backed away, a shadow in her eye as she tugged again at his hand. He frowned as he released it but remained sitting near her. "What did I say?" He ran a hand through his hair in frustration. "Peter and Cole were the ones who excelled at flirting," he muttered.

"Flirting?" she whispered. When he nodded, she leaned forward again. "I fear … I fear ye'll only be interested in me a short while. That ye can no' truly want me for long."

Frederick's gaze was intense as he met her chagrined stare. "In that, we share the same fear." He nodded at her shocked stare. "I will try to court you, Sorcha. I'm not sure how in this awful winter."

She shrugged and then lifted one shoulder in a flirtatious manner. "I'm sure ye're smart enough to think of something. Or ye can ask one of yer men."

He laughed. "Please leave them out of it." Delight lit his eyes as he stared at her, then shook his head. "Courtship should end with a kiss, not begin with one." He sighed as he backed away, although a mischievous delight filled his eyes as she was unable to hide her disappointment that he would not kiss her. "I wish you a pleasant evening, Sorcha."

CHAPTER 7

The following morning, Sorcha sat at the kitchen table with the men as breakfast was served. The platter of eggs, bacon and toast was passed around, starting with her. However, in front of where she sat was an empty bowl next to her plate. When Frederick entered the kitchen, wearing a clean cranberry-colored cambric shirt with a brown waistcoat, he nodded to his men. His black hair was rumpled, as though he had recently gotten out of bed, but his blue eyes were alert. He raised an eyebrow, and Slims gave a grunt before marching to the stove for a pot. Slims grumbled as he stirred the contents once, then picked it up and brought it over to Sorcha.

"Boss thought you might want porridge," Slims said as he scooped out a few spoonfuls into her bowl. He turned his back, hiding his expression from Frederick and winked at Sorcha before marching back to the stove to replace the pot on top of the stove with more grumbling.

Sorcha fought a smile and lost, pleasure at this small gesture brightening her mood. "'Twas *verra* thoughtful," she said as her accent thickened a moment. "Thank ye, Frederick."

He nodded and sat with the men as they talked about the unremitting cold, the concern that the hay they'd set aside for the horses and the milk cows would not last, and the likelihood that Bullet would have her foal soon.

"I want someone in the barn at all times. When she does foal, I want to be informed immediately. I will be there." Frederick looked at each of his men. He smiled with approval as they agreed with him.

"Why would ye call a mare Bullet? Seems like a daft name for a filly," Sorcha said. She flushed as the men stared at her as though she were insane to criticize Frederick and any of his horses.

Frederick laughed, relaxed after the warm meal and the well-brewed coffee. "Peter named her, and he has no sense when it comes to naming horses."

Dixon laughed. "He's better off with his cattle." The men chuckled. "When are they comin' home, Boss?"

Frederick shook his head. "I'm not sure. Not before the thaw."

Sorcha looked at them a moment. "If yer brother Peter named one of the horses, did Cole name one too?"

The men chortled, and Sorcha watched them with avid curiosity as Frederick flushed. "Yes, he did, much to my chagrin. We call her Butter, although her real name is Buttercup."

"We love hearing Frederick call out to her in her full name in his sweet voice," Slims said as he chuckled over by the stove.

Sorcha giggled as Frederick swore under his breath.

Soon the mealtime ended, and the men rose to begin their work. Frederick remained with her in the kitchen, along with Slims. "Sorcha, I wanted to ask you something."

She smiled as she took a sip of coffee. "Aye?"

"Do you have any interest in cooking?" He ducked as she threw her napkin at him and then laughed as Slims gave a groan of dismay. "I think that answers your question, Slims."

"Why should ye believe I'd be achin' to use that … that monstrosity of a stove when I could be doin' anything else that would be more enjoyable?"

Slims slammed a pan down on the stove again. "I hoped you were like most women and that you liked cooking."

"If I did no' like ye as much as I do, I'd throw my mug at ye," she hissed. "Do ye think only women can cook?"

Frederick grabbed her hand, preventing her from following through on her threat of tossing her half-filled cup of coffee across the room or from standing up too soon and potentially hurting her leg. "Sorcha, all we did was ask, and you answered. There is no expectation that you cook."

"I dinna want ye believin' I canna cook," she said with a mutinous tilt of her chin, her hair seeming more red than brown in that instant as her cheeks were flushed and her eyes bright with indignation.

"Of course not. Cailean has spoken of the meals you have prepared for the family. It's why I had hoped you'd be able to help out Slims a few times a week, so he could spend more time in the barn with the horses."

She frowned. "Ye dinna expect me to cook every meal?"

Slims shook his head. "Two or three suppers a week would be helpful."

She sighed and slumped her shoulders. "Fine. I'll try to make a few a week, but I dinna ken if I'll have the strength. Will ye be here the first time I cook?" she asked Slims.

Slims beamed at her. "Yes, Miss Sorcha, I will."

"Thank you," Frederick whispered to her, his fingers tracing her cheek before he rose. "I'll see you later today."

Sorcha watched him leave, her gaze following him until he was out of sight. "What had ye planned tonight for dinner?"

Slims shrugged. "More of the same. Slop or stew."

She shook her head. "Nae, I have somethin' else in mind." She rose, grinning at Slims.

That afternoon Sorcha sat in the rocking chair in the corner of the kitchen near the stove, sipping a cup of tea. Slims was about to head out to the barn for a few hours. A quiet contentment filled

Sorcha as she rested her head against the back of the chair and gently rocked to and fro.

"May I ask you something, Miss Sorcha?" Slims asked as he sat on one of the benches by the long kitchen table. At her nod, he said, "Why did you agree so quickly to help me?"

She smiled. "Do you ken anything about what is occurrin' between Frederick and me?"

"He's courting you."

"Aye," she said with a satisfied smile. "I realized this mornin' that I needed to court him too."

Slims chuckled. "Never doubt, Miss Sorcha, that you are the perfect woman for my boss."

She studied him a moment. "He's your friend as well, aye?"

"Aye," he said. "And I've known him since he was a little tyke. Always chasing after his brothers, desperate not to be left behind." He saw her understand what he said. "I think he's come to realize that the best thing they ever did was leave him behind."

"Aye," she whispered. "They gave him all of this."

"Well, it's not all his," Slims said. "When they're here, it's theirs too. But they don't have the love of this land the way Frederick does."

She smiled at Slims absently as he slipped out the side door to head to the barn. After a few moments, she rose to check on the loaves of bread rising in their pans. When she determined that it was time for them to go into the oven, she set them in and then stirred the pot of three-bean stew flavored with pork on the stove.

After the bread was out of the oven and on cooling racks, she grabbed a new cane that Dixon had whittled for her and walked toward the parlor. Frederick stood at the door, his eyes closed and head tilted back, a look of supreme pleasure on his face. "Bless you," he whispered.

"Why?" she asked, moving to a chair to sit down.

"For making a dinner not prepared by Slims." He met her laughing smile. "He's a decent cook but has a limited repertoire." He sniffed again at the air. "And there's fresh bread."

She giggled at the wonder in his voice. "Aye, I can bake bread. I dinna ken that it was such a rare occurrence."

His delighted gaze made him look younger as all of his worries had disappeared in those few moments of speaking with her. "It is. Believe me, it is."

She burst out laughing. "Oh, I ken how arduous a task it can be. When I first moved to Bear Grass Springs, my bread was so hard I thought Alistair would lose a tooth biting into it. Now, since I've learned from Annabelle, 'tis much better." She met his appreciative gaze. "How was yer day?"

He sat next to her, reaching for her hand. His fingers played with hers, earning a shiver. "Good. I like knowing you are here. At the ranch." He waited for her to say something sarcastic, and, when she remained quiet, he relaxed into his comfortable chair. "I don't care what you do, Sorcha. Knit, sew, write letters or daydream. I simply like that you are here."

"Ye'd want more than that at some point," she whispered.

"Do you know why I've rarely had anyone here doing chores, like cleaning up after us?" He met her curious stare. "First, I think it's important for all the men, including myself, to learn how to clean and cook and wash our clothes without expecting a woman to do it for us. But mainly it's because, if the woman is unmarried, she often has ideas of wanting more from me or one of my men."

"I doubt yer men would disapprove," she said wryly.

He laughed. "I doubt it. But I had no desire to feel as though I were a vole evading a hawk on my own ranch."

"Ye dinna mind Helen bein' here," she whispered.

He stroked his thumb over her palm. "I knew she loved Warren. And, for a few weeks, we ate like kings." He sighed with pleasure. "Then I had the idea to hire a male cook, and that was a disaster." He shuddered.

"What happens after ye wed?" she whispered.

"Well, after *we* wed"—he raised an eyebrow to see if she protested his wording and nodded when she remained quiet—"I don't care who comes here to work. As long as they actually work. I'll have you, so no woman would be foolish enough to believe she could compete with my wife."

"Frederick," Sorcha whispered, flushing with pleasure at his words.

"Why is it so hard for you to believe I am sincere in what I say?" he whispered. He raised her hand and kissed it.

"Thank ye," she murmured, leaning toward him and kissing him softly on the lips.

"That comes at the end," he teased.

"I ken, but I couldna help myself." She cupped his jaw, her fingers scraping over his stubble. She dropped her hand and rose from her chair as the door opened to the men entering. "I'll see ye at supper."

Two weeks after her brothers had visited, Frederick paused in the parlor. Although early March, winter had maintained its stranglehold on the land. However, Frederick had noted that the days were slightly longer than the nights, and neither were as brutally cold as in February.

Before entering his office, he heard quiet, haunting singing coming from a back room in the house. He walked down the hallway, passing Sorcha's empty bedroom, and continued to a room he considered a storage area and off-limits. He paused outside the partially open door, his breath catching as Sorcha's voice rose as she sang of lost love and the desire to reunite with her love. With eyes filled with passion and hope, he pushed open the door.

In an instant, his contentment faded. "What in God's name are you doing?" he snapped, his anger bursting forth.

Her head jerked up at his voice, and the pleasure at seeing him faded with his evident ire. "Are ye daft? I'm spinnin' wool on this fine wheel."

"Give it to me," he demanded, marching toward her to tear it away from her. However, she gripped it tight, her foot on the pedal.

When he attempted to pull it away, she leaned over it and screeched at him. "Ye have no' right to take this from me! It is no' as though ye cared about it, tossing it aside as though a piece of kindlin' in this old room." She panted with anger mixed with disappointment and confusion as she saw him control his fury.

"Why can you never be content with what is given to you? Why must you snoop around, getting into things that aren't yours? Things that should never be found again?"

A flicker of concern flashed in her eyes as her ire faded. "I dinna understand. This is a fine spinnin' wheel. An' the wool is old, aye, but I've missed makin' my yarns." She watched as he gave a growl of frustration and stomped out of the room. "Frederick?"

He ignored her call, continuing to his office. Once there, he slammed the door shut for good measure. "Damn interfering woman." He ran a shaking hand through his head and took calming breaths. Images of his mother, smiling at him while she worked at the wheel, flashed through his mind. He groaned as his door opened.

"You've the strangest notion of how to court a woman," Dalton said as he entered with a cup of coffee for Frederick. "Gen'rally, the yellin' comes after you marry. Thataways, she doesn't realize what a sorry bastard you are before she binds herself to you."

Frederick shook his head and shared a rueful smile with his friend. "I told anyone who listened that I wasn't meant to court her."

Dalton eased onto one of the chairs in front of the desk. "From what I've seen, and experienced, the most successful courtships have to do with gettin' to see if you suit. And part of that is talkin' about your past." He slurped from his own coffee mug and met his boss's forbidding stare.

Frederick nodded and pointed to the coffee. "Thanks."

"Anytime, Boss," Dalton rose, understanding he'd been dismissed.

Frederick swiveled in his chair and stared out the window, although there wasn't much to see with the windows half-glazed with snow-encrusted ice. He envisioned summer, with the range grass growing high and blowing in the gentle breeze. Cattle lowing in the fields, fat and contented. Meadowlarks singing. And flowers blooming once again in the flower garden that had lain dormant since his grandmother had moved to town. His breath caught, as much as when he heard Sorcha singing, with the realization that Sorcha would bring beauty to the ranch again. "She'll bring me to life again," he whispered.

With a heavy sigh, he rose and walked with purposeful steps down the hallway to the room where he had left her. Rather than her beautiful singing, he heard sniffling. "Sorcha?" he whispered as he poked his head in.

"Go away!" she demanded as she turned from the door, hiding her face.

He entered the cluttered room, shutting the door behind him. "No, I already made that mistake too many times." He pulled out a rickety stool and perched on it, letting out a breath when it didn't collapse with his weight. "I'm sorry."

She twirled to face him, her gaze filled with amazement at his words. She scrubbed at her face, wiping at the tears that fell.

"Don't cry," he whispered, his expression tormented at the pain he'd caused her. "I'm sorry." He ran a thumb over her cheek, smearing her tears away.

"Why were ye cruel?" She sniffed and accepted his handkerchief.

"I become irrational when I am reminded of my mother. When the past comes flooding back. I'm sorry I lashed out at you because of it."

Her expression softened at his quiet words.

"Will you listen?" When she nodded, he whispered, "Will you promise not to gossip about what I tell you?" He closed his eyes as she traced a hand over his face and then cupped his cheek.

"Aye, Frederick." Her breath caught as he turned his face and kissed her palm.

"My parents ..." He opened his blue eyes, sparkling with bitterness and betrayal. "My father married my mother while he was in St. Louis. She had never thirsted for travel as she loved the society there, the close proximity to shops, and she loved being a sought-after young woman." He flushed. "When she dallied with my father, and became pregnant with Peter, she realized she'd have to have an appetite for adventure, for my father was not a man to leave his wife behind to receive sporadic letters updating him about her and his child's welfare."

Frederick paused a moment and then continued. "We eventually ended up here, with every member of the family who was of eligible age taking out a homestead and proving up our acres." He smiled. "I thought it was a wonderful adventure, to be away from Fort Benton. To have the romance of raising cattle, with roundups and branding, and teaching horses how to do the work."

"Yer fascination with horses began at an early age," Sorcha whispered.

His eyes glowed at her comment and the supportive tone in her voice. "Yes. But my happiness was equaled by my mother's bitterness. Her anger at being forced to live on a ranch with no neighbors and no friends, with few opportunities in the year for social gatherings ..." He shrugged. "The town wasn't big then, and we were busy trying to create a prosperous ranch."

"What was yer da like?"

Frederick closed his eyes. "Strong, competent, kind and decisive, unless it had to do with Mother. Then he became weak and spiteful and mean. They'd say things to each other meant to hurt. I didn't understand why when I was a child. I realize now how miserable they were together."

Frederick paused, and it seemed as though he wouldn't say anything further.

"What happened?" Sorcha prompted.

"The man I considered uncle, my father's first cousin, moved here." His gaze filled with loathing, and he looked at Sorcha. "Tobias."

She nodded as she was well acquainted with his miserly relative who ran one of the general stores in town known as the Merc. "I'm certain he was as unpleasant then as he is now." Her eyes widened with shock when Frederick shook his head in disagreement.

"No, he was amiable and kind and welcoming. He never failed to make us laugh and was charming." He clamped his jaw shut for a moment. "So charming that he sweet-talked my mother into leaving my father and moving to town with him."

"What?" Sorcha gasped. "I've never heard a word about any such gossip."

Frederick shrugged. "We don't speak of it much, and now that both my mother and father are dead, there is little reason to bring up the scandal that ensued. My grandparents insist that, if they remain friendly with Tobias, then we will suffer less censure from the townsfolk."

Sorcha leaned forward and ran a hand over his shoulder, giving it a gentle squeeze. "Why should ye suffer? Tobias should be the one to suffer!"

Frederick closed his eyes. "It has been said, numerous times, that my father was a brute and a beast and a bully and incapable of keeping a woman satisfied. That no woman would desert her sons and a prosperous life on the ranch unless she had been forced to." Frederick watched Sorcha to see her reaction.

"I dinna ken yer father. I wouldna ken how he was." She paused, taking a deep breath. "But I do ken ye, an', if he was anythin' like the son he raised, then only a fool would believe such words."

"What?"

She watched him with compassionate understanding. "Ye are a good man, Frederick. Ye have a short temper, aye, but ye are loyal. Ye show kindness to yer men, even when I ken ye are frustrated with them. Ye inspire loyalty in them. Something a man who was a bully or a brute wouldna do." She smiled at him as he sat, dumbstruck on his stool. "Ye dinna see yerself as others see ye." She paused and took a deep breath. "I am no' yer mother."

He frowned at her last statement and shook his head in confusion.

"I was no' born in a big city. I was raised on a farm on the Isle of Skye." She shrugged. "I do no' care for society." She flushed. "Although I do gossip with my family when I work at the bakery." Her gaze was earnest as she looked at him. "I ken I havena spent much time on the ranch, and this winter has been brutal, but I ken I already love it here."

"Do you?" he asked. "Do you think you could be happy here?"

"Aye," she whispered.

He leaned forward, kissing her softly before groaning and deepening the kiss. The rickety stool he sat on crumpled, and he tumbled to the floor.

Laughing, Sorcha slipped from her chair and joined him on the floor. "Kiss me," she whispered as she threaded her fingers through his hair.

He tugged her close, kissing her for many minutes as he ran his hands over her back and sides. Finally he broke the kiss. "I have to stop, or I won't be able to." He frowned as he saw the flash of shame in her eyes.

"Aye," she whispered, pushing herself up and away from him. "I ... I should go."

"Sorcha," he whispered, his hand snagging hers and preventing her from leaving. "Thank you for listening to me."

"Dinna worry. I will keep yer confidence."

He frowned as she left him sitting on the floor, never turning toward him, before she opened the door and exited the room. He collapsed onto his back, staring at the ceiling. "What just happened?" he muttered, letting out a sigh.

A few weeks later in mid-March, Sorcha sat in the room that had previously been a cluttered mess, looking around at the now-pristine space. While Slims had occupied her in the kitchen with an attempt to give her a lesson on how to better use the large stove, the rest of the men and Frederick had cleaned out the untidy room. Now light-blue curtains bracketed the freshly washed windows; the floor was swept clear of any dust, and two lamps on end tables brightened the room on cloudy days. A comfortable chair sat behind the hand-pedaled spinning wheel. Baskets of wool to spin sat around the wheel too.

She glanced to the door as Frederick poked his head in. "How? Why?"

He smiled. "I wanted you to have a place that was yours, other than that room you've been sleeping in. You are becoming well-known for your wool as you sell them in Annabelle's store, and I thought it a shame that you were denied something you enjoy."

When she remained silent as she stared at him, he flushed and rubbed a hand through his black hair. "If you don't like it, you don't have to ..."

"No," she rasped, standing and wobbling a moment before she found her balance. Then she rushed to him and threw herself into his arms. "Thank ye." She held him close. "Thank ye so much."

He pulled her tighter, burying his face in her neck. "I want to bring you joy."

She backed up, a broad smile enhancing her beauty. "Ye do. Ye have no idea." She stood on her toes and kissed him, sighing when he groaned and tugged her closer.

They would have continued kissing for many minutes, except for an amused chuckle sounding in the doorway causing them to spring apart. Frederick turned, standing in front of Sorcha. His glower faded to annoyance when he saw Warren Clark in the doorway.

"I should be unsurprised to find the rumors were correct," Warren teased. "Hello, Frederick." He tilted his head to one side. "Sorcha."

"Why are ye here, Warren?" she asked, pushing around Frederick to hug Warren.

"Helen wanted to visit you after she spoke with Cailean and Ewan." He shrugged. "I did not want her traveling alone, and I wanted to see how you were."

Frederick stood tall as he glared at Warren for hugging Sorcha. "As you can see, we are fine."

"More than fine," Warren joked as he winked at Sorcha. "Helen is in the parlor, if you want to join her."

Sorcha gave a quick glance over one shoulder at Frederick and then slipped past Warren to join Helen. She paused a moment in the hallway to smooth a hand over her hair and dress. After taking a few deep breaths, she entered the parlor to find Helen looking at the books in one of the bookcases. "Helen!"

At her name, Helen spun and smiled at Sorcha. Her assessing gaze roved over Sorcha, and her smile widened. "I'm sorry to say that I believe we interrupted something."

Sorcha flushed and waved at her friend to sit down. "Ye did no'."

Her cheeks reddened further at her friend's laughter. "Do ye want tea?"

Helen shook her head. "No, although we may stay a few evenings, if that is all right?"

"I would think so, but ye'll have to speak with Frederick. I dinna ken as much as I should about the house."

Helen sat beside her, smoothing her fine sage-green woolen skirt. "If you are merely a guest, I shouldn't think you'd need to know much about how this house runs." She waited and raised an eyebrow. "Unless you plan on becoming more than a guest."

"Dinna start," Sorcha muttered as she leaned against the back of her chair, tugging a pillow to hold to her chest. After a moment she whispered, "What are they sayin' in town?"

"Well, it didn't help that Alistair tried to drag the preacher here when your brothers visited. That supposed man of God will have his day of reckoning with his penchant for gossip." Helen let out a disgruntled sigh. "However, now that it's been three weeks since your brothers were here, with still no word of a marriage, the rumblings that you are … enjoying that which is generally reserved for marriage are becoming louder."

Sorcha groaned and rested her head against the back of the chair. "I can no' say I miss town. I enjoy life out here." She met Helen's curious gaze. "The men have their squabbles, aye, and there are times I'm a little lonely for the stories and laughter from the bakery. But I dinna think I'd truly miss it."

Helen smiled. "You're the opposite of me. I liked my time here, and I enjoyed the sense of accomplishment when I managed to cook a good meal on that stove. But I always wanted to return to town."

"Aye, because Warren was no' with ye." Sorcha flushed at her friend's knowing look. "Aye," she murmured at Helen's inquisitive stare. "Aye."

"Will you marry?" Helen asked.

"I dinna ken. He has no' asked me." She sobered as she stared at the flames flickering in the fireplace.

"Then he's a fool."

"Nae," Sorcha said as she readily defended him. "He's afraid, and I ken well enough what that feels like." She took a deep breath and changed the topic. "Why are ye here?"

Helen looked at Sorcha a long moment and then tactfully changed the subject. "Cailean mentioned you are having trouble with your leg. I wanted to examine it again and ensure you are well. I know I taught you exercises the last time I was here, and I want to see how you are doing with them. We had to wait for a break in the weather before we could venture to the ranch." She smiled at Sorcha. "And I brought letters."

"Letters," Sorcha whispered. She smiled as she held out her hand for the small packet from her family. "Thank ye, Helen."

"Come. Let's get our work done, and then we'll have time to catch up." Helen rose, and soon they worked their way through the exercises together, chatting, laughing and enjoying each other's company.

Warren met Frederick's challenging stare as he stood in the doorway to Sorcha's new spinning room. "What's the matter, Frederick?"

"How would you feel if I hugged Helen?" he snapped.

"I already know how that feels. I had to live with the fact that you sheltered her here last winter for almost two months. And then tried to separate us when I returned with her because you thought I would only bring her harm."

"If you recall, I didn't object for long. Only until Helen assured me that she wanted to marry you." His eyes lit with humor. "Helen and I have only ever been like brother and sister."

Warren nodded. "Yes, just like Sorcha and I. I've never had romantic inclinations toward her, no matter what the idiots in town think." His gaze flared with a warning. "However, if you harm her or do not have honorable intentions, you should know I'll be as bad as any of her brothers."

Frederick jerked his head in agreement. "I would expect no less."

He ran a hand though his hair and then shook his head. "I don't know what more to do. She said she wanted a courtship. I've tried, but I'm no good with romance."

Warren chuckled. "What man is?" He looked around the room, noting small touches a woman would appreciate, such as the piece of fine lace on a table, the framed picture of a mountain valley and the ironed curtains. "You set up this room for her. Seems a fine way to court her."

Frederick groaned. "I had to after I acted like a fool a few weeks ago." He shared a chagrined smile with Warren. "I found her in here, using my mother's spinning wheel. I was not kind."

Warren's gaze was filled with understanding. "I imagine anything to do with your mother is unwelcome."

Frederick shrugged. "At times I act as though I never had a mother. When I saw Sorcha in here, using her wheel, singing as my mother used to ..." His gaze was distant. "I was unable to see the present for the vision from the past had blinded me."

Warren looked around the room. "Well, it seems to me that you've apologized for any perceived transgression. And, from what I witnessed when I knocked on the door, she's more than forgiven you."

Frederick smiled.

"When will you marry her?" His expression sobered. "The gossip in town is becoming vicious."

"I ... I try to avoid thinking about town and their gossip when out here." He sighed and then spun to pace. "I haven't asked her yet."

Warren gave an exasperated shake of his head. "Don't you think you should? Courtship is fine, but it must come to an end at some point. Besides, you two have been courting in your cantankerous way for the past few years." He laughed as Frederick glared at him. "Watching you and Sorcha come to near blows as you have verbal sparring matches while dancing at town events has been very entertaining."

Frederick smiled. "Well, she was the only person who could entice me to attend those functions."

Warren chuckled. "Watching you glower at each miner she danced with was one of my favorite ways to pass the time." He smiled at Frederick. "However, I doubt you noticed how her brothers had to hold her back when you danced with the young ladies in town. She hated it."

Frederick brightened at that news. "She did mention me flirting with Leena. I think she could have been jealous." Frederick lowered his voice, fighting a smile as he heard Sorcha and Helen laughing together. "What have you learned about Walter?"

Warren shook his head. "Not much. I think it would be wise to talk with Helen. She might have some insight." He gave Frederick a warning glance. "However, I don't want her anywhere near her brother. She's already suffered enough at his hands."

"I agree," Frederick said and slapped Warren on the shoulder as they moved down the hall toward the parlor and his office.

"If you don't mind, we'll be here a day or two. Helen wants to have time to help Sorcha." Warren grinned. "And perhaps you'll have the sense to plan a wedding while the lawyer has come to call."

March 15, 1887

*D*ear Sorcha,

It seems like forever since you have been at home. Since you have been at the bakery. I still turn, looking to the door to hear your voice as you discuss town gossip or something that has caught your interest. Your joy in life, your interest in all of us and the delight you have in being an aunt, is greatly missed.

Cailean assures me that you are well at the ranch. I know that Frederick is an honorable man, but I hope that you feel free to choose him because he is whom you desire, not because you feel that you must marry him. I know I married your brother out of necessity, and my greatest gift, other than Skye, has been to find true happiness and love with him.

I want the same for you, Sorcha. You deserve to have a man as devoted to you as you will be to him. You deserve to have your life filled with laughter.

With happiness. There will always be sorrow, but the sorrow is more bearable when we do not have to carry it alone.

I miss you, but I know that, unless something goes terribly wrong, you will not return to live with us. Do not mourn that, Sorcha. You have spent enough time living in your brothers' shadows. Living in the shadow of your past. You need to forge your own future, as all of your brothers have done, and know that all of us will always delight in everything you do.

With love,

Annabelle

❧

Sorcha poked her head into Frederick's office. She stilled when she saw him frowning over a document. "What is it?" she whispered.

He jerked up, staring at her. "I'm trying to find a way to write my grandparents a letter. I need to inform them about how badly things are going on the ranch."

Sorcha's gaze softened as she approached him. "I'm certain they are well aware of what is occurrin'. Dinna fash over what ye dinna yet ken. Ye'll lose sleep over it soon enough." She sat on the chair across from him.

"How is your visit with Helen?" Frederick's gaze roved over Sorcha, taking in the soft blush in her cheeks, the shine in her hair and the sparkle in her eyes. Her plain auburn dress enhanced her subtle beauty.

"Oh, wonderful. She's like a miracle worker, aye?" Sorcha glowed with contentment. "She is no' satisfied with me acceptin' havin' a weak leg forever and will help me find a way to strengthen it."

"I should think it better not to overwork your leg." Frederick frowned. "I don't want you to suffer any more harm or pain."

"Aye, I ken. But Helen insists 'tis the opposite. If I suffer a little pain now, I'll be stronger later." She shrugged. "Her advice sounds daft, but I dinna want to be an invalid."

"You'd never be an invalid, Sorch," he said, his gaze filled with tenderness. After a long moment, where they spent the time staring into each other's eyes, he whispered, "These are the times I dream about. Quiet times where we share and talk."

She nodded. "Aye."

He rose, moving around his desk to sit beside her. "I know I should kneel. I know that's the ritual." He kept a firm hold on her hand and remained seated next to her. "But I want to enter our marriage as I want it to always be. As equals. As partners. Where we share our hopes and dreams with each other. Where we are honest about our fears so that we don't use them to push the other away." He paused and took a deep breath, staring into her eyes. "Will you marry me, Sorcha?"

"I've never liked the idea of a man kneeling at my feet as though no more than a beggar," she whispered, her eyes tear brightened. She took a deep breath, and a tear coursed down her cheek. "Will ye listen to what I have to say and then ask me again if 'tis still truly what ye want?" She squeezed his hand as he nodded.

"I'm no' who ye think I am." She paused and cleared her throat. After a short pause, she whispered, "I'm only half sister to the MacKinnon brothers." She met Frederick's gaze, relaxing as no censure or disgust was found there. Instead he watched her with love and patience as he waited for her to speak.

"My brother's mother and Da dinna have a good marriage. I always kent they dinna have an affinity for each other. I dinna ken, until after my brother's mother died, that I was the cause." She closed her eyes, as though envisioning that moment. "While I remained at the croft, awaiting the money from Cail and Alistair that would bring me here, a man visited me. A man I dinna ken."

"Who was he?" Frederick asked, tracing a finger over one of her cheeks.

"My uncle. But he was no MacKinnon and no' from my mother's people." She shook her head as though in frustration. "'Tis the irony. He *was* from my mother's people. My real mother's people. My father had had an affair with Mairi MacQueen, and I was the result."

In the ensuing silence, the wind blew on the shutters outside, and sounds from inside the house filtered in through the closed door. Frederick ignored it all, wholly focused on Sorcha. "How did you come to be raised by your father?"

"My mother died. An' I was to go to an orphanage. One of my mother's brothers—Mairi's brothers—wrote my da and informed him what had happened, and he came to find me. An' I never kent."

Frederick was silent a long moment, his gaze downcast. "Your stepmother, your brothers' mother, treated you differently your whole childhood?"

"Aye, I always kent she dinna like me. I thought it was because I was no' a boy. A lad can do more work on a croft. I never understood why she did no' want me." She rubbed away a tear with her free hand.

"How fortunate you were to have your father," Frederick whispered. "And your brothers adore you."

"They dinna accept I'm a bastard."

Frederick's eyes flashed with anger. "Because you aren't. Your father claimed you." He let out a deep breath. "I hate that you think about yourself like this."

She shrugged. "So now ye ken."

He gripped her chin and tilted her head up so her gaze met his. *"What* do I know? The reason why you think I should not marry you? That you believe you are not good enough for me or anyone?" He shook his head, his eyes filled with passion and devotion. "I want you, Sorcha MacQueen MacKinnon and no other. Will you marry me?"

Her hands rose, touching his lips as he said her name with MacQueen in it. A smile bloomed. "Aye. Yes, I'll marry ye."

She gasped as he swooped forward, kissing her breathless. He tugged her, pulling her onto his lap, breaking the kiss. "Is this why you fear passion? Because of your mother?" At her shrug, he stroked a hand over her back.

"I dinna want anyone to believe I was a shameless hussy."

He kissed her head. "Having passion, sharing passion with someone you care about, does not make you shameless. Or a hussy. It makes you human." He cupped her cheeks in his hands. "I hope you will come to believe that with me."

She flushed. "Ye are the only man I've ever felt such madness with."

He laughed and pulled her into his arms to hold her close. "Good."

$\sim$

That evening Sorcha and Frederick sat holding hands near the fireplace while Warren and Helen curled up next to each other on the settee. When Sorcha squeezed Frederick's hand and gave him a gentle nod, Frederick cleared his throat. "I—we—have a favor to ask of you."

Warren shared a secret smile with his wife and then looked at his friends. "Yes, we will."

"Yes, what?" Frederick asked.

"Yes, I will marry you. Yes, Helen will act as one of the witnesses, and, yes, we will proclaim it to anyone in town who can hear that we celebrated your wedding with you."

Frederick chuckled. "Thank you."

"Ye've always been too smart for yer own good," Sorcha teased Warren. "Thank ye."

"You must understand, no matter what we say, there will be those who believe you should have been married earlier or that your wedding is a sham," Helen said. "Too many believe the preacher must be present for it to be valid."

Frederick looked at Warren. "But it doesn't, correct?" At Warren's subtle shake of his head, Frederick relaxed, his thumb playing with Sorcha's. "I spend my life on the ranch, with very little of it in town. As long as our marriage is legal and those I care about know that I am married, I can't say that I care to court town opinion."

Warren was silent a few moments. "Unfortunately there may come a time when you need to court the good opinion of those in town."

"Why should marryin' me cause Frederick to lose any good opinion?" Sorcha demanded. "I should think 'twould only raise his estimation in their eyes."

Frederick chuckled and kissed her palm. "You're correct, for I'll finally no longer be acting like a fool."

Warren shook his head at them and kissed Helen's head.

Sorcha focused on Warren and stilled. "Why are ye no' as relaxed as ye should be, Warren? Ye seem … uptight, even for ye." When he did not answer immediately, she said, "Is there a case in town that is botherin' ye?" Her gaze flew to Frederick when he stiffened beside her. "What are ye two no' tellin' me?"

After Frederick gave Warren a subtle nod, Warren spoke in a soft voice, "I'm worried about you, Sorcha. Not because you are marrying Frederick. I'm relieved you're marrying him."

"Relieved?" she asked. "I could understand happy or delighted but no' relieved. I've done nothin' wrong."

Warren looked at her with such intensity that her indignation flickered out. "I'm worried about your safety, and I know that Frederick, and his men, will do as much as your brothers to keep you safe."

"An' why should ye believe I would no' be able to keep myself safe?" she demanded, dropping Frederick's hand and leaning forward, her ire rekindled at his words.

"You're capable, strong and intelligent," Warren said. "But no match for a man intent on harming you. No woman is."

Sorcha paled. "Ye ken who caused Sugar to spook. Who loomed over me." Her eyes flashed with fear.

"We *suspect*," Frederick rasped, clasping her hand again and squeezing it.

"Walter Jameson," Warren said, his hold firm on his wife as she gasped in his arms. "We think he has some plan to further harm you to get back at Frederick. Or that he's rustling your cattle. We're not sure yet, and, until we are, there isn't much we can do."

"Why do ye suspect him?" Sorcha asked. She watched as Helen swiped at a tear. "An' why do ye no' defend yer brother?"

"I can't defend him. Ever again. He's a horrible, mean man, and he will do whatever he needs to for money. Or for revenge."

Sorcha shook her head in confusion. "He has no reason for revenge with me," she sputtered. "We glare at each other when we pass in town, content in our mutual disregard."

Frederick explained further. "He hates me for helping Helen. For giving her a place, other than her mother's house, to go to last winter."

Helen shuddered. "If I had returned home, I would have been forced to marry Bertrand."

Warren growled. "No you wouldn't have. I would have dragged you off the altar before that man ever had a chance to touch you." He turned crimson with rage at the thought of Bertrand March, her cousin and convicted murderer, ever having the opportunity to hurt his wife.

"What are we goin' to do about Walter?" Sorcha asked them all.

"We'll marry, and you're safer here at the ranch than in town. You'll visit your family when you can, but you won't spend much time in town. And someone will always be with you." Frederick looked at her with confusion as she stiffened beside him.

"When?" she whispered. "When did ye learn about Walter?"

"During the chinook. At Helen and Warren's last visit." Her hand was limp in his as he held it.

"An' ye informed my brothers of yer concerns?" After he nodded, she rose. "Forgive me. I ... I ..." She raced from the room as fast as she could with her uneven gait. Her bedroom door slamming echoed down the hallway.

"Excuse me," Frederick said, leaving Helen and Warren to talk quietly on the settee. He raised his hand to knock on the door but then decided to ease it open. His step faltered when he saw her sobbing on her bed.

Rather than pull out the chair, he sat beside her on her bed, running a hand over her quivering back. "Sorcha, love, don't cry so."

"But I'm no'!" she exclaimed as her sobs intensified.

Rather than try to have a conversation as she cried, he sighed and lay down beside her, tugging her into his arms. He cooed and whispered soothing words to her as he waited for her to calm. When she lay with only a hitching breath, he whispered, "May we talk now?"

"Why would ye want to talk now when ye dinna talk to me afore?" She did not fight him as he eased her onto her other side to face him.

"Oh, darling," he whispered as he saw the devastation in her eyes.

"I'm sorry. I didn't want to worry you, and you were finally happy." He closed his eyes as though seeing her sadness was too much to bear. "I hate that I've already been a failure to you."

She gave a grunt of disgust. "Ye have no'. Cease yer mindless prattle about bein' a failure. However, ye did fail me, Frederick. But 'tis different."

He looked deeply into her eyes and saw a deep-seated fear. "What is it? What are you afraid of?"

"Are ye only marryin' me to protect me from Walter? Out of duty?" She sniffed. "Did my brothers only change their mind about ye courtin' me because of the threat to me?"

He swore. "Dammit, Sorcha, if I'd known you'd see things this way, I'd have told you everything from the beginning." His devoted gaze bored into hers. "I promise you, in the future, I will share everything with you. My fears. My hopes. My dreams. Everything. I won't keep something from you because I fear it will take away your happiness or because I'm trying to protect you. I want us to be equal partners in our marriage, and I hope you want that too. But you can't be my partner if I don't share with you."

She smiled at him and cupped his cheek. "Thank ye."

"But I need you to fight me when you know I've done something wrong, not run away in disappointment to cry alone. I might not always know I've done something stupid or hurtful, and I need you to tell me. Please."

At his quiet entreaty, her eyes filled again. "You do no' displease me, Frederick." She moved closer to him as he caressed her cheek. "I never kent a man would want such a relationship with me."

"Any man who didn't is a fool." He took a deep breath. "Why were you so upset at the news?" He gazed deeply into her eyes.

"I had dreamed our marriage was more than duty or necessity."

He stared at her for many minutes in silence. "Do you know what the thought of you being harmed does to me? The thought that you will know one moment of fear or pain because of your association with me?" His eyes glowed. "I nearly came to body blows with your brothers over who had the right to punish Walter or whoever it is who threatened you."

She frowned. "I dinna understand."

"I love you, Sorcha. I have since we started our little dance in town." He met her startled gaze. "I love you."

Her hand shook as she raised it to cup his cheek. "How do ye ken?" she whispered. "I'm no' an easy woman to care for."

He laughed. "You are when you aren't being prickly. You're kind and generous and smart. Your laughter, singing and mere presence fills me with joy. When I open the front door and sense that you are here, I calm because I know you are near."

Her eyes filled as she watched him with wonder, and then she pulled him into her arms.

"I marry you because I have to, Sorcha. I have to, or I'll go mad."

"Oh, so 'tis passion then?" she teased.

He chuckled. "Passion and so much more." He relaxed in her arms. "Someday I hope you'll love me too."

Her grip on him tightened, and they lay in each other's arms for many moments before he rose to speak with Warren and Helen, leaving Sorcha to her thoughts.

CHAPTER 8

The following afternoon, Sorcha stood in her bedroom, her hand tracing over the worn hem of one of her two dresses. She frowned at the dresses laid out on her bed, uncertain which one to wear. She had tried to remember which one Frederick had seen her in the least and then decided that road led to lunacy. Now she attempted to discern which one was less worn. She sighed as the evergreen wool had a faded hem, thinning fabric at the elbows and torn lace at the wrists. If possible, the navy blue dress was in worse shape as she fingered missing buttons down the front, a frayed hem that she hadn't realized needed mending until now and a seam coming apart at one shoulder.

She pulled on a shawl to cover her scantily clad self and moved to the door when she heard a knock. When she saw Helen on the other side, she let her in. "What do ye have there?"

Helen smiled as she saw the dresses on the bed and Sorcha still in her underclothes. "Frederick is already pacing, even though you aren't late yet. I thought you might have dress difficulties." Helen set down her package and untied the string covering the burlap. "I didn't even tell Warren about this as I feared he'd ruin the surprise and would share this with Frederick."

"Ye should no' have worried about that. The man ye married can keep more secrets than ye can imagine."

Helen smiled. "I know, but sometimes he doesn't believe these little things are important secrets to keep." She smiled as Sorcha gave a gasp of delight at seeing her mint-green dress.

"Oh, thank ye, Helen," she said as she pulled Helen close for a hug. She then tugged the dress out and held it up. "This is my dress, but it looks different."

"Fidelia added a little lace here and there. She wanted something new to be on your dress." She pulled something else out. "Annabelle sent you a matching ribbon for your hair, and Leticia sent you her pretty pearl earrings to wear." Finally Helen flushed. "Jessamine sent you a garter."

Sorcha blushed beet red and then laughed. "That sounds like Jessamine. She's a perfect match for Ewan, aye?"

Helen laughed and agreed. "They knew that you'd most likely marry with Warren present. And, although they are devastated that they won't see you wed, they wanted to be with you in some small way."

Sorcha swiped at her cheeks. "I canna believe I willna have them with me."

Helen wrapped an arm around her. "I know. But they will have a wonderful celebration for you in town when possible." She smiled. "And I imagine Frederick feels much the same because his grandparents and brothers aren't here."

Sorcha sniffled. "If I were sensible, I'd say we should wait for the thaw, but I dinna want the gossip to worsen. And I dinna want to wait to be his wife."

"You love him," Helen said with a smile. "Why should you wait?" When Sorcha froze at her words, Helen frowned. "What did I say?"

"Why do ye believe I love him?"

Helen laid out the small pile of treasures sent from town by Sorcha's family and then sat on the bed. "If I misspoke, I'm sorry. I thought you'd come to realize how you felt."

Sorcha held a hand to her heart and shook her head. "I dinna ken how I feel."

Helen sighed. "You will. One day you will." She smiled mischievously. "Now there is one more surprise from Fidelia. She wanted you to have a beautiful nightgown for your wedding night." She pulled out a fine linen nightgown with lace strategically placed.

"That's scandalous!" Sorcha rasped.

Helen laughed. "If I were to wear something like this, I know Warren would love it. And I suspect Frederick will too. However, you might not feel bold enough on your wedding night, but I suspect, one night soon, you will." She folded it up and wrapped it again. "Keep it somewhere safe, Sorcha."

Sorcha flushed red and then placed it in a drawer. "I'm movin' my things to Frederick's room after the weddin'. A few days from now."

Helen nodded and motioned for Sorcha to drop her shawl so she could help her get ready. "Come. You're making Frederick wait long enough."

Sorcha gripped Helen's hand. "Thank ye, Helen, for comin' to the ranch. For ensurin' I was well and for bringin' Warren to marry us."

Frederick paced in front of the fireplace as his men stood around and chatted among themselves. Warren stood near Frederick but seemed to understand that he was in no mood for small talk. His gaze roved to the hallway entrance every few seconds, worried that he would miss her entrance, and equally concerned that she had decided against marrying him.

"There's no need to panic. She'll come. Helen's with her and will ensure all is well," Warren murmured.

"I hope you're right." Frederick ran a hand through his hair, silently chastising himself for blurting out his feelings last night to her. And trying to batten down his disappointment that she did not feel the same way about him. He battled long-held fears that he was acting like his father, a man who loved his wife more than she could ever love him. But, just as his thoughts had raced over and over again in his mind during the long sleepless night leading up to his wedding day, he could imagine no other way forward than marrying her. For he did love her, and he could imagine marrying no other.

He heard Slims sigh, and Frederick glanced up. His doubts and fears were momentarily banished as Sorcha stood in attire more appropriate for a summer wedding. The mint-green dress cinched her waist, showing off her figure, and had lace at her waist, wrists and hem. The gentle color of the fabric made her red-brown hair shine even more as it hung loose over her shoulders, held back by a simple ribbon. He absently noted pearl earrings before he focused on the joy and hope in Sorcha's gaze when she stood there, as though waiting for some sign from him.

He beamed at her, his chest so tight he thought he might be having a heart attack. With that smile, she moved toward him, walking from the hallway unescorted. She never took her gaze away from his, and then she stood beside him, with her hands in his.

"I should have flowers for you. Something to match your beauty," he whispered.

"I dinna need flowers," she murmured as she stood on her toes, and it looked as though she were about to kiss him. "I just want ye."

His blue eyes flashed with desire and something much deeper as Warren cleared his throat and began to speak. Frederick paid little attention to what Warren said, Frederick's entire focus on the woman who would shortly become his wife. She met his gaze the entire time, seemingly as taken with him as he was with her.

When Warren jabbed him with the Bible, Frederick jumped, earning chuckles from his men. "Repeat after me," Warren said again.

Frederick smiled at his friends, and they soon finished the ceremony.

"I now pronounce you husband and wife. You may kiss the bride," Warren intoned.

Frederick swooped forward, kissing her for a long moment. Only when he heard a *whoop* from one of his men did he back away. The promise of more passion was in his eyes when he met Sorcha's—his wife's—gaze. He tensed subtly as he saw the same promise in her gaze.

Warren slapped Frederick on his shoulder, and Helen raced forward to hug both Frederick and Sorcha. Then Frederick's men circled around them, all of them eager to congratulate their boss and his new wife.

"Congratulations, Boss," Dalton said as he shook Frederick's hand and then kissed Sorcha's cheek. "I hope you have many years of happiness."

"Thank ye, Dalton," Sorcha said as she squeezed his hand.

Slims pounded Frederick on his shoulder and then pulled Sorcha in for a quick embrace. "Good to see you decided not to let her get away."

When the initial congratulations were done, they moved into the kitchen, where Helen and Slims had prepared a dinner of venison stew and biscuits to be followed by a small wedding cake.

"Oh, how I've missed your cakes," Frederick said as he saw the cake on a small table across the room.

"It's nothing like Annabelle makes," Helen protested.

"They're delicious," Frederick said as he pulled Sorcha against his side.

After toasts were made, they ate their fill, and then Dixon pulled out a fiddle to entertain them. Helen and Sorcha danced until they thought they'd fall over. Finally Sorcha said, "No more. No more."

Frederick looked to Dixon, and the music turned into a slow waltz. "Dance one more. With your husband." He delighted in how her cheeks reddened with pleasure at being able to call him her husband.

"Yes," she murmured in a husky voice. "Only slow dances with you."

She took his proffered hand and followed him to the center of the kitchen floor. They ignored the murmurs as he pulled her into his arms.

He twirled them slowly about in a small circle, holding her close, breathing in her scent. "You are beautiful, Sorcha."

"Ye have Helen to thank," she murmured as she rested her head on his shoulder, utterly relaxed in his arms. "She brought this dress. Otherwise ye would have seen me in one of the dresses I've nearly worn out."

"No matter what you wore, you would have been beautiful." He kissed her head. "Are you ready to retire?" He smiled as she stiffened slightly in his arms.

"Aye," she whispered, raising her head to meet his gaze. "Very."

He fought a groan and kissed her. "We have two options." He kissed her cheek. "We can cease dancing and thank everyone individually and leave here in about an hour as they'll do their best to detain us because they are all rascals. Or I can waltz you out the door."

"Waltz me out the door," she breathed.

His grip on her tightened, and he whispered, "Hold on."

He spun her quickly twice, and they were in the parlor. After releasing her, he grabbed her hand, half-listening as the fiddle playing came to an abrupt halt, and stools and benches scraped the floor when the men stood up. "Run!" he gasped on a delighted chuckle.

They raced down the hall to a small staircase and then up the stairs. At the top, he led her to a large front bedroom that overlooked the ranch and the drive leading to the main house. He slammed shut the door behind them, latching it closed.

"Where are the men sleeping tonight?" she whispered.

"They moved back to the bunkhouse yesterday," he said with a smile. "Warren and Helen are moving to your room downstairs tonight. This whole floor is ours."

"Thank ye," she whispered.

"I thought about taking you to one of the foreman's cottages, but I didn't want to expose you to the winter." He shifted as though uncertain. "I hope this is acceptable."

"Acceptable?" Sorcha paused and looked around the room. It was easily twice as large as her room downstairs with a big bed in an iron frame along one wall. Three windows had heavy curtains covering them to prevent the cold from seeping in. A large bureau with a mirror on top was across from the bed, while in the corner of the room was a seating area. "It's a lovely room. Although rather cold." She shivered.

He nodded. "I know. I'm working on that." He held his hand out to her. "Come here, my love."

Her eyes flashed with pleasure at his words. She took his hand and then squealed as he tugged her to him, holding her close. After a few moments, she whispered, "I dinna ken what ye expect of me."

He backed away a few inches, dropping his head to pepper her face with kisses before kissing her lips for long moments until they were both breathless. "My hope, darling, is that you will be as honest with me in your passion as you are in everything else." He ran a finger through her long hair, smiling as he touched it. "It's like silk. Like spun fiery gold in my hands."

"Frederick," she pleaded as her eyes filled with tears. "I want to please ye. I dinna ken how."

He kissed her again. "You please me by being in the same room with me. You please me by smiling at me. You please me by challenging me and by fighting with me." He smiled. "But I know that's not what you mean." He took a deep breath and stepped away. "Let me undress you. Let me kiss every inch of you. Let me show you how much I love you."

She stared into his mesmerizing eyes and nodded. "Aye. Let me do the same."

He groaned as he pulled her close, his mouth covering hers in a drugging kiss as his fingers pulled at the buttons on the back of her dress. When he had only unfastened one-third of them, he broke the kiss and spun her around. His nimble fingers worked on the buttons, and soon her lovely dress pooled at her feet. In seconds, he had freed her from her corset cover, and then he went to work on her corset. His mouth kissed her neck and upper back, nudging aside her long hair as he loosened the strings. Finally that was thrust aside, and he felt her take a deep breath.

She turned to face him, and he ran a finger over her arm, frowning to feel her shiver. "I'm sorry about the cold."

She smiled at him and batted her eyes. "Warm me, husband."

He groaned again and tugged her shift over her head. "Kick off your knickers and climb into bed."

"No," she whispered, standing in front of him naked from the waist up with only her drawers covering her. "You undressed me. Now it's my turn." She met his startled gaze and reached for his necktie, pulling it loose. She stood on her toes and kissed the skin bared to her.

When she dropped to her feet, she looked at him for a long minute. "Ye asked me to share my passion. To believe that to feel like this is human. Not wantonly."

He nodded, his hand rising to cup her cheek. "Yes, Sorcha. Share yourself with me as I give myself to you."

She beamed at him and then bit her lip as she freed him of his waistcoat and then his shirt. Her breath caught at the fine muscles of his shoulders and chest. Her hands reached forward, tracing the dusting of hair on his chest and abdomen. When his muscles jumped, she stilled her movements.

"No, love, keep touching me. I love your touch." He tilted his head back in ecstasy as her hands played over him.

"I canna believe I can touch ye like this. That ye want me to."

He looked at her and smiled. "Never doubt how much I want you. Nor how much I want you to find joy in our time together." After a long moment, he leaned forward and kissed her soundly. "Come to bed with me."

She shivered at the promise of passion in his voice and nodded. Giggling as she leaped into bed, she shivered as her skin touched the cold sheets. After a moment she wriggled about under the covers and tossed her drawers onto the floor.

"Oh, how you tempt me, wife," he said as he shucked his pants and drawers. He joined her under the covers and pulled her to him. "You've skin like satin."

"How do ye ken what satin feels like?" she asked on a gasp as he kissed her shoulders and then worked his way down her chest.

"I'm not a complete country bumpkin," he teased. He raised his head and ran a hand over her head. His eyes lit with joy to see his joy mirrored in her gaze. "Show me what you like. Tell me what you don't like." He smiled as she gasped at one of his caresses. "Let me love you."

"Please, husband, please," she whispered as she arched into his touch.

B right sunlight shone through the curtains, casting shadows through the patterns of the fabric. Sorcha lay in Frederick's embrace, listening to his gentle snore. She squirmed in his hold and then sighed as his hand on her hip moved up and down over her side, hip and leg.

"No need to be so restless this morning, Sorcha." His body shook as he stretched behind her, and then he relaxed into her again. "We can stay abed all day if we choose."

"We can no'!" she exclaimed, turning over with such haste she elbowed him in his belly, provoking a grunt. "What would they think?"

"They already know what we did all night long," he teased, running a hand over her brow and into her disheveled hair. "I think they'd be disappointed if we make too early an appearance." His grin faded as she belted him on his shoulder. "Why are you so upset?"

"I dinna like gossip. I dinna like the men talkin' about us in such a way."

He sighed and met her embarrassed gaze. "Love, it's a fact of life that everyone knows what we did last night. There's no reason to feel ashamed." He grabbed her fingers and kissed them.

"Will yer men always gossip about me? About us?"

He nodded. "Yes, as we will about them. And they are your men now too. When you need something done, you have every right to ask them for help. There may be times when we are too busy on the ranch to help you at that moment, but they will always aid you, as I will."

She furrowed her brows as she stared at him.

He paused and then took a long breath. "Do you regret last night?"

Her eyes widened, and she pushed herself toward him, toppling him backward until she had crawled over him and straddled him. "Nae!" She kissed him and ran her hands through his black hair. She broke away only to kiss his whisker-roughened cheeks and neck. "Never." She flushed crimson. "I never kent I could feel like that."

He smiled as he caressed her back. "It will only get better. The longer we know each other." He kissed her chin. "Trust each other." A kiss to her shoulder. "Love each other." He paused and then kissed her other shoulder. "It will only get better."

"Love me again," she whispered.

"As long as you love me too," he gasped, losing himself to her touch and passion.

When they emerged from their room in the late afternoon, Sorcha gripped Frederick's hand as they entered the parlor. However, it was empty of the men, and she remembered that Frederick had had the men return to the bunkhouse, even though winter continued outside. "I want us to have time to get to know each other with some privacy in our own home before my brothers return," he had whispered to her last night. However, as she stood in the vacant room, she missed the quiet conversations and the sounds of the men that had made the house feel like home.

"'Tis too empty," she whispered to Frederick.

"It'll be loud enough again soon," he murmured. "Don't forget. The men will still eat with us."

She walked into the kitchen and came to a halt, with Frederick bumping into her from behind. "I dinna expect to see ye here still." She flushed as she met Helen's gaze.

"Oh, Warren and I thought we'd stay another day to make sure you had what you needed. I've food warming for you, if you're hungry." Helen smiled as Sorcha's stomach grumbled. "I knew I should ignore Frederick's command and bring food upstairs to you. But he insisted no one was to come up those stairs until you descended them."

"If you'd brought us food, you wouldn't have seen us until tomorrow," Frederick said, earning a gasp of embarrassment from Sorcha and a chuckle from Warren, who sat at the kitchen table.

"Well, I remember you kept us well fed when we were here after our marriage," Warren said. "If I remember correctly, it was a few days before you saw us outside of that caretaker's hut."

Helen flushed, but her eyes sparkled with pleasure as she looked at her husband. "I've never seen anyone so thankful for a blizzard."

Warren laughed. "Gave us the perfect excuse to remain holed up inside together." He sighed with contentment. "It's one of the reasons I'm so fond of this ranch."

Frederick smiled. "Well, we weren't so lucky as to have as mild a winter like last year's or I would have had us spend our honeymoon in one of those homes." He looked at Sorcha, and he saw her relaxing at Helen's and Warren's conversation and subtle proclamations that passion in a marriage should be celebrated.

Helen smiled at Frederick and Sorcha, placing on the table two plates she had pulled from the warming oven. The dishes were filled with scrambled eggs, bacon, baked beans and toast. "Who's to say your honeymoon is over?" she asked with a wink.

Frederick sighed. "There's always work to do on a ranch."

Warren nodded. "And you have competent men who can take care of things for a few days." He looked up as Slims entered the kitchen.

"Hello, Boss, Missus," he said with deferential nods. He looked at them as he always had, and Sorcha relaxed a little more as she ate her meal. "Thanks to Miss Helen cooking, the horses are well cared for, and there's no need for you, Boss, to come to the barn today. Or tomorrow." Slims took a long sip of coffee. "Ah, heaven. Are you sure you don't want to return to the ranch and work as our cook?" he asked Helen.

She laughed and swatted at him with one of the drying towels. "Very. It's only taken me two days to remember how hard the work is. Although I do miss all of you."

"But I'd miss her more," Warren interjected.

Slims looked from Warren to Helen. "What do you do in town?

Does Miss Helen cook all the time? I'd think seeing patients would make that hard."

Helen shrugged, moving toward Warren to clasp his hand. "I cook when I can, but there are times when I am away from home, attending a patient. Then Warren goes to the café. Or to the MacKinnons."

"Or we go together sometimes because Helen is too tired to cook even if she is home. Her pursuits are as important as mine." Warren squeezed his wife's hand.

Slims shook his head. "Seems odd to me. A wife should cook and clean and have babies."

Helen flushed; Warren glowered, but Frederick spoke up. "Those are all important things for both men and women to do, Slims. Except having babies of course. You remember my grandparents. They shared the work."

Slims nodded as though in understanding. "Yeah, and the towns-folk need Miss Helen, with or without a competent doctor." He took another sip of coffee. "Take it easy, Boss. All is well on the ranch."

Frederick watched the large man leave and then faced Helen. "This is why you are staying. So you can cook and ensure that Slims is helping with the horses."

"If he weren't in the barn, you'd have to be there," Helen said with a shrug. "A few more days out of town won't hurt Warren's business or mine. A doctor is there now." She smiled. "Consider it our wedding gift."

CHAPTER 9

Two weeks after their mid-March wedding, Sorcha stood in the kitchen, staring proudly at a cake. She set it on a cooling rack and then turned her attention to making a stew from the remaining stores that had been stockpiled to get the ranch through winter. She looked out the window at the muddy, impassible road leading into the ranch and sighed that there would be little chance to replenish their supplies anytime soon. After making a potato and bacon soup, she left it to simmer and then picked up her knitting needles.

Although Frederick had cleaned out the old storage room for her as her own private workroom, she had found she preferred working in the kitchen when she knitted because it was warmer. She shrugged as she admitted to herself that being in the kitchen also afforded her the opportunity to see Frederick when he came in to have a quick cup of coffee. She relished any opportunity to see her husband. "Like a lovesick calf," she muttered in disgust about herself as her needles *click*ed together.

Soon she sang her favorite songs and lost track of time. While she sang, she thought about the first few weeks of their marriage. The passionate nights spent in his arms. The quiet evenings in his office as they shared favorite memories or dreams for the future. She relished the few times he had opened up and discussed his fears for the ranch. Only when she heard the creak of a floorboard did she look up to find her husband in the kitchen doorway, watching her. "Frederick! How long have ye been there?"

"Not nearly long enough," he said with a smile before he moved toward her to give her a quick kiss. He leaned over her with both hands on the rocking chair arms. "I love hearing you sing. It's like another window into your soul."

She flushed and then shook her head. "Flatterer."

"Aye," he said as he mimicked her with a broad smile. "When you sing, I know you are happy. And that fills me with joy."

Before he could rise and move away from her, she gripped his arms and arched up, kissing him more deeply. She broke away from him with a bright flush at Slims's grunt of dismay in the doorway.

"Lovebirds again," he grumbled and then winked at Sorcha as he entered the kitchen.

Her gaze shot to the clock above the stove, and then she pushed Frederick away. "Why did ye no' tell me it was time for dinner? I've yet to set the table."

Slims motioned for her to relax and grabbed a set of plates. "There ain't nothin' to worry about, Missus. We're used to setting the table." Soon Sorcha ladled the soup, and the men passed around slices of her fresh bread.

She sat beside Frederick and listened to them discuss their day. Bullet's foal was sickly, and no one was certain why. "Do ye no' have someone who specializes in animal husbandry?"

"We do, but it's difficult to travel this time of year. And I continue to hope she'll improve on her own." Frederick squeezed Sorcha's hand under the table.

After the men finished dinner, Sorcha rose and brought out the white sheet cake she had prepared. At their smiles of delight, she preened. "I kent ye loved Helen's treats, so I thought I'd try to make one. I think I followed the recipe correctly."

She set it down and began to slice it. After she served the first piece, her face fell. "I dinna understand," she whispered.

"What's the matter?" Frederick asked as he peered over her shoulder and then made a face. "Looks like it didn't fully cook."

"I gave it all the time it called for," she said as she put her hand on her hip and glared at the cake.

"Looks like it's oozin' its guts out," Dixon joked. He sobered when Sorcha pointed the knife at him.

"Ye make one more comment about my *puir* wee cake, an' ye will no' have an opportunity to eat a piece of the next one I bake." She slammed the knife down in frustration. "I told ye I was no cook."

Frederick ran a soothing hand over her shoulder. "All that matters is that you tried, love. And next time it will be better." He glared at his men to make conciliatory noises or comments, and they quickly complied. He held her as she turned into his arms.

"I wanted to have somethin' nice for ye after ye worked all day."

"And we did. A wonderful meal that was different from what Slims cooks us. It gives us something to look forward to on the few days a week you cook." He kissed the top of her head as the men left the kitchen, murmuring their thanks for the fine meal as they departed.

She let out a deep breath. "I'm sorry I'm a disappointment in the kitchen."

He cupped her cheeks and stared with a reverent intensity into her eyes. "You never have been, nor will you ever be, a disappointment. Not to me." He kissed her. "I hope someday you will learn that you do not have to earn my love. You already have it."

She stared at him in wonder. "I ... I dinna understand."

He pulled her close. "Someday you will."

Sorcha stood on the front steps as the wagon rolled to a halt. A gentle breeze blew as spring attempted to push out winter still hanging on into mid-April. Drifts of snow remained in shadowy areas, but large swaths of prairie were visible. She waited every day for her first sighting of a robin. She focused on the wagon, holding a hand over her eyes as she watched Frederick run out of the barn to greet his grandparents. In the month since they were married, they had not received a letter from them, and Sorcha's anxiety about their approval had mounted with each passing day of silence.

She saw her husband tease his grandmother, earning a laugh and an affectionate swat to his arm as he helped her from the wagon. Slims had joined Frederick to greet Harold and Irene, and Slims would take the team to the barn. After Harold had jumped down from the wagon and hugged Frederick, he looked around. When Harold saw her standing on the porch, he frowned and waved at her. "What are you doing up there? Come and give your grandparents a hug!" he hollered.

She scampered down the steps and threw herself into Harold's open arms. Sorcha then turned to Irene, who embraced Sorcha and kissed each of her cheeks.

"Finally you are family," Irene said, cupping Sorcha's face and beaming at her. She dropped a hand and reached for Frederick. "You will never know how happy we were to hear the news that you had wed."

"But I insisted that we tell you ourselves. Not waste it in a letter," Harold said as he pulled Sorcha close to him, tugging her to his side and kissing her head.

"Thank ye," Sorcha whispered, fighting tears.

"Now there ain't no reason for tears unless this boy of ours ain't treatin' you right," Harold said. He winked at his grandson. "But I know he isn't that foolish."

"No, sir," Frederick said as he looked at his wife in adoration. "I can't believe you'd leave the café to come out here now."

Irene smiled. "Well, we wanted to bring you supplies, and I needed a break." She smiled. "I reckon the townsfolk will appreciate us even more when we return."

"Or another café will have started in our absence," Harold muttered.

"'Twould no' matter," Sorcha said loyally. "No one could cook as well as ye nor chat with the locals like ye do," Sorcha said as she spoke first to Irene and then Harold. "Besides, ye make the best coffee in town."

Irene flushed with pleasure at Sorcha's words, and Harold puffed out his chest. "If you think Irene's resting here on the ranch, you're a fool. I know she'll be cookin' for you and the men from sunup 'til sundown."

"And loving every minute of it," Irene said with a smile. "Besides, we decided, if you were not coming to town, we'd have to come to you. A month was already too long to wait to celebrate your wedding."

They moved to the house, cleaning off their boots on the boot scraper outside and then shucking their coats to hang on pegs by the front door. Sorcha watched as Irene looked around the parlor. Little had changed since Sorcha had married Frederick, although she had moved furniture around to have better conversation areas and more seats near the fire. The desk that had been crammed into a corner of the room now sat in a place of prominence along one wall. A small lamp stood on one corner of the desk, while writing paper and an inkwell was at the ready.

"Oh, you've made it a home," Irene breathed. "At last." She shared a smile with Harold.

"We can't tell you how sorry we were to miss your wedding. But we were delighted to hear about the festivities from Warren and Helen." Harold looked at the newlyweds with approval. "Very smart to have the lawyer wed you. Few will go against him, especially after they made fools of themselves last year doubting his credentials."

Sorcha smiled. "I still remember Mrs. Jameson's dismay when she read Jessamine's article. Can ye imagine Warren kennin' a man on the Pennsylvania Supreme Court?" She moved into Frederick's embrace at the mention of Mrs. Jameson.

Harold chortled. "Mrs. Jameson's a menace, but her power is waning in town."

"What is her son doing?" Frederick asked.

Harold shrugged. "Oh, he skulks around, flashing coin here and there. I've heard he's been barred from the Boudoir after nearly killing a Beauty."

Sorcha shivered. "Why should the Madam care this time when she didn't care about Fidelia's welfare? The Madam never cared when Fidelia was abused by patrons."

Irene gave a *tsk* of disapproval. "Seems she came to realize finding profitable girls is a challenge. Ezekial enjoyed his chance to plant a facer on Walter."

Sorcha frowned at the name, and Frederick whispered, "Ezekial's the bouncer there." He froze when he realized he'd walked right into her trap. "Not that I know the man or the Boudoir."

She stood with her hands on her hips. "Then how do ye ken who the man is? It's no' as though he frequents respectable establishments in town."

Frederick took her face between his palms, ignoring his grandparents as they moved into the kitchen. "The men talk. And I've seen him in the Watering Hole a few times."

"Ye promise?"

He nodded and then chuckled. "It does me good to see you jealous."

She gave a sound of disgruntlement and moved into his arms. "How would ye feel if I'd been at the Boudoir?"

His arms tightened around her. "Like a rabid wolf. I don't know how Warren handled it last year when he rescued Helen."

Sorcha nuzzled her husband's neck and then backed away. "He managed because his love was stronger than anythin' else." She clasped Frederick's hand and walked with him to the kitchen. "Come. We're ignorin' our grandparents."

The following day, Frederick and his grandfather rode out together to survey part of the ranch. Although Frederick attempted to chat with his grandfather, he found it difficult to focus on anything but the empty ranch land, barren of cattle. The only hopeful sign was the green shoots of early grass sprouting from the muddy earth. After a few minutes, he turned to his grandfather. "I'm going to be horrible company."

"I'd expect nothing more," Harold said. He nodded to a coulee. "Let's look there."

They steered their horses in the direction of the deep ravine and then brought them up short and dismounted as the stench permeating the air reached them before they looked into the protected area. Willows and shrubs grew out of the hillsides, and scattered along the ravine and in nearby gullies were rotting carcasses of cattle. Frederick pulled out his bandanna and covered his nose.

"What should we do?" Frederick asked as he stared into the coulee at the dead cattle. When visible, all had the distinctive MBR brand on their haunches.

"Leave them," Harold said, staring at the sky and the circling buzzards. "If we find some near water, we should pull 'em out and burn 'em. Otherwise, let them fertilize the prairie." He swatted at a fly and followed Frederick back to the horses.

The scene repeated itself over and over, until finding live cattle became a surprise. Those cattle were skeletal and seemed as though a stiff wind would knock them over. However, they were feasting on the early shoots of the prairie grass pushing through the mud.

After hours riding across acres of the ranch, they returned home. Rather than the quiet conversations, the tall tales or the interesting stories they usually shared, Frederick and Harold remained silent after reaching the barn. Frederick jumped off his horse and grabbed his grandfather's reins to lead both horses to the barn. "I'll curry him. Thanks, Grandpa." He nodded to his grandfather as he was slapped on the back and then watched as Harold walked toward the house. Frederick turned his horse to the barn, tugging Harold's horse behind him.

In the barn, he glared at anyone who came near him. He curried both horses, fetched water and oats, and ensured their stalls had fresh hay. And then he looked around for more work. He began to muck out stalls, only stopping when Sorcha blocked his wheelbarrow full of muck that he was about to push outside. "What are you doing here?

You should be in the house with my grandparents." Frederick glared at her as she put her hands on her hips and met his glower.

"Ye mean, ye want me tucked away, an' ye'll come to me when ye've worked through whatever it is ye saw on the prairie today?" She shook her head. "Nae, that isna how this marriage works. Ye are my husband, an' ye need to share with me as I am to share with ye."

"Dammit, Sorcha, don't push me," he rasped. "Not now." He looked over her shoulder and saw Slims prodding Dalton and Dixon into leaving the barn, thus allowing them privacy.

"I have to push ye. I will no' be locked out of yer life. For 'tis my life too." She stood bravely in front of him, her red-brown hair catching rays of sun that entered through a window.

"Do you want to know what I saw?" He shook his head as though to banish the images flooding his memory. "I saw more cattle dead on the range than I've ever seen. Cattle with my brand rotting in the sun." His eyes glowed with impotent anger. "I saw absolute ruination. There's no way this ranch will survive, Sorcha. You've married a failure."

"Do no' dare speak of yerself in such a way." She moved around the wheelbarrow and hit him in his chest with both of her hands, propelling him back a step. "Ye are no failure. Ye will find a way."

He looked at her with panic and fear. "What happens if I can't? Will you still want me if we can't live here anymore? If you can't be the madam of the ranch?"

She gaped at him, momentarily at a loss for words.

"Will you still want me when we are poor?" he whispered.

Now she glared at him. "Do ye think my love so fickle that I will no' stand by ye? That I will no' fight alongside ye to regain what was lost? That is no' marriage. That is no' love." She battled tears in her dismay.

He breached the step that separated them and cupped her face, his eyes watching her with ardent intensity. "What do you mean?"

"I love ye, Frederick, an' I canna stand the thought of ye hurtin' as ye are. Please let me comfort ye as ye would comfort me. Please ..."

Anything else she would have said was lost as he covered her mouth in a passionate kiss.

He yanked her full-bodied to him and twirled until they were in a cleaned-out stall. Horses nickered nearby and were their only company in the barn. "Make love with me in my barn."

She arched into him. "'Tis scandalous," she whispered as she met his kisses and as her hands raced over him. "Aye, husband," she said as she followed him down into a clean bed of hay.

Afterward, she lay curled around him, with her clothes rumpled, her hair in disarray and her fingers making hearts on his chest. "I love ye," she whispered against his throat. His arms tightened around her, and she pressed herself more tightly against him. "Dinna doubt I want ye, Frederick. Never the ranch. Never anythin' more than I want ye."

"When did you know?" He kissed her head. "It seems as though I've waited forever for you to tell me, but it's only been a little over a month since we married."

"I kent I loved ye when we wed, but I feared tellin' ye." She pushed herself up so she could meet his gaze. "I dinna ken why." She shrugged. "But I canna bear to hear ye call yerself a failure. Ye will never be one in my eyes, ye ken?" She kissed him softly, her hands caressing his face. "Ye are good and strong. Loyal and kind. Ye are patient and forgiving. I dinna care where we live, as long as I am with ye."

He closed his eyes at her words and then whispered, "I want to provide you everything your heart desires. If I'm poor and destitute, working at my grandparent's café or mucking out stalls in your brothers' livery, how can I provide for you?"

She shook her head and crawled over him. "Why can ye no' understand? *Ye* are my heart's desire, Frederick. Ye—an' nothin' else."

He groaned and pulled her down to him. "I never want you to regret marrying me."

She held on to him tightly. "I am no' yer mother. I could never regret my life with ye. I could never regret marryin' ye." She held him as his tears trickled into her hair, and he silently mourned what he had seen earlier.

"I don't know how I'll tell the men," he whispered. "How I'll ever bear to leave."

"Nothin' is certain yet. Harold told me that ye must wait for the roundup."

He held her close. "I will, but I already know what we'll find."

She gripped his hand. "Remember. Whatever ye do find, I will no' let ye down. I will love ye still."

They remained together on the bed of hay, dozing and cuddling for long minutes until Frederick urged her to stand. "Come. I should return to the house to reassure my grandparents."

She rose, running her hands through his hair and over his shirt, freeing him from stray pieces of hay. "Nae, ye dinna need to worry about them. For they understand ye, Frederick, an' the love ye have for yer home."

She smiled as he plucked hay from her hair and then kissed her forehead. After they had put themselves to rights, Frederick washed up at the hand pump, and then they walked hand in hand to the house.

When they entered, they heard laughter coming from the kitchen as Harold told a tale, and the ranch hands hooted at his embellishments. The scent of fried chicken filled the air, and Frederick rubbed at his stomach. "I forgot how hungry I was."

"Come," Sorcha urged, tugging him to enter the kitchen.

"There you are!" Irene said with a knowing smile as she took in their rumpled clothes. "I'm glad you could join us for dinner. Fried chicken is always better warm." She motioned for them to sit down, but Frederick kissed her on the forehead first before finding his seat beside his grandfather.

He sat, listening as Harold started another tale about his brother Cole.

"Now Cole liked to believe he didn't need no one to tell him what to do or to teach him how to do things. And he certainly didn't need no help from his youngest brother." Harold smirked in Frederick's direction. "But Cole's impatient, and he doesn't always believe that all steps are necessary. Why waste time doing three things, when two would be just as good?"

Harold chuckled. "Now that might be a good philosophy some-times, but it don't work when you're saddlin' a horse. Peter had already raced from the barn, and they had a bet about how many cattle they could gather into a herd. The winner had his stalls mucked out for him for a week."

Harold nodded to Frederick. "Now he was the wisest one. He never followed along with his brothers' antics. Just enjoyed being in the barn and accepted that muckin' out stalls was part of workin' with horses. Peter and Cole hated it. But Frederick wasn't about to take on their chores so they could spend more time outside.

"As Peter hurtled out of the barn, Cole ran to his horse. Rather than listen to his baby brother about the proper way to cinch on a saddle, Cole insisted he'd invented a new way that was twice as fast but just as effective."

Harold slapped his hand in amusement. "You should have seen that boy kick his horse into motion, only to have his saddle careen to the side and have him plop into a pile of fresh horse apples."

Frederick continued the tale. "He came up sputtering and yelling at me for not helping him." Frederick laughed as he shook his head. "It took Slims to keep him from pummeling me."

"They always loved the adventure to be had but never the ranch. Never the work that was required to keep it running," Slims said.

Frederick took a deep breath as he absently noted his grand-mother serving the food. "It may all be lost." He met the gazes of his men and the understanding in their stares. "We saw … horrible losses on the range today."

"We know, Boss," Dixon said. "We lived through this winter with you."

Dalton sat forward. "I'm speakin' for myself, but, if all I got was room and board for a while, I'd be happy to stay on here. This is a good place to work, and you treat us well." He looked around the table. "And, if we were this hard hit, so were other ranches. There won't be much work to be had for a man like me."

Frederick stared at his men as they nodded their agreements.

"Thank you," he whispered. "But I don't know if we'll survive with enough cattle to continue be abel to continue on the ranch."

Harold looked at Frederick. "You may have some lean years, son, but, no matter what, this ranch will survive. This land will not be lost to us."

Frederick relaxed as Sorcha squeezed his hand and leaned into his side. Soon their happier dinner conversations restarted, with Dixon and Dalton sharing stories, and the mood lightened as a faint hope rekindled in Frederick.

❧

Frederick sat in his office and wrote a letter. He paused as the door creaked open. He expected to see Sorcha, but, when his grandmother poked her head in, he beamed at her. "Hello, Grandma," he said, rising to embrace her. After she had settled in a chair in front of his desk, he sat beside her.

"Who are you writing?" she asked.

He squirmed. "I thought you could bring a letter back for me. To Cailean MacKinnon." He pointed to the letter. "I regret that no one from either family was at the wedding, and I know Sorcha is saddened by the fact that Cailean was not here to give us his blessing or to walk her down the aisle." He looked at his grandmother with barely contained anger. "But it's been a month. Over a month. I thought he'd write and wish her well. Doesn't he know how much his silence is hurting her?"

"Oh, Frederick," Irene said as she leaned forward and gripped his hand. "Annabelle has been sick. Deathly ill." She blinked as she fought tears. "They asked me not to tell you because they know you have enough worries. But I realize now that was wrong."

"What is wrong with her?" he whispered.

"She lost another baby. And almost died again." She held her grandson's hand. "You may not know, but that is how Cailean's first wife died—in childbirth. And twice now, Annabelle has almost died after losing a child."

"But they have a child," he whispered. "A beautiful daughter."

Irene nodded. "Yes, Skye. But I'm not certain if they will ever have another." She paused a moment. "Should I tell Sorcha?"

He shook his head. "No, I want to. I want to comfort her when she hears the news. And then I want to be with her when she insists we travel to town." He looked at his grandmother, a woman who had always supported and loved him. Who had scolded him when he needed to learn a lesson but had never faltered in her love for him. "Thank you for coming to the ranch."

She smiled. "You know I love it here. And I wanted to see for myself how your marriage was." She squeezed his hand. "I'm delighted to see that you are even happier than I had hoped."

He looked at his grandmother with wonder. "She loves me," he whispered. "I never thought she would."

Irene cupped one of his cheeks. "Your mother's leaving hurt you the most, I fear. You were the youngest and the most in need of her love." She stared into his blue eyes. "I'm saddened to hear you ever thought yourself unworthy of loving."

He leaned forward and pulled his grandmother into his arms for a few moments and then released her. "I must tell Sorcha about Annabelle."

"Yes, you need to speak with your wife." She stroked a finger over his cheek and then rose with him as he left his office.

When he entered the bedroom he shared with Sorcha, he stilled to find her asleep under the covers. After he shucked his clothes, he climbed under the covers, easing to her side and sighing with relief as she cuddled up beside him.

"I thought ye'd stay in yer office forever," she murmured. "Why were ye gone so long?"

"My grandmother visited," he said as he kissed her head. "Were you asleep?"

"Nae, I'm talkin' with ye," she said as she pushed herself farther against him as she always did when she was about to fall asleep.

"I need to tell you something, and it isn't good news. It has to do with your family in town."

In an instant, she jerked awake and sat up, the blankets falling around her waist and her upper body beautifully bared to him.

However, he ignored her nakedness as he focused on the panic in her gaze. "*Shh*, ... love, no one you love has died." He ran a hand through her long hair and then gripped her shoulder, urging her down beside him again and under the covers. He propped himself up on an elbow as he ran a finger from her hairline, down her cheek, neck and shoulder and then back up again. "Cailean hasn't written," he began.

"Aye, I ken. He's sorely disappointed in me." Her breath hitched as though fighting a sob.

"No, he hasn't written because Annabelle has been sick." Frederick held Sorcha close when she convulsed, as though she had been physically injured. "She lost another baby. And nearly died again."

"Nae!" she screamed. "Nae," she said more softly as tears began to course out. "Why did he no' write? Why did he no' let me go to them?"

Frederick shook his head. "I can't answer for him. I imagine he was wholly focused on her improving. On ensuring he didn't become a widower. Again."

She fell against Frederick as her tears poured out. "Take me to them. Please? Oh, please, Frederick. I ken ye have work on the ranch, but please don't keep me from them."

"*Shh*, ... my love, we will go tomorrow and stay as long as you need. The roundup can wait. My grandparents will stay to help run the ranch in my absence."

She clung to him. "I canna imagine the fear Cailean has been feelin'."

Frederick held her even more tightly to him. "Nor can I. I'd rather never have a child than suffer Cailean's torment."

Frederick cradled his wife, murmuring his love into her ear as she cried until she had calmed and fallen asleep in his arms. And then he continued to hold her, his hands caressing her back as he held her against him, giving thanks for the chance to love her and to hold her close.

The following morning, Sorcha rose early. She packed a bag for herself and Frederick, then waited impatiently for him to ready a team of horses. She kissed Irene's cheek the moment before she raced out the door to join Frederick in the wagon. Harold helped her up into the seat and waved them away.

As they rode into town, Sorcha ignored her husband's few attempts at conversation. Her mind was filled with what she would find when they arrived at the livery and Cailean's house. She ignored the brilliant springlike day, the bright blue sky, the green hills, the sparkling stream and snowcapped mountains in the distance.

When they reached town, she saw little had changed in the months of her absence. The church still needed a fresh coat of paint. The schoolteacher still lacked any semblance of control over his students. The street still bustled with carts and wagons and townsfolk going about their daily business. And then Frederick parked the wagon in front of the livery. He helped her down, and, before he could say anything, she raced to Cailean's house next door.

"Cailean!" she shrieked as she thrust open the door. Inside, the house was silent. The kitchen had an air of disuse about it, and she frowned as Fidelia should still have been cooking. Sorcha spun and raced up the stairs. At her brother's bedroom door, she gently knocked. When she heard no noise, she edged open the door.

Her breath caught when she saw the empty space. A gaping hole in the room where the bed should be. "No," she gasped as she fell to the floor to her knees. "Oh, dear God, no."

A hand on her shoulder gave her a start, and she glanced backward. "Annabelle!" she yelled, jumping to her feet to pull her sister-in-law into her arms. "I thought … I thought this meant …" Her tears prevented her from saying anything more.

"No," Annabelle said with a tired smile. She tugged on Sorcha's hand and led her to what had been Ewan's room. "The bed was ruined during my illness. We have to replace it, but we haven't been able to yet. We are sleeping over here." She sat with a groan of relief on the bed before lying down again.

"Where's Skye?" Sorcha asked.

"Staying with Jessamine and Ewan," Annabelle whispered as her eyes closed. "I don't have the energy ..." She was asleep in a few moments.

Sorcha found a throw blanket she had knitted and tucked it around Annabelle. "Rest, Anna. Recover yer strength." She sat beside her for long minutes, only turning to the door as it creaked open again to find her eldest brother, Cailean, staring at her.

"Sorcha," he whispered, "how is she?"

"Tired. More tired than I've ever seen her." She ran a hand over Annabelle's forehead. "But I dinna believe she has a fever."

He nodded. "That broke a few days ago." He motioned for his sister to follow him. "Come." He led her downstairs to the kitchen. The oven was cold, and no coffee sat brewed and ready to drink on the stove.

"What are ye eatin'?" she asked as she sat at the table.

"Leticia and Jessamine bring food over. Fidelia has been too busy caring for her sister to worry about cooking." He leaned his head back against the wall as he sat in a chair, closing his eyes with a heavy sigh.

"Why did ye no' write me? Or have Alistair or Ewan inform me what was occurrin'?" She was unable to hide the hurt in her voice.

"You'd just married, Sorcha." He opened his eyes, and a momentary happiness filled his gaze. "You finally married Frederick. After all that time spent circling around each other, and then your courtship, I didn't have any right to think you'd come into town and interrupt the first month of your marriage."

"But ye're my brother. Ye're my family." She blinked away tears.

"Frederick is your family now, Sorcha. How would he feel if you ran to us every time we had a small crisis?"

"Annabelle nearly dyin' is no' a small crisis!" she snapped. "Do ye ken how it made me feel?" she asked as she glared at Alistair when he entered the kitchen, his gaze shadowed with guilt and worry. "It made me feel as though ye felt relief that ye had finally freed yerself of yer

160

responsibility to me." She took a gulping breath. "That any joy ye felt was because ye no longer had the carin' of me."

Cailean's eyes flashed with anger, and he reached for her fisted hand. "Never, Sorcha. Dammit, I was mad with grief and fear over Belle and our lost child. Dinna make me pay for a mistake when I only wanted ye to ken joy, no' sorrow." His eyes glistened with tears as he met her hurt gaze.

She took a deep breath and studied her brother. Devastation, fatigue and worry shrouded him. She gave a small sound of distress and rose, throwing herself into his arms.

He pulled her onto his lap and held her close.

"I'm sorry, Cail. So sorry for the wee bairn."

He he shuddered a few times. "All that matters is that Belle improves. That I dinna lose Belle." His accent had thickened with the deepening of his emotion. "Forgive me."

"Always," she whispered as she held him. She looked to Alistair and held a hand out. "I hate bein' separated from all of ye."

Alistair nodded. "I ken. I hate it as much. But ye have yer own life now, Sorcha. Ye're a married woman. Ye must focus on yer husband."

She shook her head. "That doesna mean I'll forget my brothers." She sniffled. "Promise me ye'll always tell me the truth in the future. That ye willna keep anythin' from me. Please?"

Her eldest brother nodded. "Aye," he whispered as he kissed her head and then pushed her to stand. "Aye." He took a deep breath. "If ye dinna mind, I'm goin' to spend a few minutes with Belle." He rose and slipped up the stairs to join his wife.

Sorcha watched him leave and then looked to Alistair. "How bad was it?"

"Worse than the first time she nearly died." He shook his head. "Helen and the doc did everything they could, and they still nearly lost her."

Sorcha bit her lip. "Irene told Frederick they may never have any more children."

Alistair nodded. "Aye, but I dinna think Cail cares. All he wants is Belle better."

Sorcha looked at her second-eldest brother, noting the toll the past month had taken on him. "How are ye? Leticia and the children?"

"Missin' me," he said. "I'm workin' long hours because Cail canna focus on work. He's with Anna or Skye. I dinna blame him, but I'm bone weary." He shrugged. "I ken it will change. Anna is slowly improvin', an' soon it will all be a sad memory."

Sorcha shuddered. "Skye is with Jessamine?"

"Aye, an' she's flourishin' with her aunt and uncle. Jessamine's taken to writing one paper a week right now, as she does no' have as much time as she'd like to focus on her reporter duties." A smile flit as he thought about Skye. "I think Jessamine doesna mind the interruption to her life. Jessamine adores Skye."

Sorcha gripped Alistair's arm. "I'll be back soon, but I want to see Skye, and then I'll stop at the Merc to pick up supplies. I'll make Cail something to eat."

Alistair pulled her into an embrace. "Thank ye for comin'. We've missed ye."

Sorcha kissed his cheek and then rushed from the house, barely remembering to grab the basket for groceries. She smiled at those she passed, ignoring the shocked looks or the women who glared at her. She walked past the shuttered café, the bakery and the print shop and then cut to a back street to go to Ewan and Jessamine's house.

When she arrived at the well-built one-story home, she knocked on the door, fighting her desire to barge inside. When her brother Ewan yanked it open with a growl, she beamed at him. His distemper fled at her appearance, and he pulled her into his arms.

"Sorcha!" he exclaimed. "I never thought to find ye on my doorstep this morning." He kissed her cheek and then led her into the house before patting at a smeared area on the front of her dress. "Sorry," he apologized as his shirt was covered with splatterings of porridge. "Wee Skye is havin' too much fun with her food today to eat it."

Sorcha laughed and gripped his arm as she followed him into the kitchen area. Jessamine sat in front of Skye, making faces at her as Jessamine coaxed her niece to eat. Jessamine had a white clump of porridge stuck in her brilliant red hair.

"Sorcha!" Jessamine exclaimed as she grabbed a rag to wipe at her hands. "Oh, what a wonderful surprise. How are things at the ranch? How is life with Frederick?"

"Give the lass a moment to relax," Ewan teased his wife. "Always in reporter mode."

Jessamine swatted at him with the rag. "No, I'm not. I'm worried about Sorcha, like a sister should be. She's been away too long." She watched as Sorcha moved toward Skye. "But I can see you are well. I can barely discern a limp."

"'Tis thanks to Helen and Bears that I've no limp, although I've walked too much today, an' it's startin' to pain me. Helen taught me what to do to strengthen my leg," she said with a smile. "Now, how is my little angel?" she asked as she accepted a cloth from Jessamine and helped clean up Skye's face, neck and hands. Then she picked up her niece and held her high, earning a squeal. "Oh, how I've missed ye, ye wee bairn."

"She's no' so wee anymore," Ewan said as he ran a hand over Skye's back. "She's a wee devil and reminds me of ye when ye were young."

Sorcha smiled at her brother. "Then that only proves her intelligence." She kissed her niece on the forehead and then walked into the adjoining living area.

Skye squirmed to be let onto the ground. Once on the floor, she played with dolls and wooden blocks that had been left there for her.

"She's thrivin'."

"Aye," Ewan said as he looked at his wife, "but she misses her mother and father. I'll miss her when she goes, nae doubt that, but she needs them."

Sorcha looked at them, sensing a secret grief. "I ken Cail is thankful for all ye've done for Skye. For allowin' him the ability to focus on Annabelle."

Jessamine smiled. "It's what you do for family." She took a deep breath. "I'd worried you'd be much angrier at us for not writing you. For not congratulating you, as we wanted." She sobered. "Every letter I wrote turned into a melancholy mess, and I feared you would interpret that to mean I was saddened you'd married Frederick, when I am truly delighted for you."

Sorcha smiled at her sister-in-law. "I spoke with Cailean. Yelled at him. An' I ken now why ye acted as ye did. I am no' admittin' I agree, but I understand." She took a deep breath. "I hope ye'll like Frederick."

Ewan laughed. "We do. We always have. Ye were the one who insisted on a courtship."

Sorcha laughed. "I'm glad I did. Although I'd lived at his ranch for months, that time afore we married allowed me to ken him better. To ken the man I'd marry." She smiled with contentment.

"And it kept him on his toes. Something that is always important in a relationship," Jessamine teased. "You don't want him to take you for granted."

Ewan rolled his eyes and rose. "I must change, and then I need to join my foreman, Ben, for a few hours." He kissed Sorcha on the forehead. "I dinna ken how long ye are stayin' in town, but I am delighted I saw ye. Jessie an' I will visit the ranch soon."

"Please visit," she whispered. At her brother's nod, a little of her anxiety eased.

After Ewan had departed for work, Skye became fussy, and Jessamine laid her down for her morning nap. When she emerged from the middle bedroom that they had turned into Skye's nursery, she saw Sorcha watching her intently. "What is it?" Jessamine asked.

"I ken I've been away for months. I've missed more gossip and goings-on in the family than I'll ever be able to make up." She paused as she bit her lip. "What's the matter between ye and Ewan?" she blurted out.

When Jessamine paled, Sorcha stood and held her hands out, as though asking for forgiveness. "I dinna mean to cause ye pain. I only want to understand. To see if I could help ye in some way."

Jessamine rubbed at her hair, pulling clumps of porridge free before rebraiding it. She gave a humorless laugh. "There is nothing for you to do, and I'm surprised Anna or Leticia didn't write you about us." When Sorcha shook her head in confusion, Jessamine motioned her to join her at the table. She put on a kettle for tea and wiped up the remains of Skye's breakfast from the table. "Ewan and I can't have children."

Sorcha gave a gasp of distress and grabbed Jessamine's hand that scrubbed at the tablecloth. "Ye dinna ken that for certain. Ye've been married a little over a year."

Jessamine paled further, highlighting the redness of her hair. "Do you ever know certain truths, even though there are no facts to back them up?" When Sorcha nodded, Jessamine whispered, "This is one of those truths." When Sorcha began to protest, Jessamine shook her head. "I've already lost three pregnancies, Sorcha. Ewan knows about two of them." She took a deep breath. "The first one, I didn't realize what was happening, but now that I've lost these other … bairns," her voice broke. "Now that I know, I realize I've lost more."

Sorcha bit her lip. "What does Ewan say?"

Jessamine swiped at her eyes. "That he doesn't care if we never have children as long as he has me. That he doesn't care how we have a family, as long as we are together." She sniffled. "I try to believe his words, and then I see how he is with Skye. He'd be such a wonderful father."

"He would, aye," Sorcha whispered. "But he loves ye more than anythin', Jessamine. 'Tis a tremendous gift."

Jessamine smiled. "Yes, and I have to keep telling myself that he won't regret it."

Sorcha shook her head instinctively. "Nae, never. He's as devoted to ye as Alistair is to Leticia and Cail to Annabelle."

Jessamine took a deep breath. "Now tell me about life on a ranch. I imagine it must be boring compared to town."

Sorcha laughed. "That's where ye would be wrong," she said. She spent the next hour chatting about her life there, the daily challenges and joys. Finally she departed for the Merc.

Frederick entered the livery and waited a moment for his eyes to adjust to the dimness inside. He nodded with approval to see a tidy well-run barn where the horses were well cared for with stalls cleaned out on a regular basis. He'd always liked the MacKinnons and thought they ran a good livery. Now that they were family, he was proud to be associated with them.

Bears moved out of the tack room and saw him standing in the center aisle. "Wrangler," he said. "What brings you to town?"

"My wife is worried about her family," Frederick said. He watched Bears give a small nod of approval and then moved with lanky grace toward him. His long black hair was braided down his back, and his brown eyes looked black in the darkened interior of the barn. "I have two horses that need tending. I'm uncertain if we will depart today."

Bears nodded again and followed him outside to help unhitch his horses from the wagon. When the horses were stalled and curried, Bears stood beside Frederick in contemplative silence, then spoke. "She'll be as mad as an upturned hornet's nest."

Frederick gave a grunt of agreement.

"They would not interrupt your first month together. In the midst of their sorrow, they wanted her to know joy." Bears looked at Frederick. "In her hurt and anger, she might not understand that, Wrangler."

After a few moments of silence, Frederick asked, "What news of Walter Jameson?"

Bears shrugged. "He bides his time, like a snake before it strikes. I wouldn't underestimate his hatred of you. Or his desire to hurt everything and everyone you hold dear."

Frederick shook his head. "I don't understand why."

"There are men who don't need a reason to hate. And when they find something or someone to hate, they feed it as others feed an empty belly. But that hunger will never be satisfied." He looked at Frederick with an intensity in his gaze. "No matter who he hurts or what he destroys, it will never be enough."

Frederick shivered. "Thank God Helen escaped him."

Bears nodded. "Yes, but now his focus is on you. I'd be careful, Wrangler. I'd keep my womenfolk close."

Frederick paused, his gaze distant as he again relived the scene last fall when he had found Sorcha, fallen in the forest with a broken leg. "What did you see when you found Sorcha?"

Bears shook his head. "No, what did you see?"

Frederick took off his hat and ran a hand through his hair. "I saw her lying on the ground. Her head bleeding. And her leg broken." He paused and frowned. "But where was the rock that she was to have hit? Where was the bloody rock where she hit her head?"

Bears nodded. "Someone moved her there. A quarter-mile away was a bloodstained rock and a patch of her deep-red skirt on a boulder. That's where she fell." He met Frederick's angry gaze. "Someone hurt her but then thought she was dead and decided to dump her body. They never thought she'd be found."

"But they left her on a path," Frederick said.

Bears waited a moment and then said, "Which tells you the man you're chasing is a lazy one. Couldn't be bothered to move her farther. And an arrogant man. Didn't believe anyone would miss her or look for her."

Frederick shook his head. "I don't know how this helps me at all."

"If there's one thing I know about Walter Jameson, he's a lazy man. He'll do whatever he can to earn an easy dollar. He'll sell his sister to the Madam. Steal from his mother. Bet on a losing hand, hoping to bluff his way to winning the pot. Speak against his cousin for bounty money." He watched Frederick impassively as Frederick watched him in shock. "But that also shows the extent of his greed and that he has no loyalty. To anyone."

"Which makes him a very dangerous man," Frederick whispered.

Bears gave a *click*, either in agreement or to one of the horses.

"Why didn't you tell her brothers about her being moved?" Frederick asked.

Bears gave a grunt of disgust. "Look how they acted when they heard the rumors that a man had slept in her bedroom." He half-chuckled as though recalling the morning when the brothers had stormed into the barn and then dragged the pastor to the livery. "They're as hot-headed as Sorcha but like to deny it." He looked at Frederick. "Besides, if my woman had been treated in such a way, I'd like to be the one to wreak vengeance. I wouldn't want to hear of it from her brothers." He pushed away from the railing and moved toward Sugar. "Keep Sorcha close. You've entered Walter's lair by coming back into town."

Frederick watched as Bears walked away to work with Sugar. Frederick lost track of time as he thought through his conversation with Bears.

A long while later Alistair entered the livery, and he smiled at Frederick.

"How is Sorcha?"

"Irate, but not irrational. She forgave us," Alistair said with a sigh. "Said she'd cook for Cail too, which she doesna have to do."

"It will bring her pleasure to be able to do something for him," Frederick said. "I should go with her to the Merc."

Alistair shook his head. "She's already left. Over half an hour ago."

"What?" Frederick gasped. "You can't let her wander the town on her own. What about Walter?"

Alistair watched him with amusement. "Ye may have better luck tellin' my sister what she can an' canna do as her husband. I pick my battles with her." Alistair slapped Frederick on the back and moved to help Bears.

Frederick waved to them both and bolted from the livery to find his wife, praying that she would find no mischief while she wandered town alone.

～

Sorcha left Jessamine and Ewan's home and walked to one of the two general stores in Bear Grass Springs. After she had learned about Tobias Sutton's affair with Frederick's mother, she had no interest in shopping at his store, called the Mercantile or better known as the Merc. Instead she headed to the other General Store that stood near the Stumble-Out Saloon.

As she entered the store, conversation among the patrons inside ceased. A moment later a quiet murmur began as she perused the shelves. After months on the ranch, she enjoyed staring at the varying items for sale. She wandered the room, attempting to find something to purchase for Frederick as a belated wedding gift, but her concentration was broken as she overheard the women near her gossiping.

"They say she broke her leg, but she walks without a limp," one woman said in a carrying voice.

"If she'd broken her leg as badly as the MacKinnons proclaimed, she'd need a cane or a crutch. She'd be a cripple," her friend proclaimed.

"I imagine all that was bluster to excuse her absence on the ranch. Although I don't know why we'd expect differently when all the women of that family act shamelessly."

When Sorcha approached them to confront them about their hurtful gossip, they turned their backs on her as though she did not exist. Sorcha looked around the store and noticed the other patrons acting in the same manner.

Irate, she marched up to the counter to place her order. However, the man behind the counter shook his head. "I'm sorry, but I don't serve your kind."

"Excuse me?" she asked with a stomp of her foot. "The kind of woman who's married to a successful rancher?" She leaned forward as she glowered at him. "Ye'd better think carefully afore ye offend a man like Frederick Tompkins."

He shook his head, his smile transforming to one of patronizing indulgence. "I imagine you envision yourself married to him. But we know you're not."

Sorcha gaped at him. "Have ye no' spoken to the lawyer, or are ye callin' Warren Clark a liar too?"

At this, the man lost his smug smile and frowned. "He's a respectable man."

"Aye, an' he's the one who married me. To my respectable

husband." She shook her head. "Ye'll be sorry." She spun and stormed out of the store, barreling into a man as she turned to walk toward her brother's house. She stilled as she heard him chuckle and then froze when she heard his voice. "Let me pass," she whispered.

"So you've returned to us at last," Walter Jameson said as he remained in front of her, one hand gripping her basket handle. "I've had to wait a long time for the pleasure of your company."

"Let me pass," she whispered again, her voice quavering.

"Sorcha!" Frederick yelled as he raced toward them. When he stood beside her, he ran a hand over her shoulder, frowning when he felt her quiver. "Let go of my wife's basket, Walter."

Walter sneered. "You don't expect us townsfolk to believe you've actually married her. You had her for months without a need to marry her."

At Sorcha's whimper of dismay, Frederick took a warning step toward Walter, forcing the man backward and dropping his hand from Sorcha's basket. "You will treat her with the respect she is due as my wife. As a respected woman of this town."

"Respect must be earned, Tompkins." Walter tipped his hat at them and spat a wad of tobacco at their feet. "Seems you've finally got something you wouldn't want to lose." His eyes shone with delight as he sauntered away and entered the Stumble-Out.

"Come," Frederick whispered to Sorcha. "Come with me."

"Not to Cailean's," she whispered. "He's enough to worry about."

Frederick looked up and down the town's main street and then nodded. "Come." He gripped her hand and walked with her across the street to the bakery. As the door jingled with their entrance, Leticia walked in from the back room.

"Sorcha!" she exclaimed, running around from behind the counter. "Finally you are home." She hugged her, frowning as she felt her shuddering. "What happened?" she asked as she looked at Frederick.

"I don't know. Is there a space here that is private where we can speak? I remember a back room at one point."

Leticia nodded and led them to the kitchen area. Fidelia washed dishes while Leena cooked. They looked as exhausted as the MacKinnon brothers as they attempted to keep Annabelle's business afloat during her illness. Sorcha nodded to Leena and then held her arms open as Fidelia gave a small screech and flew across the room to pull her into a tight embrace.

"Sorcha!" Fidelia said as she leaned away, her blue eyes sparkling with tears. "I'd begun to fear we'd never see you again."

Sorcha pulled Fidelia close again for another quick hug and then released her. "Ye canna be rid of me that easily," she teased. "'Tis wonderful to see ye again."

Fidelia swiped at her cheek. "The house has been too quiet without you. I listen for your singing and have to remind myself that you're not there." Fidelia looked to Frederick. "I hope you realize what a treasure you have."

He nodded and gave Sorcha a squeeze. "I do. And I would miss her singing more." He kissed her brow. "If I'm not being too rude, we need to discuss something in the back room."

Fidelia nodded and stepped away. Sorcha and Frederick followed Leticia into the back room. Angus slumbered in a crib, but a rocking chair and another chair were near a potbellied stove that sputtered out heat. "Don't forget to talk with us when you're done." She squeezed Sorcha's shoulder as she left them alone.

Sorcha stood, swaying in place for a moment, and then threw herself into Frederick's arms. "Hold me," she stammered.

He held her as she clung to him, her shaking finally subsiding after many long minutes. "What happened?" he asked. "Why would you go into town without me?" He leaned away and bracketed her face with his palms. "You know I would want to be with you. To walk beside you as you faced the criticism and skepticism of the townsfolk about our marriage."

She shook her head. "I wasna thinkin' like that. I've lived here for a few years, and this has been my home, aye? All I thought about was seein' Skye an' Ewan an' Jessamine afore I went to the store to buy food to cook for Cail." She shrugged. "I dinna think about them doubtin' I'd been injured because I dinna walk with a limp."

He frowned. "They think your injury was fabricated? That your time at the ranch was uncalled for because you weren't really hurt?"

"Aye," she whispered. "The women in the store said I was shameless, and the owner refused to wait on me. He only seemed mildly worried when I said ye'd be displeased."

Frederick closed his eyes. "Damn." He sighed. "I refuse to do business with a place that maligns you." He saw her understanding in her gaze. "But I can't imagine giving my uncle any business again. I've enjoyed denying him my patronage since the second store opened." After a moment he whispered, "What did Walter say that upset you?"

"Nothin'." She grabbed his hand when he paced away in frustration. "Nae," she protested, clinging to him. "He only had to speak. To say a word and I kent." She shuddered as she closed her eyes, and a tear trickled down her cheek. "I kent he was the one who hurt me."

Frederick froze. "You recognized his voice?"

"Aye," she said as she met Frederick's gaze. "Aye. An' I was terrified of him. Of the pain I remember feelin'. I … I dinna ken what I would have done had ye no' come. I've never stood frozen like that in my life."

He ran a finger over her cheek. "You did nothing wrong, Sorcha. Nothing. He fed off your fear. Relished in knowing that you recognized him." Frederick pulled her close, breathing in the subtle scent of her as he reassured himself that she was well.

She buried her face in his shoulder. "I want to go home," she whispered against his neck. "I want to go back to the ranch."

He stroked soothing hands over her back. "Of course, my love. But first, the town must see us as a couple. They must see my love for you. Otherwise, they will have a hard time believing we are truly married."

She snuggled into his embrace for a few more moments and then murmured her agreement.

They emerged from the backroom, and he stepped aside as the women enveloped Sorcha in a group hug. She was covered in flour and kisses and was soon swiping at tears again.

"I never thought I'd miss your chattering as much as I have," Fidelia said as she gave Sorcha's arm a squeeze before moving back to the sink. Rather than continue washing, she leaned against the counter and looked at her friend.

Leena gave Sorcha a quick hug. "We've missed you."

Sorcha gave her a searching look. "How are things with Karl? I read a worrisome letter and then not much more news afterward due to the harsh winter." She flushed. "And then I was preoccupied."

Leena laughed. "Karl and I are good, *ja?*" She patted at her stomach. "We'll have a reason to celebrate in the summer."

Sorcha gave a little squeal of delight and pulled Leena close again. "Oh, I'm so happy for you!"

Leticia laughed as she wrapped an arm around Sorcha's shoulders. "Ewan has been busy helping Karl build a larger home for them. Karl wants the perfect home for Leena and the baby."

Leena flushed. "He doesn't understand the perfect home is the one wherever he is."

"A lucky man," Frederick said. He chuckled as the women startled at his voice. "Leticia, we have a favor to ask. May we stay in this small room tonight?"

She smiled. "Of course." She found the spare key to the back door and handed it to Sorcha. "I know Annabelle would be delighted."

Sorcha flushed. "An' do ye think ye could bake us a basket of treats to bring back with us tomorrow as we go home? I ken Irene is at the ranch, but I'd like to bring somethin' special for the grandparents and the men."

Leticia looked at Leena. "What do you think, Leena? You're the baker right now."

Leena smiled. "*Ja,* I can make you a little basket. It won't be ready until midday."

Sorcha gave a relieved smile. "Thank you. It will be a wonderful surprise for them." She gave each woman another hug and then clasped Frederick's hand.

When they stood on the boardwalk, Frederick hitched out his elbow, and she looped her arm through his. He began a slow promenade up and down each side of the boardwalk. With every townsperson they met, he paused and made a point of introducing

Sorcha as his wife. If they were strangers to Frederick, he introduced them both to the townsperson. Soon he had those in town congratulating them on their marriage and commiserating with him about how long it took him to convince her to marry him.

After they had walked up and down the boardwalk, returning to their starting point in front of the bakery, he took a deep breath. "Now to the Merc," he muttered.

She gripped his arm, and they strode into the Merc to face his uncle together. The bell rang as they entered, and Tobias stood behind the counter, watching them enter. Tobias's store was much like the other Mercantile, although it was larger and better stocked. "Hello, Tobias," Sorcha called out as she approached him. She placed her empty basket on the counter. "I've supplies I need for Cailean."

Tobias looked from her to Frederick and then back again. A flicker of emotion glinted in his eyes. "I suppose I should offer my congratulations." His brown hair was more gray, as was his beard, although it remained with splotches of brown. He wore a clean white apron over his cambric shirt and black pants.

"That would be acceptable," Frederick said as he met Tobias's hard stare.

"Congratulations on finally wedding," Tobias said. He waited with raised eyebrow for her order. When she had rattled off a list of foodstuffs for Cailean, he moved around the store to fill her order. When her basket was filled, he tallied up the order.

Sorcha looked through the basket and frowned at a can of sardines. "I did no' order this." She held up the can.

He flushed. "I know. I heard Mrs. Clark talking about how an increase in iron helps after blood loss. I thought those might help Mrs. MacKinnon."

She stared at Tobias, slack jawed for a moment, before nodding her thanks. "Cailean will thank ye for anythin' that might help Anna."

Tobias brushed away her thanks. After they had paid their bill, she and Frederick left, deep in thought.

"I never kent he could be thoughtful," she whispered when they stood on the boardwalk outside the Merc.

"That's how he was when I was a boy," he murmured. "He was caring and considerate. Doing things for my brothers and me without anyone having to ask it of him." He looked at her with mournful eyes. "I hadn't allowed myself to miss him until now." He caressed her hand holding on to his elbow before reaching down to take the basket from her. "Come. Let's help your brother, and then we'll return home tomorrow."

~

Sorcha squeezed Frederick's arm, and he remained in the kitchen with Fidelia and Bears as she rose to follow Cailean. "Cail," she whispered as he entered the living area. "How are ye?"

He looked at her in confusion and then shrugged. "You should worry about Belle, not me." He ran a hand through his thick brown hair, making it stand on end. After a minute, he collapsed onto the settee, a deep sigh escaping.

"Of course I worry about ye." She sat beside him, taking his hand. "Ye were forced to live through yer worst fear again."

He nodded, his eyes closed, as his head rested against the back of the settee. "I wanted that bairn, Sorcha. I want a son who I can pass all this down to. Another daughter so that Skye can have a best friend like I have with Alistair, aye?" His eyes sparkled with torment. "But, when I saw Belle, nearly bleeding to death again, none of that mattered. Nothing but Belle."

Sorcha tugged him to her so she could embrace him. "I'm so sorry, Cail," she whispered as he shuddered in her arms, mourning what he'd lost. "I can't imagine …"

"Ye can no'," he whispered. "Ye will never ken what it does to a man to stand by helpless as he watches the woman he loves fight for her life, kennin' there is nothin' he can do to help. Kennin' that, if she dies, his life ends too." He swiped at his face as he leaned away and met her gaze. "Dinna be too harsh on yer man, for he loves as we do. With a madness that is all-consuming."

Sorcha took a deep stuttering breath. "We are no' speakin' about me an' my marriage."

Cailean cut her off with a shake of his head, his voice thick with emotion as he stared at his baby sister. "We should. I wish I'd been there, Sorch. To walk ye down the aisle. To tell ye how proud I was of ye and the man ye'd chosen on yer wedding day. To give a blessing to ye both." He ran a hand over her hair and cupped her cheek. "I wish ye every joy ye ever dreamed of while singing yer songs and staring at the lochs on Skye. I wish for yer days to be filled with happiness, laughter and love. I pray ye never ken sorrow." He kissed her brow. "Learn to forgive as readily as ye love, Sorcha. For, in marriage, ye need both in equal measure."

Sorcha nodded, her eyes bright with tears at receiving Cailean's blessing. "Thank ye, Cail."

He nodded. "I know Belle wrote ye. She wanted to write again when we heard from Helen and Warren that ye'd wed. But then ..." His gaze shadowed with the memory of nearly losing her. He took a deep breath to calm himself, and his Scottish accent faded. "Forgive me for wanting you to have time with your husband before coming to town. I knew you'd come the minute you heard."

Sorcha gripped her hands together. "It wasn't because you didn't want me here?"

"Don't be daft," he rasped. "We'll always want you here. And even though the ranch isn't far from town, it's still too far for my liking." He smiled. "Although I wouldn't like having you live again with us and having your husband here. 'Twould be awkward, aye?"

Sorcha bit her lip. "We may have to," she whispered. "We may lose the ranch after the horrible winter. Too many cattle have died."

Cailean sat as though poleaxed. "How could that happen? You have the most profitable ranch in the area."

She shrugged. "We'll ken more after the roundup. But I ken Frederick worries."

Her brother gripped her shoulder. "Never fret, Sorch. You'll always have a place to go, and Frederick can work with us. He's a master with horses and rivals Bears." Cailean glowered. "But there must be a way to save your ranch."

"If there is, he'll find it," she whispered. "But he's losing hope."

At the commotion in the doorway, they turned to see Jessamine entering with Skye. Cailean leaped to his feet and reached for his daughter. "My darling," he whispered as he held her to him, nuzzling the top of her head. "How you've grown in a day."

Skye giggled and batted at his cheeks before kissing him. "Da!" she said, earning a chuckle from Sorcha.

Sorcha saw Cailean duck his head, hiding tears at his daughter's word.

"Come, love. Let's visit Mama," Cailean said as he tickled his daughter's belly. He looked at his sister and then Jessamine, before walking upstairs with his daughter to seek out his wife.

Jessamine joined Sorcha in the parlor. "How is he?" she asked.

Sorcha shrugged. "Mournin' what he's lost but thankful for what he still has."

"Sensible man," Jessamine said as she sat with a sigh of relief. "I never realized how much a child would exhaust me." She shared a chuckle with Sorcha as the two of them sat in companionable silence.

F rederick watched Sorcha leave the kitchen to speak with Cailean and had to fight an instinctive desire to accompany her. He stilled when he saw Bears studying him. The kitchen was warm with the stove pumping out heat, and he held a cup of coffee between his hands. Fidelia left to check on Annabelle.

"You are wise to give her time with her brother. There are still hurts that must be healed," Bears said. He sat back and sipped at his coffee when Ewan burst into the room.

"I never kent it would stay as cool as it has," he grumbled and shivered. After taking out a cup, he poured himself some coffee and sat with Bears and Frederick. "Where's Sorcha?"

"Talking with Cailean." Frederick nodded with his head to the room on the other side of the hallway. "Sorcha ran into Walter today in town." He nodded as Ewan became more alert, and Bears focused on him. "She recognized his voice."

Ewan flushed red, and Bears nodded.

Frederick met Ewan's irate gaze. "I have no doubt that it was Walter who hurt Sorcha."

Bears gave a grunt. "Unfortunately that proves nothing."

"Nae, but we ken the truth," Ewan said as he glared into his black coffee. "An' we ken our adversary." He shook his head in frustration. "I try to keep an eye on him, but he seems to disappear for days at a time."

Bears frowned at Ewan's words. "Where would he go? He hates living outside of town."

Frederick shook his head. "I don't know, although we did have a straggler on the ranch a few months ago. I've asked the men to keep watch for Walter, but none who know him have reported seeing him. I don't have any new men working the ranch, but not all of my men know who Walter is." He tapped his fingers on the tabletop. "What do you think, Bears?"

His brown-black eyes were unreadable. "I fear there is little to do until he acts again. We have no proof it was Walter who attacked Sorcha in November. She thinks she recognizes his voice, but that's no proof he did anything."

Frederick sighed with frustration. "I know."

"Jessie's forbidden me from attackin' the man. Or playin' poker with the man an' beggarin' him." Ewan shook his head in frustration.

"But you haven't played poker since you won Fidelia," Bears said, unable to hide the shock in his voice.

"I'd do what I must to ensure Sorcha was safe." Ewan glowered at the two men.

Frederick pointed at his brother-in-law. "You remember that Walter is mine to deal with."

Bears sighed as he stared at the two men glaring at each other. "All that matters is that Sorcha is safe. Make that your focus."

∾

Sorcha pulled out the key Leticia had given her and fit it in the lock to the back door of the bakery. As she and Frederick stepped inside, she breathed deeply of the sweet scents permeating the air. "Heaven," she whispered.

Her husband chuckled behind her, closing and locking the door. His hands snaked around her middle, pulling her against him. "*This* is heaven," he whispered. "You, all to myself, with no one nearby, for an entire evening." He kissed the side of her neck as she shivered. "No concern for a foaling mare." He felt her chuckle as their lovemaking had been interrupted a few weeks ago as Biscuit had her foal. "No concern about my grandparents."

She gasped as his hand began to roam. "Let's start the fire, or we'll be cold tonight."

He kissed her neck again and released her to follow her into the back room. Colder than the main kitchen area, he shivered before kneeling in front of the potbellied stove to light a fire. "This will only take a few minutes," he said, while she lit a lamp on the wall.

She turned to look at him with a seductive smile. Her fingers played with the buttons on the front of her dress. "Come warm me, husband," she said as she slipped a button loose.

He strode to her, pushing aside her hands as he took over freeing her from her dress. "It's never enough," he whispered. "Every time I'm with you, I want you more than the last time." He kissed her passionately, backing the two of them toward the freshly made bed.

He shivered as Sorcha fought with his buttons, her fingers tickling his chest as she tugged him from his clothes. He gasped when she kissed his chest and ran her hands over his muscles and then around to his back. "I love how you touch me. How you show me you want me."

"Never doubt I want ye as much as ye want me," she whispered as she met his ardent gaze. "Ye've taught me there is no shame in desirin' my husband."

He smiled and kissed her. "Good. For I have no shame in wanting you." After stripping her of all her clothes, he hitched her up onto the bed and crawled over her, losing himself to her touch and their shared passion.

~

He held Sorcha to his chest, his fingers playing in her long hair. He kissed her forehead and smiled as she wriggled to get closer to him. "I've heard this is a place used as refuge for women fleeing the men in their lives."

Sorcha giggled. "'Tis true that's how it's been used in the past." She looked up at him, her smile radiant as she met his contented gaze. "I'm glad I'm no' fleein' ye."

He caressed her cheek. "So am I." He sighed as she settled again on his chest. "I wish we could stay here longer."

"I dinna," Sorcha whispered. "I dinna miss livin' in town."

He ran a soothing hand over her shoulders and back. "You know I don't care what they said about you, right? That I know it was said out of spite and jealousy?" He met her startled gaze. "I'd bet hard-earned money, which I don't have right now, that the majority of those women have daughters who they wanted me to marry. And they were angry I foiled their plans."

"Doesna give them the right to treat me like they did," Sorcha said. "I never kent I'd feel so ... dirty."

He urged her to meet his gaze. "Please don't allow those women, or anyone, to sully what we have." His gaze filled with a passionate intensity. "I would hate for you to believe you needed to act in a proper manner and then lose this passion we have between us."

She shook her head. "I'm no' good at actin' proper. An' I dinna want things to change between us, Frederick."

He smiled. "Good." After a deep breath, he whispered, "There is something I must tell you. I promised to never keep anything from you, and I will not break that vow." He waited as she propped herself on his chest and continued to stare at him. "I spoke with Bears today. About the day you were injured."

"Aye? I dinna think there was much more to be said about that day."

He shook his head. "In that you are wrong. Bears is observant. It's what makes him a good trapper. A good hunter. He sees things that everyone else overlooks." Frederick paused a moment. "That day, all I focused on was you. Your injury. And fighting my panic that you were hurt." He flushed. "I already loved you."

She stroked her fingers over his cheek and stubble. "Oh, love."

"But Bears wasn't hindered by deep emotions, no matter how much he worried about you. He saw that you had been moved. That you hadn't fallen where we found you." He gripped her hand as she shuddered. "You'd been thrown from your horse farther up the trail."

"Why move me? It makes no sense," Sorcha whispered. "I dinna remember any of it."

"How could you? The pain of being moved on a pallet caused you to faint. Being carried on a horse would have been so much worse." He ran a finger over her cheek. "We don't understand any of it, but it's something we need to figure out."

She shuddered and lay down once more against his chest. "I want to go home," she whispered.

He kissed the top of her head. "We will." He smiled as she snuggled into him.

"Why are ye relieved?" she asked as she felt him relax under her.

He stroked a hand over her back. "I worried you'd see your family and remember how much you missed them. That you'd realize you'd rather be here with them than on the ranch. With me."

She pushed herself up and cupped his cheek. "Oh, Frederick. Nae." She shook her head as she blinked away tears. "I want this life we are buildin'. I willna lie to ye an' say I dinna miss my family. I do. An' I hope we can visit town often. But I dinna want to live here. I want to live on the ranch. With ye."

He wrapped his arms around her and buried his face in her hair. "Thank you." He held her for many minutes until they tumbled into sleep.

~

Sorcha giggled, looking over her shoulder at Frederick as she walked out the front door to the bakery. She gasped as she ran into someone, jerking backward. "I beg yer pardon."

"As you should," Mrs. Jameson snapped. "I should have known that this would be how you'd act. Running off and acting like a damsel in distress. Couldn't convince a man to marry you unless he believed you weren't the feisty beast we all know you to be."

"I'd watch your tongue if I were you," Frederick snapped as he stepped behind Sorcha, placing a hand on his wife's quivering shoulder. "I won't have as much clemency as Mr. Johansen for your defamation of his wife's good character. I'll have no regrets over beggaring a woman like you."

Mrs. Jameson stood as tall as her small frame allowed, her thin shoulders shaking with indignation in the black dress and jacket she wore. "How dare you threaten me! I'm a respectable woman."

"Simply sayin' the words doesna make it fact," Sorcha said. "Yer actions must match what ye say."

Mrs. Jameson leaned forward with a satisfied gleam in her eyes. "Yes, they must. Just as everyone here knows what you were doing the many months you were on that ranch."

"Aye, I was recoverin' from the accident yer son caused." Sorcha glared at Mrs. Jameson, her cheeks red and her blue eyes flashing with dislike. "Yer daughter had to risk her own welfare a few times to visit me an' teach me exercises so I wouldna walk with a limp. She kent I wouldna want to use a cane or be crippled my whole life."

"A likely story," Mrs. Jameson said with a snort and roll of her eyes. "Everyone knows my daughter has limited skills."

Frederick shook his head. "How can you speak of your daughter in such a manner? What I know is that she is highly esteemed for her skills as a healer. And that anyone who doubts her abilities is a fool."

Mrs. Jameson thrust her shoulders back and tilted her head up in defiance. "You have no right to say such disparaging things about my

Walter. If you only knew how he's suffered. How hard he's had to work to survive." She swiped at her tear.

Sorcha gaped at her and shook her head as though momentarily struck dumb.

"I fear few in town share your sentiments," Frederick said in a low voice filled with warning. "We know what Walter is and what he attempted to do. If he comes on my land again, I have every right to shoot him on sight." He watched Mrs. Jameson pale. "Feel free to share that news with him."

He nodded at her in a mockery of deference and grabbed Sorcha's hand. "Good day. And thank you for your congratulations on our marriage." The last sentence he said loudly, so the loitering townsfolk could overhear. He winked at Sorcha as they walked hand in hand to Cailean's house for a brief visit before heading home to the ranch.

I rene poked her head into Sorcha's workroom, pausing as she listened to Sorcha sing in Gaelic. "What is your song about?"

"Losing love and then refindin' it," Sorcha said with a smile. "Please, come join me."

Irene wandered in, her gaze moving over the homey room. "I can't believe this is the same room we used as our junk room," she marveled. "What did Frederick do with all the stuff?"

"I think he found a spare room in the barn," Sorcha said with a giggle. "He was courtin' me at the time an' desperate to prove he was a worthy man to marry." She shared a smile with his grandmother. "I already kent it, of course, but I enjoyed the courtship."

Irene gave a huff as she sank into a comfortable chair. "Courtship shouldn't end simply because you've married."

The younger woman smiled at Irene. "Ye an' Harold are an example to us all."

Irene laughed. "Oh, don't think there aren't days I don't want to bash him over the head with one of my frying pans!" She sighed as she settled into her chair. "But I couldn't imagine this life without him.

He's my best friend, and he knows how to calm me when I get excited."

Sorcha stared at Irene in confusion. The day was chilly for late April, and a small potbellied stove pumped heat into the room. The stove was a new addition to the room, and it sat on bricks in one corner to prevent starting a fire on the wooden floor. "What had ye riled in town?"

Irene gave her an exasperated look. "How about how they were discussing my grandson and the woman he loves with no respect or regard for my feelings? Too many seemed to find joy in disparaging you both."

"They were only too happy to continue to speak poorly of me when they saw me in town a few days ago," Sorcha said. "Ye ken I worked hard with Helen to strengthen my leg?" At Irene's frown, Sorcha said, "Many claim I faked a broken leg to remain here to act like a Boudoir Beauty."

Irene shook her head. "They have the common sense of a herd of sheep. And that isn't saying much. If anyone bothered to speak to the doctor, they'd know the truth. The only problem is, after that last charlatan was run from town, too few have any faith in doctors. It'll take time for him to build up his reputation and regard."

Sorcha set aside her spinning wheel and focused on Irene. "We saw yer nephew," she whispered. "He seemed different than afore."

"What did you see when you looked at my nephew?" Irene asked.

Sorcha flushed. "Ye may call me daft, but I saw a man full of regret. No' a man gloatin' over Frederick havin' to shop in his store because his wife had been poorly treated at the other mercantile."

Irene nodded. "You've an ability to see to the heart of the matter, Sorcha. I appreciate that in you. Do you know, Tobias used to be my favorite? He was kind and funny and generous. Not the mean, miserly, bitter man he is now. Before he paid a fool's ransom for his passion, he was well loved by all."

"An' now he's loved by none," Sorcha whispered. "I think Frederick misses him. Or he misses what was."

Irene smiled sadly. "We always miss what was lost. And Frederick remembers with great fondness his outings with Tobias. He always showed Frederick great patience and encouraged him with his horses." Irene took a deep breath. "When his mother ran away, Frederick lost three people he loved that day. His mother. His uncle Tobias. And his father. For his father was never the same again."

Sorcha sniffed and swiped at her cheek. "How sad. Do ye think he could reconcile with Tobias?"

The older woman shook her head. "I doubt it. Too much time has passed, and too much bitterness lies on both sides." Her gaze was distant for a few moments. "Don't allow your anger and pain to keep you separated from someone you love, even if you have right on your side. If too much time passes, you may well find it too hard to reconcile and that more was lost than you ever thought possible."

CHAPTER 10

O n the first morning of the belated spring roundup, Dixon, Slims and Frederick rode out in the early light with the newly hired men, looking for cattle and calves in a large expanse of rangeland far from the ranch house. Dalton had headed out the day before to set up a small camp and to get the branding irons hot. Cowboys from the two neighboring ranches would join them, and they'd help each other brand the calves with the correct mark.

Although the days were longer and warmer, a distinctive chill remained to the air, and it never felt warm until midafternoon, even with the sun shining. Streams flowed at capacity to overflowing with the runoff from the snowmelt on the mountains, and the muddy conditions impeded easy travel in a wagon. Trees had begun to bud, although their limbs remained skeletal.

Sorcha, Harold and Irene rode in the chuck wagon, driven by Harold, slowly following the rapidly disappearing silhouettes of the men on horseback. Sorcha rocked to the slow sway of the wagon and looked out at the vast expanse of land. "Ye own all of this?" Green shoots of fresh grass sprouted up as the sun shone down. The verdant hills gleamed in the distance on one side with the snowcapped majestic mountains on the other. Willows and cottonwoods had begun to leaf out in a nearby creek bed.

Irene smiled. "Yes." Her voice rang with pride. "Much of it we proved up on, but then we bought other's claims as they gave up and moved on to other areas."

Sorcha shook her head. "I canna imagine givin' this up."

Harold gave a grunt of satisfaction at her words. "Well, it takes a lot of work to keep a cattle ranch goin'. And more than the 160 acres you could prove up on with a single claim."

Sorcha looked at him in confusion.

"The Homestead Act of 1862 allowed men and women to own a 160-acre parcel of land as long as they proved up on it," Harold explained. "They had to show improvements to the land. It's why we have the ranch house in the middle of our land rather than by the hills, which would have given us some protection from the winter storms. The main house is on one parcel. The foreman's house is on another parcel, and yet another parcel is not far from the bunkhouse. We had the parcels drawn up so the three would meet there."

Irene laughed. "It was very irregular, and the man drawing up the deeds was put out. He liked things done in a linear fashion, with blocks of land of similar dimensions. But we were the first ones here, so he agreed to the oddly shaped parcels."

Sorcha looked at one and then to the other. "I ken there's more to the story than ye're tellin' me."

Harold shrugged. "There's always more to any story." He winked at her. "And never discount the value of a good bottle of whiskey."

Sorcha laughed. "Who was the third?" At their blank expression, she asked, "I ken ye were one claim, an' yer son must have been the other. Who was the third?"

The couple shared a long look, and then Irene sighed. "Tobias was the third. He lived on the ranch for years and had his own place."

"Is he no' part owner?"

Harold's expression clouded, and he shook his head. "We bought him out. He'll never be welcome on the ranch again."

Irene rested a soothing hand on her husband's arm. "We're friendly to him in town. As much as we can be. But we will not have him on the ranch, bothering our boys."

"Is that how he had money to start his store?" Sorcha asked.

"Yes," Irene said. "He used the money from the sale of his part of the ranch to start the mercantile. And has resented his loss ever since."

Sorcha frowned as she stared at the beautiful scenery, her mind awhirl and filled with questions. However, she sensed that Harold and Irene had no interest in talking any further about their nephew. "What happens at a roundup?"

"They lasso the calves and see which cow bellyaches the loudest to determine which one is the mother. That way, they can tell which ranch can claim the calf and which brand to use. It's hard, sweaty work," Harold said.

"What happens if there is no mama cow?"

"The unclaimed calves will be kept aside, and they'll be auctioned off to the ranches doing the roundup. Some won't want more cattle as they'll have enough. Others will want as many as they can get."

"Who gets the money?" Sorcha asked.

"The ranchers divide it among themselves," Harold said. "It's the best system that's been worked out so far."

"Our role is to keep the men fed. Yours is to keep Frederick from fretting too much," Irene said with an affectionate smile.

Sorcha nodded and remained lost in thought as they made their way to the first day's roundup. When they arrived, the men had formed a large circle with their horses that looked like an impromptu corral. Inside were the cattle in the process of being culled. Cattle lowed and tried to escape but were thwarted by the experienced cowboys.

"They're so thin," Sorcha whispered as she looked at the emaciated cattle.

Harold's jaw tightened as he nodded. "Yes, and there's far too few of them." He pulled the wagon up next to another chuck wagon and helped Irene and Sorcha down before he chatted with the other Cookie.

Sorcha grimaced and spun as a calf bleated as it was roped and then branded. She gripped her hands together until the cowboy released the calf. The calf leaped to its feet, shaking out its hind legs and ran to its mother.

"How long does it take to brand them all?" she whispered as the same sequence of events was repeated again and then again.

"Generally all day." Irene shook her head in consternation. "Looks like we could be done here by noon today."

"Are these all the cattle on the ranch?" Sorcha asked in a barely audible voice.

"No, we'll move around to three or four other sites and repeat the same process. But the first day is an indicator of how well the roundup will go." She nodded to her grandson who sat glowering at the small herd from his saddle.

Harold joined them. "At a glance, I'd say we're at least 50 percent short this year."

Sorcha blanched and shook her head. "I ken that is no' normal. What do ye usually lose?"

Harold pushed his hat back as he stared at the scene playing out in front of him as though he were in a bad dream. "Oh, 10 or 15 percent. Maybe 20. Never this much."

Sorcha looked to her husband as though willing him to look at her. However, he remained focused on his job. "I dinna ken how to soothe him."

"Your presence will help him," Irene said as she patted Sorcha's arm.

⁓

Due to the small herd they had found to round up for the first day, they moved to their second spot early in the afternoon to prepare for the second day. Dalton packed up and moved the branding equipment while Irene and Harold packed up the chuck wagon. That evening, Frederick stood away from the camp, staring at the moon as a cool breeze blew over him, and listened to the cattle low. He hoped for a better second day, but the anxiety gnawing at his stomach would not ease.

He tensed at a soft hand on his shoulder and then relaxed. "Sorcha," he whispered. "You should be in bed."

"I find I canna sleep without my husband beside me," she murmured, wrapping her arms around his belly and heating his back with her front. She rested her cheek on his back. "Let me ease ye, husband."

He trembled and shook his head. "I'm wretched company, my love."

She ran her hands over his chest and smiled against his back. "I ken. Yer grandparents explained yer fears. But ye must have hope that tomorrow and the following days will be better, aye? Ye canna give up hope."

He grabbed her hands and eased from her hold, turning to pull her tight against him, his arms wrapped around her as tightly as hers had been around him. "I don't know what to do."

Her fingers clenched into his back. "I ken. No one kens what to do, Frederick. All ye can do is yer best." She traced a pattern over his back and whispered. "Come to bed, my love. Take comfort in what we have."

He groaned and kissed her. "Yes." He backed away and smiled, his first smile of the day. "I'm glad you insisted our tent be far from the others." His smile broadened as he felt her cheeks flush under his fingers, and he bent his head to kiss her.

Three days later Frederick sat in his office with the door shut. He stared at the bottle of whiskey his grandfather had set on the corner of his desk with the added caution, "You'll feel better for a moment, but then you'll only multiply your worries." Frederick sat with his head in his hands as he thought about the roundup.

They had brought in one-third of the number of cattle that had been set loose onto the prairie the previous fall. He shuddered as he had expected to lose half. He had found a way for the ranch to survive with that staggering a loss. But he could not conceive of survival with only one-third of the herd.

They were emaciated, bare-boned, and many remained near death as they docilely followed the movement of him and his men. No energetic cattle made a mad dash to escape. They seemed to move with the hope they were being led to a greener pasture.

He rubbed at his head as he envisioned the mountain pasture they could move the cattle to in a few months. However, before he could contemplate moving the cattle there, he had to wait for the snow to melt at the higher elevations. He stilled as he heard the door handle on his office rattle, and he ignored Sorcha calling to him as he had locked the door. He wanted no company this evening.

As he contemplated the future of the ranch, he thought about his horses. He had yet to sell many of them, but he knew he could ask a fair price for them. He had always turned down nearby ranchers' offers to buy his horses, but now Frederick knew he needed to sell some of them. With that in mind, he made a list of his stock and which ones he could bear to part with. Of the twenty-three horses, only six were listed as possible sales, and even those he had little interest in selling.

"Sentimental fool," he muttered about himself. He rose, deciding to walk the ranch to calm his emotions rather than opening the whiskey and stumbled as he strode out his office door. Sorcha had sat in front of his door, and he'd tripped over her. "Why in God's name are you down there?"

She glared at him, rubbing at the bruised flesh of her thigh that he had kicked. "Ye would no' answer yer door. I ken ye should no' be alone tonight." She shrugged. "I decided to wait ye out."

He sighed and put his hands on his hips. "Sorcha, go to bed. I need …"

"Ye need to cease yer ruminations," she said as she rose, gasping her thanks as he held her steady as her leg failed her for a moment. "Ye need to remember all that ye do have, no' all that ye dinna."

He glared at her. "And I suppose that means you? That I should

ignore all that is going on around me and drop to my knees in gratitude because you're a part of my life?" He glared at her. "How in God's
name am I to care for a wife when I can't even care for myself? I
should never have married you." He paled as he saw how his words
injured her. "Sorcha ..."

"Nae," she rasped. "'Twas silly of me to think I could comfort ye."
She pushed past him and rushed from the room to the hallway and
stairs at the back of the house. He waited a moment, listening for her
in their bedroom above the parlor, but he didn't hear her footsteps.
He stilled, forcing himself to quiet his anger and fear, and calmed.
When he still did not hear her after a few moments, he followed her.

He looked in her old room, but it remained vacant. Her new workroom sat in ready for her presence tomorrow. He took the stairs two
at a time, and, when he entered their bedroom, he knew instinctively
that she was not in it. "Where did you go?" he asked.

He spun on his heel and went downstairs. At the back of the hall
was a door rarely used to go outside, and he pushed it open. It creaked
with the motion and clanged shut when he let it go. His gaze searched
for Sorcha, but he did not find her. "Sorcha!" he called, but a soft
breeze was his only reply. After racing from the root cellar to the
chicken coop to his barn, he shook with fear. "Where did you go?"

He returned to the house and the room he shared with her, hoping
she had rejoined him, but the room remained empty. He sat on the
edge of the bed, staring at the door, waiting for her to return.

❧

Sorcha raced from the room, determined to seek out a place
where he would not find her. She grabbed a blanket from her
workroom and eased out the back door, knowing that it often clanged
shut. After she closed it softly, she moved to the abandoned garden
tool shed that she had been cleaning out in preparation for her flower
garden. She eased inside and pulled the blanket around her.

Curling onto her side, she sobbed. The days of the roundup had
been difficult. She had known the numbers of cattle gathered were

low and that the men's spirits continually dropped as each day they found fewer and fewer living cattle. Frederick had sought comfort in her arms each night, and she had relished her ability to ease some of his torment. However, tonight he had not wanted her comfort. He had wanted only to cause her pain rather than to accept her succor.

She dropped her hand to her waist, her sobs intensifying as she cradled the baby she knew she carried. The baby she feared he would not want. Not when his regret at marrying her had been so clearly expressed. "Oh, what am I to do?" she whispered.

She fell into an exhausted sleep, failing to hear him calling her name.

~

The following morning, Sorcha woke as the rooster crowed before the break of dawn. She jerked awake, pulling the blanket tightly around her as she had no recollection of where she was. After a moment the ache returned at the memory of Frederick's words, her flight from the house and sobbing herself to sleep. She rose, her body sore and her heart broken, emerging from the small hut near the woodshed.

She stumbled across the uneven ground in the darkness and into the house through the back door. She entered her workroom and sat at her spinning wheel, her hands and feet working unconsciously. After a few hours, she heard the house wake up. Harold's and Irene's voices. Frederick's panicked voice. She continued to work without calling out to anyone.

Harold poked his head into her room and glared at her. "Do you have any idea what you've done to him?" He yelled for Frederick, and his steps could be heard pounding down the stairs.

"Sorcha!" Frederick said as he came into her room. He stilled at her vacant stare, void of any emotion. "Where have you been?"

"I fell asleep outside," she said as she turned her focus to her spinning wheel. "I hadna thought ye'd be concerned."

Frederick looked at his grandfather and nodded for him to leave them alone. Irene's voice could be heard in the hallway, and Harold moved to intercept her to allow Frederick and Sorcha time alone.

"Didn't you hear me calling for you last night?" he asked. "I ... I sat awake all night, worried about you."

She flit her gaze to him a moment before concentrating again on her activities. "I found shelter. I was plenty comfortable."

He growled as he came closer, ripping the wheel from her and pushing it aside. He maintained enough restraint that he did not throw it and turn it into kindling as he was inclined to do. He ignored her moan of distress as he sank to his haunches in front of her, clasped her face between his strong hands and forced her to look at him. His voice shattered with regret when she closed her eyes. "Don't shut me out. Please, love, don't."

She shook her head. "I'm no' doin' anythin' different than ye did yesterday," she whispered, her voice thickened.

"You have a temper," he said. "You know what it is to say something you don't mean. To regret it the instant you say it."

A tear coursed down her cheek. "That is no' something you say to your wife. That ye wish ye had never married me."

"I said no such thing!" His hold on her strengthened as she struggled to free herself. "I said I should never have married you." He swallowed. "And that is very different."

"I dinna understand ye," she said in a weary voice. "An' I find I'm tired of our battle of words." More tears slipped down her cheeks. "I thought we were past them by now."

"We've had our first fight as husband and wife," he entreated. "Forgive me."

She shook her head. "I canna, Frederick. I canna. Because ye did no' fight fair." She opened her eyes, and he saw the devastation and grief in her gaze. "Ye told me ye dinna want me last night. I can no' fight against that fear."

She pushed past him and left the room, leaving him on his knees.

Harold pushed open the door to the office and came to an abrupt halt. Rather than his grandson sitting with his head in his hands, staring vacantly as though his world had ended, he saw his son. His only child. His heir who had never recovered from the loss of his wife. Harold blinked and focused again, finding Frederick. After shutting the door behind him, Harold moved to sit so he faced Frederick without the desk between them.

"So you lost your temper," Harold said as he sat.

"I lost much more than my temper." Frederick rubbed at his eyes. "I lost Sorcha. I lost what we were building together."

"Hogwash. You had your first real fight. Not that namby-pamby fighting you did before your marriage that was to conceal your attraction to each other." He met his grandson's startled gaze.

"I hurt her," Frederick whispered and then closed his eyes as he admitted, "and I wanted to. I wanted her to hurt like I was hurting."

Harold gripped his arm. "I never raised you to be a fool, boy, but that's exactly what you've been. You had bad teachers in your parents, but I expect you to look to your grandmother and me." He met his grandson's gaze filled with shame. "We fight. We yell. But we never go for the soft underbelly. We never intentionally hurt each other."

"How do I make it better?" A tear tracked down one cheek. "Did you see how she looked at me?" He saw acknowledgment in his grandfather's gaze but still had to say the words. "Her gaze was as filled with disdain as any gaze my mother had for my father."

"Apologize—and mean it. Show her that you'll never act like that again. It will take time, but she'll forgive you." Harold sighed. "You hurt her. She'll take time to get over her hurt. But don't give her too much time. You don't want to allow hurts to fester because then they can become a poison between you."

CHAPTER 11

By the last week of May, Harold and Irene had left the ranch, and Jessamine and Ewan were to make a visit. The lilac bushes on either side of the house were just coming into bloom, and the tulips Irene had planted years ago in beds in front of the house were in full color. A warm breeze blew large puffy clouds across a light-blue sky. Robins built nests, while sparrows swooped overhead, and a meadowlark serenaded from the nearby prairie.

Nearby the creek gurgled with freshly melted snow from the mountains, and the prairie grass grew tall and plentiful. The days lengthened as the memory of the harsh winter faded with the arrival of true spring weather. Sorcha cooked in the kitchen of the ranch house with a window open, preparing a meal for her brother and sister-in-law as she awaited their arrival. When she heard the wagon on the drive, she leaped to her feet and ran out the door.

"Ewan! Jessamine!" she called out, waving madly at them. She saw Frederick's graceful lope as he walked from the barn, but Sorcha ignored him as she had done since that dreadful night of their fight two weeks ago. She waited until the wagon had come to a halt before rushing to its side. Ewan leaped down, grabbing her in a fierce hug, and then he helped Jessamine down. She immediately pulled Sorcha in a hug, although Jessamine frowned when she looked closely at Sorcha's face.

After a moment they exchanged greetings with Frederick, who moved to the barn with Ewan, while Jessamine and Sorcha walked into the main house. Sorcha brought her to the bright kitchen where she had been interrupted in chopping carrots.

Jessamine laughed. "I can't believe you are cooking for all your husband's men."

Sorcha shook her head. "Nae, he hired a cook last week. They now get their meals in the bunkhouse. I prepare meals for Frederick and me and our guests. On the nights I dinna want to cook, Cookie will send over food for us too."

Jessamine smiled. "That is a nice luxury. I wish I had someone willing to cook for me." Her teasing smile faded as she saw Sorcha's attempt at forced joviality. "What's wrong? I could tell something had happened the moment I saw you."

Sorcha finished chopping the carrots and added them to the stew pot. "No' here," she whispered. Once the stew simmered, she led Jessamine to her private sitting room toward the back of the house.

"This is quite a home you have," she remarked. "I thought Cailean's home was large, but this is impressive."

Sorcha shrugged. "They did well for years with the ranch, an' many of them lived here at that time. They needed a large home. Now it seems odd with only the two of us in it." She shut the door behind them and motioned for Jessamine to choose a chair.

"Frederick had his men clear this room and make it mine when he was courtin' me," she whispered as her throat clogged with tears. "When he did no' regret marryin' me."

"What?" Jessamine gasped. "I can't believe the man I saw in town last month has any regrets in marrying you. He was devoted and smitten."

"The cattle died, J.P.," Sorcha said, reverting to Jessamine's nick-name before she married Ewan. "They needed to find half their cattle in the roundup to have a hope of survivin' the last winter. They found one-third instead." She sniffed. "Frederick is devastated. Doesna want to lose the ranch. His horses. Doesna want to be considered a failure." She took a deep breath. "An' he regrets takin' on the responsibility of a wife."

Jessamine was quiet for a long moment. "If he said such a thing, I know he must have said it in anger. A man is only that stupid when he is riled."

Sorcha failed to smile. "Aye, he was angry. Angry because I wanted to comfort him." Tears seeped out. "But I dinna ken what to do. And I dinna want to stay in a marriage filled with regret."

Jessamine leaned forward and took Sorcha's hand. Sincerity lit her cognac-colored eyes. "The only regret he has is in hurting you. In speaking a lie in anger rather than a truth."

"But to say it at all means he must have thought it. Must believe it a little bit," Sorcha argued.

Jessamine shook her head. "Do you want to push him away? Do you want him to resent you?" She met her sister-in-law's shattered gaze. "Not because what he said was true but because of your inability to forgive him?" She took a deep breath. "I said horrible things to your brother. Pushed him away. Lashed out in my fear. And then I had to hope his love for me was stronger than his anger at me. Don't make the same mistake, Sorcha. Talk with him."

She sniffed. "He used the one fear I have no defense against," she whispered. "I am terrified of being unwanted."

Jessamine squeezed her sister-in-law's hand. "Then tell him that. He can't change and make sure he never says something so thoughtless again unless you tell him and explain how he hurt you." As a knock sounded, she looked to the door. "Yes?"

Frederick's voice was heard through the wood. "The stew's bubbling over on the stove."

"Dammit," Sorcha muttered, rising. She faltered as she hopped up quickly, grabbing on to Jessamine a moment before she fainted.

"Frederick!" Jessamine yelled. A few seconds later the door burst open, and Frederick moved to his prostrate wife.

"What happened?" he asked as he ran his hands over her. "What did you do to her?" He flinched as Jessamine hit him on his shoulder.

"I didn't do anything to her. We talked, and then she stood up quickly to attend the stew, and she fainted." She ran a hand over Sorcha's clammy forehead. "I wonder if she's coming down with an illness."

Frederick looked to Ewan in the doorway. "Can you bring a wet cloth?" Ewan nodded and was gone. "Sorcha, come on, love. Wake up," he coaxed. He breathed a sigh of relief when she stirred. "How do you feel?" he asked as he ran a hand over her head. He moved so that her head was pillowed on his lap. "What can I do for you?"

She struggled to rise but was held firmly in place by Frederick. When a wave of nausea hit, she closed her eyes and breathed deeply. After a few moments she opened her eyes and whispered, "I dinna feel well. I should lie down." Frederick looked into her eyes, and she saw concern, love and despair mingled together in his gaze. "Let me rise, Frederick."

He nodded and helped her to stand. By the time Ewan returned with the cloth and a pitcher of water, Frederick and Jessamine were helping Sorcha upstairs. She looked at her brother. "I'm sorry to miss yer first dinner at the ranch."

"Dinna be daft, Sorch," Ewan said with fond exasperation as he kissed her forehead. "Ye get better, an' then we'll celebrate."

Sorcha shook her head in confusion at his words but then followed her husband and Jessamine to her room. When she arrived, she allowed them to help her change into a nightgown and ease her into bed. Jessamine shooed Frederick away.

When Sorcha lay on the bed, taking deep breaths, Jessamine held her hand. After long minutes passed, Jessamine whispered, "When will you tell him?"

Sorcha's eyes flew open. "I have naught to tell him."

Jessamine shook her head in disappointment. "I know that's not true. You're acting like a woman who is in expectation of a blessed event. Am I wrong?"

Sorcha closed her eyes in defeat. "No' yet, J.P. Please, no' yet."

Jessamine smoothed the covers around Sorcha. "He loves you, and he'll love your babe. Don't deny him this happiness because of your fears, Sorcha. It isn't fair to you or to him." She kissed Sorcha's forehead and eased out of the room.

Frederick opened the door to his bedroom, his gaze immediately going to Sorcha. She lay curled on one side, facing away from the door. He shut the door with a barely audible *click* and moved about the room. He kicked off his boots, hung up his pants on a peg with his shirt over it and crawled into bed in his underclothes. He lay on the opposite half of the bed, refraining from reaching out to her or touching her.

Moonlight spilled into the room, and he looked at the soft tufts of her hair as they curled around her face. He frowned as he saw a tear slip down her cheek, the silver track glistening in the moonlight. "Sorcha," he whispered as he leaned over her. "Oh, Sorcha, please."

She sobbed as she rolled over and pushed herself onto his chest, her hands beating against him as she let out weeks' worth of pent-up anguish. "Why did ye have to say that?" she rasped. "Why did ye have to bring my worst fear to life?"

He wrapped his arms around her, holding her as tightly as possible. "I suffered,and I wanted you to suffer too. It was selfish of me. And I've never regretted anything more in my life."

"Did ye mean it?" she whispered.

"Dammit, no!" He swiped at her face, looking deeply into her eyes. "I was feeling sorry for myself. Sorry that you'd marry such a pathetic excuse for a man. A man who couldn't even provide for you for more than a few months of marriage. I hated that you might regret marrying me."

She sniffed as she watched him. "So ye thought to provoke an argument so I'd reassure ye?" She shook her head as fresh tears coursed out. "Dinna manipulate me like that again."

"I won't, my love. I won't." He kissed her cheeks. "You have no idea the torment I lived through that night when I couldn't find you. The visions I had of you in danger and alone on the prairie. The thought that some animal would find and hurt you and that I had caused you to be harmed." His hands roved over her as he tugged her even closer. "And then, the next morning, when you looked at me with no emotion."

"I couldna handle ye hurtin' me again," she whispered. "I'm no' that strong."

"You are strong, Sorcha. You're the strongest woman I know."

She kissed his lips, fleetingly, earning a groan from him at the first show of tenderness from her in weeks. "Do ye no' ken that ye have the ability to strip me of all my strength?" She kissed him again. "To render me defenseless?"

He swore and pulled her closer. "I'm so damn sorry," he whispered. "These last few weeks have been hell for me too." He pulled away so he could meet her eyes. "I may have brought your worst fear to life, but I've also created my own." He shuddered. "That morning, after I found you sitting in your workroom, spinning your wool, when you looked at me as though you had never cared for me ..." He closed his eyes. "It was as though I were my father and you my mother. It's how she always looked at him."

"Oh, Frederick," she whispered, tracing a line in his brow. "Then ye must ken she cared for him deeply."

He shook his head. "Not deeply enough to reconcile. Not deeply enough to forgive whatever had gone wrong between them." Frederick met Sorcha's compassion-filled gaze with wonder. "It took everything I had not to shatter that spinning wheel that morning. To render useless the barrier you put between us."

She sniffled as she arched up to kiss him again. "I needed something to defend myself against ye. To separate myself from ye."

He nodded in understanding. "Please don't do that again." When she murmured her agreement, he cupped her cheeks and sobered. "I can't stand that you've been so unhappy that I've made you ill."

She laughed, her joy startling him, and kissed his neck. "Well, I've made ye start comin' to our bed with yer clothes on. I far prefer ye scandalous." She kissed him again.

He shuddered and pushed her away so that he could look into her eyes. "I refuse to make love with you when you fainted and were so ill that you couldn't join us for dinner tonight. I love you too much."

Sorcha's eyes filled with tears. "An' I love ye, Frederick." She took a deep breath. "Do ye ken why yer words were so devastatin' that night?" She held a finger to his lips so he would not respond. "It was no' just because of my greatest fear. It's because I'm carryin' our bairn." She gasped as he pulled her into his embrace. "I thought it meant ye did no' want either of us."

"Oh, love, forgive me," he said as he kissed her and then met her gaze. "There is nothing more that I want in this world than to have you and our baby." His voice broke on *baby*. "I never thought I'd be so blessed." His hand dropped to her lower belly. "Do you think she can hear us?"

"Nae," Sorcha whispered as an intense love for him filled her heart to overflowing. "Nae, but 'tis never too early for him to learn his father's voice."

"I love you, little one. I'll love you forever," he whispered reverently. He gazed at his wife as his voice cracked. "Thank you, Sorcha, for forgiving me."

She cupped his face, swiping away his tears. "Jessamine helped me realize that I had to tell ye how I felt rather than freeze ye out." She took a deep breath. "My brothers' mother excelled at freezin' out those she did no' like or those who had disappointed her." She held her husband's face between her hands. "I promise ye, Frederick. I promise ye I will no' do that to ye."

"And I promise I'll never use your fears against you again." He cupped her face. "I won't cause an argument so you'll soothe me." His smiled softened. "I could have saved us weeks of agony if I'd let you comfort me from the start."

"Aye, husband," she whispered as she kissed him. "Comfort me some more."

The following morning, Sorcha and Frederick joined Ewan and Jessamine in the kitchen. Cookie had prepared bacon, eggs, potatoes and fried bread and had left it in the warming oven. The coffeepot was full, although Sorcha requested tea.

"What's the matter with ye, Sorch?" Ewan asked as he watched Sorcha pale at the mention of coffee. "Ye always liked coffee."

"It does no' sound good to me right now," she whispered as she closed her eyes and took a few deep breaths.

Ewan looked at his wife in confusion as she elbowed him in his side. He then sat as though thunderstruck, and a broad smile spread over his face. "Are ye expectin' a bairn, Sorch?" Absolute delight lit his face at the idea.

She smiled and nodded. "Aye." Her hand reached out for Frederick and clasped his before coming to rest over her belly. "Aye, we're to have a bairn, although 'tis early yet. We should no' speak of it until I'm more certain."

Ewan rose and pulled her into his arms. "I wish ye every happiness in yer marriage. Ye will be a wonderful wife an' mother, Sorcha. Look to the love ye have inside ye, an' ye will no' go wrong." He kissed her forehead and then swiped her cheek as a tear trickled out.

"Thank ye," she whispered. After a moment she asked, "Ye mentioned celebratin' last night. What are we to be celebratin'?"

Ewan laughed. "Well, yer bairn would be reason enough, but no one in the family has ever celebrated yer marriage. Jessie an' I thought it time for a party, even if it is a small one."

Frederick smiled. "Thank you. We would enjoy any reason to celebrate our good fortune." His eyes shadowed at that as he thought about the precarious future of the ranch. "I wish more of our families could be here."

Ewan shrugged. "Anna is still too weak, although she is recoverin' well. An' Leticia is too weak, but because she's expectin' another bairn. Yer bairns will be about the same age." He wriggled his brows in delight.

Sorcha studied him, as though attempting to discern if he were envious of his siblings having children. All she saw was joy. She gripped his arm and then pulled him close. "Thank ye, Ewan."

He laughed. "For bein' yer favorite brother?" he teased as he kissed her forehead. "Ye take care of yerself and listen to yer husband when he wants ye to rest. He only wants to care for ye an' yer bairn." He waited until she nodded, and then Ewan winked at Frederick.

Sorcha sat at the table after Frederick urged her to rest. He served the plates of food and then joined them. "How is Fidelia?" Sorcha asked. "She seemed quiet when we were in town."

Jessamine shared a long look with Ewan, who shrugged. "She and Bears have had a falling out."

"What?" Sorcha asked. "They were always friends. Seemed to understand each other well."

Ewan tilted his head to one side, looking pained. "I canna say for certain what happened, but I think Bears wanted to be more than a friend to her. An' she panicked."

Sorcha munched on a piece of bacon as she thought through all Ewan said and didn't say. "They would be perfect together. Anyone can see that."

Jessamine chuckled. "Perhaps, but they are the ones who must see it, not us."

"Bears seemed his usual self when he spoke with me," Frederick said. "Wise but not overbearing with it."

Ewan shrugged. "He has a way of shutting part of himself away. I've never seen that before. Especially not among the MacKinnons." He winked at his sister.

"Boss!" Dalton yelled as he stormed into the kitchen. "Boss, you gotta come see this now!" He looked at Sorcha. "You too, Missus." He ran out the door as fast as he had entered.

Frederick looked at his guests and gave an apologetic smile as he abandoned breakfast. "I'm sorry, but it seems we are needed outside."

Ewan held out his hand to Jessamine. "I dinna see why we canna come along." Soon they had donned light jackets and hats and walked to the paddock. Sorcha nearly ran beside Frederick, who walked with long steps.

When they reached the paddock, he stopped short. In the distance, a herd of cattle was driven toward the homestead. Frederick's breath caught at the sight of them. Healthy, well-fed cattle with plenty of meat on their bones.

"How?" he whispered. "Where did they come from?" He looked to Slims, who rode up to him with Boots saddled. He saw Sorcha wave away any apology from him, a brilliant smile on her face as she watched him with pride as he mounted Boots to join his men.

He raced toward the herd and the man who had worked diligently to bring it in. "Shorty!" he yelled. "I thought you went south!"

Shorty gave a hoot, taking off his hat and waving at his boss and friends. Dalton, Slims, Dixon and Frederick were all working to round up the herd in one area. Shorty matched his nickname, but he had the strength of a bull. He was fiercely loyal to Frederick and the MBR.

Shorty rode his horse beside Frederick and shook his head. "Nah, I was riding around in November, seein' where the cattle were holin' up and got caught in a mountain pasture during that first real winter storm. Good thing you keep that cabin up there well stocked."

Frederick cast his gaze over his friend. "Doesn't seem like it was well-stocked enough. You've lost weight."

"Had to ration what I had, but I made it, didn't I?" He shrugged. "Worst part was I ran out of coffee and tobacco." He shook his head in disgust.

"I don't understand," Frederick said as he looked at the healthy cattle, lowing in front of him. "How did they survive the winter?"

Shorty shrugged. "Wasn't no different than any other winter up there on the mountain. Harsh but with plenty of food to eat. They dug around and ate what they needed, and then I let 'em fatten up a bit afore I drove 'em down." He scratched at his head. "Is it May or June?"

"End of May," Frederick said. He shook his head. "You don't know what this means." He stared at Slims as he joined them. Frederick had always thought of them as the oddest of best friends. Slims, huge at over six-and-a-half-feet tall, and Shorty barely reaching five feet in his cowboy boots. "This should save us," he said to Slims.

"Why do you need savin', Boss?" Shorty asked. He sighed with pleasure as Slims handed him his bag of chewing tobacco.

"The winter was brutal down here in the valley. Only one-third of our cattle survived to make it to roundup." He smiled. "Until now."

Slims looked at the number grazing in front of them. "This should get us well over half, Boss. And they aren't scrawny buggers about to be felled by the faintest wind." He looked at his friend. "You did good, Shorty."

The two men rode off together as they prepared to brand any with a bare haunch, ensuring the cattle were theirs. Frederick spun his horse around and rode back to Sorcha and his family. He saw Sorcha, standing at the paddock fence, watching him approach with delight.

"Sorcha!" he called out as he jumped off his horse, tying Boots to the rail. He laughed as she threw herself in his arms. "We're saved!"

She cried and clung to him. "I dinna ken how or why, but I'm so happy for ye."

He held her and whispered, "Happy for us, love. For all of this is ours."

She pushed back and traced his eyebrow. "I ken. But ye have worked so hard for this. Ye have carried the burden of the ranch's survival, more than anyone else in yer family." She kissed him softly.

That evening, after the men had branded the cows and calves, the sound of a fiddle and men singing was heard from the main house. "What are they doin'?" Ewan asked as he looked out the side door from the kitchen.

Frederick smiled as he sipped at his coffee and played with Sorcha's fingers. "They're celebrating. Although we had the roundup in late April, there was no point in celebrating then. Now that they know the ranch will not fail, they are having a party."

Jessamine shared a look with Ewan and smiled. "Shouldn't we join them? You are their boss."

Ewan sighed and tugged her close. "Ye want an excuse to twirl around in a cowboy's arms."

She giggled and rested her head on her husband's shoulder. "No, I want to twirl in your arms."

Frederick looked at Sorcha. "What do you think, love?"

Sorcha rose and held her hand out to Frederick. "For a little while. It will be fun." She flushed as he swooped down to give her a quick kiss.

When they walked to the small fire the men had lit in a circle of rocks, the music momentarily stopped before starting again with a few more *whoops* from the men. In an instant Sorcha was dragged away to dance with Dixon, while Jessamine was spinning around the flattened grass with Ewan.

Frederick stood and watched his wife laugh at something the young ranch hand said, and Frederick's breath caught at her beauty.

"Seems she's over whatever mad she had," Slims said.

"Last night," Frederick murmured. "Before the fresh herd arrived."

Slims gave a grunt of agreement. "Good. Thataways you know she's happy to be with you no matter what. I never thought that woman was interested in you for your money or for the land, but now you have no doubt. She was standing by you through the worst of it."

Frederick gave a satisfied smile at Slims's words.

Slims handed Frederick a glass of beer. When he raised an eyebrow at the beer, Slims shrugged. "Ewan knew we'd want to celebrate. Sent a note with one of the boys to the Stumble-Out for a keg."

Frederick shook his head again. "There will still be work to do in the morning."

"We know, Boss. We're celebratin' that we will have work. Too many in this state don't."

Frederick shivered and nodded. "I know. I've heard that about half the spreads are going to fail." He smiled at Shorty. "I'll never be able to thank him enough."

"Shorty don't want no thanks. He's like the rest of us. We never thought to have a place that was like home for us, and you've given that to us." Slims paused and took a deep sip of his beer. "Have you thought about buyin' up land while it'll be cheap?"

Frederick shook his head. "I've barely realized that we won't be among the ranches that failed." He looked at Slims. "Any word on those in the valley? I'm always interested in land in the valley."

Slims shrugged. "The Hendersons are in trouble. If you gave them a decent offer, I know they'd sell."

Frederick's eyes gleamed at the prospect of buying the large tract of land beside his with a creek running into it from the mountains. "That's fine land. Almost as good as ours."

Slims laughed. "Almost." He backed away as a breathless Sorcha approached her husband. "Missus."

A light sheen of sweat lined her forehead, and her eyes were bright with delight as she stared at her husband. "Come dance with me, husband." She held out her hand to him, and he thrust his half-filled glass of beer at Slims.

The older man chuckled as the newlyweds moved to the makeshift dance floor, where Ewan had been replaced by Dalton. Jessamine chatted with him, but her gaze continued to wander to her husband. When Ewan cut in after a few notes of the slow waltz, she pulled him close.

Sorcha rested her head on Frederick's shoulder as the strains of the waltz faded into the background for her. She listened to his soft heartbeat under her ear, the gentle breeze, the men's voices as they laughed and chatted. She sighed with contentment. "This is home," she whispered.

"Yes, with you in my arms, it is," he said as he kissed her head.

CHAPTER 12

A week later, Sorcha sat on the front porch with her spinning wheel between her legs. Ewan and Jessamine had brought her fine wool to spin, and she enjoyed the feel of it after months of spinning rough wool. She hummed, rather than sang, as Frederick had teased her that her singing was a distraction to the men. They often ceased their work to listen to her, and she knew this was a busy time of year at the ranch. More men had been hired, and the bunkhouse was at full capacity. However, she did not know the new men like she knew Slims, Dixon and Dalton. Although she was cordial, she maintained a formal distance from them.

Ewan joined her on the porch, pulling over a chair to sit beside her. He kicked his legs out in front of him and let out a contented sigh. "Ye are fortunate to live in such a place, Sorch."

She smiled at him. "I'm fortunate to have married the man I love."

He nodded. "Aye, ye are. I'm glad Cailean an' I did no' scare ye away from him. I ken ye can be skittish at times." He laughed as she belted him on his shoulder. "Ye are happy, are ye no'?"

She set aside her spinning wheel and wool, and focused on her brother. "I will no' lie to ye an' say we've no' had arguments. We have. But I am happy, Ewan."

He looked into her blue eyes. "Ye have a temper. Ye have to remember he does too. It may no' be just like yers, but it's there, an' it may hurt ye when ye do no' expect it to." He smiled as he looked at his sister. "Never forget what ye feel now an' fight to regain it."

She shivered. "I hate our fights."

He chuckled. "Aye, they are no' fun, but the makin' up is always enjoyable." He kicked her foot as he teased her. "Never forget, Sorcha. Dinna gamble with more than ye are willin' to lose. That doesna apply only to the poker table."

She nodded and was silent a few moments. "I hate that ye have to leave tomorrow."

He shrugged. "I've left Ben alone for too long, an' Jessie's deprived the fine citizens of Bear Grass Springs of a newspaper for far longer than is healthy. They'll start to concoct their own gossip, which we ken is no' a good idea."

"Ewan, how can ye be happy for me?" she whispered.

He looked at her, his brown eyes startled. "Are ye daft? Ye've a bairn on the way, an' ye're married to a fine man. How could I no' be delighted?"

She took his hand. "Jessie told me about not having children." She saw his eyes cloud with grief. "I'm sorry. I should no' speak of such things."

He shook his head. "No, Sorcha, ye should. I should. 'Tis difficult, because I am filled with joy for ye and sorrow for myself, all at the same time. Do ye ken how that is possible?" He smiled. "But it's as I told Jessie. I willna ever want more than her."

Sorcha pulled him close, sniffling on his shoulder. "I want ye to have this joy too, Ewan. I'm selfish."

"Nae, ye are no'. 'Tis 'cause ye care as ye do that ye want us all to be as happy as ye are. That is no' selfish." He swiped away her tears. "An' I ken, someday, I will be a da." He kissed his sister's forehead and rose, walking down the front porch to look over the paddock and the rolling hills of the ranch.

≈

S orcha had just finished using the privy near the main house when she heard a slithering noise. She frowned and looked down and then scrambled up, balancing her feet on either side of the privy opening. Her hands on the walls gave her purchase, although she worried she would fall when her legs began to shake with fear.

"Frederick!" she screamed. When she heard nothing, she continued to scream. Over and over again she yelled, as the rattlesnake wound its way around the privy, its tongue flashing out at times. "Frederick!" she screamed again. She banged one hand on the privy wall and began to cry as it seemed she was trapped inside with a rattlesnake and no hope for escape. She couldn't remember if they crawled up things, but she raised her skirts as best she could as she didn't want it to become entangled in her skirts.

"What in God's name is the matter in the privy?" she heard Frederick mutter as he walked near.

"Get a shovel or a rock," she yelled.

He pulled open the privy door, momentarily blinding her as the sunlight streaked in. "What are you doing standing atop the privy? With your skirts up?" He froze as he saw her panic and tears. "Sorcha?"

"Rattlesnake," she whimpered.

He swore. "Stay calm. You're safe right now. I'll be right back."

"Dinna leave me," she begged. "Please."

"Slims!" Frederick bellowed. He turned and kept his gaze on hers, his calm helping her recover her composure. "You will be fine, love. I'll let nothing happen to you."

Slims came, panting from his sprint from the paddock. "Boss?" He tilted his head in confusion at the sight of Sorcha standing atop the privy.

"Get a shovel. A rattlesnake is in there." Frederick looked around and saw the tail but not the head. It had slithered behind the seat. "Sorcha, I want you to trust me and to reach for me."

She shook her head. "I do trust ye, but I ken they strike with movement. Dinna ask me to move. Please."

He saw the panic returning to her gaze and nodded. He stilled as he saw the rattlesnake move, slithering into the sunlight now that the door to the privy was open. "Stay still," he whispered to her. "It's moving."

Slims returned with the shovel, and Frederick nodded to the rattlesnake. Its head was now visible outside of the privy. Slims waited a moment longer and then slammed the shovel down, decapitating the snake, its headless body continuing to writhe across the privy floor.

The minute the snake was dead, Frederick leaped forward, grabbed Sorcha and hauled her from the privy. Once outside, they fell to the ground with her on his lap. "*Shh*, ... love, I've got you. You're all right. It's over."

She shook as he held her, her tears soaking his light-blue cambric shirt. "I dinna want that to be the way I die. In a privy with a rattlesnake," she said with a disgruntled shake of her head at the ignominy of the idea.

He chuckled. "Only you would worry about what your obituary would say." He sobered as he held her closer. "I couldn't bear to lose you and our child. Please be careful."

She hit his back with her fist. "If ye think I went to the privy to have tea with a rattlesnake, ye're daft." She relaxed into his arms, their foolish conversation soothing her more than anything else would have. "I love ye, Frederick. Thank ye for comin' to help me."

He shuddered. "I'm just thankful I heard you calling. I was walking to the house for a cup of coffee, or I would never have heard your scream." He clutched her more closely. "And none of the men would dare to approach that privy if they knew you were inside."

She kissed his neck. "Perhaps ye should instruct them that, if I'm screamin' for help, they should always render aid."

He kissed her. "A sound idea, my love." He eased her away and then helped her to stand. "Are you well?"

She knew he was worried about the baby, and she smiled, cupping his cheek. "I'm fine. I might take a nap after my adventure, but I am well." She stood on her toes and kissed him. "Go away with ye now, and do whatever work needs to be done."

He shook his head. "Nothing will ever be more important than you." He raised her hand for a kiss and then followed Slims back to the paddock.

~

By late June, the summertime heat had arrived, and Sorcha spent most of her afternoons on the back porch in the shade. Any chores she needed to do were completed before the heat of the day. Most afternoons she sat on the porch, spinning wool or knitting as she listened to the sounds of the ranch. The clang of horseshoes on the anvil as the blacksmith worked. The men calling to each other. The chickens clucking in the nearby chicken coop. She always prayed a gentle wind would blow, but today the air was mostly still. A trickle of sweat ran down the center of her back, and she shifted in her seat as she spun wool. Every few minutes she ran a cloth over her brow, and she paused to drink a sip of water.

She looked with pride at the garden, thriving behind the tall fence. The men helped her water it, and, although they grumbled about the extra chore, they seemed to delight in her success. Near the garden, sunflowers dozed under the intense sun. A deep contentment filled her as she stared out at the ranch and the land behind it. "I'm building a life here," she whispered to herself.

Her attention was caught as she heard a wagon leaving the barn. Rather than listening to it rattle down the drive toward town, it stopped in front of the house.

"Sorcha!" Frederick called out. The front door opened and closed, and, after a few minutes, he poked his head out the back door. "There you are." He smiled as he saw her busy at work and joined her on the back porch.

"Where are ye goin'?" she asked as she arched up to meet his soft kiss.

"We are playing hooky." He grinned at her as he held out his hand. "Come, my love." He helped her gather up her things and led her inside. "No, I'm not telling you where," he said in a teasing voice.

"I'm to make supper tonight," she protested. "I canna leave."

He kissed her again, the soft teasing kiss deepening as he held her in his arms. "Aye, you can," he whispered as he nibbled at her neck. "I've spoken with Slims and the new cook, and they've worked something out between them." He winked at her and tugged her behind him out the front door.

A wagon pulled by one horse awaited them, and he helped her onto the high seat. "I would have preferred riding horses, but I'm uncertain if that is safe in your condition."

She ran a finger over his cheek and smiled. "I wrote to Helen. She said, as long as I did no' ride at a gallop but at a walk, I should be fine on a horse. Do ye want to change plans?"

He shook his head and gave a soft *click* to the horse and a gentle flick of the reins, and the wagon rolled away from the house. "No. I've everything I need in the back of the wagon. We'll have to walk a few minutes, but we'll be fine."

They rode the short distance across the rangeland, with the golden prairie grass blowing in the faint wind. The mountains were a deep evergreen, while their peaks remained white from a smattering of snow. When the wagon stopped, Sorcha spied a wounded bird. "What's wrong with that wee bird?" Near the wagon, a brown bird walked as though a wing were broken, looking over its shoulder to see if they were following it.

Frederick leaned over and smiled. "Nothing. That's a killdeer. It acts like that to distract us and to keep us away from its nest."

Sorcha watched it and smiled. "What a brave wee thing." She waited until Frederick came around to her side of the wagon and held onto his arm as she climbed out of the wagon.

She grabbed his free hand as he hefted the basket from the wagon. He led her into the forest and over to a spot by the creek bed. A flat area with tall grasses stood by the creek with a large deep pool, inviting them to jump in. "Oh, what a magical place."

He smiled at her, walking over the tall grasses to flatten them. He spread the blanket in a shaded area and set the basket on one corner. "Come," he said, holding his hand out to her.

"Will we swim?" She looked from him to the creek to him again.

"Do you know how?"

"Of course I ken how!" She gave him a nudge with her shoulder as she sat beside him. "I lived next to the ocean. On fine days, I'd sneak to the small beach and swim. Cailean warned me that I had to be careful and not allow a selkie to steal me."

He frowned. "A selkie?"

"Aye, a creature that is seal in the ocean but human on land. I ken a man who claimed his wife was a selkie, an' he had hid her pelt to prevent her from goin' back to the sea. She was never more content than when she was lookin' out to sea."

"Are there selkie men?" Frederick asked.

"Oh, aye, an' they're rumored to be the most handsome of men. They ken when a woman is dissatisfied with her life an' seduce her." She flushed. "I dinna meet a selkie, but I saw plenty of seals."

Frederick shook his head. "Do you think that man had a selkie wife?"

Sorcha shrugged. "I dinna ken. Ol' Man McClure was a miserly man who kent nothin' about keepin' a woman happy. I heard the women gossipin' that his wife looked to the sea because her lover was a fisherman." She flushed as her husband chuckled. "This doesna mean I do no' believe in selkies, aye?"

He wrapped an arm around her shoulder and gave her a squeeze. "I'll keep you far from the sea. I want to ensure you're never stolen from me."

She sighed as she snuggled into his side. "I have nae desire to leave ye." She closed her eyes as he kissed her forehead.

After a moment he said, "Come. Let's swim, and then we can have our lunch and relax before we have to return." He rose and helped her to stand. They undressed each other to their underclothes, and then Sorcha batted away his hands.

"I'm no' swimmin' naked!" She sighed as he kissed her.

"There's no one to see us, love. You'll be much more comfortable if you don't have to hang your shift over shrubs to dry." He kissed her again. "Come. Frolic with your husband." He winked at her and shimmied out of his underclothes before jumping into the creek. He gave a *whoop* at the cold water and then dunked his head. "Come join me, wife."

She bit her lip as she saw the hope and love in his eyes. Taking a deep breath, she gripped her shift and pulled it over her head, dropping it on the blanket. She walked to the creek bed, wincing as small pebbles dug into the soft soles of her feet. Frederick stood and helped her ease into the water. "Oh, 'tis as cold as the water on Skye!"

He chuckled and pulled her to him, pressing their chests together as he floated around the large pool. "Take a deep breath," he said a moment before he dunked them.

Sorcha hit his back with her hands, and he brought them above the surface after only a moment under the water. "Oh, I never kent I'd be this cold again." She shivered as she wrapped her arms and legs around him.

A few moments more and he eased her away. "Come, love. We have to get out, or you'll get too cold." He helped her from the pool and yanked open the basket, revealing a large towel. He pulled it out and scrubbed her dry. He then dried himself and wrapped it around her. He sat on the corner of the blanket, now in the sun, and held her as she shivered in his arms.

"How long have ye been comin' to this spot?" she whispered as she kissed his neck.

"Years. Ever since I was a boy." He tilted his head so she could kiss her way up to his jaw. "I've never seen the water this cloudy this time of year. Runoff was in May and early June."

She turned in his arms and pressed herself along his front. "The water was plenty clean for us today, husband."

He groaned as he sank his hands into her red-brown hair, kissing her soundly. "Make love with me, Sorcha." He gave a grunt of pleasure as she wriggled on his lap.

She pulled at the towel so that it was wrapped around both of them and then met his delighted gaze. "I dinna want ye catchin' cold," she teased as she traced her hands over his back.

He gripped her closer. "I'll be six feet under before I'm cold around you." He kissed away her shiver at referring to his demise and swallowed her shriek of delight as he tickled her and then made love to her.

~

In mid-July, Sorcha departed the house soon after Frederick rode out onto the range for the day. She had heard a few of the new cowboys talking about huckleberry bushes in the nearby hills, and she wanted to surprise Frederick with a huckleberry treat. She donned an old dress, an apron, pulled on a wide-brimmed hat and carried a large basket.

She trudged across the range for what seemed like miles until she reached the base of the mountains. She didn't want to ride a horse because then Frederick would learn of her surprise. Panting from exertion and thirst, she entered the forest and sighed with pleasure at the slightly lower temperature and the sweet smell of the forest. She followed the sound of running water and smiled with delight to find the small creek running near the path she walked. She paused to dampen her handkerchief to wipe her sweaty brow, and she cupped her hands for long sips of water. After a few minutes of rest, she moved farther up the path until she found a patch of huckleberry bushes, bursting with berries. She had gone berry picking the previous summer with Bears and Fidelia, and she knew what to look for and what to avoid.

Soon she sat in the middle of a huckleberry patch, filling her basket while, at the same time, eating her fill. Her fingers were stained purple, and she sighed with pleasure. She swatted at insects and wished she had some form of repellant for the annoying pests. Tilting her head up to the sky, she was filled with joy in the moment.

"Well, look what I've found," a deep voice said.

She stilled as she heard the voice from her nightmares.

Sorcha rose, gripping her berry basket. "Walter," she said in as forceful a voice as she was capable. "What are ye doin' on Frederick's land?" She stood as tall as possible, but he was taller and stronger than she was.

"I was just passin' through." He sneered at her. "Seems you have a desire to see me. You're always about when I'm passin' through."

She shook her head in denial. "I never have any wish to see ye." She took a step back when he lunged toward her. "Stay away from me!"

"You're trouble," he whispered. "But I don't know what to do about you yet."

She shook her head in confusion. "I dinna ken what ye mean."

"Should I take you with me?" His eyes shone with delight at the fear in her gaze. "Or should I just kill you and be done with it?"

She straightened her shoulders. "If I go missin', the whole ranch ... the whole town will come lookin' for me. An' ye will no' like what will be done to ye when they find ye." She tilted her chin up in defiance.

"If you're already dead, they'll be too busy mourning you."

She gave a small scream and swung her basket at him, hitting him on the head and shoulder. Dropping the basket, she ran from him, only making it a few steps before he tackled her to the ground. "Get off me!" She bucked and hit at him.

"Oh, so this is what you desire?" he asked with a lascivious sneer. He chuckled as she froze beneath him, her breaths emerging in pants. "I'd be happy to oblige you."

"Nae," she gasped. "Nae, please God, nae." Tears coursed down her cheeks as he ran a finger over one brow and then down her nose to her lips.

"I wonder if your husband misses you yet. How long do you think it will be before he searches for you? It's hours until noontime." His fetid breath washed over her. "Did you even tell him where you were going?"

She struggled, trying to move her legs so she could kick him, but his weight was on her, holding her immobile. "He'll kill ye for darin' to touch me."

"Oh, I already know I'm a dead man," he murmured. "I have more than one man after me."

She froze as he moved and pulled out his pistol. "If ye are no' smart enough to ken that my husband, my brothers and Bears will track ye down and skin ye, then ye are daft." She met his glare, although she couldn't hide her tremors of fear. "They ken it was ye who hurt me last fall. They ken ye are doin' somethin' illegal on this land."

He frowned. "But they don't know what, do they?" He held the pistol to her head when she remained silent. "Answer me, dammit!"

"Nae," she whispered as tears poured down her cheeks.

He grinned as she whimpered. "I love the fear." He looked into her eyes. "Good night, Sorcha." He slammed the butt of the gun against her head, knocking her out.

Frederick walked to the house for a mid-morning cup of coffee and to steal a few moments with Sorcha. He shook his head as he knew his brothers would tease him if they knew how much he liked to see her throughout the day. Hearing her sing or having a battle of wits with her for a few moments lifted his spirits and reenergized him for the long hours of work needed to run a successful ranch.

"Sorcha!" he called out as he entered the house. He stilled as he waited for her to call back to him. He canted forward, listening for her singing. After sniffing the air and not smelling anything baking or cooking, he walked to the rear of the house, expecting to find her lost to her wool in her sitting room. When that room was empty, he poked his head out to scan the back porch, to find that vacant too. He frowned and then smiled. "I imagine our babe is wearing her out. She must be resting."

Walking on his toes so his bootheels wouldn't wake her, he climbed the stairs and eased open their bedroom door. He let out a puff of breath to find the bedroom as empty as the rest of the house. Giving up any notion of stealth, he raced downstairs and looked into every room in the house. Soon he ran to the barn, calling out for his men. Many of them were on the range, but those who were there came at his call.

"What's the matter, Boss?" Dixon asked.

"When is the last time you saw Sorcha?" he asked them. His gaze searched theirs for any sign of guilt or culpability and saw instead confusion and concern.

"Last night," Dalton said.

Slims nodded next to him. "Yes, Boss. Last night, when she tried out baking another cake." The men hid a smile at another of her disastrous attempts to create an edible cake.

"Did any of you say anything that would have made her run off?" Frederick watched them with wild eyes.

His men shook their heads. Then Dixon said, "I mentioned the huckleberries were in season."

Frederick looked to Slims. "Do you think ..."

Slims nodded. "Yes, it sounds like something she'd do. I wouldn't be worried, Boss. She won't be happy with you if you ruin her surprise."

The men laughed and wandered off to continue their work as Frederick stared at the house. Slims remained beside him. "What worries you, Boss?"

"Something's not right. I don't know how I know. But I do."

Slims nodded. "None of the work we're doing won't keep until tomorrow. If you want to go search for her, go."

Frederick looked at him. "Saddle two horses and pack rifles. I want you with me."

Slims nodded and moved to the barn. Soon they were on horseback, racing to the hills.

Hours after her encounter with Walter, Sorcha woke and opened bleary eyes. Staring around her, she heard the roar of the creek and saw tall pine and fir trees. However, she squinted because they seemed to merge and split as she stared at them, and she closed her eyes at her blurry vision. When she opened her eyes again, she did not recognize where she was and did not see the huckleberry patch where she'd been collecting her berries.

She touched the side of her pounding head and groaned as both hands moved together. She gave an indignant yank at her wrists and whimpered at the pain of the rope burning into her flesh. Her fingers probed at her head and came away bloody. After attempting and failing to tie her bandanna around her head, she stuffed it in one pocket, wincing as the rope dug deeper into her sensitive skin.

"If I'm dead, then why do I hurt so much?" she muttered. She focused a moment on the area around her. A small circle of rocks was nearby with charred wood and a pallet next to it. She glanced to the sky and saw blue, but she knew it was no longer early morning.

She tugged on her wrists again and grunted in indignation to find that, although her legs were not tied together, she was strapped to a tree. She could bend forward but could not free herself. The rope around her middle was tight, and the more she struggled, the more it chafed against her clothes.

"I do love to see a woman struggle. It brings me such joy," Walter Jameson said from a nearby rock. He perched on it, polishing a knife with long strokes. Each swipe of the knife made a distinctive sound that caused Sorcha's hackles to rise. "Is it because you miss my attentions?"

"Stay away from me!" she said. "I dinna ken what ye want with me, but I ken ye will no' live long once my husband finds me."

He laughed. "Oh, my dear, why are women always so delusional? Why do you believe your husband will worry one second over you?" He moved toward her with the knife pointed toward her. "He will find another woman, more biddable and to his liking after he's playacted his mourning period."

Sorcha glared at Walter and shook her head. "Ye lie." The sound of his bootheels scrunching on pebbles as he approached caused her to arch away, but she had nowhere to go. Soon he crouched in front of her, and she stilled any movement as he held his knife up against her cheek.

"I tell an all-too-common truth. One that few wish to hear." He smiled as a tear leaked down her cheek, and he chased it away with the dull side of his knife. "Women always believe in the fairy tale."

Sorcha turned her head, focusing on the faint trail leading away from him. Searching for Frederick. When the trail remained empty, she closed her eyes.

"Closing your eyes doesn't change that you're my … guest," he said with a laugh. He rose and walked away. "I look forward to hearing you beg."

Sorcha bit her lip before declaring she'd never beg. She feared that, by the time she was free of Walter, she would break such a vow.

Frederick and Slims entered the forest and slowed the pace of their horses. Frederick paused as his eyes adjusted to the dim light before leading Slims to the huckleberry patch he knew about. He saw a flattened area and frowned. "Where is she?" He dismounted his horse, tying it to a nearby tree.

"It looks like she sat here for a bit," Slims said as he shook his head in confusion. He froze as he saw an overturned basket in the distance. "Boss." He nodded in that direction, and Frederick ran to it.

"Sorcha," he whispered. He looked around, but there was no sign of her. "Where would she go?"

Slims met Frederick's wild gaze. "What if she wasn't alone in the forest?"

Frederick nodded. "Come. Let's follow that trail. We shouldn't ride as it's too narrow, but I don't want to leave our horses behind. You never know who could be here now, and I don't want the horses stolen."

Slims nodded, and they walked single file up a path. After a short distance, it branched into two trails.

Frederick stood, staring at each. "Logic says I should take the more traveled trail. But I don't think so. Not today."

He led them up the steep path, pushing bushes and brush out of the way as they fought for footing. After a short distance he halted as he heard voices. Slims' strong hand on his shoulder prevented him from bolting forward.

"Steady, Boss. You don't know how many men there are. You want to help her, not harm her. *If* she is there." Slims pulled a rifle from his saddle as Frederick did the same. Slims took Boots' reins and his horse's reins and tied them both to a nearby tree. "I've got your back, Boss."

Frederick nodded and crept toward the small clearing where he had heard the voices. He stopped short when he saw Walter Jameson with a knife, leaning over Sorcha, ribboning her clothes as he taunted her about doing the same to her flesh later that night.

"Imagine how the wolves will enjoy feasting on you," Walter said with a maniacal laugh.

"No, please, no," Sorcha gasped and then whimpered as his knife cut into her shift. The next thing to be cut would be her skin.

Sorcha whimpered again, and Frederick burst into the clearing. "Get away from my wife, Jameson!"

Walter spun to face Frederick. "So she is important to you, Tompkins. I wondered what you'd do if I finally had something you valued."

Frederick raised his gun, but, before he could fire, Slims' shot rang out, hitting Walter in the arm holding the knife. The knife fell to the ground, barely missing Sorcha's leg. Walter howled in pain and ran into the woods as he saw lethal intent in Frederick's and Slims' gazes.

Frederick raced to Sorcha, grabbing Walter's knife to cut her free. "My love," he gasped. "My darling."

She sobbed as he sawed through the thick rope around her middle and then at her wrists. Her clothes were in tatters, and she had shallow scratches on her arms and chest where the sharp knife had bit into her flesh. "Frederick, hold me an' dinna let me go."

"*Shh*, love. I have you. You're safe now. You'll always be safe now." He sat, lifting her gently to sit on his lap. "We'll take you home, make sure you are well."

"Yes. Home," she whispered. "But I dinna think I can walk."

Frederick looked to Slims. "I'll be sentry. Can you carry her?" Frederick grabbed his gun and watched as Slims gently lifted Sorcha.

Frederick moved around the camp and found Walter's gun, emptying it of bullets and jamming it into his waistband.

"You'll be fine soon, Miss Sorcha. Another adventure to tell your little 'uns about," Slims said as he looked at Frederick.

They walked as quickly as possible down the trail to their waiting horses. Frederick slipped the rifles into the saddlebags and mounted, holding his arms out for Sorcha. "I'll hold her on the way home." When she was as comfortable as she could be riding with him, he began the journey home, walking the horse carefully, crooning in her ear the entire way.

"Ye only sing to me when I'm injured," she whispered against his neck. "The last time ye sang to me I was wild with pain from my broken leg."

"After you recover, I'll sing to you every day," he murmured, kissing her head. As they approached the ranch, he sped up the pace. "I'll have you home and comfortable soon, my love," he said.

Dalton saw them arriving and ran from the barn.

Frederick yelled, "Go to town and get a healer. Now! And once the Doc is on his way, find the Sheriff and tell him he's needed out here." He handed Sorcha down into Slims' arms.

Slims carried her into the house and laid her on the bed, Frederick close behind them. "I'll return with water and with the healer when he arrives."

"Thank ye, Slims," Sorcha said.

"Anything for you, Miss Sorcha," Slims said before he slipped from the room.

"I'm sorry," she whispered as Frederick remained silent. "I dinna mean to cause calamity." A tear trickled down her cheek. She looked to him and reached a hand up to trace his cheek. "I only wanted to make ye a huckleberry pie."

"Are your pies any better than your cakes?" he attempted to tease, but his voice broke as he fought a sob. "Don't put me through this hell again, Sorcha. I know it's not your fault, but I nearly went mad when I couldn't find you here. The house never seemed more like a tomb than when you weren't here. And then to find your basket overturned in the forest with you nowhere in sight?" He shook his head as he fought tears.

"I'll be fine, husband," she whispered as she traced his cheek and dug her fingers into his beard.

"I don't know if I ever will be," he rasped, falling forward to rest his head on her shoulder a minute. "What did he do to you?" His fingers roved over her head, and she flinched at his soft touch. He frowned as his fingers came away sticky and blood smeared. He rose up to probe at her head wound.

She winced as he pulled her hair away from the wound. She jerked at the knock on the door, and it opened.

"Here's water and a cloth," Slims said. He met her gaze, and he stood with his hands on his hips as he looked at her lying on the bed. "Dalton will return soon with a healer."

"I dinna need a healer," Sorcha protested and then hissed in a breath as Frederick washed her wrists and then wrapped linen around them.

"You may need stitches," Frederick said as he pressed a cloth to her head. "Bring Doc here the minute he arrives," he told Slims as he turned to leave.

The door opened and closed again, and she was alone with Frederick. "I'm sorry," she whispered. "I wanted to surprise ye. I never thought he'd be there."

Frederick gave a grunt of frustration. "There's no reason for him to be in that area." He dampened the cloth and cleaned her wound. "Tell me, love."

She reached for his hand and took a deep breath. "He seemed to think I planned to be there when he was. That I was trying to interfere with his plans. At least that's what it appeared to me."

He kissed her hand. "He has to know that he's a dead man now, after the way he's mistreated you a second time."

She whimpered. "He threatened to kill me. Raised his pistol and put it to my head." She opened her eyes and met Frederick's horrified gaze. "Said ye'd be too busy mournin' to look for him." She shrugged. "An' then I dinna remember anythin' else. He must have hit me hard on the head. I woke up, an' I kent I wasna dead because ye shouldna hurt in heaven, aye?"

He chuckled because he knew that was what she needed, but no humor lit his gaze. "No, you shouldn't." He traced her cheek. "Thank God you were smart enough to talk him 'round."

"Why did he no' kill me? I dinna understand." She shivered. "When I woke up, he had me at his camp. I dinna ken what he planned to do."

Frederick shook his head. "I don't care what his reasons were. What he taunted you with will give me nightmares until I'm ninety."

She shuddered. "I ken. They'll haunt me too. But I only thought of you. I kent ye'd come for me. That ye'd worry about me and find me." Her eyes swam with tears.

"How did you know that?" he whispered, smiling at his wife.

"Because I would have done the same for ye. I never would have given up."

Still smiling, he cupped her cheek. "Yes, I love you that much," he whispered as he kissed her softly. "Thank you for being so brave. Thank you for never losing faith in me. For not listening to his malicious words." Frederick kicked off his boots and climbed in bed beside her, slinging an arm over her belly. "Is the baby all right?"

She sighed. "I think so. I hope so."

"This is why we need Helen or Doc," he whispered. "To make sure your head is looked after." His arm around her waist tightened. "And to reassure us that our baby is well."

"Dinna cry, darling," she murmured as she kissed his wet cheek. "I'm all right."

He shook his head, burying his face into the cradle of her shoulder and neck. "The thought of him holding a pistol to you … The image of him holding a knife to you …" He took a deep, shaky breath. "I couldn't bear it if anything happened to you, Sorcha, or to our babe."

She rolled to her side, groaning as her head hurt and the world spun with the movement. After she regained her sense of place, she hitched her leg over his, slung an arm around his broad chest and tugged him closer to her. "Feel me. Feel that I am all right," she urged as her hand ran soothingly up and down his back. She continued to murmur to him as he calmed.

"Dammit," he said as he cleared his throat. "I should be the one easing your fears after your ordeal. Not the other way around."

She chuckled and kissed his cheek. "Nae, we comfort each other. An' holdin' ye in my arms has done more to soothe me than anythin' else could have."

"I love you, Sorcha," Frederick whispered as he kept a firm hold on her.

"I ken." She cupped the side of his face and eased him back so she could look into his eyes. "I ken ye love me, as I love ye. Which means ye will no' kill the man." She watched with patience as he glowered at her. "I will no' have ye sent to prison or hanged for it." She waited as he stared into her eyes. "I will no' allow ye to separate us like that. To leave me to raise our bairn all by myself."

His indignant bluster faded, and he relaxed in her hold. "Aye," he whispered, leaning forward to kiss her. "I will concede that I will not kill him. However, I will not promise that he won't wish he were dead."

She smiled. "I wouldna want it any other way." She settled onto his chest as he rolled onto his back, resting in each other's arms as they awaited the healer's arrival.

The door flung open, and Ewan stormed inside. "Sorcha!" he bellowed, gasping from the mad dash from the wagon. His anxious gaze roved over his sister resting with her husband, and he frowned at the peaceful scene.

"Would ye stop yer yammerin'?" she demanded, holding one hand to her temple. "My head hurts enough without ye addin' to the pain."

Ewan let out a deep breath as some of his panic abated. "Ye are well?"

"If ye call *well* seein' double an' a wound over my ear that will no' stop bleedin', then aye, I'm the picture of health," she grumbled. She made a sound of distress as Frederick eased out from underneath her.

Frederick kissed her forehead and murmured, "I'll ensure everything is on hand for Helen or the doc."

"'Tis Helen. An' Warren. An' Bears," Ewan murmured, sharing a long look with Frederick. "We thought Bears would be needed for tracking." At Frederick's nod, Ewan said, "Alistair and Cailean were convinced to remain in town, takin' turns workin' the livery and ensurin' Annabelle and Leticia an' the bairns are safe. Never doubt they wanted to be here, too, aye?"

Sorcha nodded, watching as her husband slipped out the door.

After Frederick left, Ewan approached the bed, blanching when he saw her head wound leaking through the bandage. "He's a dead man."

"Nae," Sorcha snapped, reaching out to grab her brother's hand. "If I will no' allow my husband to kill him, then ye are no' allowed to either." She met his mutinous glare. "Ye are no' that man, Ewan."

Her brother shook his head. "You don't know what I am." He fought to conceal the extent of his rage as he looked over his sister. Softly caressing her shoulder, he whispered, "The bairn?"

"I dinna ken. I think the bairn is fine." She met her brother's tormented gaze. "I hope Helen can tell me." She fought tears. "I promise I dinna mean mischief! I wanted to pick huckleberries for my husband. To make him a surprise treat." She sniffled as Ewan eased onto the bed, tugging her into his arms. "I dinna ken the man was in the forest. Why would he be?"

"Aye. Why would he be?" Ewan murmured. "Ye are strong, Sorcha. Whatever happens, ye will recover. Ye will have all of us to help ye."

Ewan held his sister as her tears fell, his mind racing with images of what could have happened as his desire to avenge her and her unborn bairn grew.

At the gentle tap on the door, Helen poked her head in. "I fear I must interrupt," she said with an apologetic smile. She wore a serviceable brown cotton dress with a thick apron over it. Her wheat-colored hair was pulled back in a sensible bun. Clean linen cloths were draped over her arm, and she carried a basin of water.

Ewan rose, stilling his movement as Sorcha grabbed his hand.

"Promise me, Ewan," she demanded. She met his stare. "Promise."

He closed his eyes, and then his shoulders relaxed. "Aye, I promise ye that I will no' kill anyone."

"No' today, no' ever," she said.

"Aye, no' ever." He traced a finger over her cheek as he leaned forward to meet her gaze. "It doesna mean I dinna think ye are no' worth it, ye ken? Ye are worth one thousand of him. I will find some other way to avenge ye."

She grabbed ahold of his finger, holding tight when he would have slipped from the room. Tears tracked down her cheeks at her brother's avowal of love. "I dinna want revenge, Ewan. I dinna want ye or my husband to waste yer time on it. It only ever brings pain and sufferin'."

He shook his head. "I will do what I must to ensure that man doesna hurt you again, Sorch. As will your husband. That's no' revenge." He gave her fingers a squeeze and then slipped from the room.

He headed downstairs where Slims pointed to Frederick's office. "What do ye have planned?" Ewan asked as he entered.

Bears watched Ewan with patience. "You can't return to the woods like this." He looked from Ewan to Frederick. "Any clues about which way Walter went will be lost to you as you storm about in your rage."

Ewan closed his eyes and gripped his hands together by his side. "I ken ye are tryin' to help, Bears. But ye dinna ken what it's like to see Sorcha hurt. To know her bairn was put in danger too."

Bears watched him implacably. "I know what it is to watch someone I love suffer. I also know the importance of keeping a cool head." He shared a long look with Ewan. "If you want to try to find Walter, you have to promise to follow my lead."

Ewan nodded. "Aye, 'tis an easy promise. Ye're the best tracker I've ever kent." He looked at Frederick. "Do ye agree?"

Frederick gave a swift nod. "Yes. But I want it known that I am the one who metes out punishment. She is my wife."

Bears sighed. "I am not aiding you so you can murder the man." He waited, but both Frederick and Ewan remained quiet. "If that is your plan, you can find Walter yourself."

Frederick let out a long sigh and collapsed into the chair behind his desk. "No, I promised Sorcha that I wouldn't kill him. Although she was fine if I made him wish he were dead." He saw a flash of amusement in Bears' expression before it became impassive again.

"She did no'!" Ewan sputtered. "She just gave me a speech about how revenge never accomplished naught." He shook his head in disbelief.

"Seems she wants her husband to have the right to rough up Walter," Bears said with a chuckle. "We should go."

"For the record," Warren said, sitting calmly on a chair in one corner, "I'm coming along to ensure no laws are broken and to further ensure no one is killed." He met Ewan's and Frederick's stare. "I want Walter punished as much as any man, but murder is not the way."

Frederick took a deep breath and nodded. Helen had been abused by Walter for years and then had been tricked into becoming a Boudoir Beauty because of Walter. "I know we all have our reasons to hate the man, but Sorcha is my wife and his most recent victim."

"As Helen is my wife and his most prolonged victim," Warren countered. "We will see what we find. There are other ways to hurt a man that are not physical."

"Spoken like a *bluidy* lawyer," Ewan muttered with a rueful smile.

"Let's go while we still have daylight," Bears said.

Frederick rose, and they filed out of his office. Slims awaited them in the parlor. Frederick met Slims's gaze, who nodded.

"The horses are ready, and there are provisions," he said. "Good luck, Boss."

Frederick slapped him on his shoulder. "Thanks, Slims. Make sure she remains safe."

"We all will," Slims vowed. He stood on the front porch steps, watching as the four men mounted fresh horses and galloped toward the mountains where Sorcha had been injured.

Helen set the basin on the bedside table and frowned at the fear she saw in Sorcha's gaze. "You know I'll do everything I can to not hurt you, Sorcha."

Sorcha reached her hand out for her friend. "I ken. It's just …" She firmed her jaw as it quivered. "I dinna ken if the bairn suffered."

Helen let out a breath and eased onto the bed to sit, facing her friend. "Are you bleeding? Like you have your monthly courses?"

"Nae," Sorcha whispered. She dropped a hand over her belly.

"Does your belly hurt?" At Sorcha's confused look, asked, "Like you were kicked in your belly?"

"Nae, I've no pain there."

Helen let out a relieved breath. "Thank God," she murmured. "I feared my brother had turned into the Devil himself and had done more than bash you over the head. I feared he had beaten you when you were senseless." Helen rose to examine Sorcha's head.

"I dinna ken what he did," Sorcha whispered.

Helen stilled her movements. She met Sorcha's terrified gaze. "Were your clothes askew? Do you hurt anywhere else but your head?"

Sorcha shook her head. "Nae. 'Tis only my head that aches. An', when I woke, my clothes were no' rucked up."

Helen closed her eyes in relief. "Good," she whispered. "I think all he did was strike you." She opened her eyes and met Sorcha's gaze. "I'm not implying that isn't horrible. But it could have been so much worse."

Sorcha nodded. "Aye. I dinna share this fear with Frederick. He was already terrified about the baby and your brother holding the pistol to my head. He has to live with the vision of Walter holding me at knife point." She bit her lip at her rash words as Helen paled. She reached forward and grabbed Helen's hand. "I'm sorry, Helen. I ken he's yer brother."

She sniffled. "Yes. But he's not like yours. I feel no kinship to him."

After a moment of awkward silence, Helen let go of Sorcha's hand and untied the bandage around Sorcha's head. It stuck where the blood had dried, and she rose to wet a cloth. When she successfully loosened the bandage, she sighed with remorse. "I'm sorry, Sorcha, but you need stitches. This is a deep gash."

Sorcha nodded. "I ken."

Helen held a clean cloth to her wound and then pulled Sorcha's hand up to hold it in place. "I'll be back in a moment." Helen scurried from the room, returning with Slims, her medical bag and a bottle of whiskey.

"I dinna ken if now is the time for drinkin'," Sorcha joked.

Helen shook her head. "No, I'll use it to help clean the wound." She looked around the room and brought a lit candle over to the bedside table to give her more light. She set out what she would need and then wet another cloth with whiskey. She held it to Sorcha's wound, earning a small hiss of distress.

"Slims, come here with the bottle," Helen said. She held the linen below the wound and instructed Slims to pour the whiskey onto the open wound. The linen would sop up most of the whiskey and blood that overflowed.

Sorcha whimpered, fisting her hands, and clamped her eyes shut at the pain. "Ye wee demon," she groaned. "They say I'm a demon, but ye truly are. Ye say ye are a healer, but, mother of God, ye are no'!" Tears poured down her cheeks, and Slims held one hand on her shoulder to keep her in place.

When Helen was satisfied the wound was clean, Sorcha relaxed. "Forgive me, Helen. I never meant to say ye were no' a healer."

Helen chuckled. "I've been called much worse. I thought you'd be more colorful in your swearing at me." She smiled as she teased her friend. "You still have plenty of time to practice as I stitch up your head."

"Slims!" Sorcha thrust out a hand. "Give me that whiskey." She grabbed the bottle, swallowing down a mouthful before gasping. "It burns as badly goin' into my gullet as it does on my head. Why do my brothers like drinkin' it?"

Slims eased the bottle from her grasp. "I believe it's an acquired taste, Missus. And I hope you have no reason to acquire it."

"Aye, neither do I." She closed her eyes and gave a grunt of thanks as Slims held onto one of her hands as Helen stitched Sorcha's wound together. Rather than rant and rail, Sorcha whimpered. When Helen whispered, "Done," Sorcha burst into tears. "Thank ye, Helen. I dinna ken how ye can do that. Ye harm someone to heal them."

Helen ran a hand over Sorcha's shoulder and met her friend's pain-ladened eyes. "Yes, but that is true of all of us at times, Sorcha." She squeezed her shoulder. "Rest. I'll be here for a few days to ensure you don't develop a fever."

Sorcha met Slims's worried gaze. "He left, aye?" At his nod, she slumped farther into the bed. "Stay in the big house. Make sure we are safe. Until he returns."

"Of course. He already asked me to." Slims released her hand. "I'll be by soon to see if you want any supper."

"Thank you, Slims," Sorcha whispered, already tumbling into sleep.

Bears led the silent party up the narrow trail through the forest. He followed Frederick's instructions and led them to the abandoned camp. Bears motioned for them to wait for him, and they stood in silence, with guns at the ready as Bears went into the woods. Bears returned an hour later.

"His trail isn't hard to follow, but he has quite a head start. If you want, I can follow it and find the man. I don't know how I'll bring him back to town without … inflicting more damage."

Warren sat on a log and looked around the camp. "Why would he be here on Frederick's land?"

Bears pointed to another small trail. "I suspect the answer lies up that trail." They tugged their horses behind them and continued on a path up a hill with the stream trickling beside it. "The water shouldn't be this cloudy this time of year," Bears commented.

"I said that to Sorcha when we were out here recently," Frederick said.

They walked along a small trail carved through the woods.

Someone had cut out the dead and fallen logs, allowing them to walk easily and for their horses to travel without impediment. The air was thick with the scent of pine and fir trees, and the sound of the creek became louder. They walked the short distance uphill with Bears in the lead. He came to an abrupt halt as he crested a small ridge. "This is why," he said and led them to a makeshift placer claim. Water from the creek had been diverted to help filter sediment in the search for ore or other minerals.

"Do you own this land?" Warren asked Frederick.

"Yes. My father always said our land went to the top of the mountain. He wanted to make sure we had the rights to the water that came out of this creek."

"Smart man," Ewan muttered.

"Difficult land to prove up on," Warren muttered.

Frederick shrugged. "The bottom part of it was flat." He pulled out his pistol before he wandered around. He poked his head into a small miner's shed but found it empty. There was no horse, and Walter was nowhere to be found.

Bears had wandered to a small pool built above that would feed water as needed into the sluice and allowed an even flow for the small mining operations. "What do you want to do?"

"Destroy it. Destroy it all," Frederick said. "I might not do physical damage to Walter, but I will hurt him every other way."

"And he most cares about finances," Warren said. "As your lawyer, I will be able to say you were merely protecting your property rights." He nodded in agreement as Ewan found an ax and hacked at the wood making up the sluice. Bears stood in the shallow pond, removing small stones that had blocked the creek's natural flow. Soon the water freely flowed down the creek again, and the pond shrank in size.

Bears joined Warren as he watched Frederick and Ewan release their pent-up frustrations and anger as they tore apart the small mine. "They'll still want to do him bodily harm," Bears murmured. "But this brings them a few moments of peace."

Warren shrugged. "Sometimes that's all you need to calm the rage within."

After the claim looked as though a small tornado had ripped through it, Frederick and Ewan collapsed on rocks near Bears and Warren. They panted as they nodded their heads in satisfaction, while they surveyed the destruction they had wrought. Frederick sucked on a thumb in an attempt to loosen a splinter, and Ewan put pressure on his bleeding finger.

"Come. Let's get going. Helen can tend your wounds, and I'm sure Sorcha will want to know you are well," Warren said. "I doubt we'll make it to the ranch before dusk."

"There's little more to do here." Bears hesitated to join them. "If you want, I can continue to track his trail."

Frederick paused. "No, come back with us. We've destroyed whatever reason he had for being on my land, unless he's rustling my cattle. Regardless, he'll resurface. He's injured, and he needs a healer. We'll be ready for him when he does reappear."

Ewan nodded. "Aye, we will."

Helen rushed to the front porch at their arrival. Rather than ride to the barn, they stopped at the house, hitching the horses to the post.

"Helen?" Warren asked as he ran up the steps. "What's the matter?"

Frederick nearly pushed him aside. "Sorcha?" he asked, his gaze wild with fear.

"No, no, it's nothing like that. The sheriff is here. Slims is standing guard at the entrance to the hallway, while Dalton is glaring at the man. The sheriff wants to interview her and doesn't accept that she has a severe head wound and is asleep. He thinks I've concocted the tale since I was injured in a similar fashion last year."

"He will show you respect," Warren growled.

"And he'll leave Sorcha be until she's ready to speak with him," Frederick snapped. "If he needs an account of what happened, Slims and I can speak with him."

Bears sighed, walking to the front door to block their precipitous entrance. "Calm down." He spoke in his low forceful voice. "You aren't helping anyone with your tempers."

Ewan glared at him. "There will come a time, Bears, when ye are no' always calm an' rational."

Bears' gaze glinted with acknowledgment of Ewan's words even though he shook his head at his friends. "If you march in there like a pack of rabid wolves, you'll antagonize that man and prevent him from believing that Walter is the problem. The sheriff already has a fragile-enough sense of right and wrong as it is."

Warren took a deep breath and rolled his shoulders. He calmed further as Helen stroked a hand down his arm. "You're correct of course, Bears. It's difficult to always be rational."

Bears nodded, but his gaze was now on Frederick.

"I will be with my wife when he questions her," Frederick said in a tone that brooked no argument.

"I doubt the man would bar you from the room," Bears said. "Be reasonable and act like you're placating his ego."

Frederick tilted his head as though studying Bears. "It's how you've managed to outmaneuver most of the townsfolk, isn't it? Soften them up with sweet words, and then you can do what you please."

Bears rolled his eyes. "I don't talk to the townsfolk. I speak with their horses." His tone implied the horses were the ones with sense.

Frederick looked to Warren and Ewan and saw that their momentary ire and fear had passed. "Come. Let's see the sheriff." After Bears stepped aside, Frederick opened the front door to see the scene as Helen described it. Slims stood as a glowering hulk, guarding the hallway and stairs from the sheriff. Dalton, never a very loquacious man, glared at the sheriff, while Dixon spun yarn after yarn about life on the ranch. The sheriff roamed the parlor, his bootheels *thunk*ing on the floor as he paced.

Frederick gave a nod of thanks to Slims and Dalton before focusing on the sheriff. "I am glad you came so quickly at the behest of one of my men. Slims and I will give you witness accounts as to the harm done to my expectant wife and how one of our bullets hit Walter's arm."

The sheriff stared at him in confusion.

"I have Walter's gun for you to inspect. And the knife he used to torment my wife."

The sheriff waved away the offer to see the weapons. "I did not come here at the request of one of your men. I am here because I must speak with your wife. Perhaps you'd care to explain to me why I was barred from seeing your wife." Sheriff Sampson stood at his full six foot height and glared at the party who had just entered. He stroked his brindle-colored mustache as he took in their united front. "I can see I won't get far with any of you."

"I don't understand what you mean," Frederick said.

"I believe that your wife is the last person to have seen Walter Jameson before he fled town. I know this because the healer was called, and the townsfolk like to gossip." He held up a slip of paper. "I have here a warrant for his arrest. You're impeding my investigation and could lead to his escape. And such actions could be construed as a desire to aid that man."

Frederick flushed red with anger. "If you believe we would aid him, you are a fool. We were away from the ranch because we were tracking Walter after he kidnapped my wife this morning and ran away from us. Slims shot him in the arm when we rescued him from her." He took a warning step toward the sheriff as he vibrated with anger. "Imagine how I felt when I saw my wife, tied to a tree, with him taunting her with a knife. Threatening to kill her." Frederick glared at the sheriff as the sheriff stared at him as though unimpressed by what Frederick had said.

Bears hissed in a breath and made a sound like he did when he needed to calm an uptight horse.

Frederick ignored him and focused on the sheriff. "My wife is upstairs with a severe head wound that required stitches and I will not be made to feel guilty that I don't care for the sheriff to be in her room, interrogating her while she is in such a fragile state."

"Sorcha MacKinnon hasn't been fragile since the day she arrived in Bear Grass Springs. That woman is a hellion," the sheriff snapped.

"Ye be careful how ye speak about my sister, ye ken?" Ewan bellowed.

"And she's Sorcha Tompkins, *my wife*," Frederick said with a step toward the sheriff. "Helen arrived to care for her. She's the only one who I allowed in her sick room."

"Then why does your hulking man have blood on his shirt?" the sheriff asked.

Helen stepped between the men who were acting like circling pugilists, waiting for the opportune moment to strike. "I needed Slims to help me hold Sorcha in place while I stitched her head wound."

"So others *are* allowed in her sick room," the sheriff said in triumph. He looked toward the large man whose glower had deepened.

"Only to aid my wife, not to harangue her or to pester her. She suffered enough already today. I only sent for you, Sheriff, to take Slims' and my witness statements and to ensure you understood what occurred this morning," Frederick said. He took a deep breath, closing his eyes a moment. "I will check on my wife. If she feels well enough to speak with you, then I will allow you a short time with her as long as I am present. Then you may ask Slims and me whatever you'd like to know."

The sheriff nodded. A short time later, the sheriff entered the bedroom where Sorcha sat propped against a pile of pillows. A white bandage covered her wound, already bright red with blood behind her ear, and she squinted at the sheriff.

"Why are you looking at the bureau?" the sheriff asked.

She focused on his voice and blinked. "I see double right now, an' I thought ye were over there." She sighed and closed her eyes. "Ask me what ye want, but dinna expect me to look at ye."

The sheriff frowned at her, and Frederick glared at him as he sat beside his wife, holding her hand. "Are you sure?" He smiled as she patted his hand.

"What were you doing in the forest?"

"Collecting huckleberries."

"Where are these huckleberries?" The sheriff sat on a chair and made notes on a small pad of paper.

"Scattered on the floor of the forest. I imagine a bear is eatin' 'em," she said as she opened her eyes to look in the sheriff's direction. "I threw my basket at Walter in an attempt to get away from him."

"What did he do?"

She shuddered. "Tackled me. Held me down. An' then he must have bashed me on my head. I dinna remember anythin' until I woke up."

The sheriff frowned. "Why didn't he kill you?"

"I dinna ken. I told him that he was a dead man for touchin' me." Her hold on Frederick tightened as he stiffened next to her. "He said more than one man wanted him dead. I dinna ken what that means."

"It means he's a desperate man, ma'am, and I'd count myself fortunate if you escaped with only a head wound and a few scrapes to your wrists and with your clothes in tatters." He focused on Frederick. "What did you find when you returned to the forest?"

He paused and then shrugged. "We returned to Walter's camp, but he had quite a head start on us. Bears could have tracked him, but it's not Bears's responsibility to bring him to justice." He met the sheriff's stare. "From the camp, we took another trail, and we found a small placer mine. It's no longer functional."

The sheriff's eyes glinted with interest. "I had heard a rumor that the existence of a fake MBR brand was to put you off the real reason he was on your land. It seems that rumor was correct."

Frederick's gaze sharpened as he stared at the sheriff. "Does this mean that no one is rustling my cattle?"

"I can't guarantee that, but I do know that no blacksmith in town has made a new brand. Few see a profit in rustling just now." The sheriff sighed and rose. "If you don't mind, I might borrow the Indian to help me track Walter."

Frederick glared at the sheriff as Sorcha bristled next to him. "Bears is his own man. You'll have to ask him if he has any inclination to aid you."

The sheriff rose. "I'll get brief statements from your giant and the

241

healer while I am here. Then I'll be leaving, unless you have further information to add at this time."

Frederick shook his head, and the sheriff left, closing the bedroom door behind him.

"Do ye think Bears will help the man?"

Frederick kissed her head and smiled. "The only way he'd help the man is if Bears thought he'd be aiding you in some way." He kissed her again and then stood. "I must see the sheriff out, and I'll be back."

After the sheriff had left, and Helen had redressed Sorcha's head wound, Frederick eased open his bedroom door. The curtains remained pulled back to allow the cool night air to enter the open windows. Faint moonlight lit the room, and he shucked his clothes before moving to the bed. Sorcha lay on her side, facing him with her eyes closed.

Rather than crawl into bed, he knelt on the floor and watched the slow cadence of her breathing. The new white bandage enhanced the beauty of her red-brown hair, and her hair was loose around her shoulders. After a moment he reached forward and took a lock between his fingers, playing with the silky strands for a few moments.

"Are ye done starin' at me yet?" she whispered. Her mouth turned up in a half smile, although she didn't open her eyes.

"I'll never have my fill of looking at you. You are the most beautiful woman I've ever seen, my love." He leaned forward to kiss her cheek.

"Daft," she said, but her voice was filled with pleasure. "Come to bed, husband. I want ye to hold me."

He lay beside her, sighing with contentment as she rested her head against his shoulder. "Why didn't you braid your hair tonight?"

"It tugged too much on the wound. Hurt," she muttered. She ran a soothing hand over his chest as he tensed at the word. "I'll be fine."

"As long as you don't get an infection. As long as ..."

"*Shh*, love," she said as she kissed his chin. "Helen is here, and she willna allow anythin' to happen to me." She smiled. "Nor will ye." She frowned as her words failed to ease the tension in his body. "What is it, Frederick?" She attempted to lift her head to look at him but groaned and put her head down again. "I want to look at ye, but I canna."

"*Shh*, love. Don't make yourself dizzy." He held her close, his hands roving over her as he kissed her head. "What else, Sorch? What else did he do to you?"

"Oh, my love," she rasped as her tears soaked his chest. "Nothin'. I promise ye. All he did was bash me on the head, cut my dress and taunt me with his words. Naught else."

"You swear?" he asked. "For you know I'd love you, no matter what happened."

She swallowed a sob and pushed herself more tightly into his embrace. "I ken. And ye canna ken what a gift that is. He threatened me, Frederick. I willna lie an' say he dinna. But I spoke with Helen, and I dinna have any pain except for my head. I would feel somethin' if he had attacked me, aye?"

Frederick let out a pent-up breath, although his hold on her did not ease. "And the bairn?"

She kissed his chest. "The bairn is fine. I'm no' bleedin'. I have no pains, and I have no reason to believe the bairn is in any sort of trouble." She smiled as his palm cupped her face. "We are well."

"You are my life, Sorcha. You and our babe. I'd be lost without you." He raised her hand and kissed it.

She rested on his chest for minutes, and he thought she'd fallen asleep, but then she whispered. "What did ye do today when ye left me?" She gripped his arm. "I ken I made it sound like I would be all right if ye beat the man." She shook her head, stilling her movement when he rested his hand gently on her shoulder. "I dinna want ye comin' to any harm, Frederick. An' I dinna want to give that sheriff any reason to arrest ye. To separate ye from me and our bairn."

Frederick murmured into her ear, and she calmed.

"What did ye do? You do no' seem as filled with rage as afore ye left."

"Do you remember that day we went swimming in the creek, and you told me about selkies?" He smiled as she gave a little giggle. "I said the creek seemed too dirty for that time of year. Well, we discovered that Walter had built a small mining operation farther up on our land. He'd diverted the creek to help with the cleaning of the ore."

"What did ye do?"

He kissed her temple. "Warren watched us as Bears destroyed the small dam, and Ewan and I took turns with an ax destroying the wooden sluice. Walter won't be mining again anytime soon on our land."

She traced her fingers over his chest. "Did it help ease yer rage?"

"A little. I no longer have a desire to murder him. I don't know what I'll do if I see him though." His arms tightened around her. "He threatened you, my love, and I'll never forgive him that."

She kissed the underside of his jaw. "Aye, I ken. But dinna let yer anger at him consume ye. He'll suffer justice someday soon. I ken it."

CHAPTER 13

In early August, Sorcha knelt in the dirt and paused in her digging. She rubbed an arm over her forehead, smearing both with dirt, and grunted in dismay. The garden had been planted in May, and now shoots of green sprouted up in the orderly rows. However, weeds attempted to choke out her vegetables, and she fought a never-ending battle to allow her vegetables the room and nutrients they needed to grow. She worked early in the morning before the heat of the day and knew she would soon need to go inside. She would return that evening.

In the large fenced-off area of the garden, she had planted rows of carrots, beets, potatoes, green beans, onions and cabbage. She had discussed gardening at length with both Harold and Irene, when they had visited in the spring, and hoped she would have as great a success as they had when they lived here. In the past few years, Frederick had left the garden fallow, and his men had grumbled at having to till it again. However, once the healthy soil was readied for her seeds, Sorcha had eagerly planted her garden, following her grandparents' instructions.

She paused at having mentally called Harold and Irene *her grandparents*. They had wanted her to consider them as her grandparents from the moment they had come to the ranch after her marriage, and she realized she did. She'd barely known her MacKinnon forebearers in Scotland, and she knew little about Mairi MacQueen and her people. Sorcha sighed with pleasure at the thought of all of the family she now had.

After she finished weeding the carrots, she moved to the beans. Her arms and back ached, and she glared at the large pile of weeds that grew beside her. "I ken how to grow weeds," she muttered to herself.

She shrieked as a deep voice chuckled and a large shadow blocked out the sun's morning rays. She sat on her heels and held the spade in front of her as a weapon. "Who are ye, an' what are ye doin' in my garden?"

A tall slender man with brown hair and blue eyes stared down at her, his cowboy hat in his hands. The other man, slightly stouter and taller than the man next to him with blond hair and blue eyes, glared at her. "What are you doing in the garden?" asked the blond-haired man.

"Sorcha!" Frederick yelled as he ran around the side of the house to the garden. He came to an abrupt halt and stared at the two men. "Peter? Cole?"

"Who is this woman in our grandmother's garden?" the brown-haired man asked.

Frederick laughed and launched himself at his brothers. "My wife, you fools." He pulled them close. "Have you received none of the letters I've sent you?"

His brothers clapped him on his back, yet looked at Sorcha with distrust.

Frederick held out a hand to Sorcha. "This is Peter," he said, pointing to the brown-haired man with the slender build. "And that's Cole." He smiled at his stouter blond-haired brother. "This is Sorcha, my wife. We married in March."

"March?" Peter asked as his brothers shared a look. "Weren't you still battling a severe winter?"

"And how did you meet such a woman living out here?" Cole asked.

Sorcha leaned into Frederick's side and met their glowers. "'Tis a long story, but I was married to yer brother with yer ranch hands lookin' on by the lawyer, Warren Clark." Her glare dared them to contradict the validity of their marriage.

"Why did it take you so long to arrive?" Frederick asked. "It's August."

Peter shook his head. "It's not as easy as it used to be to bring a herd north. There's more fence, and too many don't want you on their land. We had to backtrack more than I'd like."

Frederick gaped at his brothers. "I thought you weren't bringing any cattle north this year."

"We weren't plannin' on it. Not after the disastrous sale in Chicago last fall," Cole said. "But then we got a herd for cheap. A man had planned to bring them north, but he got sick and didn't know what to do with them. We heard about it and made him a deal."

Peter smiled. "You know how good Cole is at negotiating." He slapped his brother on his shoulder. "The herd will be here tomorrow. It's over the rise there." He pointed to the hills in the distance. "We rode ahead because we were hoping to surprise you."

"Is Buck bringing it in?" Frederick asked.

Peter nodded. "We wouldn't have left anyone else in charge."

Frederick turned to Sorcha. "Buck is one of our most trusted men. He's originally from Ohio, so we call him Buck."

"What's his real name?" she asked.

"Obediah," Cole said and then shared a smile with Sorcha as she giggled. "He's never seemed to mind the name Buck."

"Come. Ye must be tired," Sorcha said as she motioned for them go to the ranch house.

The brothers shook their heads. "No, ma'am. We should wash first." They nodded to her and moved to the barn and the water pump.

She watched in silence as they loped away. "So yer brothers are back."

He kissed her on the forehead. "Yes, but they won't be here long.

It's already August. They'll leave in October after the fall roundup." He met her worried gaze. "What is it Ewan would say?" He smiled. "Don't fash yourself, my love. Everything will be well."

〜

Frederick walked to the barn and ducked inside. Cole and Peter stood in side-by-side stalls, currying their mounts. "Why wouldn't you wire me that you were bringing a herd?"

Cole shrugged. "We didn't think it would matter. You've the herd here with enough acreage to support more. There are plenty of hands to help with the extra work."

Peter set down his brush and stared at Frederick. "Are you telling us you'd rather focus on your horses than cattle? Do you wish we hadn't brought more cattle up?"

Frederick stared at them in astonishment. "How can you not understand how horrible the winter was?" He took a deep breath and clenched and unclenched his hands. "For months I feared we'd lose the ranch." He met his brothers' dumbfounded looks.

"You always exaggerated, Fred," Cole said with a roll of his eyes. He jumped when Frederick slammed his hand against the side of the stall, causing his horse to whinny and to shift its weight from hoof to hoof.

"Don't belittle me. Don't you dare act as though what I suffered through was inconsequential just because things turned out well." He glared at his brothers. "Do you know how many cattle survived for spring roundup?"

"A little less than usual?" Peter asked as he moved from the stall. Cole joined him in the main aisle of the barn, and the older brothers stood side by side as they faced Frederick. However, they noted that the seasoned ranch hands had angled themselves behind Frederick, silently signaling their support of the youngest brother.

"*A little less than usual?*" Frederick took a deep breath. "Try one-third left." He nodded as his brothers' eyes bulged at the number. "Yes, one-third. The rest acted as fertilizer for the range."

"What the hell happened to them?"

"Starved and froze up and died during the harsh winter we had," Frederick said, mocking his brothers.

Cole shook his head. "But, of course, you saved enough hay to keep your precious horses alive. Why spare any for the cattle?"

Frederick shook with rage. "If I hadn't saved the hay for the horses, all the animals would have died. It would have only served to increase the misery rather than lessen it."

Cole rolled his eyes again as though Frederick exaggerated.

"How are we still solvent if we lost so many cattle?" Peter looked around the barn. "You haven't sold your horses. Do you think they're more important than the ranch? You always did enjoy playing with them more than any serious work on the ranch."

Frederick gave a low growl and launched himself at his brother, catching him off guard and shoving him to the ground. He landed a few solid jabs before Slims and Dalton pulled the brothers apart and before Cole could join in.

"That's enough, boys," Slims said. He remained standing beside Frederick.

"You aren't our father, Slims. If we want to fight, we will," Peter snapped, rubbing at a sore rib.

Cole glared at Slims. "You'll always take his side."

Slims stared at the two men and shook his head "You've been here less than an hour and already you're wearing out your welcome." He watched impassively as the two brothers paled.

Frederick turned on his heel and stormed away.

Dalton gave a huff of disgust. "You owe your brother an apology. He does more than play with horses. He raises some of the finest horse flesh in the territory. Many would pay good money to have a chance to buy one of his horses," Dalton said.

"How has the bank not taken over our ranch if he didn't sell any of his horses and only one-third of the herd survived?" Cole asked.

Slims shook his head. "That's a story for your brother to tell. And, when he does, be prepared to eat crow." He turned away and moved farther into the barn with Dalton on his heels.

~

Later that evening, Sorcha waited in her bedroom for Frederick. She braided her hair and then attempted to ease her nerves as she rocked in her rocking chair, listening to the early evening sounds with the windows open to catch any faint breeze. An owl hooted in the distance, and she heard the ranch hands calling to each other as they sat outside to enjoy the beautiful evening air. Her eyes drifted shut as she rested her head against the back of her chair.

A soft hand squeezed her shoulder while she dozed in the rocker, and she bolted awake, her eyes wide and her breath emerging in a pant. "*Shh*, love, you're safe," Frederick whispered. "I'm sorry I scared you."

Her eyes filled with remorse, and she grabbed his hand. "I want to be over this fear. I'm tired of startlin' at every little noise." She flushed. "I'm embarrassed that yer brothers gave me such a fright."

He shook his head. "Don't worry about what anyone else thinks, my darling. All that matters is that you are well and that you feel safe."

She leaned forward from the rocker into his embrace until her head rested against his midsection. "I canna escape this fear that Walter will appear on the ranch. That he'll take me away."

Frederick made a low growl of disagreement. "He knows better than to ever try something that stupid. He'll hide in the woods until the coming winter, and then I don't know what he'll do. But he will never be so foolhardy as to come here and approach you on the ranch."

Sorcha nodded, running her fingers over her husband's cheek and to his shoulders. "I'm still angry he ruined my huckleberry surprise for ye."

He chuckled. "All I care about is that you are well." He held out his hand. "Come to bed, my love. You look worn out."

She rose and yawned, stumbling to bed. "I am. I thought the bairn took all the energy at the end, at the birthing, but I have no energy now."

She waited until he was next to her in bed before hitching an arm and leg over him, anchoring them together. "What happened between ye an' yer brothers? I thought ye'd have dinner together, yet ye did no' join us. I never thought I could be so bored listenin' to two men prattle on about cattle."

Frederick snorted. "No wonder they're single." He gave a huff as Sorcha patted him on his arm. "We argued in the barn. I found I had no desire for their company." He gripped her hand rubbing over his stomach. "And, yes, I ate with my men."

She continued to run her hands over him, his tension easing with her gentle touch. "What did they say to ye?"

He sighed and rolled, pulling her tight against him. "You comfort me, Sorcha, when I don't even realize I need it." He swallowed.

"Ye deserve it," she whispered, interpreting what he meant. She kissed his neck and waited for him to speak.

"Peter and Cole were shocked at how few cattle we had recovered during roundup. Claimed I was exaggerating. And they were angry that, in their opinion, I valued my horses more than the cattle or the ranch. Accused me of playing with my horses rather than working hard to save the MBR."

She growled and would have pushed away had he not held her hard against him. "Fools. I hope ye clobbered 'em."

He laughed, and his hold on her lessened. "I tried to. Slims separated us before we did any real damage to each other."

She gave a *tsk*ing noise, and he smiled as it reminded him of his grandmother. "Nae, the damage was already done. By their thoughtlessness. They dinna ken how ye suffered, worryin' over this ranch while they played cards an' whored an' drank down in Texas." She propped herself on her elbows and met his chagrined gaze. "Do ye think I dinna ken what goes on in places like the Boudoir? I'm sure yer brothers are well acquainted with such establishments wherever they are in Texas."

Frederick sighed and kissed her nose. "I fear you may be right." His fingers played over her cheek. "What should I do?"

"If I were ye, I'd kick them into town." She shook her head and let out a deep breath. "I ken they are part owners of the ranch, an' ye canna do that. Thus I'd call them into yer office. An' inform them how bad it was. Show them yer sheets with prognostications. An' show them it's *yer* office."

He chuckled. "They won't care. They never wanted the running of the ranch. The day-to-day paperwork has never interested them. They've always had a desire to be outside."

"Aye, but I ken they'll care when ye inform them ye've chosen the new foreman." She met his surprised gaze. "Ye ken who it should be, an' ye dinna want them to pick a man who doesna respect ye as he should."

He continued to stare at her in awed silence.

"Slims."

"He would never want the role."

"How can ye be so daft?" Sorcha sat up, shaking her head. "He's already doin' the work of two men. Why would ye deny him that title if he would accept the job?"

Frederick nodded. "He would be perfect. He knows the ranch better than anyone."

"Aye, an' he's loyal to ye. He kens all about cattle an' horses an' doesna believe the horses are a waste of time. Ye must protect yerself an' the ranch, Frederick."

He ran soothing hands over her arms and pulled her against him. "I will, Sorcha. I'll speak to Slims and then to my brothers. I know my grandfather will agree with your reasoning."

"An' yer grandmother. They may be silent partners, but I ken they still have a say in how the ranch is run. Ye ken she'd support ye, and that would make three in favor of Slims."

He buried his face in her hair. "I hope we don't have to resort to speaking with my grandparents. I will if I must."

"Ye have the right to have a man here who will support ye through the entire year, no' just when Peter and Cole are around." She kissed his chest.

His hold on her tightened. "Thank you, my love. For loving and supporting me."

She smiled and kissed his neck. "Of course. As I told ye before, ye are my heart's desire, Frederick. When ye are happy, I'm happy."

He buried his face in her hair. "You'll never know how much that means." He held her as she began to drift asleep. "Rest, my love."

Frederick slipped into the barn and breathed a sigh of relief that his brothers were not here. He poked his head into the tack room, finding it empty. After checking the stalls, he looked outside. Slims stood watching the gentle morning light change with the dawn. The sky subtly lightened from a dusky blue to a hint of pink and then a bright pink before the sun peeped over the edge of the mountains.

"Thought you had more sense to remain in bed with your wife. Or has the novelty already worn off?" Slims asked with a quirk of his lips.

Frederick chuckled and shook his head. "The novelty will never wear off. But I need to talk with you. Before I speak with my brothers." He paused, watching the colors reflect on the underside of the clouds. "I've missed quite a few sunrises lately."

Slims snorted. "You've seen plenty in your lifetime. And you'll see plenty more."

Frederick watched one of his horses moving around the paddock. "Are you happy here, Slims?"

Slims stiffened and frowned at him. "Is there a reason I shouldn't be?"

After slinging his arms over the rails of the paddock, Frederick looked at his friend. "No, but I wonder if you wouldn't like more."

"I wouldn't mind a woman to warm my bed. A good woman like you've found, Boss."

Frederick smiled and nodded. "I can't say I blame you for that. Have you ever wanted to be foreman?" He frowned as Slims stood stock-still.

"I was told that foremen had to come to the ranch with experience."

Frederick gave a snort of disgust. "Maybe that's something my father said when we were all greenhorns. None of us are greenhorns anymore." He looked into his friend's hopeful gaze. "I want someone here who will support me and who will tell me when I'm being a fool. I don't want someone who'll say, 'Yes, Boss,' and then go do what he thinks should be done because he thinks I'm a fool."

Slims rolled his eyes. "I'll tell you to your face when you're being an idiot."

Frederick smiled. "I know, and that's what I need. Will you be my foreman? I've never replaced Old Man Withers who left."

"Withers," Slims muttered. "Should have been called *Dithers*. Man could never make up his mind unless one of your brothers told him what to do." Slims met his boss's serious gaze. "I want to be your foreman. I think I already have the respect of the men."

"I know you do. You already have mine." Frederick pushed away from the paddock and held out his hand. "Thank you, Slims." He slapped the big man on his back and looked in the direction of the ranch house. "I should get back for breakfast. Sorcha already had to suffer through dinner with my brothers last night. I think she'd never forgive me if I abandoned her again this morning."

Slims chuckled as the young man turned to walk away.

"Oh, and, Slims? There will be a pay raise whenever the ranch can afford it. And you can use the foreman's house if you'd like."

Slims smiled at the thought of the raise and then glowered at the mention of the foreman's house. "I can't imagine bunkin' alone after livin' with the men all these years. I'll let you know."

Frederick nodded and made his way back to the house and his meeting with his brothers.

Frederick entered his office and glared at Peter until he rose from the seat behind the desk and moved to the chair beside Cole on the other side of the desk. Frederick settled behind his desk and looked at his brothers, allowing the silence to continue between them.

"Why the hell were there only one-third of the cattle alive for roundup?" Cole blurted out.

"And how are we still here at the ranch? Why didn't the bank take possession of it?" Peter asked.

Frederick sat back in his chair and sighed. "Wasn't the winter as awful in Texas?" When they stared blankly at him, he shook his head. "Winter hit Montana in November full force. As you know, summer had been too dry, and the grass on the range was weak. If we'd had a mild winter, like the one the previous year, we would have been all right." His gaze became unfocused. "But this winter was fierce. Feet of snow. Howling winds from the north."

He paused. "And then the worst thing possible happened. We had a chinook in January. Melted everything, then refroze. The cattle had no chance of digging through the icy layer over the snow. And temperatures hit minus sixty."

Frederick met their shocked gazes. "When I received your telegram, weeks after you sent it, that you weren't bringing cattle north and to keep enough alive for the fall roundup ..." His jaw clenched, and he glared at them. "I was desperate and angry and certain we'd lose the ranch."

"How didn't you?" Cole asked. "Is your wife an heiress?"

Frederick laughed. "You've spent time with her. You know she comes from a simple hardworking family from Scotland. She's no heiress, although she's everything to me." He smiled as he thought of Sorcha before focusing on his brothers again. "A few weeks after the spring roundup, Shorty rode in with a herd that had wintered up in the high mountain pasture. They were healthy."

Peter nodded. "And now we've brought more back. We'll thrive again."

Cole nodded at his brother's statement and frowned as Frederick didn't readily agree. "Quit being such a pessimist. We're fine now."

Frederick shook his head. "We're one winter away from another disaster like we just survived. Things have to change. I think they must change if we are to survive." He frowned. "I'm not certain how, but they must."

Peter jabbed at Cole with his elbow to be quiet and nodded at his youngest brother. "What do you suggest?"

"All winter, all I could think about was that, if we'd just had enough hay, we could have saved so many of the cattle. But we didn't have any put aside."

Cole rolled his eyes. "That's not how it's done, brother."

"Not how it's *been* done," Frederick said. "I think things may change." He looked at his siblings. "I know we share the running of the ranch, but I'm here full-time. I want Slims as the foreman."

Frederick waited as Cole sputtered and Peter sat back, watching Frederick with a calculated look. "You want your man in charge," Peter said.

"He's *our* man," Frederick snapped. "He'll only ever have the best interests of the ranch in mind. I work well with him, and I trust him, as do the ranch hands." He paused as his brothers glared at him. "As do the grandparents."

"You'd bring them into this?" Cole rasped, his cheeks flushed and his eyes dancing with anger.

"Yes. I put up with Withers, that pathetic excuse for a foreman, for long enough. You have no idea how excited everyone was when he left." He glared at his brothers. "Just because someone is good at bringing in a herd does not mean they are qualified to be foreman of the ranch. If you doubt what I say, you should remain on the ranch and try ranching for a year with no promise of driving a herd north." He smiled with satisfaction as his brothers shuddered at the thought.

"So you think Buck couldn't do it?" Peter asked.

Frederick rolled his eyes. "He couldn't do it because he doesn't care about the daily concerns of ranch life and wouldn't do it because he loves being on the range." He met their glares as they slowly calmed. "I lost the bet. I stayed. You can't continue to control things on the ranch when you aren't here day to day."

Peter let out a deep breath and relaxed. "Dammit, Frederick, I hate that you're right. We're still treating you like a snot-nosed ten-year-old chasing after us."

"Hard to believe you got married without us," Cole said with a shake of his head. "Can't imagine wanting to marry any woman."

Frederick smiled. "Not all women are like Mother." He relaxed into his chair. "Good. I'm glad we agree about Slims. He's delighted." He chuckled at their indignant glares as they realized he had already offered the job to the loyal ranch hand. Frederick rose but paused when Cole shook his head.

"We owe you an apology, Fred," Cole said. He looked at Peter, who nodded. "We should never have said you cared more for your horses than the ranch. It was out of line."

"We can't imagine living here all year long and taking on the responsibility of running the ranch as you do. We'd fail after a year," Peter said. "Thank you for running it as well as you do."

Frederick nodded. He reached out his hand and shook theirs. "Thank you. And welcome home."

CHAPTER 14

A week later, as Harold and Irene worked in the café kitchen with Fidelia, Leticia and Annabelle, Sorcha and Frederick set the tables in the café. Harold and Irene had closed the café for the evening for a private celebration for the newlyweds, and the tables had been pushed together so they could all sit together. Sorcha ran to Cailean as he entered with Skye, giving him a hug and kissing Skye on her cheek. Skye patted at Sorcha's head, and Sorcha giggled, tickling her niece's belly. She repeated her embrace with Ewan and Alistair, and she beamed at her husband as she stood surrounded by her brothers.

"'Tis wondrous to have us all together again," she said. "I canna believe it's been so long." Her eyes shone with tears, and she smiled as Ewan pulled her close.

"Dinna cry, Sorcha. Although I ken bein' around us is reason enough to weep with joy." He laughed as she batted him on his arm.

She embraced Jessamine, who held Alistair's son, Angus. Alistair had a tight grip on Hortence's hand. Soon Peter and Cole had joined them, and platters of food were brought in from the kitchen. Warren and Helen arrived just as they passed food around.

"I'm so sorry we're late," Helen said as she smiled a welcome to everyone. "I had a patient and lost track of time."

"'Tis no worry," Sorcha said. "I'm glad ye were able to make it."

Warren ran a hand over his wife's back, and they settled in their chairs, joining in the laughter and chatter.

"What news have you heard, Warren, about Walter?" Frederick asked. He saw his brothers focus as they had the bare bones of the story about Sorcha's most recent injuries at Walter Jameson's hands.

Warren shrugged. "Not much more than you. It seems he entered into a business agreement with a wealthy businessman in Helena, convincing that man that he knew where a secret lode of ore was." Warren nodded as Frederick and Ewan snorted their disbelief.

"Damn fool," Ewan muttered.

"His goal was to bamboozle said man out of as much money as possible, before claiming the mine wasn't as profitable as he had thought. His only problem was the man showed up last fall, wanting to see the mine." Warren nodded to Sorcha. "He was with Walter when Sorcha's horse reared. Seems he has as few scruples as Walter does and was afraid his mother lode would be discovered by someone else."

"Who is this man?" Cailean asked in a low voice laden with ire.

Warren shook his head. "I'm not about to tell you because you'd race off to Helena and make fools of yourself. I have no desire to be out of Bear Grass Springs for more time than is truly necessary." He winked at Sorcha. "Summer is my favorite time of year here, and August is far from over."

Sorcha smiled at Warren before giving a quelling look to her three brothers and squeezing her husband's arm. "Is he the one with the warrant out for Walter's arrest?"

Warren nodded. "Yes, and I wouldn't be surprised if a bounty hunter shows up at some point." He shrugged. "Walter's greed got the better of him this time."

Helen shivered next to her husband as she thought about her brother. "It will always get the better of him."

Peter looked at his youngest brother. "Will you be content with the fact he is far from town? You've ruined his reason for being on our land."

Frederick took a deep breath as he looked around the table at his family. "I will always want to rip into him for what he did to Sorcha. For what he threatened to do to her." He saw everyone sober at those words. "But I will not seek him out. I will not spend my days looking for revenge."

Irene beamed at him. "I'm so glad, Frederick. Look to your future, which will be filled with joy and hard work ..."

"And babies," Harold said with a wink.

"And love. Don't focus on the past." Irene blinked as she fought her tears as she looked from her grandson to the woman she considered her granddaughter.

Cailean cleared his throat. "Now is a good time for toasts." He nodded to Ewan.

Ewan rose, holding up his cup as he looked at his sister. "Ye ken how beloved ye are, Sorcha. Ye fill our family with laughter an' joy, an' we've no' been right without yer frequent visits. I ken ye live on the ranch with yer Frederick, but ken ye're always welcome here, an' I hope ye'll come to town for a monthly visit, or we'll die from missin' ye." He smiled as he saw a tear course down his sister's cheek. "Ye are strong an' brave, an' it's only fitting ye chose a man who is as strong as ye. As brave as ye. He took on the MacKinnons an' never suffered a beating." He smiled as those around him chuckled. Ewan raised his glass higher. "To Sorcha and Frederick. May ye only ever ken happiness an' love."

He sat, and Jessamine rested her head on his shoulder, whispering in his ear.

Peter stood, and the quiet chatter silenced as he cleared his throat. He looked at Sorcha. "I know we were not gracious when we returned. Yet you treated us with respect even though you had turned the ranch house into your home." He flushed. "Cole and I were upset we'd missed your wedding, and then we realized both families hadn't been present." He glowered at Cole as he hit his arm. "What I'm trying to say is that I've never seen Frederick happier. He smiles all the time, laughs and jokes, and isn't as serious."

Sorcha sniffled and smiled at Peter. "Thank ye."

Cole interrupted his brother. "Thank you, Sorcha, for making the ranch a place we want to spend time at again. For making it a home again. We hope you and Frederick are happy there for as long as you want to be there."

Frederick stood and hugged his brothers, slapping them on their backs, and then Sorcha gave each of them a kiss on their cheek.

After a moment Annabelle rose. "Well, I think it's time for cake and coffee."

Sorcha nodded and followed her into the kitchen.

"You're the guest of honor, Sorcha," Annabelle said as she looked to Leticia who had entered after her. She frowned as she saw Fidelia grab her shawl and slip out the back door. "You should wait for us to serve you."

"I need a moment away from all that emotion. I thought Cailean …" Sorcha said as she took a deep breath and rubbed at her cheeks. "Let the men have a moment."

"You forget that Jessamine, Irene and Helen are out there with Hortence," Leticia said.

"Aye, well, they can mingle with the men," Sorcha said with an impish smile. "Oh, 'tis wonderful to be with ye all again. But over-whelming too."

Annabelle smiled and pulled her close for a moment. "I imagine it is after months on the ranch. Although you have plenty of company with the ranch hands."

Sorcha shrugged. "They mainly eat in their bunkhouse now. Frederick and I eat alone most nights." She sighed and studied her sister-in-law. "How are ye, Annabelle? Ye look well, but I dinna ken if that's true."

Annabelle beamed at her. "I am. For the past month, I've finally felt well." She saw the unspoken question in Sorcha's eyes. "I doubt we'll have more children, but we have Skye and each other. And we'll dote on any you and Leticia have."

Leticia smiled as she patted her belly. "I wonder if we'll have our babies around the same time?"

Sorcha grinned. "They'll never ken life without the other. Will that no' be wonderful?"

"Yes," Leticia said and then gave a small grunt as they heard someone ask about cake in the other room. "Come. They're becoming restless."

Annabelle held Sorcha back a moment. "Don't worry, Sorcha. Cailean will give you a blessing." She winked at her sister-in-law as she picked up the layered cake and brought it into the main room.

~

Fidelia pushed open the barn door and slipped inside the darkened interior. She waited for her eyes to adjust, listening intently to determine where Bears was. However, all she heard was the sound of horses nickering. She walked down the center aisle of the barn and held her hand out for Sugar, smiling as she brushed her fingers over Sugar's velvety muzzle.

"Are you looking for me?" Bears whispered in her ear.

She shrieked, jumping and jarring her shoulder against the stall. She calmed as Bears gripped her arms, his touch gentle and sure, steadying her.

"I didn't mean to startle you." He frowned as she looked down and didn't meet his gaze.

"Why are you not at the celebration?" Fidelia asked him. "Don't you want to congratulate Sorcha and Frederick?"

White teeth flashed as he smiled fleetingly. "They know I'm pleased for them. I've no need to join a party that's meant for family."

She grabbed his hand, preventing him from disappearing as silently as he had appeared. "Why do you hold yourself separate? Why won't you accept the gift offered to you?"

His gaze bore into her, causing her to back up a step until she was against the stall door. "I know what I am, and I have no desire to be something I'm not. I'm a trusted friend and business partner."

"Family doesn't come solely from blood," she whispered. "Helen and Warren are family too."

"I'm not fit for company tonight, Stitch," he whispered, his nickname for her slipping out.

She frowned with concern and raised a hand as though to caress his arm before dropping it. "I ... I'd like to know why."

He shook his head and took a deep breath. "It's not something to discuss tonight." He looked at her with an intense longing as he leaned closer. "You know why I keep my distance, Fidelia. I refuse to cause you discomfort." He frowned as he saw the sheen of tears in her beautiful blue eyes.

"I miss how it was," she murmured. "Our friendship."

He nodded, taking a step back. "I will always be your friend." He took a deep breath as his eyes shone with regret and loss. "But I will always yearn for more."

She shook her head instinctively, and he backed fully away from her.

"One day," he rasped, "one day, you will come to trust that I am not like all the men you've known. I will not be another disappointment."

His whispered words carried through the barn as he disappeared from view.

After dessert, the family relaxed with cups of coffee after eating their fill of Annabelle's cake. Fidelia had disappeared after dinner, and Hortence's gaze flit to the door as she looked for Bears. Alistair ran a hand over her red hair to calm her as one of her favorite people had failed to make an appearance for Sorcha's and Frederick's party.

Sorcha smiled at her eldest brother, Cailean. "Thank ye for helpin' to organize such a feast an' celebration."

Harold and Irene bustled into the room with Cole and Peter on their heels, making the café dining room feel even smaller. "We should have rented the hall for our gathering," Harold grumbled.

"Then the whole town would have been there," Peter said.

Cole nodded. "There's no need to see those who are better forgotten."

Frederick watched his brothers tense, as though referring to their uncle Tobias. He nodded and ran a hand over Sorcha's shoulder. "I think you'll find that town sentiment is not what you remember." He shrugged as his brothers watched him disbelievingly.

"I wish Bears were here," Helen said.

Sorcha smiled. "Ye ken he's never been one for parties. Frederick an' I spoke with him afore ye all arrived, an' he was gracious an' cryptic, like always." She laughed as her brothers rolled their eyes.

"Someday he'll have to accept our advice as readily as he doles it out to us," Ewan said as he held Jessamine's hand.

Annabelle, much stronger and healthier with a bright blush in her cheeks, frowned. "I'll speak to Bears tomorrow. I don't like him holding himself apart from us."

Warren cleared his throat and shook his head. "You won't be able to do that, Anna. Bears and I are traveling to Helena tomorrow. Hopefully our journey will not be for a prolonged duration, but I cannot say when we will be back."

Alistair and Cailean gaped at him. "When did ye ken ye were goin'?" Cailean demanded.

"Ye'd think our own partner would tell us himself," Alistair grumbled.

Warren smiled, long accustomed to the MacKinnon temper. "He just found out about urgent business in Helena. I'm certain he'll speak with you tomorrow before he leaves. And his need to go to Helena with a lawyer is justified." He saw the understanding in their gazes as he referred to his previous declaration that he did not want to go to Helena to aid them in finding Walter's partner. He tilted his head in Sorcha's and Frederick's direction. "I believe Bears didn't want to ruin your celebration for the newlyweds."

Frederick frowned. "He did seem rather out of sorts when we spoke with him."

"An' he's never out of sorts," Sorcha said.

Warren smiled at Sorcha as she stared at him to expound on what he knew. "All will make itself apparent in due time."

"Dammit, Warren, ye ken that's no' an answer," Ewan said in exasperation. "Bears is our brother. If ye ken somethin', ye must tell us."

Warren chuckled and smiled. "No, I don't. Not when I'm working as his lawyer." He met their startled gazes. "It's his concern, and he must be the one to share with you what he will. Bears has as much right to his privacy as you do. You have to trust that he'll tell you what you want to know."

Sorcha made a grunt of distaste, only relaxing as Frederick rubbed at her shoulders. "Ye ken ye are only an *honorary* member of the clan," she said as she glared at Warren. "We can decide at any time to throw ye out."

He laughed, looking nonplussed at her threat.

Sorcha let out a sigh and relaxed after a moment and shook her head in resignation at the lawyer's ability to keep a secret.

"Ye ken the man would keep yer secret, Sorch," Cailean said, although his gaze was troubled.

"Aye, an' I must admit I respect him for it." She looked to Harold and Irene. "Thank ye for hostin' us here."

Irene smiled at Sorcha. "It is our pleasure. I can't believe it has taken us so long to finally celebrate your marriage, and soon enough we'll celebrate your first child." She looked from Sorcha to Frederick and beamed. "I'm delighted to have a granddaughter at last."

Sorcha's eyes filled with tears, and she hugged Irene.

"Don't go hoggin' the girl to yourself," Harold complained. "I'm delighted too." He winked at Sorcha as he hugged her and swiped at her wet cheeks. "There ain't no need to cry when you're happy."

Sorcha smiled at her family. "'Tis like a dream to me. To have us all together." She frowned as she noted Bears's and Fidelia's absence. "Almost all of us."

Cailean raised a glass. "To Sorcha and Frederick. May you always have the support of family, the joy of each other and the love to see you through anything."

Sorcha smiled at her brother as she leaned into her husband's side.

~

That evening, Sorcha lay with her head on Frederick's chest in the back room of the bakery. Peter and Cole were with their grandparents, and she had no desire to stay with one of her brothers. She traced lazy figures on her husband's chest as he breathed deeply beneath her.

"What are you thinking about?" he asked as he kissed her head.

"About ye focusing on our future rather than the past. Did ye mean it when ye said ye'd no' go chasin' after Walter? That ye'd let him be?"

Frederick sighed. "If I ran across him in the street, I'd tackle him and beat him until he wished he were dead if I could. I wouldn't be able to help myself. But I won't spend my time chasing after him, love. I won't waste what time we have being bitter and angry."

She ran her fingers through his hair as she looked at him and smiled. "Thank ye."

He lowered his hand so that his palm rested over her belly. "I will not risk you or our baby, Sorcha. I will do whatever I must to keep you safe." He kissed her. "But I want to do that standing beside you as we watch the ranch come to life again."

She cupped his jaw. "Aye, husband. Standin' together with our bairns around us as our ranch prospers." She kissed him. "I love our life."

He rested his forehead against hers. "As do I. You're my perfect match, Sorcha. Thank you for being brave and loving me."

"How could I no'?" she whispered as she peppered his face with kisses. "I've told ye before, an' I'll keep tellin' ye. Ye are my heart's desire. I'll always want ye."

He rubbed a thumb over her cheek and looked deeply into her eyes. "Just as I will always want you. Until the end of time, my darling."

"Yes," she murmured, holding him close for many long minutes, dreaming of their future together on the ranch.

SNEAK PEEK AT UBRIDLED MONTANA PASSION!

August 1887, Bear Grass Springs, Montana Territory

It was an improbable day to turn a man's world upside down. A soft wind blew, cooling the hot August heat to a more tolerable level. Warren Clark, Bear Grass Spring's resident lawyer, stood on Bears' doorstep and paused a moment before raising his hand to knock. He stared at the letter in his hand and shook his head before letting his knuckles fall onto the worn wood.

"Lawyer," Bears said as he opened the door with a frown. His raven hair hung freely to his waist, and he wore simple tan pants and a navy blue shirt with a few buttons open at the collar. "You seem to be lost. The party is at the café tonight."

Warren smiled and motioned for an invite into Bears' simple one-room home. "No. I've just received something I think you'd like to read."

The wood door closed with a *thunk* behind Warren, and Bears pointed to a chair near a small dormant stove. Warren mumbled his thanks as he sat and accepted a glass of water from Bears, his discreet gaze taking in small changes to the living area. The patchwork quilt covered bed could be separated from the room by a curtain installed by Fidelia Evans and her sister, Annabelle MacKinnon, although Bears rarely pulled it closed. A rocking chair sat near the foot of the bed, while the table with two chairs was near the stove and tiny kitchen area. A lace doily covered the table, while a framed picture of his father hung on the wall. An eagle feather rested atop his father's picture. A gentle breeze blew in through the open windows.

"I heard you had a challenging day," Warren said with a twitch of his lips, unable to hide his amusement.

Bears glared at Warren and then shrugged. "That beast should be put down. He's untamable. Untrainable." He rubbed at his shoulder as Warren lost his battle and burst out laughing. Bears had been working with Brutus, Harold Tompkins's horse, for months in an attempt to ease it of its wilder tendencies. Today, even Bears seemed to have had enough.

"I never thought to hear the tale that you'd had your pantaloons and shirt ripped open by Brutus," Warren gasped through tears.

Bears rubbed his eyes and shook his head. "He was angry because I denied him a carrot he thought he was due. He's too smart for his own good."

"Did he get the carrot?"

"He ate the whole damn bucket after I dropped it when I was virtually stripped naked by him." Bears relented and smiled as Warren swiped at his eyes. "I'll have to think of another way to train him."

"Find some other treat. Something that isn't a reward," Warren suggested. After a moment, he sobered. "As you know, talking about your adventures with Brutus is not why I came by today." He saw Bears stiffen and nodded. "I have a letter for you."

Bears shook his head. "There's no reason for you to receive a letter that would be mailed to me."

Warren set the envelope on the table, tapping the paper with a finger a few times. "It's from Sara Parker." He watched as Bears jolted as though struck by lightening. He nodded in understanding. "It's not as though you receive a letter every day from the dead woman you'd once considered your wife."

"She's been dead for some time," Bears rasped, his throat having thickened. He cleared it and his mask of impassivity was once again in place. "I don't understand why it took so long to be sent to me." His jaw tightened. "If it is really from her."

They lawyer nodded. "I understand your hesitation. However, I believe it to be authentic, although I have not read it." He raised an eyebrow to soothe Bears' sense of propriety. "I am somewhat known in Helena, and the judge there realized that I might know you and be able to deliver it. They found it when they were investigating Bertrand, and they did read it. Judge Hammond advised me that the contents of her letter helped aid in his conviction. The judge broke with propriety in this instance, as it should have been kept in the official record of material for his trial. Instead, the judge had a copy made for the court record and sent the original to you."

"Why?"

"He feared that you would believe it all a lie if you did not read the letter in her hand." Warren raised his fingers from the envelope and waited for Bears to act.

Bears' intense gaze bore into Warren's for a long moment before he reached for the letter. The ripping of the envelope sounded, and then he slipped the pages free. His eyes moved rapidly over the written lines, and his hands began to shake as he finished the letter.

Warren frowned, his hand reaching for his friend as he feared Bears would faint. "Bears? What did she tell you?"

"I have a daughter," he whispered. "All these years, I've had a daughter."

Pre-order Now!

Unbridled Montana Passion

AFTERWORD

Dear Reader,

Thank you so much for reading *Montana Wrangler*! I couldn't write it without your ongoing support.

The Winter of 1886-1887 is a winter that lives on in the memory of many Montanans. It's often called "The Big Die Up." Nearly 60% of cattle died that winter— roughly 360,000. Before that winter, there were 220 cattle operations in Montana; afterward, there were 120. It is the year that heralded the change from open range cattle grazing to the cattle grazing we are familiar with today. Although a slow change, it began due to that winter.

I know it might have seemed overly romantic when Shorty rode in with a healthy herd of cattle after the horrible winter, but that truly happened! One day, as I sat around talking about the winter of 1886-87 with friends, they told me a very similar story. It is how their family saved their ranch that winter. When Gary told me that story, I filed it away, knowing I'd use it one day in one of my Bear Grass Springs novels. Thanks, Gary!

Again, thanks for reading *Montana Wrangler*. I can't wait to share Fidelia and Bears' story with you, coming in March 2019!

Happy Reading,

Ramona

ALSO BY RAMONA FLIGHTNER

Bear Grass Springs

Montana Untamed (Bear Grass Springs, Book One)

Montana Grit (Bear Grass Springs, Book Two)

Montana Maverick (Bear Grass Springs, Book Three)

Montana Renegade (Bear Grass Springs, Book Four)

Jubilant Montana Christmas (Bear Grass Springs, Book Five)

Unbridled Montana Passion (Bear Grass Springs, Book Seven)— Coming March 2019!

Banished Saga

Banished Love (Banished Saga, Book One)

Reclaimed Love (Banished Saga, Book Two)

Undaunted Love, Part One(Banished Saga, Book Three)

Undaunted Love, Part Two (Banished Saga, Book 3.5)

With Many More!

ABOUT THE AUTHOR

Ramona is a historical romance author who loves to immerse herself in research as much as she loves writing. A native of Montana, every day she marvels that she gets to live in such a beautiful place. When she's not writing, her favorite pastimes are fly fishing the cool clear streams of a Montana river, hiking in the mountains, and spending time with family and friends.

Ramona's heroines are strong, resilient women, the type of women you'd love to have as your best friend. Her heroes are loyal and honorable, the type of men you'd love to meet or bring home to introduce to your family for Sunday dinner. She hopes her stories bring the past alive and allow you to forget the outside world for a while.

Join her newsletter at: www.ramonaflightner.com/newsletter

facebook.com/authorramonaflightner

instagram.com/rflightner

bookbub.com/authors/ramona-flightner

www.ingramcontent.com/pod-product-compliance
Lightning Source LLC
Chambersburg PA
CBHW052034240626
47153CB00006B/2082